CAUGHT LOOKING

BOOK ONE IN THE HOT-LANTA SERIES

MEGHAN QUINN

CHAPTER ONE

Jane

It's been two years today since George Lawrence broke Jane's heart. She can't believe it's been two years already. It seems like only yesterday she was picking out her wedding dress and talking to florists. Little did she know her fiancé was about to ruin her life.

This is the second time she will sit alone in her apartment and mourn the loss of one of her biggest dreams: becoming a wife. She decided last year that January 23rd was dedicated to getting absolutely plastered by herself while listening to sad old lady music and wasting her life away in pizza boxes and cartons of cookie dough ice cream. The first time she celebrated her fiancé cheating on her, she found herself waking up in the stairway of her apartment building, with blender in hand, sporting shorts, a sports bra, and one sock. Her neighbor, Mr. Mendez, woke her up by poking a broomstick at her and yelling vamanos! She pulled her pathetic carcass out of the stairway and retreated to her empty apartment. This year she decided to go for a replay, since last year was so successful.

Why is it that a guy thinks it's alright to propose to the woman he "loves" and then finds it okay to go and sleep with the office slut on many occasions? One would think that proposing means that said man wants to be with said woman for the rest of their lives, in a committed monogamous relationship. Apparently, she

1

missed the memo that cheating was okay when it came to George's proposal.

It felt like just yesterday that she had finished up with her final dress fitting and wanted to surprise George with a lunch and a lay. She wore her sexy lingerie to spice things up, since their sex life had been a little dry and thought the element of surprise would also send his shaft into high gear. Well, there was a surprise awaiting her for sure. When she walked in, all she could see was George hovering over Rebecca, the office slut, and plowing her so hard on his desk that she thought she may have seen the desk denting. God, Rebecca was gorgeous. It was hard to compete with someone who had massively fake boobs and a body toned in all the right areas. She should have known earlier, when George was working late and helping Rebecca with her new office position, that something was going on between them. Jane stormed out of the office, throwing her ring at the hooker and proceeded to move out of their beautiful home and in with her parents.

The one good thing about George and his cheating ways was it gave Jane the drive to prove to everyone that she didn't have to be a wife; she could actually succeed on her own. She took the education she earned at Duke University and applied it to her superior organizational skills to start her own event planning business, JB Events, also known as Jane Bradley Events. Although, JB Events was still a small business, she put on some great events, thanks to her gay friend, Albert Winchester, who had many connections.

Jane pulled into her apartment complex and grabbed her pizza and ice cream from the passenger seat; booze was already chilling in the freezer and she headed for her door. As she reached for her key to open her door, it flung open, startling the crap out of her. Molly, her best friend, stood in the doorway and yanked her inside.

"What the hell are you doing here?" Jane shouted. "I gave you a key for emergency reasons only!"

"Girl, this is an emergency; have you seen your eyebrows? They've become one!" Molly said. "I have come to rescue you from your January 23rd self-destruction. I will not sit back again and listen to Mr. Mendez bitch about how he had to poke you for 5 minutes so you would get out of the stairway. It's time you get out of this rut you're in."

"What rut? I'm doing fine for myself, thank you very

much. JB Events is really starting to take off!"

"Yeah, great, your business is doing well, wonderful! What about your sex life? Or how about a social life?" Molly retorted. "If I go in your bedroom right now I bet I will find a couple of vibrators with worn out batteries."

"MOLLY! Jeeze, is there a censor on that mouth of yours? So I haven't had any men lately; I've been focused on my work."

Molly stared at Jane and said, "You are so lucky and you don't even know it; you can have sex whenever you want while, here I am acting like the Virgin Mary until Luke gets back from wherever the government sent him this time. Skype and phone sex only go so far, and that's when I actually hear from him."

Jane always hated when Molly pulled the "girlfriend of a soldier card." She and Luke had the best relationship you could ever imagine. It was sort of sickening actually. They loved each other so much and had an undying admiration for each other. Luke had been out on a mission for 5 months now and it was one of the worst since he had been in the army. He had worked his way up to be on an Elite Special Forces team and now Molly not only had no clue where he was, she barely heard from him. Occasionally, she might get a letter, if she was lucky.

"When was the last time you heard from Luke?" Jane asked quietly. She knew of the stress Luke's new job put on Molly.

"Since the last time I told you. I know he loves this new job, but I'm not so sure I can take it. I started taking it out on all the kids in my classroom. I felt so bad I snapped at them; I'm just so nervous all the time that a representative of the Army is going to knock on my front door and apologize for my loss. Then on top of that, add the fact that I am so fucking horny I can barely walk. Things are looking bleak over here."

Molly was a third grade teacher, but had the mouth of a sailor. Jane didn't mind it sometimes. Before Jane met George, she could keep up with Molly's sexual banter, but George put a kibosh on that when they started dating. He really reined her in and made sure she was "more class and less sass." That's how Molly always put it.

"How you were able to become a third grade teacher with that mouth is beyond me," Jane stated. "So, why are you here again?"

"Well, first off, I need to get you back into the game! We

need to pluck that unibrow you've developed on your forehead, get you back in your sexy clothes, and go hit the town."

Jane so did not want to go "hit the town." She wanted to crawl in a hole and forget this wretched day ever happened. Sometimes she just wanted to punch Molly, but she knew she was coming from a loving place.

Molly noticed Jane's hesitation and said, "I already called Alby; he has his credit card ready and a VIP area roped off for us at Deuces."

Oh Albert Winchester, the gayest man she had ever met. He had every connection you could think of, thanks to his high-powered job in communications. No one in their group of friends really knew what he did for a living; all they knew was, he had great connections. He knew everyone and always had somewhere free to go to or something free to give. Albert also had lots of money and no one to spend it on, so he was always very generous at the bar. When going out with Albert, one could plan on getting drunk and not paying a dime.

"I love Albert, and I love you, Molly, but I'm just not up for it. I just want to sulk and be by myself."

"Too bad that won't be happening tonight; Albert instructed me to pluck those beasts above your gorgeous blue eyes and get you in that little red number you have hanging up in your closet. We are going out, lady, and we are going to get you some action!"

Jane

Jane found herself looking into her compact, applying some lip gloss, and squirming in the lacy thong Molly made her wear. She was not opposed to thongs; she preferred them, actually, but when she was wearing a red lace skin-tight dress that went a little above mid-thigh, she had a slight problem with not having much covered up underneath. After she did her hair and put some make-up on, she couldn't help but get a little excited. Maybe Molly and Alby were right, she needed to get out. As the taxi pulled up to Deuces, Jane noticed there was a massive crowd waiting to get in. Every hooch in town was waiting to dance their asses off and all the men were claiming which eye candy they planned on taking home. She hated being back in single land, but sooner or later she was going to have to jump back into the pit hole of dating again.

Molly paid the driver and then proceeded to yank Jane out of the taxi. Molly went straight to the bouncer and bypassed everyone in line, which made every hooch glare at the girls, making death threats with their over-processed smoky eyes. Jane tried to squirm out of Molly's grasp and make her way to the back to be polite, but Molly wasn't having any of it.

Pulling on Molly's purse strap, Jane said, "Come on Molly, we just can't walk up to the front. We should wait like everyone else."

"Oh, Jane, you are such a square! When have we ever waited in line? Alby has us on the VIP list, come on!" Molly said, while jerking Jane toward the door.

Surprisingly, the bouncer held the door open for them with no problem. Molly looked Jane up and down and winked at her, implying it was the dress Jane was wearing that got them access, not their VIP status. Why she bought this dress was beyond her, but it seemed to be doing the job.

They spotted Alby in the back with a couple of men, no doubt his boyfriends. He was a bit of a man-whore and they loved him for it. He was all talk, though, and no action. He lost the love of his life, Ricky, to AIDS about 5 years ago and he never really got over it. Now, he just has men around for show, but always retires alone to his house at the end of the night. Jane clearly remembered the day Alby pulled her and Molly to the side and told them Ricky was sick and only had a couple months left. She had never seen such sadness in a person's eyes. Albert made the last couple months of Ricky's life the best he could. They went to as many destinations as Ricky could handle and tried to cross as many things off Ricky's bucket list as Albert could manage. It always made Jane and Molly very sad to think about the pain Alby carried around with him, but Ricky was never talked about. As Alby always said, he was "too fabulous to be depressed."

"Darlings, finally! God, I think I grew five new grey hairs just waiting for you." Albert looked Jane up and down, giving her what he called his "gay once over."

"Holy crap! Jane, you look hot! If I was a straight man, my boner would be touching you right now!" Alby said with ease.

"I guess a thanks is in order?" Jane responded. "Molly really made me come out of my comfort zone tonight and, to be honest, I'm feeling rather sexy."

"That's my girl!" Molly said, while patting her on the back. "I knew you had it in you. Now let's get some drinks. I'm dying to get you wasted and screwed tonight."

Molly and Jane headed for the bar and ordered two fruity concoctions, which turned out to be free, thanks to the elderly gentleman with the bent nose at the end of the bar. The girls held up their drinks and blew kisses in his direction as a thanks. They turned to face the room and surveyed what they were in store for. While there were a lot of creepy men staring at the women bumping and grinding on the dance floor, there were some mildly attractive men and one table of men that were beyond gorgeous and vaguely familiar.

Jane leaned over and said into Molly's ear, "Hey, do you recognize that African American man over there, the one with the very tight shirt? Is that Michael Banks?"

"Holy shit, it is! Let's go say hi!"

"Hold on," Jane said, holding Molly back. "We've not seen him in quite some time. Do you think it's appropriate we just go say hi? I don't want to be rude and interrupt his night."

"Uh, Jane, we were roommates and best friends with him for three years in college. He would fly us out to watch him play in some of his games. Yes, we went our separate ways when George came along, but we would never have made it through our college years without each other. So, pull on your big girl panties. We're not in some country club; we can go say hi."

Jane knew Molly was right. She sighed and started walking toward the table of luscious men. He must be out with some of his fellow baseball players, but least she knew he was still playing in New York, so why was he in Atlanta? Maybe the Braves and the Mets were playing each other. Wait, no, that makes no sense...it's not baseball season right now.

As they started getting closer, she noticed the guys Michael was sitting with. Marc Sullivan, the Braves catcher and the oh-so-gorgeous Brady Matthews, the Braves first baseman and leader in home runs, RBIs and batting average, and pretty much all around stud. Jane was a fan of the Braves just because Atlanta was her hometown team, but she wouldn't consider herself a die-hard fan. The chant the Braves' fans always did with their fake tomahawks made her clench her teeth, but she put up with it whenever she went to games with Alby. She just liked to sit back and stare at Brady Matthews.

He was all man, definitely over six feet tall, pure muscle, but not bulky by any means...dark brown hair, green eyes that could melt any heart, and an amazing tan that didn't stop where his jersey met his skin. Thanks to GQ, she knew exactly what he looked like under his uniform. She might have once or twice looked at his player profile, but he was mostly known outside the sports world for his celebrity girlfriends and flings. He was a little bit of a player, but with those muscles and eyes, he had the right to be.

"Michael! How are you sweetheart?" Molly shouted above the booming music.

"Molly? Jane? How the hell are you?" Michael exclaimed "You girls look fantastic, if I wasn't married, I'd pounce you both right now!" Michael stood up and gave them both hugs.

"Married?" Molly said surprised. "Where were we when those invites got sent out? Jane, did you get one?"

"Molly, don't be rude. Did you marry Kelly?" Jane asked shyly. She was nervous to see Michael; they used to be very close, but George had cut off all friendships she had with any guys when they were dating. He said it was inappropriate to be friends with guys because, no matter what, it always led to trouble. She wasn't sure how Michael was going to react to seeing her again.

"Jane, I've missed your sweetness. We eloped in Las Vegas...went through a drive-thru chapel, one of the most romantic moments of my life. The old wife is back home right now setting up the house and spending my money on a decorator. The boys wanted to take me out and get me acclimated to my new environment."

Jane looked stunned. "Wait, you were traded? To the Braves?"

"That is correct, darlin', looks to me like the Terrible Three are back together in the same city once again," Michael exclaimed. "This has made my night! Oh crap, I'm rude. Molly, Jane these are my teammates, Marc and Brady."

Both men got out of their chairs and shook the women's hands. Jane nearly trembled when Brady looked her up and down and smiled. Oh boy, was she in trouble. She needed to make sure her intake of alcohol did not exceed her drunk limit; she didn't need to look like a sloppy idiot in front of professional baseball players.

Michael asked the girls to sit down and join them. Feeling bad, Jane looked over to Albert, who was watching the whole transaction between them and waved her off to have fun and forget about him. Looking at the crowd of men around Alby now, it seemed like he was occupied anyway. Oh, she loved her Alby. She only wished she had as much confidence as Albert right now; she could really use some so when she talked she didn't sound like a teenager going through puberty. Maybe she should drink a little more to ease her nerves. Another fruity concoction needed, pronto!

CHAPTER TWO

Brady

Brady was irritated when Marc asked him to take out the new guy with him to Deuces. It wasn't that he didn't like Michael; he actually got along with him very well and enjoyed his company. Brady was just tired of all the stories about him in the gossip magazines that portrayed him as a playboy with every girl that came up to him. None of the stories were true; paparazzi just always happened to be in the right place at the right time. He couldn't go anywhere without being followed by someone with a camera. It came with the territory though, so he couldn't be too upset. His bank account was looking rather sizeable and he got to play a sport for a living; he had no room to complain.

Despite the fact that there were paparazzi hounding the front of the club when they arrived, the guys were having a pretty decent night, but once Michael's friends from college came over, his night started to look a little bit better. He knew he shouldn't be looking, but he couldn't help himself. Jane was a bombshell. One of the sexiest women he had ever met, not even because of the blatantly come-fuck-me-dress she was wearing. She had gorgeous long brown hair, a body to die for, breasts that just screamed to be touched and eyes that bored through a man's soul. There was a certain sweetness about her with an inner sex kitten dying to come out.

When she shook his hand, he nearly split in two. Her hand

was soft and feminine and her eyes glittered with passion. He could not stop staring at her or let go of her hand; it was strange, but he felt an immediate connection with her. He reluctantly let go of her hand once everyone got quiet and stared at him.

His zipper got real tight just at the sight of Jane, which was utterly embarrassing, as if he had never seen a woman before. All he needed now was some stupid paparazzi taking a picture of him and selling it to a gossip magazine with the headline, "Brady: Boozing and Boners." Nope, he had to stop letting the gorgeous woman in front of him affect him so much.

"Isn't that right, Brady?" asked Michael.

Oh crap, what were they talking about? Great he was thinking about hiding his boner and wasn't even paying attention to the conversation.

"Sorry, Michael, I was so distracted by these gorgeous women, I wasn't even paying attention."

"That's what I thought," accused Michael. "You know, buddy, you really need to get over your infatuation with anything with two legs and a pair of tits. These women want nothing to do with a playboy like you."

Yup, thanks Michael. That's all Brady needed, his own teammate spreading wrong information about him. Granted, Michael was most likely just pulling his leg, but Brady was getting pretty sick of everyone thinking he was some kind of womanizer. Thank you Hollywood media!

"Hey, speak for yourself, Mikey! I might be spoken for, but little Jane over here is on the prowl!" Molly exclaimed.

"Mikey? Really? I thought we got over that nickname a long time ago and hey, last time I heard, Jane, you were getting married," Michael said.

Brady sucked in his breath, married? Well, of course, why would this extremely gorgeous woman be available; she would definitely have been snatched up by some lucky bastard. She was too good to be single. But then Brady wondered, if she was married, why was she in that dress drinking like a Catholic school girl released from the confines of her parents for the first time?

"Yes, last time I checked I was supposed to be married, but when your fiancé fucks his co-worker it's kind of hard to forget about that and commit your undying love to the man in front of all your friends, family, and the gardener your parents so desperately wanted to invite," Jane stated.

"Shit, I'm sorry Jane. I didn't know. What a fucking bastard. Do I need to mess him up? I know how to swing a bat pretty well," Michael said with a wink.

Jane sighed, "Thanks, Michael, but last I heard, George got fired and is now living in his sister's basement, working for himself, aka unemployed and mooching. Karma always comes back to bite you in the butt."

Brady was surprised by Jane's attitude. God, she was strong and a little feisty; he liked that. If he were in her position, he would be wallowing in self-pity. If he were in her position? He was in her position at one point in time. That Hollywood devil-bitch Laney Johnson fucked him over big time. She made it seem like she was in love with him when she wasn't, even though he gave her his whole heart. Come to find out, she was getting quite snuggly with her co-star on her latest movie. He was devastated when he found out she was cheating on him. But of course, the media spun their relationship in a whole new direction, depicting him as the asshole breaking the heart of America's sweetheart. Sometimes you can never win.

Brady's relationship with Laney was a mess from the beginning, but she had a way of trapping a man. She made it seem like she was the sweetest woman you would ever meet, but deep down, she had the devil in her. She would always get what she wanted, make promises and break them and she would use her body as a weapon. Her body was one hell of a lethal weapon. Brady had the hardest time resisting her. Somehow, she would always mess something up between them…whether it was forgetting his birthday, not showing up for a game she promised she would be at, or backing out of planned vacations. Then she would use her body as an apology and Brady always accepted, until he found out she cheated on him. That was the end of Brady dealing with her devil ways.

The group was talking about local restaurants when he tuned back into the conversation and tried to part from the bad memories of Laney. Jane seemed shy, although he didn't know why, someone who dressed like that was looking for attention. She had vixen written all over her, but carried herself in a way that was genuine and attractive. He wanted to get to know her better. He leaned over to her ear so she could hear him over all the music.

"Hey, sweetheart, can I get you another drink?"

Jane crossed her legs, showing off the most amazing bronze tan he had ever seen and said, "You can get me a drink, but by no means am I your sweetheart."

Hello! Yes, she was feisty. He called the waiter over and ordered her another drink. This was going to be harder than he thought, or maybe he was just out of practice. All he knew was that he was excited and up for the challenge. The gossip magazines always made it seem like he was dating someone new every night, but the pictures were either old pictures or pictures of him with just friends, which of course, heaven forbid he should have female friends. He actually hadn't dated anyone in two years. It was just too difficult, especially now that he was a bit of a celebrity. Women threw themselves at him just so they could have a piece of him and his paycheck.

He was interested in Jane, though; she didn't seem like the average girl. There was something in her eyes that showed innocence and purity, which he liked about her. Plus, she had a real fire to her and her body was something to drool over. Yes, he would pursue this woman. Thank you, Michael, for being little Mikey in college and best friends with these two vixens.

Jane

Oh my god, Brady was actually hitting on her. It had to be the dress. Her face must be just as red as the dress itself. What was she thinking? She was so embarrassed and so not used to getting any real attention from men, let alone from famous men. When she shook his hand, she swore they bonded right on the spot, but she was not going to fall for it…his handsome, manly ways. Yes, she was extremely attracted to Brady and, more than anything, she wanted to take him home and run her hands all over his body, but she was smarter than that. Tonight was the anniversary of the worst day of her life and she had grown since then. Why would she get involved with someone who was a known playboy? That was just asking to get screwed over once again.

There was a little voice in the back of her head telling her to let loose and have fun. Maybe she would…might as well flirt back. Nothing would come from it because, why would a professional baseball player want anything to do with her? Yes, the dress was doing wonders for her appearance tonight, but when it came down to it, he was, in fact, a player and she was just a low-key event planner. They had nothing in common, so she might as well practice her flirting and seduction. She needed to get back on the dating train sometime.

She leaned over to Brady when he handed her the drink he ordered and seductively asked in his ear, "So Brady, Fuck, Chuck or Marry: Eva Mendez, Angelina Jolie and Salma Hayek?"

Brady was startled at first, then shifted in his seat while he eyed her from the tips of her toes to the top of her head. A devilish grin spread over his face while he leaned in closer and said "Fuck Eva, she is most likely feisty like you, marry Salma because she is a sweetheart and chuck Angelina, I don't like how the whole Brad Pitt, Angelina thing went down."

Hmmm, fascinating. He thought she was feisty. Ha, if only he knew that she liked to wear her kitty cat pajamas at night while watching the Golden Girls and enjoying a good facial mask. The Brad and Angelina comment threw her off though, what did he mean? Before she had a chance to even ask him, his mouth was practically on her ear when he asked her, "Fuck, Chuck or Marry: Bradley Cooper, Ryan Gosling and Josh Duhamel."

Oh, what a handful of treats he laid out for her; how could she possibly choose? She placed her hand on his thigh, leaned over and whispered in his ear, "Fuck Bradley Cooper, marry Ryan Gosling and chuck Josh Duhamel, no one likes a cheater."

Brady stared her in the eyes and she nearly collapsed. Confidence woman, you can do this. Do not let it show that he intimidates you…that is exactly what these kind of men try to do to women. They make them feel intimidated and then make them feel good with compliments as they drag them to bed and end up leaving them hanging in the morning with a taxi fare for their ride home. Brady and Jane just stared at each other for what seemed like forever until Brady startled her when he asked her to dance.

Brady

Brady nearly fell out of his seat when she placed her hand on his thigh. Lord, this woman was doing him in. He needed to be closer to her where they could be alone and away from the rowdy table they were sitting at. Michael and Molly were reminiscing about some baseball house party they went to in college where Molly ended up breaking the house's couch because she acted like it was her own personal wrestling ring with Michael. Lord knew what they were like in college. He could imagine Jane though; she would be rolling her eyes at her two crazy friends, while sporting some sexy outfit that drew all the men's attention.

He grabbed Jane's hand and led her out to the dance floor. He was not much of a dancer, but he did it every now and then when he was either extremely drunk or needed a reason to get close to a very attractive lady; this time it was the latter.

The music was blaring and the typical re-mixes and techno tunes were playing, but with a sexy red-dressed woman in his hands, he was feeling it tonight. He wrapped his hand around her waist and pulled her close; they rocked together in perfect synchronization. Her curves melted perfectly into his in every way. It was like she was made specifically for him. She turned in his arms so her back was to him and started backing her booty up on him. He had to start thinking of his grandmother to relieve any naughty thoughts. He didn't need to embarrass himself with any tightness in his jeans right now. Yup, Grandma is what he needed to think about, but my God, Jane was a vixen. He tried to think of another way they could dance where her ass was grinding his overly-excited pelvis.

He turned her around in his arms so she was facing him again, but no matter what he did now, he was turned on, because she was running her hands up his chest and down his arms as she slowly twisted and turned and moved her way up and down his body. Yeah, he was a goner. His jeans lost any space that was left in them. Okay, maybe dancing was a bad idea. Who knew his world was going to be rocked tonight when he decided to take the newbie out with Marc?

Jane

Jane didn't know what had gotten into her, but she was having one hell of a time. She lost all her inhibitions and went for it. She moved up and down and pretty much treated Brady like her own stripper pole. It must had been the drinks in her, because next thing she knew she wrapped her arms around Brady's neck and moved against his very obvious erection, spurring him on even further. She wanted to nibble on his ear, but refrained; she just brought her face real close to his so she could encompass his electrifying scent. She felt a low groan come from the back of his throat. The sound made her feel empowered, something she had not felt in quite some time. She was getting great satisfaction out of turning this extremely attractive man on, with no thought of taking him home or taking this any further than the night club.

"You are slowly killing me, woman," Brady whispered in her ear.

"I know and I can tell you're enjoying it," she said, as she rubbed up against his crotch.

He groaned again and pulled her even closer. Uh oh, did she go too far? She hoped he didn't think this was going anywhere. What if he thought he could have his way with her, just use her for what he wanted and leave her the next morning? Why wouldn't he, it's not like they were in a committed relationship; this was what single life was like, wasn't it? Dabbling here and there and having fun? Maybe it was her turn to let loose and have a little fun. No one said she had to make a commitment or even sleep with the man. She should just let go and push all negative thoughts to the back of her head because right now she was in the arms of the sexiest man she had ever met and he was clearly turned on by her.

She tilted her head up toward him and licked her lips, clearly indicating she was ready for him to take charge. He looked at her, grinned and leaned down so close to her she thought she might pass out. They were completely still on the dance floor and he was so close to her she could practically taste him. He stayed like that for what seemed like forever, she almost threw herself at him just to get it over with, but she needed to be patient and play hard to get…not throw herself at him like some horny teenager. Finally, he started to move again and very slowly was about to place his lips on hers when there was a slight tap on her shoulder. Jane nearly jumped out of her high heels.

"Hey, chica, we have to go," Molly said.

Irritated, Jane asked why under her breath.

Molly leaned in her ear and said "George just walked in with the office hooker and I know you don't want to be involved in any drama-crazed reality show scene tonight."

All color drained from Jane's face. She completely went still and fear started seeping into the confident woman that was once on the dance floor. Molly smiled at Brady and grabbed Jane by the arm.

"Come on, Jane, let's get out of here. Alby pulled his car to the front and he's going to take us home."

Jane nodded, smiled the best she could at Brady and took off with Molly. So much for the confident girl in the red dress, she thought. The mention of George's name along with that bitch that ruined her relationship made her turn green and she was going to lose all the contents in her stomach if she didn't get out of the bar quickly..

CHAPTER THREE

Brady

A shocked Brady stood in the middle of the dance floor...what just happened? A minute ago he had the sexiest woman he had ever met in his arms, inches from asking her to go somewhere more private when, out of nowhere, her friend came over whispered something in her ear, freezing Jane completely stiff. Then her friend escorted Jane away, leaving Brady all alone and confused as hell. He was so shocked, it didn't even register to him to chase after her and make sure she was okay. What the hell just happened?

The next morning, Brady was still perplexed and it annoyed him that he cared so much. She was just another girl he met at Deuces, why did it matter so much to him? Maybe because it was the first time in a long time he was genuinely interested in someone, rather than just trying to scratch an itch he might have. He didn't even scratch as much as people thought he did. He thought about his interaction with Jane and was pretty sure she was enjoying herself last night. One clue that she was into him was when she sucked in her breath when he was millimeters away from kissing her. Damn, double damn. He needed to figure out a way to see her again, without looking too desperate. He would talk to Michael, maybe he could come up with a way to get Jane's attention.

Damn, Brady was going to catch slack for looking like

some lovesick puppy begging his buddy to set up a date for him, but he didn't care. Jane had made an impression on him. He saw something different in her from any other woman. She was sweet and sultry, but mysterious at the same time. He was intrigued and he needed more time with her; he needed to figure out why Jane twisted his stomach into knots.

Michael

Michael sat in his brand new house thinking about last night. When he was traded to the Braves, he knew he would be in the same city as Molly and Jane, but he had no clue he would run into them one of the first nights he was out. It was so good to see both of them; it brought back all the amazing memories they had together, but Michael couldn't help but feel a little bitter toward Jane. They were such good friends in college and after they graduated as well. But once George proposed to her, she cut off all communication with Michael. He had a real hard time dealing with the loss of their friendship, so he'd diverted his attention elsewhere. That was when he decided to marry Kelly and start a life with her.

He wanted to reconnect with Jane, but didn't know how to push pass the hurtful feelings he had. He would just have to talk to her about them; this was a chance for him to rekindle what he had in college with Molly and Jane and he didn't want to lose it. He knew having friends in a new city would be nice and maybe it would give Kelly a chance to meet some new people. He worried about her since the move. She was very mad and reluctant to move. All of a sudden, Michael's thoughts were interrupted by his phone ringing. He looked down at his caller ID, Brady.

"Hey Brady, how's it going?"

"Pretty good, how are you feeling after last night?"

"Good actually, I didn't have much to drink. I saw that you got a little comfortable with my friend Jane." Michael thought about how Jane was all over Brady and vice versa. It bothered him a little. He wasn't sure if it was because he didn't get to spend time with Jane last night or if it was because he had always harbored feelings for her.

"Yeah, I was actually calling you about her." Michael heard Brady clear his throat. "God, this is embarrassing. I was wondering if you could possibly set something up where we all hang out again.

I want to get to know Jane some more. She was pretty amazing, but she was also a little stand off-ish. I'm afraid if I ask her out myself, she might turn me down and say no."

Michael laughed, "A girl turning you down? I don't believe it."

"Well, in any case, do you think you can set something up?"

Michael thought about it. Did he really want Brady pursuing Jane? Well, it wasn't like Michael could pursue her himself. He was married and Jane had never thought of Michael that way. George was awful to Jane and if he could pick anyone to help Jane become herself again, Brady was a good option. He was fun, nice, and could help Jane come alive again. He was a little nervous about Brady's reputation for having so many women, but after meeting Brady and getting to know him, he seemed like a really nice guy. Why not? Jane could use a little fun.

Michael replied, "Yeah, I'll call Jane and see if she and Molly want to hang out. I miss them and it would give me a good opportunity to catch up as well."

"Thanks man, I appreciate it."

"Just don't hurt her, alright?" Michael said in a serious tone.

"You got it. I promise to be an upstanding gentleman."

"I'll text you the details later."

Michael hung up the phone and hoped the phone number he still had for Jane was the right one. He needed to push past his distaste for what happened when George and Jane got engaged and help bring the friend he used to know back from the dead.

Jane

What was she thinking last night just throwing herself at Brady Matthews like that? She was somewhat grateful George walked in and Molly escorted her out to Albert's car. She so much enjoyed the intimate and very sexy dancing she was doing with Brady, but Lord knows she would have been hurt somehow, so she was grateful their private soiree stopped before it even had a chance to begin.

She couldn't believe she had been so bold, though. When she was dating George, she really toned down her outgoing personality and eventually lost herself. She didn't realize the change in her personality until she left George…that was when she noticed how much she'd changed because of him. It was like George brainwashed her and turned her into a robot. She always thought she wanted to be a wife, who took care of her husband, and be a mother, but ever since she started her own business, her goals in life had changed. She wanted to be successful and able to provide for herself. Show the world that she didn't need George, or any man to take care of her; she wanted to take care of herself.

Her phone rang displaying a number she didn't recognize; it was an Atlanta area code so she answered it, thinking maybe it was a new client.

"Hello," Jane answered.

"Janey Bear, how are you, sweetie?" Michael's voice said from the other end of the line.

"Mikey! Hey handsome, where are you calling from?"

"Oh, I got a new number once I moved out here. Sometimes it is nice to change numbers so you can throw off the press and unwanted phone calls."

"Oh, you are such a smart man," Jane replied, "What's going on? I'm so sorry I didn't spend that much time with you last night; I got a little carried away with my drinks and acted a bit slutty."

Michael laughingly said, "Yes, you did, but it was good to see you let loose. I've been worried about you. You haven't returned any of my e-mails in quite some time…it's been a few years."

Jane cringed when Michael called her out on dropping off the face of the earth from their relationship. Michael was the one person she could count on to talk to and give her sound advice. She loved Molly, but Molly's theory was that sex solved everything. When Jane was dating George, he took over her life and separated her from her friends, Michael being one of them. She felt bad that she stopped talking to Michael; they had always been so close. Molly and Michael were crazy together and would always make sure they were the life of the party, but when it came to Jane and Michael, they were connected on an emotional level. They always leaned on each other when they needed to talk or needed advice. She didn't talk to Michael when George cheated on her because she couldn't face the embarrassment and feared how he would feel about her all of a sudden reaching out to him.

"I know. I'm sorry Mikey. I was in a bad spot after I left George and then I started focusing on my business, which seems to be really picking up now."

"Don't sweat it, kiddo, but you can make it up to me if you'd like," replied Michael.

"What do you have in mind, mister?"

"Do you have any plans tonight?"

"Sadly, no. How lame am I? Friday night with no big plans, might as well go adopt ten cats and call myself an old maid," Jane said sarcastically.

"I don't think anyone would call you an old maid after what you wore last night. Hot damn, when did you get so hot? Don't get me wrong, you've always been steamin', but every man in that club was drooling over you last night."

Jane knew Michael had always had some feelings for her, but Jane saw him as a brother, nothing more. She knew it was hard for Michael to accept their relationship as entirely platonic, but he did because she knew he cherished their friendship more than not having one at all.

"Thanks, Mikey, it was the dress."

"The dress was awesome, but the dress didn't wear you, you wore the dress and everyone knew it."

"Wow, Mikey, when did you start watching TLC? I didn't know you had a bit of gay in you," Jane said teasingly.

"Alright, settle down, jeeze. I guess a guy can't pay a compliment without being criticized. Listen, I want to hang out with you and Molly. Why don't you meet me at Dave and Busters tonight? We'll have some drinks and some friendly competition…like old times."

"Oh, I see what's happening here. You want to get a good ass whoopin' in skee-ball," Jane replied.

"Bring it, girl! I dare you. Once I made it to the big leagues, I bought my own skee-ball game and you can bet your ass I will be giving you a run for your money tonight."

"We'll see about that, mister. Will we be seeing your lovely wife?"

"No, she's hanging with her book club tonight…boring! See you tonight, hot stuff."

Jane hung up with Michael feeling surprisingly refreshed.

She was so happy he got traded to the Braves; she missed him so much. She knew it was going to be good for her soul that they had been reunited. She missed their long talks and cuddling. They were never romantically involved, but they had a general understanding that sometimes a person needed some human contact. Molly always tried to tease Jane that she and Michael would wind up together, but they both knew they were nothing more than connected by their souls.

Jane pulled out her phone and sent a text to Molly.

Jane: Hey, lady, Michael wants to meet at Dave and Busters tonight, you in?

Molly: Hell yeah, I need to get some drinks in my system. These kids are driving me insane with their inability to do their multiplication tables.

Jane: Isn't that why you're their teacher? You're supposed to help them…

Molly: Yeah, yeah, yeah oh P.S. Luke sent me a note, I read it at work and almost had an orgasm at my desk. He is so hot. I love that man.

Jane: Molly, maybe you should wait to get home to read things from him.

Molly: Where's the fun in that? See you tonight…wear something hot, I expect you to pick someone up tonight.

Wear something hot? Well, she would not be donning that red dress again. She decided on a pair of skinny jeans, a black tank top blouse to show off her arms that she worked out almost every day to achieve such tone and a pair of black stilettos that screamed sexy. She wore her hair in her natural wave and put on some natural-toned make up with a little bit of pink lip gloss. Hmm, she had been cleaning up pretty nicely recently. Not too shabby for being cheated on two years ago. Okay, time to get over it already. But how? It still hurt just as much as it did the day she ran into George on top of that slut, Rebecca. Alright, push all negative thoughts out; time to have some fun tonight with some old friends.

Molly

Molly walked into Dave and Busters with a huge smile

22

plastered to her face. Luke was hopefully coming home in a week and she couldn't wait. She hadn't seen him in months and missed him terribly, plus she missed the most amazing penis she ever laid her eyes on. She had never met another man who could make her feel so incredibly good, both inside and out and boy did he make her feel good inside. When he got home, she was going to jump him so fast he wouldn't know what hit him. She needed to make time to go shopping and get a wax. She needed to be ready for her soldier when he got home.

She brought a little excerpt of her note from Luke so she could show Jane what she was missing out on. She really needed to get her friend Jane back into the dating scene. If only stupid George hadn't show up the night before, Jane was finally letting her guard down and actually getting down with Brady. Molly had to admit, Brady was one fine piece of man meat. If she wasn't with Luke, she'd throw herself at Brady so fast no other woman would have a chance and she didn't even bother to care about the man's womanizing reputation. She bet he was dynamite in bed…good looks and his height just said he could fuck like no tomorrow. She would talk to Michael and see if they could set Jane and Brady up. The two seemed to have some serious chemistry and Molly thought it would be a shame for that kind of sexual chemistry to go to waste. So, if she had to meddle a little bit more in her friend's life, then so be it. She was actually doing Jane a favor.

Molly spotted Jane as she came through the doors. Damn, her girl was looking good. Finally, Jane was starting to find her herself again. Molly knew she was slowly losing her best friend when Jane started dating George, but there was nothing Molly could really do about it. Molly tried saying something to Jane one day, but Jane became very defensive and shut her out. They didn't talk for days, which was very unlike them. So, Molly was happy that Jane was starting to break away from the conservative shell she was in during her years with Douche McGee.

"Damn, girl, looking good. I'm so glad you decided to show off your arms tonight because, Lord knows, you'll be flexing them once you kill Mikey in skee-ball!" Molly said.

"Thanks, you know it's true; he thinks he's going to be able to kick my ass. When has that ever happened?" replied Jane.

"Never!" Molly handed Jane her note. "Here I want you to read this, I took an excerpt of my note from Luke so you can see what you're missing by being single these days."

"Molly, you know I always feel uncomfortable reading these; it's like soft porn."

"You know you like it; just read it," Molly said, thrusting it in her face. She saw Jane sigh and reluctantly open the note.

Jane

Jane hated reading Molly's private letters from Luke. They always made her feel so sad that she would never have a relationship like Luke and Molly's. They had so much love and respect for each other. Jane knew deep down inside that she could never find that kind of love for herself. They were so honest and forthcoming when it came to each other. Jane never felt that kind of connection with anyone. She opened the paper and read silently to herself...

> *I hope that previous paragraph really got you going baby* (Thank God Molly didn't include that part) *I want to tell you how much I miss you and not just your glorious tits. I miss hearing your voice, I miss touching your skin, I miss watching you struggle in the kitchen trying to make me something tasty to eat, I miss the way you wear a towel on your head after a shower, I miss the way you look in the morning and I miss the way you feel in my arms. I know this new job is more strenuous on our relationship, but I promise I will make it up to you when I get home in a week. I love you so much, baby. Love, Molly's Man*

Well that's just rich. Jane was tearing up. Luke was the perfect man, he had no shame in expressing his feelings, but he was also so manly. He fought for the country for crying out loud, doesn't get much manlier than that.

"Jesus, Molly, do you want me looking like a raccoon tonight? Why did you want me to read this? So I could cry like a lunatic?"

"No," Molly scoffed. "I just wanted to show you what you can have when you find true love. It's something so great, so wonderful, it consumes you. Don't give up girl; you will find it, I promise. You had a minor setback, but it will happen for you. I'm so proud of you for breaking out of that librarian phase you were in and so is Alby. He was really nervous he was going to have to dump your ass; you know how he's all about image," Molly said with a wink.

Jane chuckled, "Yes, I know. Alby is such a princess. Thank you for your concern and your encouragement; now let's go find that fine-ass black man of a friend we have."

Jane and Molly first stopped by the bar for some drinks, then went over to the arcade area to warm up. Jane was the all-time champion amongst them at skee-ball. She knew exactly how to score 100 points in the upper corners. Michael always hated Jane for her superb ball-placement. Their competition was all fun and games until the bets started rolling and that was when Michael, sadly, got himself in trouble; it happened every time. He always believed he was going to beat Jane so he would raise the stakes, putting himself in a world of hurt. One time, he was so confident in his ability to beat Jane that he bet her whoever lost had to go streaking through the baseball house. Thank God she won that game because she was not ready to show off her girly bits to all those horny ball players.

Jane was just beginning to roll some balls when Michael came up from behind her and slapped her butt. She whirled around to tackle him to the ground when she noticed standing behind Michael was Brady Matthews, grinning like a fool. Damn, what the hell was he doing here? She instantly became rigid and nervous. So much for a relaxing night with friends; now she had to turn on her singles game. She was not prepared to put on a production tonight. At least she was looking good.

Damn, why was he here? Michael must have set her up, he would pay for his sins later.

"Do you always slap each other's asses as a friendly greeting?" Brady asked jokingly.

"Only when we're incredibly horny," Molly replied. "Not getting any from the old ball and chain lately there, huh Mikey?"

"Ha…Ha, I'm a very satisfied man, thank you very much. My lady knows how to rock my world and pleasure her man."

Jane had only met Michael's wife once. She seemed very sweet and down to earth. They had a charity foundation together helping children. Michael said she took the foundation very seriously. Although lately, Michael's wife, Kelly, seemed more materialistic than normal. Jane thought it was a little weird that he didn't bring her with him. Wouldn't she want to come hang with his friends and get to know them better since she was new to the area? Jane shook the thoughts out of her head.

"Too much information, Michael," Jane said, pushing him to the side. "Quit stalling and trying to throw off your competition. What are the stakes tonight?"

Brady chimed in, "Stakes?"

"Jane here is the reigning champion when it comes to skee-ball and we always place a bet to make things more interesting. It's always between Jane and I; she seems to always have the edge up on me, but I plan on destroying her tonight and for a good reason," Michael said winking.

What was that man up to? He didn't look innocent at all. Actually, he looked like he'd been cooking something up in that devious brain of his.

Jane replied, "And what good reason is that Mikey?"

"If I beat you tonight, you have to go out with my boy Brady over here," Michael said, patting Brady on the back.

Jane's face drained of all color. What was Michael up to? Like Brady even wanted to go out with her. Michael was only embarrassing the both of them. She should wring Michael's neck right now and wipe that smirk off his face. She glanced at Brady and noticed the same damn smirk on his face. What was he grinning for? Cocky bastards.

"What does my dear friend Jane get from this bet when she wins?" said Molly. Thank God Molly was there to help her speak when Jane lost her voice.

"I will give her ten-thousand dollars," retorted Michael.

Jane's jaw dropped. She whipped around and stared at him. Did he know what that money would do for her business? Game on!

She stuck her hand out and said "deal." Either way, she sort of wins. If Brady doesn't technically want to go out with her, she at least would have a chance to go out with a professional baseball player or bank ten-thousand dollars. How many girls could say that?

"Fantastic," exclaimed Michael. "What are the terms? Best two out of three games or highest combined score of all three?"

"You know how I like it, Mikey," Jane replied. "Highest combined score of all three."

While Michael was picking out their machines, she got him a drink. It wouldn't hurt to get Michael a little loose so she would have a better chance of winning. Jane brought the drink to Michael, bent over and slowly pulled herself back up right in front of him. She always tried to play the distraction game with Michael, and it always worked in her favor. She was a little shy in doing so since she'd not flaunted herself in quite some time and Brady was around, so she was a bundle of nerves already, but she was able to pull off the "bend and snap" perfectly.

Michael slapped her ass and said, "It doesn't work for my wife, it's not going to work for you doll, sorry. Let's keep this fair, so don't start flaunting your body at me, even though it is hotter than ever these days."

Damn.

"Fine," Jane huffed. "I guess I'll just have to beat you like old times, purely by skill."

"We'll see. Brady, please help Molly keep score. I don't totally trust Molly not to be one-sided."

"He's right," Brady chimed in. "I'm counting on Michael to win here and I don't need you cheating on the scores."

Insulted, Molly huffed and said, "I would never cheat, how dare you accuse me of such blasphemy?"

"Do we really need to get into that right now, Molly? Case in point, beer pong championship, sophomore year. Your nipple did not just happen to slip out and distract the other team, I saw you take your bra off in the semi-finals!" Michael accused.

"A girl has to go to extremes sometimes to win a game, so sue me!" Molly retorted.

"Alright, enough with the nip slip…let's get this game going! I cannot wait to watch you write that check, Mikey. I could really use a new sign for my business," Jane exclaimed.

Jane was ready; she always beat Michael. The key to her success was to score some solid points and then go for the big points in the top corners. Michael always tried to go for the hundreds at first and never ended up scoring any points in the end. She had this in the bag.

They started shooting and Jane noticed that Michael was actually doing pretty well, too well. He was scoring all hundreds, nailing every corner shot. Crap, she needed to step up her game. She guessed he'd been practicing, but she didn't think he was going to be this good. She was on her seventh ball in her first round and she was down by two hundred. Okay, three more balls; she needed to get these next three in the hundred holes to stay alive. First one hit off the tip of the hole, damn! Oh good, Michael didn't make it either; okay, she needed to make these last two…which she ended up hitting. She was only down by a hundred going into the next game.

They rotated machines, just to make sure someone was not faring better on one machine than the other. They started the next round. They alternated shots so they could taunt and tease each other. Michael would pelvic thrust in her direction and Jane would shimmy at him, while Molly whispered sexual innuendos in his ear.

"Oh, Mikey, what big brown balls you have, can I feel them?" Molly said with a husky flair to her voice.

"Quit it, Molly…that's going too far. You can't try to give a guy a boner when he's shooting. I can't do that to you," Michael explained.

"Wait, she's giving you a boner?" Brady said. "I thought you said she's like your sister. Dude, what is wrong with you?"

"Hey, Brady, I'm trying to do you a favor here and win you a date. You really want to judge me right now?" Michael said.

"Sorry, man, please proceed."

Hmm, Jane wondered if Brady put Michael up to this whole night. It seemed rather odd that Michael made a bet for her to go out with Brady. Did Brady actually find her attractive? That seemed a little crazy. No, Michael was just trying to pair up two of his friends, probably so he could give them a hard time later. There was no way Brady Matthews wanted to go out with her; he could have any woman he wanted, and he had. He was a player and the non-commitment type. She was not interested; she did not intend to get her heart broken again because she knew, if she did go out with Brady, that's exactly what was going to happen. She was going to get her heart broken. To Brady, she was just another notch on his belt.

It came down to one shot, the score was tied and they both had one ball left. Should she go for the hundred corner or play it safe and get some points? Oh decisions. Thank God Michael had to go first. He took his ball, made Brady kiss it, making Jane roll her eyes, then he shot for the hundred. It bounced off the rim and landed in the twenty hole. How the hell did that happen? Pure luck, Jane thought, how irritating. Well, at least she didn't have to go for the hundred; she could settle for thirty points, which was her go-to shot anyway.

Molly chimed in, breaking off Jane's train of thought, "Hey, do you hear that? They're playing Luke's love song for me, 'You Lost That Lovin' Feeling.' I miss him." Molly did a fake pout look.

"I know, sweetie, but he's coming home soon. Now watch me make this shot and then we're going shoe shopping with some of the money Michael will be handing over."

Jane whipped her arm back and, as she was releasing, Molly screamed at the top of her lungs, making Jane jump what seemed like ten feet in the air. The sudden shock of Molly's high-pitched squeal caused Jane's arm to fling to the right, sending the ball straight into the gutter.

Jane stood there in shock. She lost. She lost $10,000. She lost her winning streak against Michael and now she had to go on a date with Brady Matthews, which most likely was going to be the most awkward event of her life, thanks to Michael.

"Molly, what the fuck are you screaming...?" Jane turned around and saw Molly crying. Jane looked over at the entrance where Molly was looking and saw Luke in his army fatigues, sexier than hell and smiling his movie star grin. He was seriously one gorgeous man with his golden blonde hair and steel blue eyes; his tan made everything on his body more defined. He walked with an air of confidence that made him one sexy man. They were the perfect match...Molly with her long golden hair, hazel eyes and plentiful boobs. The gorgeous couple would make beautiful babies one day. What the hell was Luke doing at the restaurant anyway and how did he know they were there?

CHAPTER FOUR

Molly

Molly was thunderstruck. She had never seen anything more perfect in her life. She ran to Luke and flung herself around him. She threw her mouth on his and started diving into him. Oh, he tasted so good, like he always had, just like mint and pure male. She was crying like a lunatic and making a scene, but she didn't care; her man was home and their song was playing…it was the perfect moment.

Luke walked her over to the group and said his hellos. Molly introduced Luke to Michael and Brady.

"So, this is the guy with the huge dong you keep talking about, well I must say, well done, Molly," Michael said.

"I thought your friend Albert was the gay one, babe," Luke joked, holding her tightly.

The group laughed and Jane asked, "Why are you home so early and how did you know we were here?"

"Well, Molly and I both have GPS tracker systems in our phones so we can always know where the other one is when we're so far apart. Although, I usually don't have my phone with me on missions, but when I do have my phone, it's reassuring. I returned home early because I have something important to do."

Molly frowned, "Are you leaving me again? You just got here."

"Actually, doll, the something important has to do with

you. I've been doing a lot of thinking and I just don't know if I can go on another mission without knowing the answer to this question."

Molly's heart dropped and she started shaking.

Luke got down on one knee and said, "Molly, you are the love of my life. You are always there for me and are a constant pillar of strength for me when I'm away. I would not be able to do what I do without you by my side. Please make me the happiest man and marry me."

Luke pulled out a ring box and flashed one huge diamond in her face. Molly nearly passed out. Luke just proposed to her. She was never a relationship kind of girl and never considered herself marriage material. She met Luke in a bar and he singled her out. He did not let her leave his sight that night and she knew she was in trouble because she didn't want to leave his sight. She didn't expect to ever get married, but once she met Luke, her life changed drastically. She fell in love and started picturing her future with him at her side. She flung her arms around Luke and kissed him senseless.

"I'll take that as a yes!" Luke laughed.

"Oh, baby, you know it's a yes!" Molly replied. "Oh, you are so going to get the best ever blow job tonight."

"And that is what we will use as their slogan throughout their wedding. No need to use monograms everywhere, oh no we will just plaster, 'oh you are so going to get the best ever blow job tonight' all over the walls and invites. If that's not romantic, I don't know what is!" Jane joked.

"Yes, and we can hand out bubblegum cock suckers as favors," Molly replied.

"Let's save that for the bachelorette party, huh?" Jane said.

"Fine, have it your way," Molly said. "Oh, and I hope you know you are our event planner and my maid of honor. You have your work cut out for you, lady."

Jane laughed and gave them both a hug. Molly could not be happier right now; she had everything she needed...her friends and her man. Now she just needed to get Luke back to her apartment and get him good and naked.

Molly felt like she was floating in heaven. She was with the sweetest man, she had the best of friends, and she could not have asked for a better proposal.

"Hey!" Molly said, swatting Luke lightly on the shoulder. "Did you have the restaurant play our song over the speakers?"

Luke gave Molly that little boy grin that made her fall in love with him and replied, "Of course, babe, do I win bonus points for that one?"

Molly laughed. "Oh, Luke, you are so on the good boy list right now, you're going to be quite the pleasured man for quite some time."

Molly heard Jane groan in the background, but she didn't care. She wrapped her arms around Luke and kissed him all over. Whenever Luke was gone, she never forgot what it felt like to have him in her arms, but when he was back with her, having him in her arms always made her feel whole.

She heard Michael clear his throat behind her. She almost completely forgot about the skee-ball challenge. Molly separated herself from Luke just enough to address Jane.

"Sorry I made you lose, sweetie, but hey, now you can go out with that hunk of meat over there," Molly said, tossing her thumb toward Brady.

Brady blushed. Was that actually a blush from Brady Matthews? Molly thought he was some over-confident prick. Not that she would normally encourage her best friend to go out with someone like him, but Jane really just needed to get back into the scene and get a good fuck in her bones. Then she would be ready to go on to the next best thing. Brady was a perfect rebound for Jane. But Molly would let her friend worry about her future date with Brady because, at the moment, all Molly cared about was taking her fiancé home for some serious private time. She could not be happier.

Jane

Once everything settled down, Molly and Luke left so they could go "bone" as Molly put it. She was a lady with absolutely no class, but Jane loved her for it. That left her with just Michael and Brady and Jane could tell Michael was itching to leave Brady and her alone. Jane prayed she wasn't going to be left alone with Brady because it would be extremely awkward. What the hell would she say to him?

She thought maybe she would just be polite and go out

with Brady to make her friends get off her back, but she really didn't want to. She knew Molly wanted her to just go out with Brady for a good lay, but what were Michael's intentions? Did he really think they would make a good match, or was he doing a friend a favor? Was this Michael's idea or Brady's?

Michael patted Brady on the shoulder and announced, "I think I'm going to take off and see how the misses is doing. Why don't you guys stay here? Maybe you can teach Brady a thing or two about skee-ball. Oh, and tough loss kid, maybe next time you can beat me."

Jane replied, "You only won because Molly screamed so loud the sound waves moved my arm to the side and threw off my shot."

"You keep thinking that, darlin'." Michael kissed her on the cheek, shook Brady's hand, and took off.

Great, now she was all alone with Brady Matthews. No doubt every girl in the place was wondering what the hell he was doing with her. Jane was mortified. Brady's face read like an open book; he looked just as uncomfortable as Jane. She knew this was going to be awful, and Brady's face agreed with her.

He wasn't even really looking at her, just scraping the ground with his shoe. Maybe she should just call it a night and take off, let Brady off the hook. That would be the best option for everyone. Jane had a feeling Michael asked Brady to go out with her, to give her a boost of confidence since things had been so bad for her in her romantic life. Well, Brady didn't have to do Michael or her any favors; she would relieve Brady of his duties. She thought that maybe she could go out on a date with the intimidating man, but she lost all her nerve when she saw the look on his face and decided to call it a night instead.

Jane yawned, looked at her watch and announced, "Well, it's getting late. I'm sure you have to get up and work out early tomorrow morning, maybe swing a bat or do something baseball related. I'll just pay my bill and we can be off."

Brady

Brady was a little shocked that Jane wanted to leave. He thought they were having a nice night with their friends. Well, now that he thought about it, whenever he tried talking to Jane

33

individually, she was either short and gave him one-word answers or she didn't answer at all. What was her deal? Women always threw themselves at him, not that he liked it, but did he repulse her? He knew he was a little nervous, but he didn't think he was giving her a bad vibe.

He was looking good tonight, was it his cologne? No that couldn't be it. Molly said he smelled like sex in heaven tonight. She was funny; why couldn't Jane be more open like Molly? Granted, Molly was a little too much for Brady. Luke definitely had his hands full, but he just wished Jane would open up more like her friend, let loose a little more, and let him into her little world.

"Hey, I thought you owed me a date?" Brady asked. Hoping he didn't sound desperate or whiney.

Jane looked a little shocked and said, "Listen, Brady, you're a nice guy and I know you're just doing Michael a favor by asking me out, but you don't have to, really. You're off the hook. I'm sure you have more famous and more attractive women to date." And with that, Jane shook his hand and took off.

Wow, that was a bit harsh. Brady was a little startled by her honesty. She barely talked to him all night and when she did talk to him, she accused him of only wanting famous women in his life and that he was too good for her. What little she knew of him. He actually would prefer to sit at home with his girl tucked under his arm, drinking some wine and talking about their day while swinging on their front porch swing. Cheesy maybe, but he grew up in a small town and cherished those memories. He didn't get many of them with all the publicity surrounding him, thanks to the worst mistake of his life: Laney Johnson.

Well he wasn't going to force Jane to go out with him. He had to make a better impression on her if he was ever going to have a shot at taking her out. He was surprised when that thought crossed his mind; he wanted to make a better impression? So, he was still going to pursue her? Even though she was giving him the cold shoulder? Well, Brady Matthews never turned away from a challenge. He was going to get a date with Jane Bradley, if it was the last thing he did.

CHAPTER FIVE

Molly

Luke swept Molly into the bedroom and she instantly melted. She missed her man so much. She made him sit on the bed while she turned on some sexy music to set the mood. Luke always laughed at her when she played music; he always thought it was corny, but she liked it because it gave her more confidence when she stripped for him.

She always wondered why Luke had fallen for her, why he chose her to be his. He was devastatingly gorgeous, like Photoshop gorgeous. His muscles rippled under his clothes and begged to be touched. He was exceptionally sculpted, their bodies fit perfectly together and, thank God, he was not a hairy man.

The music started playing and Molly started feeling the beat. She peeled off Luke's army-issued T-shirt and glided her hands down to his waist to unbuckle his belt. He stopped her and said, "Not so fast, doll; you took off my shirt, now you take something off."

Easy enough for Molly, she was wearing a black strapless dress and could not wait to get out of it. She turned around so her back was to Luke and asked for a little help. His hands glided up her backside and slowly unzipped the back of her dress. She turned to face him and let the dress fall to the ground, she kicked it to the side, while still wearing her stilettos.

"Damn, you are fucking beautiful," Luke said. "How did I

ever get so lucky to find you?"

"I was just thinking the same thing," Molly said, while leaning over and nibbling at Luke's lip and unbuckling his belt. She felt his erection already and it took every ounce of control in her not to rip his pants open and slip herself over his shaft.

"Your turn," Luke said in a low grumble.

Molly walked away from Luke so he could get the whole view of her body while she unclasped her bra and let it fall to the floor. Luke's eyes turned dark with lust; he was going to pounce on her soon, so she needed to get what she wanted before he got the chance. She went over to Luke and sat on his lap. Luke breathed in real fast with the sudden movement on his lap.

"You're killing me, woman. I can't take this slow seductive crap after being gone for so long. I'm about to explode!"

"Patience, Luke, believe me I'm so fucking wet right now and throbbing I can't take it either."

Luke growled in the back of his throat, grabbed Molly behind her neck and moved her mouth over his. They plunged into each other like raw animals. Molly slowly rocked on Luke's lap as she felt his erection getting harder and harder. She kept rocking and making out with Luke, heightening her senses until she couldn't take it any longer. She pushed him down on the bed and ripped his pants off. Thank God he took care of his shoes and socks earlier. His penis surged so high and was glistening at the tip. She just stared at him until Luke interrupted her thoughts.

"Like what you see there, hot stuff?" Luke joked with his hands behind his head.

Molly could only nod. She tore her thong off and ran her hands up Luke's thighs. God was he perfect, everything a woman could ask for. He was caring, sweet, sexy, funny, and he loved her with all his heart.

She moved her hands to the center of his being and slowly started stroking him; he made a low grumbling noise. She was never a selfish lover, she always thought pleasing her man was just as satisfying as him pleasing her because she knew she was the reason he was turned on and about to explode; that gave her all the satisfaction she needed.

She slowly lowered her head and took him in her mouth. She licked along his tip and gently stroked the bottom of his shaft. He slightly squirmed under her touch and she knew he was going to release soon. She couldn't wait any longer to fully have him. She kept stroking with her mouth and her hand and, just when she thought he was about to release, he lifted off the bed and threw her underneath him. He placed an elbow on either side of her head and stroked her hair gently.

Panting, Molly asked, "What are you doing, don't you want me to finish you off?"

"I would rather we finish together," he said gently, as he stared down at her. She felt his erection dancing between her hotness, pleading to enter. She surged her hips forward to urge him on, but he only laid flatter on her. "I want to take my time with you and savor this moment. I have the most beautiful girl in my arms and I want to make sure this lasts a long time."

Molly all but melted in his arms. Luke lowered his mouth down to hers and gently started kissing her. He roamed from her lips to her neck and down to her breasts. He sucked each one gently and used his tongue to play with her nipples. He gently lowered his head to her abdomen trailing kisses along the way and then to her throbbing center. He kissed it and then started licking her wetness. She gasped out loud and had to control herself not to surge her hips to his face. He continued to slowly lavish her until her body went completely numb. She couldn't hold it any longer, the pleasure she had was too intense and she finally gave away to the first wave of ecstasy. She didn't know how long she laid there squirming with surges of pleasure since he continued to torture her with his tongue, but next thing she knew, Luke was on top of her, kissing her mouth and spreading her legs with his knees.

"Open for me, baby." She did.

He slowly teased her core and entered one inch at a time. It was torture. She kept surging her hips toward him and she finally screamed, "Fuck, babe I need you so bad, please take me over the edge again."

On that note, Luke entered her fully and started rocking back and forth, in and out of her. Molly's senses kept building until everything turned black and she could only feel Luke and what he was doing to her. They built their ecstasy so high together they came barreling down at the same time. Luke moaned in the back of his throat and Molly screamed with desire. Luke finally collapsed on top of Molly with their bodies still connected through their centers for quite some time. He supported his weight on his elbows and just stared down at her. He put a piece of her hair behind her ear and gently kissed her forehead.

Luke broke the silence between them. "Thank you so much for wanting to be my wife, you've made me the happiest man ever."

Molly nearly cried. "Luke, you have no idea how you've changed my life with your love. I will never be the same, thank you." She really wouldn't ever be the same. Luke took her in when she was a wild child, no family, no real ambitions in life and made her dream for once, dream for a future, and dream for a family. Molly kissed him on the mouth and surged her hips up at Luke again.

Luke grinned and flipped her on top of him. "Round two already, well I'm up for the challenge doll, do your worst to me!"

Jane

Jane hadn't talked to Molly in a couple of days. Knowing Molly and Luke, they were probably still in the bedroom. The other night, Brady shook her hand and walked her to her car like a gentleman. He most likely wanted to make sure he at least treated her right so she didn't complain to Michael. He looked a little shocked when she told him he didn't have to go out with her, but he probably wasn't used to a woman turning down his offer, even if it was a forced offer. Oh well, that night is over and done with. It was nice of Michael to try, but she could do things on her own.

She had to focus on work. She got a call from a volunteer manager for Special Olympics saying their main contributor wanted to put on a fundraiser to help boost the local program and promote more awareness for the athletes. The volunteer manager, Lucy, was very set on making sure her contributor's standards were met, which were pretty high. Normally, Special Olympics puts on their own fundraising events and has their own event managers that put on the events themselves, but JB events was specifically requested by the contributor, so here she was.

The contributor asked to put on a golfing fundraiser. They made the guest list and Jane just had to make sure she booked the golf course, sent out invites, coordinated food and prizes as well make sure there was plenty of media for the event. The contributor was hoping to make a couple hundred thousand for the non-profit organization.

Jane worked her butt off, since they gave her such short notice. Putting an event together in a week was pretty difficult, but since she worked by herself, it made it almost impossible. She decided to call upon Albert for a little bit of help and resources. She dialed his number on her speaker phone.

"Darling girl, I haven't heard from you in a while. Last time I saw you, you were dancing and about to suck face with that baseball player," Albert declared.

Leave it to Albert Winchester to not let a girl live something down. "Thanks for reminding me Alby, how are you doing?"

"I take it better than you are, since you don't have a scandalous story to tell me. What happened? Did you chicken out?"

Irritated about talking about Brady Matthews Jane said, "No, I just don't want to get mixed up with the wrong guy and get my heart broken again. I don't know if I'm ready to have a relationship yet Alby."

"Oh girl, who said anything about a relationship? I'm just looking for a guy to wash out the cobwebs that have formed in that lady cactus of yours!"

"Albert! Not that it is any of your business, but I do use a vibrator on occasion, so it's not as dusty as you think it is down there." Whoa, did she just admit to using a vibrator? Where did that come from? If she said something like that when she was with George, she would have been scolded. According to George, one did not talk about bedroom activities in public. Guess he didn't mind cheating on his fiancé with Rebecca, the office slut, in public though.

"Janey, you and I both know a vibrator is nothing compared to a man like Brady Matthews rubbing his thick muscular hands up and down that luscious body of yours and pounding you until you cream."

"God, you and Molly are soul sisters, I swear." Jane felt herself blushing. Her friends were so crude. She used to be able to keep up with their sexual banter, but thanks to George, she now just became flustered when her friends teased her with their talk. She missed the days of being able to snap back a snarky comment.

Jane continued to listen to Albert talk to her about how

hot Brady was and she surprisingly was turning all hot inside just listening to Albert. She was not going to lie to herself, Brady was beyond hot and yes, having sex with him would be incredible, but she didn't think she was strong enough for a one night stand, because she knew that was all she was going to get from him. He didn't want anything more, who's to say he even wanted her at all? She was delusional to think so.

"Now that I'm all hot and bothered, what can I do for you dear?" Albert finally asked.

"I need some press for a fund-raising event I'm putting on this weekend. It's extremely short notice, but I have to make sure this event is recognized. It would be a great opportunity to build my business. There are expected to be some very influential people there."

"Sure, sweetheart, I'll set something up with my contacts, make sure you have a press release ready and I'll send it out once I've contacted everyone. Anything else I can do to help you?"

"Albert you are a doll, thank you. Would you and some of your buddies like to come golf? I know it's not your thing, but there is a contest for best dressed and it has your name written all over it."

"Count me in; you know I can't turn down a good costume party," Albert said.

Jane laughed, "It's not a costume party, Alby, it's a golf fund-raiser."

"Tomato, Tomahto. See you Saturday, sweet cheeks."

Jane owed Albert big time; he was always there for her. Maybe she'd get him one of those button-up shirts he's been raving about. Something about a pattern on the outside and a crazy print on the inside; it was all he talked about. Albert really was one of the most eccentric dressers she knew. She loved him for it. If anyone could pull off neon paisley paired with polka dot pants, he could. She feared what he might wear to the golf event.

Michael

Michael sat in his huge house; he didn't want one this big, but Kelly insisted. She said they needed to keep up appearances. Michael could give two shits about appearances. He didn't like the fountains throughout the yard, the pillars in the entrance, the marble countertops, or the five-tiered chandelier hanging in the entryway. He just wanted a nice house that didn't need any repairs and a loving wife. His house was too nice for his liking and his wife was nowhere to be found. She spent her days shopping and her nights out at different bars. He hadn't seen her in days.

Michael didn't know what to do about Kelly. He felt like he lost her a while ago. He needed to salvage their relationship somehow. She'd stopped caring about the foundation that they'd worked so hard on. It embarrassed him. He asked her a while back if they were going to go to the hospital to read to the children like they used to every Christmas, but she was too "busy." He had no clue with what, since she didn't work.

One thing he knew for sure was, he was extremely grateful for being traded to Atlanta. In a short amount of time he'd reconnected with two of his best friends and instantly connected with most of the guys on his team. He'd formed such a great support system in such a short amount of time.

It was funny to Michael that Brady took such an interest in Jane and asked him to set him up on a date with her, in a clever manner. He wasn't going to lie to himself, he was a little jealous. He'd always had a little something for Jane, but knew he could never act upon it, especially now since he was married. Still, Brady didn't strike Michael as the kind of guy interested in dating such a sweet girl. He made sure Brady had good intentions before he set them up. He didn't want to set Jane up with Brady if his only intentions were to stick her and ditch her. Brady made it quite clear that was not the plan; he really wanted to get to know Jane and Michael trusted him. How could he not? The man had been nothing but honest and nice toward him.

Michael at least hoped maybe Brady could help Jane shed that awful snooty attitude she acquired while she was with George. Maybe Brady would be able to help Jane develop into the girl he used to know: fun, sassy, and sweet. Only time will tell.

Jane

The week went by incredibly fast, but Jane was able to pull everything together. Whoever this contributor was really wanted to make sure things were going as planned and to their liking. Lucy made it very clear that this person donated, not only a lot of money, but a lot of time to Special Olympics and always made sure their events went off without a hitch. Jane only wished she had time to donate to a worthy cause. She admired this person and couldn't wait to actually meet them. There were some major high-profile people who were coming to the event today. She knew there were a lot of important people on the guest list, but she didn't know almost all of them were going to show up.

Halfway through the week, Molly and Luke came out of their cave for some fresh air and decided to come to the event, as well as Michael. Molly took some "sick" days at work to spend some more time with Luke, lucky Luke! Albert showed up with three other men, filling out a complete golf team. Each team was made up of four and had to pay a certain amount of money to compete in the tournament. At the end of the tournament, there were awards for various categories: best score, best drive and, of course, best dressed. There were athletes from Special Olympics who came out as well and joined where teams needed an extra player.

Everyone was registering around her making Jane too busy to notice anyone other than the people forming teams and donating money, so when Brady Matthews came strolling up and tapped her on the shoulder, she nearly screamed.

"Holy crap, you scared me."

Brady laughed, "Sorry about that, little lady; didn't mean to startle you."

"That's alright, are you here to golf? Did Michael tell you about the event? It was sweet of you to come," Jane replied.

"Yeah, something like that," Brady said grimly. "Uh, do you know where Michael is? We're on a team with two Special Olympics athletes. I've played with the athletes before in other fundraisers. They're amazing and will be giving us a run for our money today."

Jane smiled, hmm he had a softer side; she liked that. "Yeah, Michael is over there; you guys are in slot C to start. Good luck."

Brady gave her a devilish grin and walked off. Wow, she was surprised Brady showed up. She didn't know he made appearances at places that weren't a major highlight for the gossip magazines. Her phone made a noise, indicating she got a text message. It was from Albert.

Albert: Girl, if you do not pounce on that hunk of meat soon, I'm going to!

Jane just shook her head, laughed, and replied.

Jane: "Girl" go wax your legs or something.

The event started and the golfers took off. While everyone was golfing, Jane and Lucy were in the banquet hall making sure the rest of the event was in place, talking to press and touching up on any last-minute details. Before she knew it, golfers, athletes, coaches and families started to trickle back to the clubhouse.

The first part of the event went great, better than great. She was getting compliments from every golfer she ran into. She made sure to hand her cards out to everyone and anyone she talked to. Nothing wrong with self-promotion.

Everyone was done with golfing and headed into the big banquet hall for healthy sandwiches, baked chips and a variety of sports drinks. Special Olympics was big on recognizing healthy athletes, so at their events, they tried to promote healthy eating. Easy enough for Jane, she didn't have to coordinate some elaborate meal for a bunch of stiff shirts and fancy folk. That was one of her least favorite parts of her job: picking out the food. If it was up to her, everyone would get a hot dog, a pat on the back, and be sent on their way. Even though she was serving healthy sandwiches from the local deli, everyone seemed to enjoy them.

The day was flying by. The time came for speeches and awards and, since she'd been so busy, she still hadn't had a chance to meet the contributor; she hoped they didn't think she was rude. She was so concerned with everything going so well around her, she forgot to introduce herself. After all the awards and speeches, she would introduce herself and thank them for giving her the opportunity to make this event happen. This event was giving her a lot of exposure for her company and she couldn't be more grateful for the opportunity.

Lucy took the podium and rallied all the participants in the room. "Thank you so much for taking the time out of your Saturday to come and support Special Olympics. Our athletes are so grateful for your time and donations. Because of the success this event brought, we are going to be able to continue our programs and supply our athletes with more appropriate equipment and some new uniforms. We would like to call up one of our biggest supporters and the catalyst for this event today: Brady Matthews."

The world around Jane froze in time as she heard Brady's name called from the podium. Jane knew she looked ridiculous because her jaw fell to the floor and she had to be poked by Albert to stop gaping.

She couldn't believe it. Brady Matthews had put this event together and hired her to make it happen. He hired her! He must have thought she had some talent in order to pull this event off in a week, but he'd never seen her work, so how could he know? What were his motives? Was this another way for him to get into her pants?

Jane shook the pessimistic thought out of her head as she watched Brady hug some of the Special Olympic athletes before he made it to the podium. Maybe she should stop questioning the man and just admit that she was shocked that she was wrong about Brady; he had a heart, a very generous heart...especially after all the things she'd heard about him and what he did for Special Olympics.

An overwhelming feeling washed over Jane's body as her heart started to warm toward Brady, which was not a good thing. She needed to keep her distance from the dangerous man, but she couldn't help the way her heart reached out to him...for giving so much. Damn him.

Brady took the podium and applauded toward the audience as they applauded back toward him. Once they silenced, he began to speak.

"Thank you so much for coming out today and supporting Special Olympics. This organization has been near and dear to my heart ever since I was a kid. My neighbor and best friend, Randy Stevens, had Down Syndrome and, although he was 20 years older than me, he was the one who taught me how to throw a baseball. He would practice with me every weekend and he always told me I would make it to the major leagues one day. I always asked him why he wasn't going to try out for the major leagues and he just smiled at me and he said he was too good for the major leagues: he was in Special Olympics!"

Everyone in the room gave a kindhearted laugh. Brady continued. "When Randy was very ill and in the hospital, I was just starting to make it to the big leagues and I promised him I would make sure there would continue to be just as many, if not more, opportunities for athletes like him to participate in the sports they loved."

Jane wiped a tear from her eyes as she listened to the end of Brady's speech. God, she needed to pull it together; she couldn't be crying like a lunatic in front of all these potential clients. When she was watching Brady at the podium, she couldn't help but notice a voice in the back of her head that was saying maybe she'd misjudged Brady Matthews; maybe she was wrong to judge him so quickly.

Although…he could be a kind-hearted guy and still a player. His everyday life could be completely different from his media-pronounced active sex life. He could be a fundraising entrepreneur during the day and a man slut at night.

"So, thank you for coming out and supporting Randy's and my dream. I wanted to raise $250,000 today and we didn't come anywhere near that goal, we went over! We raised $350,000."

Jane nearly choked on her own saliva, $350,000 in a week? Holy crap…either Albert had some serious connections or someone made a huge lump sum donation and she thought she knew who it was and he was standing up at the podium, gorgeous as ever. Damn Brady Matthews and damn her rusty libido.

Brady Continued, "I have a couple of people to thank, Albert Winchester, you've been a real help this week handling all the press for us; we are very grateful. Lucy Reynolds, thank you for helping set up this event and talking with our event coordinator as well as making sure some of the most amazing athletes were invited to this outing. Finally, I need to thank Jane Bradley from JB Events; without you, we would not be standing here right now amongst all this success. Thank you for busting your butt this week and making this happen for us." Brady winked at Jane and then wrapped up his speech. "I hope you all had a good time, thank you!" Brady finished with a wave while the room erupted with applause as Brady started to walk right toward Jane.

Jane could not talk to Brady right now, she was too emotional. She dropped her clipboard on the table next to her and ran to the bathroom. Oh my God, she was such an idiot for thinking such bad things about Brady. Yes, he was still a womanizer, but he had such a big heart. Ugh, she needed to pull herself together and get back out there. She looked at herself in the mirror; she was pale and her mouth was completely dry. She sipped some water and pinched her cheeks to get some color back in them. She looked like an idiot hovering in the bathroom so she gathered herself and headed back to the banquet hall. He was just a man, a man that happened to look at her as if he was going to tear her clothes off or hold her tightly, stroking her hair all night.

When he was thanking her in front of everyone, it looked like he had pure lust oozing out of his eyes for her. Maybe Michael didn't ask Brady for a favor the night she lost the skee-ball bet, maybe Brady really wanted to go out with her. Whatever happened in the past didn't matter now because Brady sure looked interested today and she knew Michael didn't put Brady up to this.

CHAPTER SIX

Brady

Brady stood in the clubhouse of the golf course looking around for Jane. It had been an hour since the event ended. Albert, of course, was awarded best dressed. He was a vision in plaid, high socks and a sweater vest. Albert told Brady when Brady handed Albert his prize that he "took his costume parties seriously." Boy, would Brady be nervous to go shopping with Albert. He could only imagine Albert picking out a nice purple shirt with pineapples across the front and flamingo clam digger pants for Brady to wear.

Where had Jane gone off to? After his speech, he had to shake hands with a bunch of people and lost track of where she went. He hoped she hadn't taken off yet; he wanted to thank her personally instead of in front of a large crowd. Also, possibly ask her to go for a drink…a man could only hope.

Brady was taking a big risk, running a fund-raiser on such short notice, but Jane did a fantastic job; he knew he could count on her. He couldn't believe how much they raised for Special Olympics. Yes, he put in a good chunk of change of his own, but for a week's notice, they raised a lot of money. He knew Randy would be proud of him.

Brady saw Lucy wandering around the banquet hall packing up loose items so he went up to her. She was a cute girl. She looked fresh out of college, medium length brown hair, brown eyes and dark rimmed glasses. He should keep her in mind for any of his friends who were looking for a nice girl.

"Hey, Lucy, thank you again for helping out this past week; I know it was tough, but I really appreciate all you did to make this event such a success."

"No problem, Mr. Matthews, it was a joy working with you again and we are so grateful for your contributions to our organization. Because of you, our athletes are able to train in better facilities."

"You can call me Brady, and I'm glad. Do you happen to know where Jane Bradley went? I wanted to shake her hand and thank her again before I left," Brady said.

"Yes, I just said goodbye to her. She was headed for her car."

Brady yelled thanks to Lucy as he ran out to the parking lot. He spotted Jane; she was parked under a giant shade tree, his preferred parking spot as well. He always liked to keep his car in the shade and away from the Atlanta heat; he assumed Jane had the same thought since she had a sun shade in her windshield. She was cuter than ever, struggling with a giant box and trying to fit it into her little sedan. He rushed over to help her, right before the box slipped out of her hands. He lifted it up, startling her. Her eyes went big and they looked a little red. Was she crying? Brady did notice her wipe her face when he was making his speech. Maybe he actually made an impression on her today; he could only hope so.

Jane all but whispered a thank you and opened the trunk so he could place the box she'd been struggling with in her car.

"Anything else you need to put in here?" Brady asked, dusting off his shirt.

"No, that's about it, thank you though."

"Listen…hey," they both said at the same time. Brady told her to go first, but Jane gestured for him to proceed. Brady shrugged his shoulders and continued his thoughts.

"I wanted to thank you personally for helping out this week and making this happen for the organization and for me. I know I didn't give you a lot of time to accomplish all my demands, but I knew you could pull it off. Michael talked my ear off about how great of an organizer you are."

Jane shyly looked away and replied, "You're welcome." Her gaze came back to his and she smiled. "It was quite a task, but I had fun doing it and the athletes are so amazing. I admire you for spending so much time with them."

Was that a compliment she paid him? Man, maybe asking her to help with this event was turning out to be a great idea. He watched her fidget in her shoes and brush her hair behind her ears.

"Thank you, I wouldn't choose any other organization to work with." Brady took a deep breath. "I'm pretty hungry after all that work and packing up, would you like to catch a bite to eat?"

This was it, was she actually going to let her defenses down and go out with him? He saw her struggling with an answer; he just hoped it was in favor of him.

As Brady waited for her answer, he couldn't help but stare at her beauty. Even right now after working all day, outside in the hot Atlanta sun, she looked beautiful. Her eyes were as blue as the sky and her hair fell in soft waves over her shoulders. What he wouldn't give to run his hands through her mane and kiss her up her neck and across her jaw…ending right on her plump lips.

Jane looked up at him and said, "I would love to, but I have plans with Luke and Molly tonight. I haven't seen them since Molly claimed Luke was going to receive the 'best blow job ever' in the middle of Dave and Busters," Jane said, while using air quotes.

Brady laughed. She was sweet, sexy, and funny…a lethal combination. "Alright, well…" he was interrupted by Jane when she said, "You can always come along if you'd like."

Hallelujah! The heavens parted and angels began to sing in his head. Holy crap, she just invited him to go to dinner with her. He for sure thought he was going to be let down once again tonight, leading him to conjure up another way to see her. But thank God something in Jane's brain changed because he was getting his chance…his chance to finally be with her and he was not going to let go of it.

"That would be great. I'm kind of sweaty and gross. Would you mind if I went back home to take a shower? I'll pick you up at your place and then we can head on over to the restaurant."

She smiled and his heart melted; God she was beautiful. She had such a fresh, sexy look. Nothing he had seen before, throw in her sweet nature and hidden sex kitten, and she was one hell of a woman. Jane interrupted his thoughts when she said, "Sounds great."

They exchanged information and Brady turned to walk to

his car with a little bit of extra pep in his step, being careful not to trip and embarrass himself. He would get his chance with the lovely Jane. Yes, they might not be entirely alone, but if he knew Molly like he thought he did, he was sure something was going to "come up" and Luke and Molly would have to leave early, leaving Brady and Jane to themselves. This was turning out to be a great day.

Molly

Molly just got done toweling off her wet body, walked over to her very naked and very sexy fiancé, and was about to straddle him when her phone started ringing.

"Just leave it, babe, you can call whoever it is back," Luke said, while running his hands up her inner thighs and pulling her into place on top of his lap.

"Mm, your cock feels so good between my legs. You know, if I'm not careful, you're going to rub me raw."

"That's what I'm going for, darlin'," Luke said, while nibbling on Molly's neck.

"You are incorrigible," Molly said, while gently swatting the side of his arm. "If we're doing this again, we're doing it my way."

"And what way is that, sweet tits?"

Molly did a one-eighty on Luke's lap so her back was facing Luke's chest and straddled his lap. She took in his entire heated arousal in her throbbing center and started rocking up and down.

"Fuck, babe, you are so hot," Luke murmured.

"Mmmmm…you feel so good inside of me," Molly moaned.

Luke ran his hands up Molly's sides and started caressing her breasts and turning her nipples into swollen nubs. Molly arched back, giving Luke more access. He kissed her up and down her neck as Molly continued to rock up and down, occasionally pulling all the way out and then slamming back down on his length. They both moaned at the same time and Luke slid one hand down to Molly's swollen clit and started gently rubbing it. Molly nearly exploded right there.

"Oh God, Luke…mmm fuck!"

Luke started working her swollen center more, while massaging her breasts with the other hand. Molly was panting, ready to sexually combust when a heat of raw pleasure came over her, the same time Luke began shuddering. Molly screamed at the top of her lungs and then leaned back exhausted against Luke's chest. He pulled her down on the bed and gently rubbed her back as she curled into his shoulder.

Molly wasn't sure how long they laid there, but her phone kept ringing and she knew it had to be Jane; no one else would call that many times in a row. She had that big fund-raiser event, so something must have happened after she and Luke left because why else would Jane be constantly calling Molly when she was going to see her in a couple of hours in person?

"I better get that," Molly whispered into Luke's ear.

"I'm going to choke Jane when I see her. Doesn't she know I have the sexiest woman in my arms and I'm enjoying my post-sex relaxation?" Luke thought the same thing Molly did. Jane would be the only one who would call Molly that many times in a matter of minutes. Luke murmured, "My God, my cock is still throbbing…make sure you mention that to Jane when you talk to her."

Molly laughed. "I'm sure she would love to hear that information." Molly played with his throbbing center, lightly stroking him up and down.

Luke breathed in hard and said, "What you're doing right now would be a dream, but you better return Jane's phone call before she loses her mind. I'll take a rain check on the stroking, though. You have the softest hands. I wouldn't want them to miss out on an opportunity and deprive them of such satisfaction."

Molly laughed as she got up and did her sexiest strut to the phone. She glanced over at Luke. He was propped up on one elbow just gazing at her in adoration. She was so lucky to have such a loving, sexy, and honest man.

She glanced down at her phone, yup four missed calls from Jane. It must be important.

"How did you know it was Jane?" Molly asked, just making sure she was right about Luke's intuitions.

"Who else calls you four times in a row?" Luke stated.

Molly nodded her head in agreement and redialed Jane's number in her phone. Jane picked up right away and answered with a panicked voice.

"Hello?" Jane said, on the other end of the line.

"Hey, Janey Bear, it's me, sorry I missed your calls, I was busy creaming all over Luke."

"Oh, Jesus Christ, Molly, I do not want to hear about your horizontal Olympics; this is an emergency."

Molly slightly panicked, "What's wrong doll? Is everything ok? Did something happen at your event? Are you in the hospital?" The word hospital made Luke jump to his feet and throw pants on; he was ready to go. God, he was adorable.

"Everything is wrong, what was I thinking? God, I'm such an idiot." Molly was a little confused from Jane's confession.

She hesitated at first. "So, you're not in the hospital?" Luke rolled his eyes, stripped his pants off, and started doing the helicopter with his dick in front of Molly, making her giggle.

"This is not funny, Molly!" Molly stopped giggling, but couldn't wipe the smirk off her face.

"Sorry, Sweetie, I wasn't laughing at you." She swatted Luke and told him to go take another shower. "Start from the beginning, what's going on?

Jane exhaled into the phone and explained to Molly that Brady Matthews was the main contributor of the fundraising event, which Molly would have found out if she hadn't left the event early with Luke to take care of some unfinished business in the bedroom. Jane continued to tell Molly how Brady hired her specifically for the job and thanked her in front of a bunch of people and how, apparently, he was very attractive today. Molly couldn't help but chuckle at her friend's rambling. Boy, her friend had it bad for him.

"Then I was at my car about to leave and he asked me to dinner. He looked so damn sexy with his hair all messy and his green eyes cutting through me, I told him I couldn't."

"You what?" Molly nearly screamed.

Molly was just about to yell at her friend when Jane replied urgently, "I told him I was going to dinner with you and Luke. He looked so disappointed, so I told him he was more than welcome to come along and he nearly jumped out of his socks and accepted. He's picking me up at my apartment in an hour."

Molly couldn't help but smile. "That's fantastic!" Molly leaped with excitement. "So what's the big deal?"

"I think he might actually like me; I don't know if I'm ready for this. What if he is just acting like this so he can get me into bed like all his other women? I don't know if I can handle this." Jane was freaking out big time.

Molly calmly said, "Breathe, kiddo, it's going to be alright. I know he likes you; Michael told me. You just need to snap out of your funk and come to your senses. You need to realize you are a sexy little thing with a lot to offer that any man would be lucky to have. George was an idiot to cheat on you; you were the best thing to ever happen to him and now he is a loser with a sloppy-breasted girlfriend, living in his sister's basement. You have a chance to go out with a major league baseball player, who is actually very much interested in you. Who knows where it might go, but it never hurts to find out. Now pull yourself together, reach deep down inside and pull out that old Jane I know and love. I want you to wear that midnight blue strapless dress that shows off your amazing shoulders and tits, wear your hair down and put on those red stilettos you have. You are going to knock his pants off tonight."

Molly hung up the phone and charged right into the shower, surprising Luke. She felt so giddy for her friend. Finally, Jane was getting back on track with her life.

"Jane has a date with Brady Matthews tonight. We're all going out together!" Molly squealed.

"It's about time someone got rid of the cobwebs in her pussy." They both laughed, "Now, do we have time for some shower banging?"

Molly smiled, bent over and said "Always, big boy, now make me scream!"

CHAPTER SEVEN

Brady

Brady was nervous as hell, as if he had never been on a date before, let alone a group date. At least there would be other people there in case Jane went all mute on him again. He hoped Molly would bring out Jane's personality he'd seen bits and pieces of, so he could see more of the Jane he knew was hidden behind those pale blue eyes.

Brady was followed by paparazzi all the way from his house, but was able to ditch them in a housing development. Avoiding them was starting to become second nature to him. Brady pulled up to Jane's apartment complex and nodded in approval. It was a nice community. He had to remember, if this thing went further with her, not to take her back to his place until he knew she was ready because she would be intimidated...especially if she was living in an apartment. He clearly made a lot of money and he liked living in a nice home. He had all the amenities: pool with attached Jacuzzi and rock slide, movie theater, batting cages, fully equipped kitchen, and a California king bed ready for a sexy woman...one in particular he had in mind. He shook that thought out of his head for now and knocked on her door.

Jane opened the door and he nearly toppled over at seeing the goddess that was standing in front of him. She was wearing a hip-hugging dark blue dress that made her eyes pierce his soul and, what should be considered illegal, red stilettos, that had to be 3 inches high, but she was still a pip-squeak compared to his six-foot, three-inch height. Her hair was soft and wavy, begging for his fingers to be tangled in it and her smile just about cut him in half. Thank God he was so stunned because, if he wasn't, he would have had an instant erection and that would have been embarrassing. Not a great way to start off a first date with a girl who was already skittish around him.

"Jane," Brady said, stunned. "There are no words for how amazing you look."

Jane smiled dipping her head down so she just looked at him through her eyelashes. "Thanks Brady, you look pretty good yourself."

He was wearing grey khaki pants and a white and light blue plaid button-up shirt, nothing to write home about. She, though, she was definitely dressed to impress; he wished he brought his bat so he could fend off all the guys that were going to be gawking at her.

"Are you ready to go?" Brady asked, offering his arm out to her.

Jane smiled, linked her arm with his, and they headed for his car. Her hand wrapped around his forearm, which started to burn right through his skin; just the slightest touch was getting him all hot and bothered. How was he going to make it through the whole night? No matter what, he knew that, indeed, this was going to be a good night, a night that he had been thinking about for a while.

Jane

Jane was surprisingly happy now that she was wearing the dress Molly picked; she was nervous at first because, once again, it seemed like too much, but after Brady's reaction, she felt great about her choice, well...Molly's choice. Brady nearly drooled when she opened the door. It felt good to know that Brady Matthews thought she was attractive. It gave her confidence for the rest of the night, especially since he looked so damn sexy as well. Why was it that a guy could wear simple khaki pants and a button-up shirt with the sleeves folded to their elbows and still look amazing? It wasn't fair. Oh, and did he smell good. If she didn't have so much self-respect, she would have started humping him in her doorway. God, she had been hanging out with Molly too much; Jane's mind had started to meld with Molly's.

Brady opened the door to his BMW and smiled. Of course he had a BMW and she hated herself for thinking how "cool" he was for having such a stylish car. She felt like a teenager in high school all over again.

They arrived at the restaurant and spotted Luke and Molly instantly. They were the awkward couple groping each other inappropriately and making out in front of the hostess. Sometimes they could be so embarrassing.

Jane glanced up at Brady, smiled sheepishly and said, "Sorry, once they're reunited, there's no separating them, even in public."

Brady smiled back and said, "I think it's endearing. I only hope to find love like that one day." And she'd be damned if he didn't stare directly into her eyes when he said that. A shiver passed through her. She shook off the feeling, went up to Molly, and tapped her on the shoulder.

"Hey, can you stop sucking each other's faces off for a couple of hours while we're in public?" Jane asked.

Molly smiled, wrapped her hand in Luke's and apologized. "Sorry, girl. Hey, you look amazing. What do you think Brady?"

Jane almost punched her friend in the boob. Was she trying to turn Jane's face as red as her shoes?

"I think I might be in trouble tonight with all the men who are going to be panting after her."

"Don't worry," Luke said. "I deal with that every day with this vixen. I'll teach you the death stare. Every man you give it to backs off right away."

Molly leaned up and kissed Luke hard on the mouth while he squeezed her ass.

"Alright you two, let's go sit down," Jane said.

The hostess, surprisingly, gave them nice seats looking over the cityscape of Atlanta. Jane was convinced they were going to be stuck by the bathroom, thanks to the Horny Hendersons. It must have been Brady's presence that gave them the good luck in seating. Brady pulled out Jane's seat for her and gently pushed it in when she sat down. She was grateful to sit across from Molly, since she was always nervous at first to eat in front of men. Being so close to Brady sent her senses into overload, thanks to the amazing cologne he was wearing. She needed to be on her A-game and that meant no alcohol.

"How about some wine to start us off?" Molly blurted.

Well, there went that idea. There was no way Molly was going to let Jane not drink. Well, Jane just had to keep it classy and watch her consumption, simple.

They ordered their food in record time. Brady asked what she was having and ordered for her when the waitress came over. It was a very smooth move of him, maybe too smooth. It was a move that George would have made because he controlled every aspect of Jane's life. Jane tried to remind herself that Brady was just trying to be a gentleman and not take over her life.

While they were waiting, Brady asked Luke, "So, you're in the army?"

Luke replied, "Yes, sir, I'm actually in Special Forces and that's pretty much all you can know. Not even Molly knows much about my job."

"Except that it takes you away from me and I'm lucky if I get to hear from you once every couple of months," Molly said sadly.

Luke took her hand and kissed the back of it. "You know I hate it too, babe. But it's my job. I won't be in it forever and, don't forget, when I'm 45, we'll retire and live off of Uncle Sam," Luke said with a wink.

Molly looked at Luke with pure lust and was about to attack him when Jane interjected, "Molly, don't even think about it."

Molly turned to her friend, looking all innocent, and said, "What? I was just thinking about how I have to go to the bathroom and how Luke said he needed to go once we got here, but he never got the chance because we had to wait for you two." She turned to Luke and said, "Come on, Big Boy, let's go to the bathroom."

Luke got up, wiggling his eyebrows at Brady and Jane as he ran off with his soon-to-be wife. Jane just shook her head and swore under her breath, so much for Molly being her cushion.

Jane was just about to say something to Brady to cut the tension, but instead chickened out and went for a sip of wine. In the middle of her drink, Brady nearly knocked her over with his words when he turned and said, "Jane, why do you hate me?"

Jane choked on her glass of wine for a second and looked up at him. His gaze was innocent and sweet. Man, he genuinely thought she hated him. Oh God, now she felt like a complete asshole. She knew she was not giving him many good vibes because she was too scared to get involved with someone who was just going to blow her off in the end, but to make someone think she hated them? That was just awful.

Jane apologetically said, "I don't hate you, Brady; you're actually a very wonderful guy."

"Then why is it like pulling teeth to get you to talk to me or even acknowledge me? I feel like I've shown you that I'm very much interested in you. Am I coming on too strong?"

When had a guy ever been this truly honest with her? What was Brady's deal? No guy she had ever met had ever been so forthcoming with her. It made her feel incredibly uneasy. Every relationship she'd ever been in had been based around mind games. A very unhealthy way to conduct a relationship with another person, she knew that now, but then again, it felt like that was how a relationship was supposed to be at times.

Jane placed her hand on Brady's arm; he flinched at her touch and she said, "You are not coming on too strong, Brady. I've been hurt very badly in the past and I'm just always watching out for myself. I know you're a great guy, but it's hard for me to believe that an extremely sexy and famous guy like you wants anything to do with me."

"So you think I'm sexy?"

Jane smirked, "I'd be blind if I didn't."

What the hell had gotten into her? Slow it down, Jane. She just told Brady she had been hurt. She didn't want to show how desperately she wanted him to wrap her in those strong muscular arms of his and take her to bed. Whoa, where did that come from? So, now she's on team Brady? When did that switch happen? She'd told herself not to pursue him; it was too dangerous for her heart. She didn't think she would be able to just settle for a one night stand with him. He was too good to be true: kind-hearted, sexy, athletic and caring. There was just one thing that set off her warning bells; his player status.

Brady grinned like a fool, bent over to her ear and whispered, "Want to get out of here?" She tingled all over from his lips being so close.

Jane looked through her eyelashes up at Brady and nodded. "I think if don't we leave soon, we're going to be kicked out anyway because of the friendly fornicators in the bathroom."

Brady chuckled, grabbed Jane's hand, left three hundred dollars on the table, and led her out to the car. Jane was so scared. She didn't want to get hurt again, especially by Brady because he seemed too good to be true. He looked at her like she was the only woman in the world and treated her with honesty and respect, plus he announced that he, indeed, was interested in her. That made her heart rate beat faster than when she went on her six-mile runs. She just needed to be cool, calm and collected and not get lost in the manly muscles and lust that was Brady Matthews.

All of a sudden, them leaving together and getting in his car processed through Jane's head. Did he think he was going to take her back to his place or back to her place and duplicate Molly and Luke's bathroom antics? She was just about to say something when Brady touched her arm gently and said, "Don't worry, Jane. I just want to go on a walk with you and grab a little bite to eat."

Feeling better, Jane relaxed in the plush seats of Brady's car, leaned her head back and watched the great city of Atlanta pass by in her the passenger window.

Brady

Finally, Brady had Jane alone. They settled for a couple of hot dogs from a street vendor for nourishment and decided to take a walk in a nearby park. Brady made sure to hold Jane's hand the minute he could get ahold of it and did not let it go. He could tell she was still nervous around him and he needed to encourage her that he was, in fact, a good guy and was not going to hurt her.

They stood on a bridge overlooking a little creek. Jane looked even more gorgeous in the moonlight. Her hair looked so soft to touch and her eyes glistened in the moonbeams. Why some man would cheat on this woman was beyond him, but their loss was his gain.

Jane looked over at Brady and said, "Tell me more about your friend Randy, he seemed like an amazing guy."

Brady was touched that she wanted to talk to him about something so personal; maybe the hand-holding thing was warming her up a bit.

"Randy Stevens was exactly that, an amazing guy. Growing up, I didn't even really know Randy was handicapped, not that it would have made a difference. I just wanted to hang out with him because he knew so much about baseball and he wanted to play with me. I was an only child, so having a playmate right next door was like having a sibling. Of course, he was way older than me, but he didn't mind hanging out with a little twerp of a kid like me."

Jane interrupted, "I highly doubt you were a little twerp." She smiled, "I bet you were real cute, actually."

Brady brushed a hair out of her face and continued. "Randy was dedicated to his Special Olympics softball team. He played short stop and he always said that he was going to go down in history as one of the greats. Well, he did in my book. His lucky number was anything that added up to eight because according to Randy, eight was the luckiest number in the world. Growing up, I always tried to have a uniform number on my different teams that added up to eight to make Randy proud."

"Oh, so that's why you're number seventeen on the Braves," Jane retorted, but then clamped her hand over her mouth.

Brady laughed, "I see the lady has been lying to me. Seems like you know a little more about me then you tend to lead on."

Jane said shyly, "I might have looked at your player profile a couple of times in the past and noticed you were number seventeen, as well as the leader in RBIs and home runs."

"Don't forget doubles, sweetheart," Brady said, nudging her chin up so she looked at him.

Jane went to turn and continue their stroll when Brady pulled her back and up against his chest. He wanted to kiss her and was about to when someone walked past them and shouted to Brady, "Where is Laney man? I can't believe you ever let her go!"

Brady rested his forehead against Jane's and counted to ten. He did not need to get into a fistfight with some random idiot in a park. What was that moron thinking? He felt Jane tense up. She broke from his grip and walked away. Brady jogged to catch up to her.

"Please don't pull away from me right now, Jane; you're just starting to open up to me and I'm really enjoying what I'm seeing and the time we're having together. That guy is an idiot; don't listen to anything he said. You know I want nothing to do with Laney. She was the one who messed everything up between us. Please look at me," Brady said, tilting her head up. "You are an amazing woman and I want to get to know you better."

Jane's eyes glistened, "I don't know if I can, I'm sorry Brady. I don't know if I'm ready for this."

Brady didn't let her go. He tilted her head up and made her look at him. "If that's the truth, Jane, then look me in the eyes and tell me you don't have any feelings for me."

Jane

What was Brady doing to her? Of course she had feelings for him, so many feelings that it scared her. She hadn't felt like this in years. How could she not get her heart broken and at the same time tell this guy she had feelings for him? It was useless. There was no hope; either way she was going to lose.

She also could not forget about the fact that Brady was a famous baseball player who previously dated an extremely famous movie star, a movie star that people expected Brady to be with. How could she ever compete with that? If something ever transpired between her and Brady, would she ever be good enough for him? For his fans? She was never good enough for George, so why the hell would she be good enough for Brady? She needed to tell Brady the truth…that she would never be good enough for him and she wasn't interested in pursuing any sort of relationship with him. He deserved at least that much for being nice to her.

Jane looked up at Brady and held back her tears. There was courage missing from her self-esteem, but she had to do this; she had to end things with Brady before they even got started.

"I do have feelings for you, Brady. I'm not going to lie about that. I'm just scared of getting hurt again and not sure if I'm ready to get involved with someone. You are so much in the public eye and I don't know if I can handle all of that."

Brady wiped a stray tear and gently kissed her cheek. "Come on, I'll take you home."

Great, what now? What was he thinking? Was he taking her home now because she was a nutcase? Wait, she said she wasn't ready to get involved with someone. Crap, she was an idiot. He was taking her home because he was looking to just have some fun, not get involved. Well at least he was going to end her misery sooner rather than later. She got one night with Brady Matthews, well one hot dog and a walk in the park, to be exact.

The car ride home was silently awkward and uncomfortable. Jane wished she had driven herself because the crickets chirping in the background was enough to make a girl crazy.

Brady finally pulled up to her apartment complex and got out of the car. She knew she was being ridiculous for being so upset, but deep down she knew it was because she got a chance to possibly be with someone great and she couldn't get past the hold George still had on her.

Jane wiped away some of the tears that silently leaked from her eyes on the way home and tried to look her best before Brady opened her door. No such luck; she was a mess. Brady bent down and wiped away what had to be a smudge of mascara.

"Come on, sweetheart," Brady said very calmly. He took her hand, led Jane up to her apartment, and opened her door for her. She was startled when she saw him follow her inside, instead of just dropping her off. He asked where her bathroom was and she pointed him in the right direction. To her surprise, he grabbed her hand and took her with him. He grabbed a wash cloth out of the basket she had on display and made her sit on the counter. He wet the cloth under some warm water and started wiping away her makeup. She was so drained, she didn't even care. When he was done, he looked at her and whispered "beautiful" under his breath.

She almost started crying again, but held herself together, grasping on to that little bit of self-respect she had left. He led her out of the bathroom and into her bedroom, which made instant warning bells go off in her head. She had no clue what his intentions were and it scared her.

"Brady…" she started, but he cut her off.

"Don't worry Jane, I'm not going to get frisky. I'm just going to tuck you in and then I'll make sure to lock the door behind me. You might want to change, even though that might be my favorite dress ever; it might not be the most comfortable to sleep in." He winked at her.

Jane agreed with Brady's clothing assessment and quickly changed into a pair of short shorts and a tank top with no bra, might as well let the man wonder what's underneath the thin garment when he leaves her behind.

When she walked into the bedroom, she didn't miss his quick intake of oxygen and his wandering eyes that swiftly took a peek at her exposed breasts under her shirt.

Coughing, Brady said, "I deserve a medal for behaving myself tonight."

Jane gave him a little smile and went over to her bed. He turned the covers down so she could climb in and he tucked her in.

Jane could not help but ask, "Why are you doing this? Why me? Don't you have a bunch of other women who are more stable than me at your disposal?"

Brady placed a finger over her lips to quiet her. "Don't believe everything you read in those trash magazines. I picked you because you are real. You have a purity about you that is so damn attractive I don't know what to do with myself. Then you go and wear red stilettos strutting around like some sex-craved vixen; it drives me crazy. You have my mind going in so many different directions, sometimes I forget how to walk. I want to get to know you better because what I know so far I already like. Forget about Laney and anything anyone says about me and her. That's in the past and so is your relationship with George. I want to date you, Jane, but I'll wait until you're ready."

Jane couldn't help but cry, letting go of the last shred of sanity she had left in her body. He wanted to date her? Was she ready to date again? It had been two years, but she was so focused on proving she could provide for herself that she completely forgot about fixing herself emotionally. That was pretty clear tonight from her incessant crying and emotional suicide. All she could do was nod and lay her head down. Brady brushed her forehead and placed a very gentle kiss on her eyes.

"You have my number if you need anything. Take care, doll; I'll call you tomorrow. I promise."

With that, he closed her door and locked up. She wanted to scream and tell him to come back to hold her until she fell asleep, but she didn't want to look desperate. No, she would just cry like a blubbering idiot in front of him for nothing he did to her. He really was a great guy if he put up with her tonight. He promised to call her tomorrow, which gave her some hope that she didn't completely scare him away. If he did call her, was she ready for this? He didn't just want to have sex with her, he actually wanted to get to know her and date her. She shook all damning thoughts out of her head for now. Instead, she closed her burning eyes and drifted off to sleep, thinking of green eyes and rippling forearms.

CHAPTER EIGHT

Jane

Jane couldn't believe how much of a gentleman Brady had been last night. She completely embarrassed herself and he still said he was interested in her. Maybe there was more to the man than met the eye. All she knew was, she wasn't sure if her heart was ready for a relationship. She didn't know if she was ready to move past the damage George caused her and take a new step forward in her life.

Jane was just returning from her morning jog when she noticed Molly's car outside. Oh boy, this would be interesting, she thought. Molly liked to surprise Jane often. Jane should never have given Molly a key to her apartment.

Jane ran up her stairs and popped into her apartment. Molly came out of the kitchen, holding coffee and eating what looked like a jelly-filled donut. Jane's taste buds started dancing around at the sight of the confectionary breakfast treat.

"I brought over donuts," Molly announced, while looking Jane up and down. "Who goes running on a Sunday? Honestly, Jane, you can rest at some point."

"Not all of us can be as lucky as you, Molly, and be blessed with a model's body, eating donuts whenever they want."

"What can I say? Good genetics. Now give me all the glorious details, wait…" Molly looked around. "Shouldn't there be a male specimen in your bed right now? The fact that you went running this morning tells me that you didn't get any action last night because you sure as hell wouldn't be running. No, you would either be in bed with that magnificent man or you would be icing down your inner thighs from all the fucking you did last night."

Jane sighed, "Things didn't go the way you might have wanted them to, sorry lady. I'm officially a fuck up." Jane wasn't in the mood to go over the hideous details of what transpired last night, but she knew there was no way she had an icicle's chance in hell of not telling Molly what happened. Molly would just abuse the story out of Jane somehow.

Jane caved in and told Molly all about last night before Molly had the chance to dig her claws into Jane. She told Molly how she could not stop crying or open up to Brady, even though she wanted to so badly. Molly played the dutiful best friend and just sat and listened to Jane ramble on about her night with Brady and every mistake she made.

Jane thought back about when Brady made the comment 'you can't always trust those trash magazines.' The comment sent a sharp stab of guilt through her stomach. He was right. She did judge him from what she read off the newsstands, not what came out of his mouth. But, he still wanted to get to know her and date her.

Brady Matthews said he wanted to date her, little old Jane Bradley. Could she handle it, though? When someone dates Brady Matthews, they pretty much date the entire world at the same time. Her face would be on the cover of every magazine in due time. How would that fare for her business and her self-esteem? She didn't think she was strong enough to handle the lies and scandals the magazines might claim as true.

Molly gave Jane a hug and said, "It's okay, Jane. I know it has to be hard, but how great is it that Brady Matthews, starting first baseman, wants to date you? He's the hottest ticket in town and you just landed him."

"Yeah, but I don't think I can face him again; I'm so embarrassed about what happened. Who's to say he's even going to want to see me? That might have been all talk last night, just so he could be the good guy and walk out of here unscarred."

Molly shook her head. "He said he promised. Stop second-guessing him and start trying to trust him. If you like him at all, you need to start to find trust or you might as well start adopting cats because you're going to end up as an old maid with that attitude."

Jane leaned against the wall. "Molly, you of all people, know how unstable I am right now; George really mind-fucked me. I don't know if I can handle such a 'high profile' relationship. I'm just starting to remember my old self."

Molly tossed a donut in her direction. Jane caught it and took a big bite. Glad she went running just to end up putting the calories back on with the donut in her hand, but Lord, was it good.

Molly replied, "Jane you're never going to know if you're ready for a relationship until you try. You have to get your feet wet. I know you were hurt and you lost yourself when dating George, but you are slowly coming back to us and shedding that 'Stepford Wife' persona. Maybe Brady is what you need. Maybe he will actually help you find yourself again."

Jane was about to say something when her doorbell rang. It was probably Mr. Mendez wanting to complain about how Molly parked in one of his parking spaces again. Molly didn't care for the man and tested him every time she came over. It made for a great living environment for Jane. She opened the door and came face to face with a huge bouquet of flowers. The poor delivery man asked for Jane and shoved the flowers in her direction. "Enjoy Ms. Bradley."

"Oooooo!!" Molly squealed. "I wonder who those are from?"

Jane shook her head as Molly wagged eye brows. Jane picked out the card from the bouquet. She had never seen so many beautiful flowers before. The vase was full of pink and purple hydrangeas accompanied by a few filler flowers. The bouquet must have cost at least a couple hundred of dollars. She hated that she was gushing with joy and bombarded with giddiness from the beautiful delivery. She was acting like a teenager in love. The card read,

Jane,

I hope this brightens up your morning. I look forward to talking to you later today. In the meantime, there are two appointments at Salon de la Rose waiting for you and Molly at noon. Go relax and have some fun.

Brady

"Shut up!" Molly said ripping the card away from Jane. "De La Rose? Is he kidding? I've been dying to go there, but a teacher's salary does not exactly scream luxury. Ooo, girl, this boy has it bad for you!"

"I feel terrible taking advantage of his money; we shouldn't go. I don't want him to think I'm going to date him for his money and the perks that come with it," Jane replied.

"Are you serious right now? We're going. Stop being a crazy cock head right now, go take a shower, and let's get our asses moving! You are not blowing my one chance of a five star massage because, for some reason, you have a guilty conscience. The guy likes you and wants to treat you to something nice, so pull your head out of your crack and get moving," Molly said, slapping Jane's ass.

Brady

Brady got the delivery confirmation from the flower shop, letting him know the flowers he picked out specifically for Jane were now in her possession. He hoped the arrangement wasn't too much. He just wanted Jane to feel special. He wanted her to feel pampered. She deserved it. She was treated in an appalling manner by her moronic ex-fiancé, so Brady needed to show her that not all guys were dickheads. He wanted to show her what it was like to be treated the way she deserved; like a goddess.

Last night was interesting, to say the least. His heart broke for her every time he saw her crying. She must have been embarrassed as hell. No one wants to cry on a first date. Even when she was crying, she still looked beautiful; it brought out that innocence he liked so much about her. He liked everything about her. It touched his heart that she showed interest in Randy and Special Olympics. That was a big part of his life that Laney never wanted anything to do with. The evil bitch never asked how his events went or even about Randy and the special connection he and Brady had. Jane was refreshing, she was real, she wasn't out to start drama and score publicity to boost her career, like Laney.

Around noon, Brady pulled out his phone and sent a text message to Jane, just to make sure she went to the salon. Knowing her, she'd feel terrible and not go because she didn't want to take advantage of his kindness. He only hoped Molly didn't give two shits about that and made her go, which was his main reason for inviting Jane's best friend.

Brady: Hey, beautiful, I hope you're at the salon being pampered right now.

Jane: I am. You can thank Molly for that. Thank you, Brady, this is really too much. I feel bad, like I'm taking advantage of you.

Brady: I knew you would feel that way. That's why I invited that feisty friend of yours to go with you.

Jane: This is Molly—You are fabulous, Brady Matthews, thank you!

Brady chuckled to himself. Leave it to Molly to be straightforward with him. He was glad she'd convinced Jane to go. He took a risk by setting up the appointments. Jane could have taken offense to his gesture because it might have seemed like he was throwing money around, but in reality, he just wanted to give Jane a relaxing day.

Brady: Well, you girls have fun and I'll talk to you later tonight.

Jane: Thank you, Brady, you are so sweet. Can't wait to talk later.

Well, well, well was Jane finally starting to give in and let her guard down? It seemed like she was…with Molly's help. It looked like the outer shell of ice surrounding Jane was going to finally start melting away. This was going to be interesting.

Jane

After Jane's massage, manicure and pedicure, she thought she'd died and gone to heaven. An afternoon at the spa was exactly what she needed. Molly left straight from the salon because she said the massage made her horny and she wanted to try some new things on Luke. That girl never stopped when it came to her man, but Jane admired her friend for her insatiable appetite. Jane used to be out-going just like Molly and wished she could find that inner strength again. She had been so suppressed by George, she would really have to go digging for the old Jane.

Jane took a shower, put on some shorts and a tank top, her typical night time wear, and was about to pop a TV dinner into the microwave when her doorbell rang. It was another delivery man, this time with a bag of what looked like food.

"Oh, I'm sorry, sir, I think you have the wrong apartment. I didn't order any food."

"Are you Jane Bradley?" the man asked.

"Yes," Jane said, confused.

"Then this food is for you."

"Oh, okay," Jane fumbled with the bag as she tried to get her purse. "Let me just get you a tip..."

"No need to, ma'am, I've been paid plenty. Thank you and have a good night."

Jane took the food and sighed, mmm Chinese. She loved Chinese. Who would order Chinese for her? One guess came to mind and he most likely had gorgeous green eyes. Her phone started ringing. 'Gee, can't a girl relax for a second?' she thought, as she grabbed her phone and looked at the caller ID. Brady.

"Hey there," Jane answered.

"Hey there, beautiful, I'm assuming you got your Chinese."

"I knew this was your doing. How did you know I love Chinese food?"

"I have my sources," Brady said conspicuously.

"Michael?"

"Yeah, that guy is clutch when it comes to impressing the girl you're after. How was your day?"

Jane blushed. Wow, he was too much to handle. "My day was great, thanks to you. Seriously Brady, you didn't have to do all this. I was such a nutcase last night, I don't deserve this."

"That's where you're wrong, doll, you very much deserve this kind of treatment."

"Well, thank you. And thank you for taking care of me last night; you were a real gentleman."

Brady chuckled in the phone. "I can promise you this, my head was not thinking gentlemanly thoughts."

"Oh, really?" Jane teased. "What kind of thoughts were you having?" Jane realized Brady was easy to talk to on the phone, so she started to relax and feel friskier. Luckily, he wasn't awkward on the phone at all. Whenever she talked to George, it was all business, never 'How was your day?'

She pulled some Chinese out and put it on a plate, took up a seat on her couch and planted her phone to her ear. She felt like she was in middle school again, talking to her childhood crush on the phone. Her heart was fluttering and she felt like giggling every two seconds. She needed to at least try to act her age.

"Yes, it took every ounce of power in my body not to crawl into bed with you and hold you until you fell asleep. I also thought about ripping that dress off of you and having my way."

"Those are two thoughts on different sides of the spectrum, Mr. Matthews. Do you want to know something?" Jane asked.

"I like where this is going, of course."

"I so desperately wanted you to stay last night and hold me." Jane winced when she heard it come out of her mouth, but Brady was being so honest with her, she thought she should try doing the same. She just didn't want to come off as desperate and clingy. Although, since she looked deranged and crazy last night, she guessed desperate and clingy was a step up.

"Oh, doll, why did you tell me that? Now I feel like the biggest tool in the world. I should have recognized the fact that you wanted me there. I was just trying to be a gentleman. I knew if I stayed, I couldn't trust myself to keep my hands off of you."

"I didn't mean to make you feel bad, Brady. I'm sorry. I just thought I would be honest and as long as I'm being honest, I don't think I would have kicked you out of the bed if your hands started to wander last night."

Brady groaned into the phone. "You're killing me, Jane. Do you know that I dreamed of you in that navy dress all last night? I couldn't get the image of you out of my head."

"Which image, pre-dinner or post walk? There's a big difference." She chuckled to try to keep the mood light and airy.

Brady, instead, got serious. "Both images, they were both real and both you. I enjoyed seeing you let your guard down. Ever since I met you, you've had a wall up and I've been trying to break through it. Last night I got a sneak peek and I liked what I saw."

"You are one strange man, Brady, to like such a mess, but I'd like to get to know you better too. I can't make any promises, but I would like to give it a shot. What are you doing this week?

Maybe we can try to have dinner again and without the horny soon-to-be-newlyweds."

"Jane Bradley, are you asking me out on a date?"

"I do believe I am, Brady Matthews."

CHAPTER NINE

Molly

Molly woke up with an incredibly sore back. Sex on the bar in their apartment proved to be not as easy as she thought. She definitely threw her back out in the middle of her orgasm, which surprisingly heightened the sensations that rolled through her body. What she needed was a nice long hot shower. Luke was out on base doing his PT, physical training, so she wouldn't get mauled in the shower, not that she was complaining. She could not get enough of that man.

When she was in college, both her parents died in an awful car accident. Molly lost all reason to live and take care of herself. She got into some drugs and became a wild child. Jane was the main reason nothing serious happened to Molly. Jane always made sure Molly was taken care of and stepped in as her family. Michael and Jane both treated her like family.

When Luke came along, he changed her life. She finally had something and someone to live for. He became her family, family that she had been missing for years and desperately craved. Jane and Michael acted like family and loved her, but she was searching for that unconditional love you get when you find your soul mate. Luke gave light to the black and dreary life she was living. Luke meant more to her than anything in the world and she could not wait to say her "I do's."

Molly had a meeting with Jane today to go over wedding

details. She really just wanted something small. She had a big personality, but with her parents no longer around and being an only child, she didn't want to have a big wedding. It only reminded her that she really didn't have any family. Her only family members were Luke, Jane, Albert and Michael. She just wanted something small, maybe at the river or in Savannah on the beach. She was actually more interested in the honeymoon and all the naughty things she had planned for her fiancé, rather than the actual wedding.

Molly took a shower, got dressed and headed out to meet Jane. When she got to Jane's office she noticed Jane was twirling around the room, filing documents, singing to music on her computer and being in an all-around chipper mood.

"What gives, lady? You're singing, dancing and smiling. What did you do with my depressed best friend?" Molly asked.

"Hello to you too, Molly. Nothing, I just happen to have a date with Brady Matthews tonight and I'm looking forward to it."

"For fucking real?" Molly exclaimed. "Oh Jane, this makes me so happy…finally, you're getting out there."

Molly was so proud of her friend. Jane really deserved to date a good guy like Brady. Molly questioned Michael the other night on the phone about Brady. Molly had to make sure he was a good egg before she really started encouraging Jane to date him. Michael had nothing but great things to say about Brady, so that was a step in the right direction. Michael said Brady was the most well-respected guy on the team and he was a great match for their sensitive friend, Jane.

"We're going to a movie in the park tonight and Brady is bringing food so we can have a picnic. I'm scared as hell and I don't know what he sees in me, but I'm going to go for it."

Molly let out a squeal of excitement. "He sees one fine piece of ass and an incredibly sweet and hard-working girl; you deserve him. Just remember that. You better call me when you get a chance and tell me everything!"

"Oh, I will," replied Jane. "Now, let's start planning this wedding. Hey, I was thinking about hiring an assistant to help me out. I'm starting to get more business and can afford some help. What do you think?"

"Oh, Jane, I think that's great. Wow, I'm so proud of you. You've come so far."

"Thanks, Molly, I really am so excited with the way everything has been going with my business. I hate to admit it, but Brady hiring me for that fundraiser gave me a lot of exposure and, since then, I've been getting two or three calls a day!"

"Well, just tack that on to another reason to like the guy, next to stud muffin and Greek god!"

Jane just shook her head at her friend. They spent the rest of the afternoon looking up different locations in Savannah where they could have a small beach wedding. They picked beige, whites and off whites as the colors. Molly really liked the clean crisp look it offered. Jane teased Molly about having a seashell wedding. Molly just made a gagging reflex with her finger in her mouth and vetoed that idea right away. She wanted simple and classic, with a flair of vintage in the mix. It was going to be beautiful and everything both she and Luke wanted, which was mainly to be married. She could not wait.

Jane

Jane had such a great afternoon with Molly. Her wedding was going to be so romantic, just like Molly and Luke. Jane understood Molly's reasoning for keeping the wedding small and intimate and didn't blame her. If Jane ever got married she would want the same thing, since it would be the complete opposite of what George and his mom were planning. Okay, no more thoughts about George, she chastised herself. She had to focus on Brady now. She would be damned if she had another crying episode like she did last time she was around Brady.

Jane had just enough time to go home, take a quick shower to rinse her body off and get dressed before Brady arrived to pick her up. Jane picked out a pair of black skinny jeans, a dark floral silk blouse, cardigan, and yellow flats. She kept her hair down because Brady seemed to like touching her hair and it felt damn good when he did it. She applied some light make up to help her eyes stand out a little more and sprayed some perfume all over her body. She was ready for her second official date with Brady Matthews…hopefully this one would be better than the last. Hopefully, she had the strength to make it through the night without crying. Just take one step at a time, she kept telling herself. He seemed like a good guy and he seemed genuinely interested in her; it was going to be a great night.

Jane called Michael earlier in the day just to see what he had to say and get his opinion on Brady. Michael seemed slightly irritated at first. Most likely because Michael always had feelings for Jane and flaunting a new relationship in front of him must have twisted his panties in a bind, but he answered honestly. He told Jane that Brady was a great guy and had nothing but the best of intentions in pursuing her. He reaffirmed that she was not just another notch in his headboard. That put Jane's mind at ease, at least for the time being.

Brady knocked on her door and she opened it to find an oh-so-sexy man holding up a single rose with a huge smile on his face.

"Hey, gorgeous, you look amazing, but I can barely find you. You're so short, you're a little pip-squeak," he said, while looking down at her.

Jane laughed. "You've only seen me in heels. I didn't want to wear any tonight because I didn't want to sink into the ground and ruin them. They're not cheap, you know."

"Oh, I know and smart decision," Brady said. "I might just have to put you in my pocket and carry you around."

"I'm not that short. Five-foot three is a respectable height, you know."

"Yes, but compared to my six-foot three, it makes you a pip-squeak! Come on, doll, let's get going."

Brady grabbed her hand and Jane practically melted. She really needed to stay strong and not fall for him so fast. Whoa, who said anything about falling for him? No, she just had to make sure she reserved a little distance between them and didn't get caught up in his smooth operator moves. She was just having fun tonight, one step at a time.

"Hey Jane, what are you thinking about? You went silent on me."

"Oh, sorry, I was just thinking about Molly's wedding," she lied. "She came to the office today and we planned most of it; it's going to be small and intimate. She doesn't want to wait too long because she said she and Luke want to get straight to their honeymoon."

Brady laughed, "Man, they're like rabbits. Do they ever quit?"

"Not that I know of. I always hate calling her when Luke is home because she has been known to talk on the phone while having sex at the same time."

"Are you serious? That is amazing! They are quite the couple," Brady chuckled.

"Yes, they are, so what's the movie that's playing tonight?"

"It's a surprise!"

Jane mulled that over, a surprise huh? He must have set something up; knowing him and his popularity, the park would do anything for him. They drove in silence as Jane looked out her window, taking in the beautiful city of Atlanta. She always was very fond of her home town. It was diverse, interesting, and always had something new to offer. Jane focused in on where they were and noticed they passed the park she thought they were going to.

"Hey, did we just miss the turn for the park?" Jane asked.

"Nope, just sit back and relax, babe; I got this handled," Brady replied.

Yes, she liked it when he called her babe. It sent shivers down her spine. She leaned her head back against the headrest, while at the same time Brady grabbed her hand and entwined their fingers together. Jane was in heaven, this guy was too much. He was so sweet and she swore she could see a six pack through his button-up shirt. She might have to write the Braves strength and conditioning coach a personal thank you note for creating such a fine specimen.

Brady turned onto Hank Aaron Drive and Jane noticed they were at Turner Field. She gasped. Surely Brady didn't mean the ball park, right? There was no way they were going to see a movie at Turner field. Did the Braves organization let their players do whatever they wanted, whenever they wanted?

"Here we are," Brady announced.

A valet came and took the car after Brady pulled a picnic basket out of his trunk. He grabbed Jane's hand and led her to the players' entrance.

Jane stopped and whirled Brady around. "Brady, are you serious? Are we really going into the stadium?"

"Did you really think I meant a regular park?" he asked with a scrunched nose. "You're cute, Jane," Brady said, while nudging her chin.

"You know, you're going to start to run out of grand ideas

and then you're going to have to settle into being a normal person like the rest of us," Jane said.

"Yes, I know, but I'll have you hooked on me by then, so even the smallest things will impress you."

Jane all but whispered. "The smallest of things impress me now."

Brady smiled at her and guided her toward the entrance. When they got out to the field, there were two lights that were turned on, granting them some light, but they weren't too bright. That way, they didn't feel like they were under spotlights with a blanket on the ground and a folding chair that looked like was made for two. Jane didn't know what to say; everything was so romantic. It was all too much for her to process. Do not cry. Do not cry, was all she kept saying to herself.

Brady helped her onto the blanket and set the picnic basket down next to them. They both ate some sandwiches while they chatted about little factoids about the ball park. Brady seemed to really love the field and had a lot of little fun facts to share with her. It was endearing to see the passion in his eyes he had for his sport.

When they finished their meal, Brady's face turned slightly more serious. He seemed to struggle with what he was about to say, but finally cleared his throat and began. "Jane, I know you've been through a lot with your ex, and I just wanted to let you know that I know what it feels like, to be cheated on, that is."

Jane nearly choked on the wine she was drinking. Someone cheated on Brady Matthews? Who the hell would ever do something like that? This guy was perfect and he didn't seem to live up the womanizer profile that all the gossip rags claimed. Jane regained her composure and asked, "Someone cheated on you?"

Brady nodded. "Yes, Laney Johnson."

Laney? Holy crap! "Laney cheated on you? I thought reports said you came to a mutual understanding, some even said you were the one breaking her heart."

Brady shook his head. "Like I said earlier, you can't always believe what those magazines say. Laney cheated on me. Since she's known as 'America's Sweetheart' with a body to kill, her publicists paid off a lot of people to make her look like an innocent victim. I never fought it because people will believe what they want to, why waste my time?"

Jane didn't know what to say. They both knew the horrible feeling of finding out the one person you thought loved you actually couldn't give two shits about you. It was a horrible feeling and Brady was sharing his experience with her. An unspoken connection formed between them. They'd both had their hearts broken, and they both had a mutual understanding of how it felt. Jane just squeezed Brady's hand and they both knew, when looking into each other's eyes, they were sorry for the pain they had each encountered in the past.

Once they finished eating, Brady opened up the folding chair made for two and grabbed a blanket. He sat down and nodded for her to come over. Jane had to concentrate on not running over to him and climbing in his lap.

"Are we watching the movie on the mega-tron?" Jane asked, as she started to sidle up next to him. He was warm and smelled delicious. If they just sat there and watched nothing, she would have been fine with that. She just wanted to be close to him…to the man that understood her perfectly.

"Yes, we are, is that okay?"

"Uh, yeah. What other girl can say they've done this? Not many, I hope," Jane teased, while poking his side.

Brady laughed at her insinuation and said, "Believe me, pip-squeak, you're the only one I have ever done this for."

Jane melted all over again and settled in next to Brady. He wrapped his arm around her and pulled her closer.

He whispered in her ear, "The movie is about to begin. I brought chocolate covered raisins, which I know you are a sucker for, thanks to Michael, and there are some sodas in the cooler next to me if you get thirsty."

Jane didn't even need to say anything, she just nuzzled even closer to Brady, grateful that such a great man had come into her life. He genuinely cared about her and wanted to make sure she was taken care of. She had never had a man care so deeply about her, even when George asked her to marry him. George never went as far as Brady had to make her happy, even when he proposed. She thought about the pathetic proposal he gave her.

They were watching TV and he reached over her, pulled a ring box from the couch cushion, and just asked if she wanted to get married. She should have known then that he wasn't the man for her. Wait, no more thoughts of George, especially around Brady.

The lights went off, the mega-tron came on and over the loud speakers the overture of her favorite musical came on: "Singing in the Rain." She almost burst into tears right there. She propped herself up and stared at Brady. Her eyes were watering, but she couldn't help it. When she looked at Brady, his eyes spoke of pride and satisfaction. He grinned with confidence.

Brady wiped a stray tear away and said, "You can thank Michael for the suggestion. He was the one who let me know."

Something came over Jane and she lightly kissed Brady on the lips and pulled away. "Thank you Brady, for caring enough to ask Michael."

No one had ever cared enough to find out her interests, no boy she'd ever dated, for that matter. Brady was something special. He truly cared about her and wanted to make her happy. This was a night she was never going to forget.

Brady

Brady nearly shot out of his pants. Who knew some chocolate covered raisins and Gene Kelly would give him his first kiss from this incredible woman? She definitely took him by surprise when she leaned in and planted her soft, luscious lips on his, and he only wished they stayed there longer, but he knew she wasn't doing it to spur him on. She did it out of pure joy and being grateful. Any kiss from her was better than nothing.

She snuggled so close to him, he really had to control himself from losing it and pawing his hands all over her. He had to keep reminding himself to take things slow. She wasn't ready for a full-blown frontal attack from him, not yet at least.

He enjoyed the movie; his grandma used to rave about it and he always knew it was a classic. He grew fonder of Jane because a classic movie gave her so much joy. There was that innocence again that he longed for from her.

The movie ended and Jane snuggled in even closer than Brady thought was possible, squeezed him, and whispered a thank you into his chest.

"Anytime, doll. Did you have a good time?"

"This has been one of the best nights I've ever

experienced, seriously, thank you. You made me forget everything negative that's happened to me in the past couple of years."

Brady smiled down at Jane and said "Good, I'm glad. Let me get you home, it's getting chilly out here and I don't want you catching a cold, being so small and everything."

Jane playfully swatted his chest and stated, "I'm not that short, you're just the Jolly Green Giant."

"At least I'm not a Smurf," Brady retorted with a smile.

Jane

Brady walked Jane to her door. She so desperately wanted to invite him inside, but their night was so classic, she felt her invitation might ruin the date. She also needed to take things slow for her own well-being. She did not want to rush into anything with Brady, nor did she think her heart could handle rushing into a relationship. She was still finding herself and building her business, those were her main priorities.

They were holding hands when Jane turned to face Brady right outside her doorway.

"Brady, thank you so much for such a magical night. I know I sound like a girl when I say that, but I mean it. It was truly magical for me."

"Thank you for asking me out, I couldn't have asked for a more perfect date. Next time, I'll make sure to pick a place without grass, so you can wear those sexy as hell high heels so I don't have to worry about stepping on you."

Jane giggled. "So, there's going to be a next time?"

"If I have anything to say about it, there will be," Brady said, moving closer to Jane.

"Perfect," Jane hummed.

Brady

Brady tilted Jane's chin up and he closed down on her mouth. He started off slowly, nibbling on her lips and when he couldn't take it any longer, he went in for the kill. He stuck his hand through her hair and pulled her even closer, devouring her mouth inch by inch. She ran her hand up his chest, clenching his shirt at the collar and pulled him further down toward her. He felt like he could barely feel his legs, he was trembling all over from her touch. He heard a low moan rumble in the back of her throat. If he didn't leave now, he was going to tear her door open, throw her down on the floor and have his way with her.

Brady pulled away regretfully and, gasping for air, he said, "I better get going. I really want to be a gentleman here, and if I continue with what we're doing, all of my credibility is going to be thrown out the window."

Jane leaned her head against Brady's chest and nodded. She looked at him with pure lust in her eyes.

"Babe, please don't look at me like that. You're seconds away from being dragged into your apartment and getting seduced."

"Sorry, I'll make this easy on you." She pulled back and shook his hand. "Thank you for an amazing time, Brady. Have a great night."

Brady shook her hand and regretted the moment they let go. He missed her already and really just wanted to hold her for the rest of the night, but he was going to walk away and be the gentleman he was. She needed her space. Let her make the first move.

"Sweet dreams, babe."

Jane leaned in close to him, pulled his head down and whispered in his ear, "Just so you know, it turns me on every time you call me babe." And with that, she unlocked her door and blew him a kiss goodnight. Brady stood frozen in place, swearing under his breath.

He retreated to his car before he broke down her door and took advantage of the effect he had on her. Yup, he wouldn't be getting any sleep tonight. Time for a cold shower, a nice icy cold shower. He was in for a world of trouble where Jane was concerned.

CHAPTER TEN

Brady

Brady sat on the weight bench, staring into space, and dreaming about Jane and the parting sentence she said to him the previous night. He would call her babe every second if that was the reaction he received from her. He knew she was a vixen the moment she put her hand on his thigh at Deuces.

She had a wild side, but she was so guarded most of the time from being hurt that she rarely showed it. She only showed her wild side when Molly was around provoking her, or when Jane slipped up and dropped the posh attitude.

He wanted to tear down her protective wall instantly, but instead, he decided to do it brick by brick, because if he moved too fast, she would run away from him. He couldn't let her get away, not after the night they had together and not after the little slice of heaven he tasted. He really needed to spend more time with her. The biggest challenge was going to see how she was when his baseball season started up. Spring training started next week, and he would be gone for a while in Florida. He hoped they would still be able to continue whatever was going on between them.

Michael flicked Brady in the back of the head. "Hey, earth to Brady, finish up your last set. I want to get some benching in too, you know."

"Sorry, bud, just thinking about things."

"Things? I doubt that, more like thinking about Jane. How

83

did last night go?" Michael asked, nudging Brady's ribs.

"Nothing happened man, I kept it respectable. It was an incredible night, though. How you didn't fall for her in college is beyond me."

"I did," Michael said shyly. "She wasn't interested. We cuddled and shared our thoughts, but nothing more. She always said I was one of her best friends and I didn't want to ruin what we had. Plus, she was so hung up on George that I would never have had the chance."

Brady nodded. "Is George really the dick-face I think he is?"

"Yeah, he was successful for a while, but once he started banging that office slut, he lost all credibility. His company valued families, and once they got wind of what George was doing during office hours, he got canned. Last I heard, he was living with his sister. Not quite sure, all I know is that he did a number on Jane," Michael reflected. "If I ever saw him again, I would do some damage. He really fucked Jane up, to the point where she stopped talking to me, and she used to tell me anything and everything."

"The guy sounds like a total douche bag. I don't think I'd be too kind to him if I saw him either."

Brady's phone beeped, he looked down and saw that he had a text message from Jane. He smiled and read it.

Jane: Hey handsome, I thought about you last night.

Brady started grinning like a fool and Michael punched him in the arm. "You look like a cheese-dick buddy, you need to get ahold of yourself."

Brady punched him back and said, "Mind your own business dick-stick and go do some hang cleans, you need them. I saw you in the batting cage the other day; my grandma has more pop off the bat than you do."

"Fuck off!" Michael said, smiling.

Brady left Michael to finish his workout and went to go get some water. He looked down at his phone again and replied to Jane.

Brady: Good morning, beautiful, what did you think about?

Jane: Nothing too crazy, so don't get your hopes up. Just about how it felt to have you hold me in your arms last night.

Brady couldn't help but smile. He wanted to stay with her last night more than anything. It was all he thought about as the hours on his clock ticked away the night.

Brady: I thought about that all night too…as well as your parting words.

Jane: Did you, now? It was a little bold of me, but I felt like myself when I said it, and I meant it. What kind of images did you have in your mind last night?

Brady knew what she was talking about when she said she felt like herself. Michael was telling him a little while ago how Jane used to have just as a filthy mouth as Molly and they would go back and forth knocking the socks off all the guys on the baseball team in college with their sexual repartee. He couldn't imagine Jane going up against Molly's sexually deranged mouth, but he caught glimpses of her being a little vixen every now and then. He tried not to think about how she whispered against his cheek last night when she said he turned her on.

Just thinking about it, Brady started to go hard, unable to control his thoughts anymore. Yup, his workout was done; it was time to hit the showers. He poked his head in the weight room, waved goodbye to Michael and murmured something about feeling sore and not wanting to push it. Michael just shook his head and laughed.

Brady sat at his locker and stared at his phone. How honest should he be with the dreams he had of her last night? He didn't want to push her too far, but she did ask. He replied.

Brady: Naughty ones, but I don't dream and share, so you're just going to have to wonder.

Jane: Naughty, huh? I had a couple of those. I woke up all sweaty and looking for those strong hands of yours.

Brady gulped. Who was this woman? She was so sweet and innocent at times, but then had a secret sexy side that came out occasionally. He wondered if her being shy was just something she started doing because of what George did to her. She did say that George really changed her. She probably didn't want to put her normal personality out in the world for everyone to see for fear of getting hurt again. How could he help her realize that she could be her normal self all the time? He was just going to have to continue to show her that not all men are assholes. Easy enough, he loved spoiling her and treating her like royalty. It brought a smile to her face, and he could stare at that smile for days. He replied back to her.

Brady: Babe, you have me so hard right now, I can't even walk to the shower to cool off.

Jane: Oh, I do apologize. I never intended to be a cock tease.

Brady: You are such a liar, nice try though. Can you give me one hint of what happened in your dream last night?

Brady thought that was a risky comment; he didn't want to scare her away by coming on too strong, but damn if she wasn't coming on strong herself. His phone beeped.

Jane: Let's just say I felt things I haven't felt in two years.

Yup, he should not have asked that question, he was throbbing now. Time to hit the ice bath. If he didn't know any better, he would have thought he was texting Molly. He sure hoped he wasn't.

Brady: Thanks, babe, now I have to hit the ice bath to cool myself down. I'll call you when I get out. Want to meet me for lunch?

Jane: I would love to, but I have a meeting with a possible new client.

Brady: Just tell them I think you're the best, my name goes a long way and then come have lunch with me.

Jane: They're a gay couple who are very flamboyant. I highly doubt they even know who you are.

Brady: You'd be surprised. These muscles are not just for hitting a ball, they're for show too.

Jane: Awfully full of yourself today, aren't you?

Brady: Hey, you're the one who boosted my ego with your sexy dreams.

Brady loved their banter. Their date last night really helped her relax and open herself up more to him. He was extremely excited, because this new sassy side she was showing him was a huge turn on. He loved it.

Jane: Oh, I see, so it's my fault then. I'll make sure to not tell you any more of my fantasies.

Brady: DON'T YOU DARE! I promise, I'll behave.

Jane: Good, have a nice ice bath. Don't think of me too much today.

Brady: That's impossible, later vixen.

Jane

Jane sat back in her chair at her desk. What had gotten into her? She hadn't been that outspoken in a while, since before George appeared in her life. Maybe she was starting to let down her guard and she only had one man to thank. She'd only been with Brady a couple of times, but he made her feel so good about herself, like she used to before George. George sucked the life out of her and made her feel like her one sole purpose in life was to get married and be his wife and that was it. Brady actually supported and encouraged her career. He thought she was great at what she did and it felt so great to have that kind of support, especially coming from someone so damn hot.

Her door chimed up front, and in walked Molly, looking incredibly upset and crying. Jane instantly dropped her smile and fled to Molly.

"Molly, honey, what's wrong?" Jane asked.

"Luke and I just got in a huge fight, and now I won't see

87

him for I don't even know how long."

Jane wrapped Molly in her arms and sat her down. She grabbed a box of tissues and handed it to her. Was Luke going out on another mission? Jane was confused. Luke and Molly never fought before he left for a mission for the sole reason was that they never knew what would happen when Luke was out doing his job. Something strange must have happened between the two of them.

"What happened?" Jane asked.

In between sobs, Molly responded, "He...got...another...mission."

"Oh, Molly, you knew he wasn't home for good, right?"

Molly replied, "I know, but he was only home for two weeks, how is that fair? I got mad at him and told him he shouldn't leave me all the time. Then he got mad because he doesn't like to leave me, but it's his job and I should know that, then he packed and left to go on his mission. We didn't even have a good-luck-on-your-mission-blow-job." Jane cringed, Molly continued. "I know it's his job and I understand when he has to leave; it was just so soon and we just got engaged. I don't know...I was hoping he'd be able to take a little break."

"Molly, you know that's not how it works; the government doesn't give two shits about their operators' personal lives. I'm so sorry, sweetie, I know it's hard. Can you call him real quick before he leaves, so at least he doesn't leave mad?"

"I already tried calling him, he doesn't answer. I'm such an idiot, I know better than to fight with him when he gets orders. I was just so happy to have him home and got so caught up in our engagement that I forgot about the possibility of him taking off again. He's my life, Jane, I can't have him going out on a mission knowing the last thing I said to him was negative and mean."

Jane hugged her friend. "I'm sure he knows you were just upset and in the moment. Do you think you'll hear from him before he takes off? He's probably getting briefed right now and hopefully will have a sliver of time to contact you before he leaves."

"I hope...so," Molly said, still crying.

"Hang in there, sweetie, everything will be okay."

Jane wasn't sure how long they sat there on the couch in her office, but her lunch appointment came in and the two very flamboyant men dressed in matching purple velour jackets looked down at Molly and gasped in horror. Jane turned to look at Molly and was startled herself. Molly's mascara had run down her cheeks so much, she looked like her eyeballs had melted down each side of her face.

Jane nudged Molly and whispered, "Honey, you might want to go in the bathroom and wipe your face down a little."

Molly stood up abruptly, grabbed her purse, and said, "I don't give two flying fucks what I look like right now. Sorry for scaring the crap out of you gentlemen. I hope you have a very nice wedding; Jane is the best. I'll call you later, Jane." And then Molly flung herself out of Jane's office, only tripping once on the slight lift of the door frame and disappeared.

Once Molly left, Jane cleaned up the soggy tissues that Molly had flung around everywhere and looked apologetically at the men, hoping they would understand.

"I'm sorry about that; my friend is having a rough day. Please, come sit down, I want to hear all about how the proposal happened and all the plans you have in mind.

Jane listened to her hopefully-new clients, but couldn't help feeling sick to her stomach for Molly. She knew how much Molly fretted when Luke was gone. She always put on a good front, but deep down, Jane knew she was scared and nervous as hell. She couldn't imagine falling head over heels in love with someone who risked their life for their country every day. Jane always thought it was the loved ones at home who had it the worst. At least the soldiers knew what was happening when they were overseas. Loved ones had to wait around at home, staying positive, and praying for safety.

Molly was one of the strongest women she knew. She could say goodbye to the one she loved and not see him for weeks on end, but Jane, pathetically, couldn't get over the fact that her ex-fiancé cheated on her...God, she was a sorry excuse for a human.

Molly

Molly went straight home and lay in bed. She obviously called in sick to work, not being able to face the responsibility of teaching a group of third graders. She kept her phone next to her at all times while she wasted her day away in bed, but it didn't ring, no text messages, nothing. Molly's heart was breaking. She would never send Luke on a mission without giving him a proper goodbye. She couldn't stop feeling like she was a cold-hearted bitch. Why did she pick a fight with him? She was being selfish; she knew when he was home she needed to enjoy every minute of it, because he would soon be leaving again.

Molly thought about how her life had changed so quickly when Luke came home. She realized that when Luke proposed, she thought they were actually going to have a normal relationship. Maybe, just maybe, things were going to be like she dreamed, not only seeing him on occasion and the rest of the time wondering where he was and if he was safe. In her mind, she thought he wasn't going to go on any more missions, he was just going to go to work like a normal person, then come back home safe into her arms every night.

When Luke asked her to marry him, thoughts of normalcy bled into her mind and implanted themselves there. She convinced herself that life was going to finally be normal. That was why she was such a bitch to him when he announced he was taking off again. Damn her ring and her stupid head. Well, no, not damn the ring. The ring meant the world to her, because Luke wanted to become one with her. She just wished becoming one meant having a normal life as well.

Molly's phone beeped, causing Molly to whip her head around to her nightstand and look at her screen. Fuck, it was from Jane.

Jane: Hope you are doing alright and sorry if you thought this was a message from Luke.

Molly hated and loved her friend at the same time. Jane was so sweet for checking on her, but Molly also hated her because she wished it was a message from Luke instead.

What the hell was he doing? He should have messaged her by now. He was definitely gone, somewhere in the world, putting his life on the line, while knowing that his soon-to-be-wife was a rotten bitch. With those thoughts swirling through her mind, she slowly drifted to sleep.

A little while later, Molly was awakened by the sound of breaking glass. She nearly crapped her pants from the loud noise that vibrated through the silent room. She grabbed the bat that was next to her bed and held it up to her chest. Someone was in her apartment. What did Luke always say about intruders? If you keep swinging, they'll leave you alone?

She slowly got out of bed, walked up to her bedroom door and heard somebody rustling around. Oh my God, this was really happening, someone was actually breaking into her apartment, and Luke wasn't here to save her. Why couldn't this disgusting criminal have chosen yesterday to do this? Luke would have had the intruder's head ripped off by now.

Molly slid behind the cracked door, realized she was only wearing her bra and underwear, and hoped she wasn't an open invitation to the thief. She decided on the count of three she would charge out to the living room, screaming like a lunatic, and beat the crap out of whoever was in there.

One...two...three...

BANG!

The bedroom door flew open and knocked her dead in the face. She saw stars and fell to the ground. All she could think about before she passed out was great, now she was going to get raped and there was nothing she could do about it.

Jane

Jane was lounging on her couch, watching her latest crazed reality show and finishing off her very bland but semi-healthy Lean Cuisine when her phone rang.

Brady.

"Hey there, how's it going?"

"Hey gorgeous, it's going alright. How was your night? I wish we could have met up today at lunch."

"I know, me too. My night was pretty lame compared to a movie at a ballpark."

"Mine was lame too, since I didn't get to cuddle with you in my arms."

Jane's stomach did a little flip-flop, making her smile. "Such a smooth talker, did you take a class on that?"

Brady laughed, "Yeah, it's required when you make it to the big leagues. You take classes on how not to say the wrong things in an interview after a game, as well as how to make all the women swoon."

"Well, I'm not quite swooning yet, so maybe you need a refresher," Jane joked.

"Oh, I'm not even through chapter one with you, just you wait."

"I'm ready for it, Brady Matthews, make me swoon!" They both laughed. She continued "What are you doing this week, are you ever going to ask me out again, or was the movie a one-time thing?"

Brady sighed and Jane instantly went up on the defensive. Why did he sigh? Oh my God, it was a one-time thing. Oh no, look at her throwing herself at him. This was exactly why she didn't want to let her defenses down; now she felt like an idiot.

She quickly added in, "Sorry, that was a little forward. I had a great time the other night, but I don't expect you to take me out again. I know you must have other more important things to do, other people to see. I'm just going to go, sorry..."

Brady cut her off, "Jane, sweetheart, slow down. I most definitely want to go out with you again. You are what I think about twenty-four-seven. I'm just mad right now because my manager signed me up for a three-day conference, where I go talk to different coaches and give tips on hitting and how to teach a proper swing."

"Oh, well that should be fun," Jane replied, blushing with embarrassment.

"I guess, but I had other plans to spend time with you. I have to report to spring training next week, and that only gives me Saturday night and Sunday morning to spend any time with you before I leave."

"Gee, I almost forgot you had a job," Jane laughed. "How long is spring training?"

"Spring training is a month and a half...and it's in Florida."

Jane's voice raised slightly louder, "Florida?"

"Yeah, Florida. It's not too far away, and I'll have some days off, so it shouldn't be too terrible."

Florida? For a month and a half? So, whatever was going on between her and Brady was going to turn into long distance. Could she do that? She was barely strong enough to handle what was happening between them now. Maybe she should just cut all strings with him and save the heartache. He was such a great guy, but he didn't need to worry about a nutcase back home when he was trying to get ready for the season. Lord knows the media would plaster her face all over the gossip magazines and accuse her for Brady's lack of performance. She didn't need to carry around that kind of guilt.

"Uh, Jane, are you still there?" Brady asked.

"Yes, sorry. Well, I'm sure you'll have a lovely time at spring training. Give me a call when you get back from your conference, maybe we can have a bite to eat before you take off again. Talk to you later."

Jane hung up her phone. Yup, she just blew him off, and she knew he sensed her panic. She felt like such a jerk, but sometimes she just had to consider herself first. She could not get involved with Brady Matthews. She wasn't strong enough for him. He needed somebody solid, who he didn't have to worry about; someone he could go home to when he was back from the road and just sink into without having to answer any questions. Jane knew she couldn't be that girl right now...she was still too sensitive. She would have one last night with him for her own selfish reasons when he got back from his conference and then cut things off with him completely. She was doing it for Brady.

CHAPTER ELEVEN

Molly

Molly woke up in her bed. How did she get here? What happened? Then it all came flooding back to her; there was a robber in her house and, when she was about to make her attack on him, she got knocked out by her own door.

Where was he now? Panic swept her body when she heard heavy breathing next to her. She felt around and nearly pissed her pants when her hand came in contact with a large human-like mass next to her. She screamed bloody murder and started swinging her arms in every direction they would fly. She could hear someone telling her to stop in the distance, but she just kept swinging.

"Baby, it's me. Calm down."

Baby? Molly opened her eyes and made eye contact with Luke's steel grey gaze. She broke down and started sobbing. He was home; he was with her. Was she dreaming? Luke scooped her up and laid her on his lap, stroking her back.

"Shhh, everything is okay. I'm here."

"I…thought…you…were…a…rapist," she forced out in between sobs.

Luke chuckled at her almost-incoherent words and pulled her in closer. "I'm sorry, babe. I didn't mean to scare you. I didn't want to turn on any lights and wake you up."

"What are you doing here? I thought you were sent on a mission."

"We were called in, but when we were about to be sent off, another team was close enough to take care of the mission instead. They sent us home, but said to keep close in case they needed back up. By the time I found out, I thought I would just come home instead of calling you, since it was so late."

Molly sobbed into Luke's chest and hugged him. "I thought you left and I didn't get to give you your goodbye blow job."

Luke threw his head back and laughed out loud. "Oh, Molly, I love that's what you were concerned about. I was more worried that we left on a bad note. I don't ever want to leave in the middle of a fight."

Molly sniffed, "I was worried about that too. It tore me apart that I sent you out there thinking I was some evil bitch."

Luke lifted Molly's chin and stared into her eyes. He placed a very gentle kiss on her lips and said, "I would never think that. I knew you were upset that I was being asked to leave again so soon."

"I was, but that's never affected me before. I know it's part of the job. I think I was just upset because, when we got engaged, it was such a normal thing to do, and our relationship has never been anything close to normal. I thought that our relationship was finally going to be like everyone else's and I ingrained that in my brain. When I found out you were leaving, I lost it because, why would you leave if we were going to live a normal life?"

Luke sighed and pulled Molly down on the bed spooning her back while caressing her bare stomach with his thumb. "Baby, we won't have a normal life for a while, but I promise you, when I retire, I will be all yours to do with whatever you like. We'll buy a house and sit on the porch in our rocking chairs, making fun of all the kids that walk by."

Molly giggled, "That sounds like heaven. I love you, Luke, more than you will ever know."

"I love you too, baby. So…we just had a fight and made up, I'm wondering doesn't something usually come after that?"

Molly turned toward Luke and smiled. She ran her finger tips along his very chiseled and strong jaw. She gently licked her lips and ran her tongue across his lips. She felt him getting hard next to her and his throat made a low grumble of appreciation.

"Are you cashing in on the goodbye blow job?"

"I think I want to cash in on a lot more than that. When I found you on the floor wearing only your underwear, I had to control myself not to rip everything off and drive myself into you. You have one sexy body, babe."

"I have to in order to keep up with you," Molly said, while dragging her hand down his chest, across his stomach, and straight to his manhood.

Luke grunted and threw her on her back. "You are in trouble, little lady, because you upset me and now you have to make it up to me," Luke said jokingly.

"Oh, poor baby, how's this?" Molly tore her underwear and bra off and spread her legs.

Luke gulped and said, "That will do."

Jane

Jane was startled awake by a loud pounding on her door. What time was it? 2:30am? Where was her wasp spray? She was told wasp spray worked just as well as mace when there was an intruder, plus she could shoot it from a distance.

She reached into her nightstand, grabbed her spray and slowly crept out into the living room toward the entryway. The pounding got louder and her heart sank. Why didn't she take that self-defense class Luke asked her and Molly to take? She could use some self-defense tips right now. She tip-toed to the front door and put her eye up to the peephole. Her heart sank when she saw two brightly colored green eyes staring back at her. What was Brady doing at her apartment? She opened the door and ushered him in.

"What the hell are you doing here? You scared the living daylights out of me."

It wasn't until Brady's eyes swept over her and turned into hot molten lava that she realized she was only wearing a lacy nightgown that she honestly found comfortable to sleep in, even though it looked like she was trying out for the next call girls movie. She bashfully pulled her nightie down and grabbed a blanket to wrap around herself.

"Brady, what are you doing here?" she asked again.

Brady shook his head and cleared his throat. "I came to see you. I didn't like how our phone conversation ended."

She didn't know what to say, so she just blurted out, "That was a few hours ago. Is this some sort of booty call?"

She instantly regretted the words as they flew out of her mouth. Brady's face went completely stone and his eyes almost turned entirely black.

"Is that the kind of opinion you have of me? You really do think I'm some sort of player, don't you? Have I not been a gentleman since I met you? Have I not stopped myself from ripping your clothes off and pounding my dick into you after our dates? Have I not touched you since I've been here, even though you're wearing that...see-through lace thing?" Brady said, while gesturing up and down her body.

Jane sighed and grabbed Brady's hand, pulling him to her couch. "Brady, I'm sorry, I don't know what got into me. I shouldn't have said that. You've been more than a gentleman to me. You've been so sweet and kind, and you've made me feel so incredibly good about myself, thank you."

Brady's face lightened a bit. "Well, I like to treat my woman well."

Jane startled, "Your woman?"

Brady let out a frustrated huff. "Listen, Jane, I don't know how I can be clearer. I like you, a lot. You put a smile on my face even when I'm not near you. You are a fresh breath of air for me, something that contradicts this media and fan-crazed life I live in every day. I want to get to know you more, and I want you to get to know me. I don't know about you, but I can't stop thinking about you and that means something to me. I haven't felt this way in quite a long time and I like how it feels. You make me happy and I want to date you. I want you to be my girlfriend."

Jane just looked at him in disbelief. She didn't know what to say. Brady continued.

"I know this is hard for you, babe, and like I told you, I will take this slowly, but you have to know that I'm willing to make this work and help you through any insecurities you might have or doubts you might be facing. I need you to put your trust in me, though, and not freak out when something difficult comes along."

Jane couldn't help but shake her head in disbelief. "It's just too hard, Brady. George really fucked with my head."

"I know, sweetheart," Brady said, lifting Jane's chin up and stroking her cheek. "But I want to help you, please let me help you."

Jane shook her head, "You're too good for me. I'm going to ruin your concentration and then Atlanta is going to hate me because you won't be the leader in home runs anymore."

Brady couldn't help but chuckle. "Jane, you are so cute." He pulled her in close. "I separate my personal life from my work life, just like everyone else, and I'm not too good for you. We are perfect for each other."

Brady

Brady held Jane for a while without her saying anything. He was not going to take no for an answer. He knew she cared about him and liked him. It was all over her face. She was just too scared to admit it and take that first step toward a new relationship.

Spring training would be a bitch to get through, especially since their relationship was so fragile right now. He was a strong guy, though, and he knew he could help her through it. She was cute for being concerned about his batting statistics; he could care less if he was a leader in anything, he just wanted to contribute to his team and help them win a championship.

She finally pulled away from his chest and looked up at him. "You sure you want to date a crazy like me?"

Brady laughed in response and said, "I wouldn't have it any other way. So, are you saying you're going to be my girlfriend?"

Brady waited in anticipation when she didn't answer. She merely stood up and entwined her fingers with his, leading him to the bedroom. Oh God, he had been waiting for this moment for a long time. He was already starting to get hard when he realized this was not the right time. He wanted his first time with her to be wonderful, when they had fresh minds and weren't in the confusing limbo of what was going on between them.

He stopped her, turned her around and started to say, "Jane, I don't know…"

She put her finger over his lips and said, "As much as I would love to jump your bones right now, I really just need to be held tonight by my boyfriend. Is that okay?"

Boyfriend? A sense of relief washed over Brady. She called him her boyfriend. He couldn't be happier; their relationship was going to be hard and have its ups and downs, but he looked forward to every minute he was going to spend with her.

Brady sighed in relief, "I would love, to sweet thing."

CHAPTER TWELVE

Jane

Jane woke up to the faint smell of French toast. Was that really French toast she smelled? Jane looked to her side and noticed that Brady, that glorious man, wasn't next to her. Jane slipped out of bed, put her slippers on and skipped out to the kitchen, then stopped dead in her tracks.

Brady was in her kitchen cooking her breakfast without a shirt on. It was the sexiest thing she had ever seen. He had massive pecs that spanned across his chest, absolutely no hair to get tangled in, and an actual six pack. The man was the epitome of an athlete. He even had those little indents in his stomach that were sexy as hell and basically dragged your gaze down to his crotch. She couldn't help but drool a little. She couldn't believe she was going out with this guy.

"Like what you see, gorgeous?" Brady asked. His question interrupted her very naughty train of thought.

She went over to him and wrapped her arms around him so his back was facing her. She placed a gentle kiss on his shoulder blades and said, "Now that is a sight to see in the morning. I think I almost got pregnant just looking at you."

Brady gripped the counter and let out a low growl then swung around. "Pip-squeak, you are going to get yourself into some serious trouble with that kind of talk."

"Oh yeah, what are you going to do? Spank me?" Jane

teased, while running her hands over his chest.

Brady picked her up by her waist and flung her over his shoulder. Her heart started to flutter as she started laughing. He put her on the ground and straddled her waist. He pinned her arms to her sides and lowered himself so his elbows were on either side of her face. He lowered his head down so he was mere centimeters away from her face. Jane breathed heavily in anticipation of his next move. One of his hands stroked her forehead as he moved in a little bit closer.

He stared deep into her eyes and whispered, "Have I mentioned lately how fucking beautiful you are?"

Jane could barely move, let alone speak, so she gulped and just nodded her head yes. He lowered his lips to hers and gently started kissing her. He tasted like coffee and he tasted so good. She couldn't get enough of him. She so desperately wanted to take her hands, wrap them around his neck and caress the back of his head, but he trapped her, blocking any attempts of her wandering hands.

He kept kissing her softly until she lined his lips with her tongue. The green in his eyes went completely dark and all she saw was pure male rawness. He wanted her and he wanted her bad. She felt his erection on her stomach as her heart rate picked up speed. She tried to wiggle free, so she could run her hands up and down his body and into his pants. She wanted to feel his protruding bulge, but her hands were pinned down so tightly they weren't going anywhere.

He pulled his head away just enough so she could no longer kiss him. "I suggest you go take a shower, while I finish making your sweet-ass breakfast."

"Don't you want to join me in the shower?" she asked coyly.

He groaned, "Babe, you're not making this easy on me. I have plans for our first time and it's not going to be like this, although, I would prefer for you to wear something just as nice as this lace number you have on."

"What's wrong with right now?" Jane pleaded.

"You have to go to work, and I have to catch a plane in a couple of hours; I want our first time to last all night."

Jane gulped, "All night?"

Brady kissed her along her neck to her collarbone, around her jaw and up to her lips while saying, "All...night...long."

He released her from his leg trap, helped her up, gave her a good slap on the ass and told her to go take a shower. She didn't know how he could have such self-control. She surely didn't have any because, as she was walking away, she pulled her top off, revealing everything except a thin thong that left nothing to the imagination, turned around with her arms barely covering her breasts and said, "I like my bacon extra crispy." Then she proceeded to the shower.

Brady

Brady sat in the airport while waiting to board his airplane when the image of Jane's backside came flying back into his memory. Damn, she had a fine-ass body. He had to relieve himself in the shower when he got home because there was no way he would have made it otherwise. He had a hard on from the time she took off her top until he got back home and in the shower.

She was a little temptress and she enjoyed it. It was nice to see her relax and have fun. He saw her opening up more and more, showing him the Jane that Michael and Molly talked about.

When she called him her boyfriend last night, a huge weight was lifted off his shoulders. He knew he liked Jane and wanted to get to know her better, but he didn't know it mattered that much to him. His phone beeped, making him look to see who the message was from.

Jane.

Jane: Are you sure you have to be gone for three days?

Brady smiled and texted back.

Brady: I miss you already too.

Jane: You caught me, yes I'm missing you, but mostly I'm so horny right now and the only medication I know of is you. I can't stand your teasing anymore!

Brady laughed out loud.

Brady: Oh, is that so?

Jane: Yes! I feel like my lady bits are about to fall off from neglect.

Brady: Well, Jesus, we can't have your lady bits falling off. Can your lady bits hang in there until Saturday night?

Jane: I don't know. I think it might be a little touch and go.

Brady: Is there anything I can do to help in the meantime, since I have the secret medication?

Jane: Yeah, when you get to your hotel you can send me a picture of you, shirtless. I wanted you so bad this morning when I saw you without your shirt on in the kitchen.

Brady: Ha, well I tend to have that effect on women.

Jane: Women? Who are these women you speak of? Do I have to come twist some bitch's face off?

Brady laughed. He could only imagine Jane in a fight. She was too sweet to do any harm to anyone, plus she was a tiny little thing. She would get trampled on. She would most likely fling her arms around, hoping to hit someone or something. Or she would bust out her wasp spray.

Brady laughed to himself as he remembered the terrified look on her face, in her lacy nightgown, holding a can of wasp spray when she opened the door. Smiling, Brady sent her a message back.

Brady: I would love to see a little pip-squeak like you get in a fight.

Jane: Don't let size fool you. I might be petite, but I pack a lot of punch, and don't you forget it.

Brady: Ha, threat received. We're about to board. I'll call you tonight. Miss you, babe.

Jane: Miss you, handsome.

Michael

Michael had to leave for spring training in a couple of days, so he decided to put together a nice dinner for Kelly. He wanted to reconnect with her before he left. He wasn't just going to let their marriage fail. He was going to do whatever it took to rekindle the love they had for each other.

Michael decided to set up a nice dinner at the dining room table they never used and grabbed their old cribbage set. They used to always play cribbage and eat dinner together while drinking wine and listening to oldies on their old record player. Those were the good days, before Kelly's activity of choice was going out and getting her picture taken by whomever. Michael enjoyed the simple times they used to share and thought his dinner gesture would help bring them back together. At least he hoped it to be a start to a conversation about their marriage.

He ordered dinner from Mario's Italian Cuisine. Kelly loved Italian food, especially lasagna. He would have cooked if he knew how to even turn on the oven, but that wasn't an option. Kelly needed top-of-the-line appliances when they moved in and the oven that was in their kitchen was digital with no labels on the screen, so he had no clue where to even turn the damn thing on. Whatever happened to knobs? Everything had to be touch-screen nowadays.

He ordered a pan of lasagna, salad, garlic bread and tiramisu for dessert. The dinner was not one of his favorites, but Kelly loved it, and he was doing everything for Kelly tonight. He set the table with candles and red roses he got from the local florist. A very classy dinner for two, he thought. He was just about to go get dressed when his phone beeped.

Kelly: Hey, won't be home tonight. Talk to you later.

What the fuck? Michael instantly got furious and tried calling her, but she didn't pick up. Nothing razzed him more than when someone just sent him a text message, but then didn't pick up his phone call a second later. He sent her a message back instead.

Michael: Kelly, I had a nice surprise dinner planned for you. What are you doing that is so important? I'll be leaving soon for spring training and wanted to spend time with you.

She sent him a message back. Apparently, she was only capable of text messaging and couldn't be bothered to hold an actual conversation on the phone, like a decent human being. Irritated, Michael read what she had to say.

Kelly: Sorry, had prior plans with friends. Hopefully will see you before you leave. Don't wait up.

Michael picked up the vase of flowers he bought for her and threw it against the wall in the dining room. Fuck. How could he make things right if she wouldn't even give him the time of day? She was slipping away from him, and there was no use trying to get her back. She would have made the effort in the past to come home. She was done with him, and Michael knew it. He needed to get drunk tonight.

Molly

Molly decided she needed a girls' night out. She'd had one hell of a night with Luke. She didn't think their lips ever stopped moving. She was exhausted, but completely satisfied. Before he went to training this morning, he made sure to tell her how lucky he was to have such an understanding soon-to-be-wife and he promised never to leave again without his goodbye blow job. That made her giggle. He said he didn't want to deprive her of such a thing. Besides her lady cactus, Luke's favorite thing was a goodbye blow job; he said it always put him in the right frame of mind, and she reveled in being able to make him squirm with pleasure.

Luke was doing some overnight training, so she thought it would be the perfect opportunity to catch up with her girls: Jane and Albert.

She sent them both an e-mail.

To: Jane, Albert
From: Molly
Subject: Bitches Night!!!
Hey Hookers,

I'm in desperate need of some girl time. I just fucked myself through the night and got all the testosterone I can handle. Meet me at Deuces at 8pm sharp. Albert, I assume you will take care of our VIP status. Jane, bring your big barf bags. We are getting wasted tonight!
TGIF
Xoxo - M

Molly's phone beeped instantly with a reply. She opened her e-mail.

To: Molly, Jane
From: Albert
Subject: Re: Bitches Night!!
Oooo, girl, I'm jealous. I wish I had a man like Luke to suck me dry. You girls are all set, just strut your stuff and you're in. See you tonight. I'm ready to dance your tits off!

Jane replied right after Albert. Molly was shocked when she read it.

To: Albert, Molly
From: Jane
Subject: Re: Re: Bitches Night!!
I'm in, sluts! I promise to wear something real revealing and low cut, have to make my new boyfriend jealous for being out of town! Plan on taking pictures with my phone, bitches! Can't wait!
The Old Jane

Molly had to read her e-mail a couple of times before the words actually settled in her brain. Jane was officially going out with someone? She assumed it was Brady. He'd been chasing Jane around like a little puppy. What really got Molly was the fact that Jane was transforming back into her old self again, sweet and caring, but so scandalous. When she was with George, she was still herself for the most part, but she became very shy, isolated and soft-spoken, not the same Jane that Molly and Michael went to school with. Molly was so happy, she grabbed her phone and texted Michael.

Molly: Our old Janey is starting to come back to us, thanks to your first baseman!

Michael sent her a message back.

Michael: I knew he could do it. He is head over heels for her.

Molly: I could tell. Well, he's doing a good job. He better not fuck things up or I'll rip his dick off.

Michael: You and me both sister. What are you doing tonight? You guys want to hang out?

Damn, she hated to turn down Michael, but they planned a girls' night and, unless he had some lady flaps hiding in those jeans, he was not invited to their festivities tonight. Albert was only allowed to go because he claimed he had a man-gina, so that put him in the classification of able to attend girls' night.

Molly: We are actually having a girls' night with Albert. If you want to wear a dress and a wig and join us, we would love to have you.

Michael: Does Albert have to wear a dress and wig?

Molly: No, he's more feminine than Jane and I put together!

Michael: Ha, I'll pass, but make some time for me soon. I miss you girls. I'll be reporting to spring training next week, but I'll be back on some weekends.

Molly: We will, miss you too. Give our best to the misses.

Molly got home and got ready for the night; she couldn't wait to let go and have some fun. She had been so wrapped up in Luke since he got back home that she started to forget there were other people in her life that cared to see her as well.

The same thing always happened when Luke got back, she became self-absorbed and forgot about everyone else around her. Well, not tonight; she was going to have some fun with her friends. She noticed a note on her mirror when she walked into the bathroom to fluff her hair so it wasn't clinging to her face. It was from Luke.

If any guys hit on you tonight, consider them dead. I'll be thinking about your tits all night. Love you Baby – Molly's Man

Jane

Jane decided to wear a pair of Olivia-Newton-John-tight pants and a shirt with a neckline down to the middle of her stomach. She donned her hot pink stilettos and paired them with a light shade of lip gloss on her lips. She knew Brady would have an instant hard on if he saw her in her outfit, so she decided might as well send him a picture on her phone. She loved to tease him, mainly because she enjoyed his reaction. She took a picture in the mirror, slightly leaning forward, so he could notice her abundance of cleavage trying to come out. She added a comment with the picture.

Jane: Eat your heart out, handsome. Just a little reminder of what you're missing back home.

Jane almost didn't send it because she thought it might be a little too much, but then said screw it and sent the picture. She used to do things like that all the time, and she was starting to feel like her old self again. Brady texted her back.

Brady: Are you freaking kidding me? You're going out like that?

Jane smiled; he must be dying right now. She had to admit she looked pretty hot and very slutty. She had not worn the shirt she had on in years, but it still fit like a glove and was, surprisingly, still in style. Although she guessed slut was always in style at the night clubs. All one had to do was either show some tits or ass and they were trend-setting at the clubs. Her phone rang, startling her from her thoughts. It was Brady.

"Hey Brady," Jane said innocently.

"Jane, I'll have you know I'm currently sitting on my hotel bed, watching a college basketball game with a fucking boner."

Jane laughed out loud. "I'm sorry. I just wanted to show you my outfit."

"That is quite the outfit, babe. Damn, I want you so bad.

Are you sure you're not secretly flying out to California to surprise me?"

Jane shivered. Brady wanted her. She knew they were dating, but hearing him say those words sent heat down to her center. She still couldn't believe she was dating him; it still seemed so crazy. One minute she was about to get lost in pizza and alcohol while drowning in her own sorrows, and then the next minute she was getting lost in Brady's brilliant green eyes.

"I wish! We're having girls' night, Molly, Albert and me. Molly told me to get slutty. Did I do a good job?"

Brady gulped, "I'd say, damn you look hot. I wanted to titty-fuck you through the phone."

Jane giggled, "Oh, you're a titty-fucker then? That doesn't surprise me. I'm always catching you staring at my chest."

"Do you blame me? You are such a little thing with an excellent rack. I can't help myself."

"Understandable. I do feel that my boobs are quite perky and round. Who would have thought I'd be sporting a 32C?"

Brady coughed and said, "Alright, this conversation is over. I need to go take care of myself. Thanks for the picture; it'll come in handy."

Jane was taken aback at first. Wow, Brady wasn't shy at all. He just told her he was going to go masturbate to her picture. If he wasn't so hot, she might find that a bit creepy, but he was just a man with a healthy libido that she kept teasing. She wished she was in his hotel room to help him relieve himself. She couldn't wait to see him the next day. She knew he had something grand planned and couldn't wait to find out what it was.

"You're welcome. I can't wait to see you tomorrow."

"I can't wait either, sweet thing. Be safe tonight. I expect some wild texts from you."

"You can count on it, and don't worry about other guys, I only have one on my mind right now and he has the sexiest green eyes that melt my heart."

"Mmm, see you tomorrow, gorgeous."

Jane hung up the phone and threw her head back on the couch as she waited for her taxi. Oh boy, this was not good; she had it bad.

CHAPTER THIRTEEN

Jane

Molly's taxi picked Jane up and they headed over to Deuces. Molly looked good, like always. She chose to wear a mini skirt to show off her amazing legs and a teal top. Her shoes were strappy stilettos that Luke bought her as a present for making it through another mission together. He always got her something really nice when he got home. This past mission's present clearly was a beautifully large engagement ring.

Jane envied Molly. She had such an amazing and loving relationship. Luke and Molly were the perfect match for each other; they were both horn dogs, but they understood each other. They knew each other's past history and loved one another for where they came from and who they were. Luke always made sure Molly was taken care of when he was with her and when they were apart. Jane only hoped she could have half the relationship they had.

Jane felt pretty good with the way things had been going with Brady. It was still very new and they had been somehow able to stay out of the limelight, but Jane knew she was going to get caught up in some tabloid sometime soon. Brady always wound up in the tabloids. Needless to say, if she was dating Brady, she could expect her face to be plastered all over the grocery check-out stands at some point. Brady said he would do his best to make sure they didn't get ahold of any of her personal information, but there was only so much he could do. He was sweet because he didn't want any gossip magazines to mess with her new business.

The bouncer at Deuces waved them in and, as they walked up, he said he would like for them to come around more often. Jane and Molly laughed together. Women have such an advantage over men, they flash a little side boob and they can get whatever they want.

Deuces was crowded. It was fun to see all the different types of people who came out. There were the couples who wanted to go out and have a good time, maybe she would bring Brady here one night and redo their first night together. There were the single ladies who practically wore bikinis they showed so much skin and there were the single men on the prowl, who stood in the corners of the club or leaned against the bar watching the girls gyrating with each other, aka the perverts of the crowd.

"There are actually some very attractive men here tonight," Molly said. "Usually all the single guys here end up either being gay, which is a shame, or beyond creepy with their button-down shirts and gorilla hair climbing up their necks."

Jane chuckled, "Eh, the men are alright, nothing to write home about."

"You're only saying that because your eyes are so glazed over with infatuation for Brady Matthews. I bet you if I got on top of the bar and shouted that you were Brady Matthews' new girlfriend, every girl in this bar would tackle you and rip your pubes out one by one."

"I would wish them good luck in finding any."

Molly playfully pushed Jane to the side. "You didn't?" Jane nodded "You got a Brazilian? FINALLY! I have been telling you to get one for years now. How was it?"

"It was God-awful, but I can't wait for Brady to see me in all my glory."

Albert waved them over to his plush little VIP area. They walked over and ordered drinks from the waiter as they sat down next to their very fabulous friend.

Before Jane could even say hello to Albert, Molly shouted, "You mean to tell me you haven't boned Brady yet?"

Heads from people around them turned and looked at Jane. "Can you please keep your voice down?" Jane said in a whisper. "No, we have not 'boned' yet. Believe me, I want to, but he's taking things slow and I know it's because he's sensitive to my situation of getting over George, but I swear I've become a virgin again from waiting. I can't take this much longer."

Albert kissed them both on the cheek and said, "Honey, if I was you, I would just strip and stand in front of him and see what he does then. There's no way he would be able to resist you."

"He's coming home tomorrow from a conference, and he said he has something great for us planned…and he also mentioned something like fucking all night long," Jane said with a smile.

Molly and Albert's jaws both dropped and then they cheered. "Our Janey is back!" Albert exclaimed.

"I told you she'd become feistier, just like the girl we know and love," Molly said.

"I know. I'm sorry you lost me for a while, but Brady is really helping me put my George complex behind me and helping me find myself again."

She thought about that for a second. Brady really had helped her come back from the death that was George. She should reward him for his efforts.

"Well, that calls for a shot," Albert said. "Here's to sexy baseball players."

They lifted their glasses together and all took a shot of tequila. Jane cringed as the burning liquid slid down her throat. She had not had straight-up tequila in quite a long time. She concluded that it was going to be a rough night.

Jane corrected Albert. "Baseball player, Alby, only one for me."

Albert nodded ahead of them and said, "Well, I see baseball players."

Jane's heart fluttered and she turned to look for Brady, but she didn't see him. Instead, she spotted Michael, Marc and another guy, whom she had never met before.

The very athletic looking men were headed their way. It was supposed to be a girls' night, so their appearance was contradicting the purpose of their night. Maybe the guys would just say hi and then leave. That was wishful thinking; Michael was a chatty guy with a crush on Jane. She knew he always had a thing for her and it confused her that, ever since he was traded to Atlanta, they hadn't seen his wife once. She hoped they were not having problems.

Michael walked up to Jane, gave her a once-over, smiled,

and kissed her on her cheek.

"You guys look hot tonight, including you Albert," Michael said.

Albert smiled brightly and said, "You sure know how to make a girl blush."

Michael laughed, "Do you mind if we join you for a little? I know its girls' night, but I thought we could at least buy you ladies a shot."

Molly chimed in, "Well, if you're giving out free shots, you're more than welcome to sit down, but don't expect to stay too long. We need to get our talk on, and you men will hinder our ability to be candid."

"When have you ever not been candid, Molly?" Michael laughed.

He ordered 12 lemon drop shots, two for each person. Jane started to get nervous; she was about to get real loose with all the drinks in front of her.

Michael took a seat next to Jane and introduced everybody. Marc was with him, who was one of Brady's best friends and the guy she'd never met turned out to be a rookie looking to make it on the team this year; his name was Austin Lee. He was 'born and raised' in Texas and apparently conceived in Austin, hence the name. He had a very sexy drawl to his voice and kept calling her ma'am. Wasn't he cute? If she had a single friend, she would totally try to hook them up.

Michael leaned over and whispered in Jane's ear, "Take a picture with me?"

Startled, Jane smiled and said, "Of course, Mikey."

He pulled out his phone, leaned in so they were cheek to cheek and took a picture of them together. At the last minute, he turned his head and kissed her on the side of her mouth while he snapped the picture. He smelled of pure alcohol. How long had he been here drinking?

He handed her a shot and told her to drink up. They all clinked glasses and downed their second lemon drop. All of a sudden, Jane started to feel her drinks. She was a little thing and didn't have much tolerance, so one drink and three shots made her feel good. She kept thinking about Brady; she missed him and wished he was with her right now, sitting next to her instead of Michael.

She loved Michael, as a brother and nothing more. They'd always had a special connection, but she'd never had romantic feelings for him.

Michael leaned into her and said, "Jane, you're really looking good tonight."

Blushing, Jane thanked Michael. Jane was starting to get a little uncomfortable, so maybe it was time for the boys to go. Michael seemed to be getting a little too friendly when he slid his arm from her shoulders to the small of her back. She looked over at Molly, trying to get some help, but Molly, Mark, Austin and Albert were playing some sort of drinking game. Damn, what happened to girls' night? All of a sudden, her phone beeped. She looked down and saw a message from Brady; her heart fluttered.

Brady: Hope you're having a good night and Albert is beating away the guys with his dick.

Jane laughed out loud, causing Michael to lean over and ask if the message was from Brady. Jane started to get irritated with Michael. It was none of his business who was communicating with her. Why was he so nosy?

She didn't let her irritation show and instead replied, "Of course, thank you so much for introducing me to him; he's amazing."

Michael rolled his eyes and said, "He sure is."

Jane turned to him and asked, "What is that supposed to mean, Michael?" What was he getting after? Was he trying to tell her something, or was he trying to get in her head?

"Nothing," Michael mumbled and turned away.

Jane shoved him so he was facing her again and said, "No, not nothing, what are you not telling me?"

Michael shook his head and said, "You're right, Jane, he is amazing, that's the problem. He doesn't even give anyone else a shot at trying to be with you."

Jane was stunned. Did Michael want to be with her? He was married to Kelly, though. Last time she knew, they had a great relationship. Although, she did find it quite weird that she had not seen Kelly since they moved down to Atlanta. She decided to call him out.

"Michael, you're happily married. What's going on?"

Michael looked dead into her eyes. He looked so sad. Why had he not said anything to her if things were not going well between him and Kelly? Was it because she stopped talking to him when she was with George? She thought they cleared the air about that.

He smiled slightly and looked at her lips, she accidently licked them when he was looking at them and that was all he needed. He started to swoop in to kiss her. She quickly turned her head, so he missed her lips and kissed her ear instead. He grunted out of frustration, tossed a shot glass to the side and got up.

Jane was so stunned, she didn't know what to do. Molly looked over at her perplexed. Jane shrugged her shoulders in confusion and went after Michael. She chased him outside and called after him.

When she finally caught up to him she asked, "Michael, what the hell are you doing?"

He whipped around so fast and pinned her against the outside brick wall, she barely had a chance to steady herself. His hands straddled her face and he was inches from her nose. Jane started to shake; Michael wouldn't hurt her, but she didn't like the darkness in his eyes.

"You don't get it, Jane. I waited around for you. I was your best friend and cuddle buddy for years so you had someone to go to when things went wrong in your life. I watched you ruin your life when you were with George and now Brady comes around and he has saved your life. What about me? I was the one who was there for you, through everything and yet you still just look at me as a brother. Why don't I get the attention Brady does?"

Jane tried to push him away, but he was rock solid; there was no moving him. "Michael, aren't you married? Why are you treating me like this? How am I supposed to be with you if you're married? I am not a cheater or an adulterer, so what do you expect from me?"

Did Michael really expect her to go after him romantically when he moved to Atlanta? Even if she did harbor romantic feelings for Michael, which she didn't, she would never do anything about them because he was married. There must be something going on with his wife for him to act out like he currently was.

Michael threw his arms up and yelled, "Nothing, I'm out of here. Sorry for ruining your night."

Michael took off so fast Jane couldn't even try to chase after him. She walked back into the club and sat down with everyone; they looked at her awkwardly and Albert finally broke the silence and said, "What flew up his dick hole?"

That was why Jane loved Albert; he always took the tension out of things. She shook off what happened with Michael and tried to enjoy the rest of her night. She had another shot, courtesy of Austin and started feeling a little too good. She grabbed Molly and went out on the dance floor. She loved dancing, especially when it was just her and her girl. She did enjoy dancing with Brady, but with Molly, she didn't have to make sure she was sexy. She could just let her limbs fly about, let loose, and have fun.

A man tried to come up behind Jane and grab her waist to dance, but Albert, thankfully, finally pulled himself away from the baseball players and pushed the creep to the side. They were just three girls having a blast. Jane ended up having two more shots and one more drink. Within an hour, she was having a hard time focusing.

She pulled out her phone and saw she had three text messages, all from Brady. Uh oh. She went to the bathroom, climbed in a stall, sat down and read her messages.

Brady: Hey babe, just making sure you're okay. Michael texted me and said he was breaking up your girls' night.

Brady: Michael is texting me weird things. Is he doing okay? He's not bothering you, is he?

The last message read…

Brady: Why did Michael just send me a picture of him kissing you and say "I'm moving in on your girlfriend?"

When did he kiss her? He didn't kiss her, did he? Maybe her cheek or was it on the mouth? She couldn't remember…either way, she thought he took a picture of them smiling together. She was so confused and couldn't think straight. She needed to go home and call Brady to clear things up. She met Molly and Albert out on the dance floor and told them she was going home. They both gave her a hug, and Albert made one of his bouncer friends make sure she got a cab successfully and was taken care of.

Jane climbed up her apartment stairs and finally made it to her apartment after what seemed like a huge struggle in her intoxicated state. She unlocked the door, pulled herself out of her clothes and stretched out on her bed. The room was spinning big time. She couldn't focus on anything, and when she closed her eyes to make the room stop spinning, it felt like it started spinning even faster. She grabbed her phone and attempted to dial Brady. It took her five tries, but finally, her phone started ringing. She laid the phone on the pillow and laid her head on top of it.

Brady

Brady's phone started ringing. Thank God, Jane was finally calling him. He wanted some answers. Michael was being a huge douche bag and Brady wanted to know what Michael's deal was. Brady answered.

"Hey, Jane, are you okay?"

"Hey, sexy," Jane slurred "I miss you…you're so fucking hot. Did you know that?"

"Thanks, sweet thing, but are you okay? Where are you?" Oh boy, was she drunk.

"I'm drunk Brady. The room keeps spinning."

"What room Jane? Are you home?"

"Yes, I'm home. I'm lying on my bed wearing only my thong. I don't know what happened to my bra, but these sheets feel so good on my skin."

Brady had to keep himself from being turned on. He needed to make sure Jane was okay and then find out what happened between her and Michael, but it was kind of difficult to not focus on the sexy tone of Jane's voice and the picture she was painting for him. Damn, now was not the time to picture her rolling around in those satin sheets of hers, naked. He groaned and swore under his breath.

"I'm glad you're home. What happened with Michael?"

"Brady, I wish you were here. My nipples are so hard for you right now. Mmm, let's have phone sex, Brady. I'm so turned on right now just hearing your voice. "

Brady knew talking to her right now was going to be completely useless. She was too drunk to remember anything. He

117

wasn't about to have phone sex as one of the first erotic things they did together, so instead, he decided he needed to get off the phone or change the subject. He decided to try to get off the phone. She was safe at home, in bed. She was okay.

"Well, I'm glad you're home, Jane. I'll let you get some sleep."

Jane started to sniff. Was she crying? Brady asked, "Are you crying, sweet thing?"

Jane didn't reply. Brady asked again a little louder. Still nothing. Brady started to get frustrated until he heard Jane say, "Brady, I'm so sorry."

Brady's heart dropped. Did something actually happen between her and Michael? Before he could respond, Jane hung up the phone. Fuck! What the hell was going on? He tried to call her back, but he knew she was passed out. She wasn't going to answer. He slammed the hotel remote against the wall in frustration. He needed to get home.

What the hell was Michael thinking? Brady was going to kill him. He was planning Michael's death sentence when he got a text message. He looked at his phone to see who it was, and the number was one he didn't recognize. Who had his phone number? He hoped Jane wasn't so drunk she was giving away his phone number. He opened the message.

Hey sexy, I've missed you so much. I want to meet up with you and run my hands all over your body, anything you want.

Did Jane have another phone? Brady was so confused. He sent a message back to the strange number.

Brady: Jane? Is this you?

Who the fuck is Jane? This is the love of your life, Laney.

Fuck! Double Fuck! How did she get his number? When they broke up, he changed all his information so she couldn't get in touch with him. What should he do? Should he text her back? He didn't want Jane to know he was texting her, but Laney needed to know she didn't have a chance with him. He decided to send her a message back.

Brady: Where the hell did you get my number?

Laney: I have my sources. How about it Brady? I miss your dick and could really use a good fuck.

Brady: Go to hell and leave me alone, you fame whore.

Brady turned his phone off. He didn't want to deal with Laney anymore. What a messed up night. Just when he thought everything was going right for him, he leaves for a couple of days and his friend, or who he thought was his friend, was hitting on his girlfriend and his ex-girlfriend was trying to weasel her way back in his life. Well, Laney could go to hell for all he cared, and Brady needed to get to the bottom of Michael's intentions, because hell if he was going to be sharing Jane. She was his.

CHAPTER FOURTEEN

Jane

Jane woke up to a beeping noise in her ear. She lifted her head and groaned from the pounding that vibrated through her head. Okay, small movements, that would help that jackhammer making a mess of her brain.

Ugh, she had way too much to drink last night…damn those lemon shots.

Beep.

What was that noise? She tried to place the irritating sound, but couldn't focus. She moved her hand around and touched something smooth, oh her phone. She opened one eye because that was all she could muster at the moment and peeked at her phone. Three missed calls from Brady, shit. Did she talk to him last night?

She checked her text messages. She re-read the three she got from Brady and noticed something must have happened with Michael. What the hell? Then it all came flooding back to her. Michael was extremely close to her last night, confessed his feelings for her, got touchy and something about a picture? Oh, for fuck's sake. All of the sudden, there was a pounding at her door.

She got up and noticed she was only wearing a thong. Too lazy and in too much pain to dress herself, she pulled the sheet off her bed around her and answered the door. She nearly got run over by Michael when she opened it.

"Michael, what the hell are you doing here?" Jane asked.

Michael ran a hand through what little hair he had and came toward her.

"Stop right there, buster. I have a feeling you got me into

some trouble last night with Brady and you have some explaining to do."

Michael's shoulders sagged and he broke down emotionally. "Shit, Jane, I'm sorry. I don't know what came over me. Things haven't been good at home and reconnecting with you brought back all these old feelings. I was drunk and lost control. I sent a picture to Brady last night of what looked like me kissing you, but I swear, nothing happened. I tried to kiss you, but you turned away. I tried calling Brady this morning and sent him a million text messages trying to explain. I haven't heard anything from him. I'm so sorry."

Michael looked terrible. She didn't know things were bad at home. She pulled him into a hug then grasped his head in her hands and looked in his eyes.

She said, "You need to talk to me Michael; you can't keep things all bottled up…"

She was about to let go of him, but she was interrupted by Brady stepping into her apartment and saying, "What the fuck is happening here?"

Jane's heart dropped to the floor. Oh my God. This so did not look good. She had a sheet tied around her body, while her hands were holding Michael's head, showing off what looked like a lover's embrace. Brady's eyes blazed with fire. His fists were clenched at his sides, and he looked like he was about to punch Michael so hard his face would fall off.

Jane was extremely nervous. If a fight broke out between them, there was no way she would be able to break them up, especially only wearing a bed sheet. She would have to go next door, grab Mr. Mendez and have him poke the guys with his broom stick until they stopped.

Michael stepped away and said, "Dude, I swear this is not what it looks like. I came over here to apologize for overstepping my boundaries last night. I swear, nothing happened."

Brady closed in on Michael, inches away from his face. Jane's heart started to pound incredibly fast. She didn't know what to do. Should she throw herself between them? They wouldn't hurt a girl; they'd probably just push her to the side and take each other out.

Brady breathed heavily and gritted out, "Get the fuck out of here."

Michael didn't say another word. He looked at Jane apologetically and took off. Brady just stood there, looking out the door. He turned to Jane and blackness filled his eyes. She thought he might actually combust. He was so not happy. She couldn't lose him over something so stupid. He turned away from her and started to walk toward the door.

Jane tripped over her sheet while grabbing Brady's arm and pleaded, "Brady, please don't go. Let me explain."

Brady looked her up and down and that was when she realized that when she tripped over her sheet, she actually stepped on it, making it fall off completely. She was standing in front of Brady with only a thong on. The fire in Brady's eyes turned from anger to pure lust. Jane just stood there frozen, breathing as if there was an anvil on her chest. Brady kicked the door shut with his foot and charged toward her, separating them only by inches. His hands skimmed up her arms and then down her sides, scraping the side of her breasts with his thumbs, and then he stopped at her waist. He wrapped his fingers under her thong and pulled her close.

Jane had to focus on breathing because, if she didn't, she would pass out. She wanted this man so badly.

Brady lowered his head toward Jane's and started to kiss her, deeply. He had never kissed her like this before, as if he couldn't get enough of her. He skimmed his hands over her bare butt and ran one hand all the way up her back and into her hair, sending chills down her spine. He pulled her head even closer and drove his tongue further in her mouth, claiming her as his. She was throbbing everywhere, begging to be touched in places she hadn't been touched in a while.

A low moan crept out of the back of her throat and the hand that once was on her ass, she found cupping her breast and kneading her nipple. Her knees started to go weak and, in one fluid motion, Brady swept her up into his arms and carried her to the bedroom, still kissing her like he never wanted to let go.

He placed her gently on the bed and covered her up. Wait what was happening? He wasn't kissing her anymore. She reached for his neck to pull him back down, but he stopped her hands and put them back down by her sides.

Brady started to get up and she cried in frustration. "Brady, please believe me, I swear nothing happened. Please don't be mad at me."

Brady turned around and pushed a lock of hair away from her face and said, "I'm not mad at you, sweet thing. I know nothing happened. I trust you. Michael explained everything in the million voice messages and texts he sent."

"Then why did you look like you were going to blast him through the wall?"

"It was very unnerving walking in on the two of you. I didn't like how it looked. Plus, sometimes you have to make the other guy think you can kick his ass, so he doesn't try pulling another stunt like that." Brady smiled.

Jane was confused. "So, you aren't mad?"

Brady didn't answer for a second, which made Jane nervous. He looked her in the eyes and said, "I can't lie and say I wasn't mad, upset, angry, jealous, and all those other feelings that go along with the idea that your girl might be with someone else, but instead of reacting, I decided to look at the facts. I know you wouldn't cheat on me, and Michael apologized for his actions. When I saw you two this morning with you only in your sheet and your hands cupping his face, I thought I could only see red, but I calmed myself before I attacked Michael."

"Then why did you stop kissing me and touching me if you're not mad? Do I repulse you?"

Brady sat right next to her and gently stroked her hand. "By no means do you in any way repulse me, baby. I brought some hangover remedies for you and I was going to go grab them. I want you ready for our date tonight. I was just giving you a little sample of what's to come."

Jane groaned in frustration. She thought only girls were able to cock tease men. She didn't know men could be pussy teasers. She flung her head back and then groaned in pain and grasped her head.

"Brady Matthews, you are slowly killing me. I'm not going to last at all tonight with all the pussy teasing you've been doing."

Brady gave her a hearty laugh and repeated, "Pussy tease? Well, I've never heard that one before." He placed a kiss on her forehead and said, "I'll be right back, sweet thing; just lay your head down and relax. I have a masseuse coming over around two this afternoon to help replenish your body. I want you in top form tonight."

Jane sat up, exposing her breasts and took Brady's head in

her hands; she lightly licked his lips and then kissed him the sexiest way she knew how. Brady gulped and lightly grabbed her boobs, caressing the sides of them and barely rubbing her nipples with his thumbs. Jane started to pull him closer and arch her back toward him when he pulled away and rested his forehead on hers, breathing heavily. They both sat there for a couple of minutes before he got up and announced he would be back with a cheeseburger, Advil, and some PowerAde…his favorite hangover remedy.

Brady

Brady came back shortly and made sure Jane was somewhat conscious before he took off. He took one last look at her perfect body lying in her welcoming bed before he left. God, he was an idiot; he could have her right now if he wanted. She just stared up at him with her big blues eyes begging him to touch her. She moved slightly under the covers, once again revealing her gorgeous breasts. She smiled in a seductive manner and pulled the sheets down even further. Brady just stood there and drooled. He was acting like a teenage boy. Jane looked down at his crotch, licked her lips and smiled. Jesus Christ.

He shook his head and said, "Save it for tonight, pip-squeak." He reluctantly left her in her bed, alone.

As he walked out the door, he reminded Jane to pack an overnight bag and said he would be at her apartment around seven to pick her up. Jane flashed him one of her sexy grins and blew him a kiss goodbye.

He needed to talk to Michael and make things better with him. He suspected things were not going well with him and his wife. Brady thought the move away from her family had made it difficult on their marriage, but he wasn't quite sure. Michael never really talked about his personal life. Brady gave him a quick call.

Michael answered, "Hello?"

"Hey, it's Brady."

"Brady, God, I'm so sorry; I feel like a real douche bag. You've been nothing but nice to me and then I go and pull a stunt like last night. Please tell me everything between you and Jane is okay."

"Everything is fine. I trust her and know she would never

do anything to hurt me. I know things aren't easy for you right now, and I just wanted to let you know if you need to talk about anything, just let me know. I'll take you out for a beer and we can bitch about how women drive us crazy."

Michael laughed, "I'll take you up on that offer. When we get down to Florida, that is; I'm sure you're going to spend as much time with Jane as possible until we have to report in."

"You're right about that. I'm actually getting ready for a date tonight with her. I plan on knocking her socks off."

"I know you will." Michael was silent for a second, but then continued. "Brady, thanks for bringing Jane back to us. She isn't fully recovered from the wrath of George, but it's great to start seeing little pieces of old Jane coming through again. You did that, man."

Brady sighed, "I'm only treating her the way she deserves to be treated. Hey listen, just so you know though, if you ever fucking try to move in on Jane again, I'll make sure you'll be out for the season. I don't take well to people trying to take what I have."

Brady heard Michael gulp on the phone. "Understood, I'm sorry again. I was out of line."

"Thank you for contacting me earlier, so I didn't lose my mind completely. I'll see you on Monday, bud, have a safe trip down."

"You too, have fun tonight," Michael said, and they hung up.

Brady was still a little irritated with Michael and cautious about his intentions with Jane, but he knew he had to give the guy a little slack. Michael was in a new city dealing with a bitching wife, most likely, and the last thing he needed was for Brady to be pissed off at him and giving him the cold shoulder. It did chap Brady's ass, though, that Michael had feelings for Jane. No man likes to deal with the fact that another guy has feelings for his girl. It was going to put Brady on edge every time Jane and Michael were together. He trusted Jane, but he didn't fully trust Michael to not try anything again.

Enough thoughts about Michael and Jane, Brady had to get ready for his date. The masseuse should arrive at Jane's at two, and then the package he sent her should be there shortly after. He planned on spoiling his little lady tonight. He wanted it to be a perfect night. She deserved a great night and he really wanted to leave a lasting impression on her before he took off for spring training.

God, why couldn't he have met her earlier? Brady hated the fact that he had to leave for a month and a half and leave Jane behind, especially since their relationship was so new. He was going to do his damnedest to keep things going between them when they were apart. He'd already planned some romantic get-a-ways. They usually only got one day off at a time, but he could weasel his way around that. He also planned on flying Jane down to Florida, maybe convincing the organization to hire her as an event coordinator for some of the events they put on during spring training. It would be okay.

He also needed to make sure that Laney kept to herself. He didn't want to change his phone number, but if she started getting crazy again, he might have to consider a switch. He thought about telling Jane about Laney contacting him. He always believed in being open and honest in a relationship, but Jane was still very sensitive; he wasn't sure how she would react to hearing news about Laney. Maybe for now, he would keep it to himself. It wasn't like she'd tried to contact him again since last night. Hopefully, she got the hint.

Molly

Molly woke to a light rubbing on her back and felt a cold surface on her cheek. She couldn't open her eyes because that meant her head was going to explode. Where was she? She groaned and tried to move, but big strong hands grabbed her and lifted her up.

She moaned and then her head was plastered against a very strong and very bare chest.

"Molly, it's me. I'm just going to move you off the kitchen floor and into our bed."

Kitchen floor? Oh, good, she was home. Albert must have dropped her off. Oh boy, she was going to lose her cookies if Luke didn't put her down soon. He slowly laid her down in their bed and stroked her hair to the side.

"Babe, do you want me to change your clothes for you?" Luke asked.

"I don't think I can move. My head is throbbing as hard as your dick was the other night."

Luke laughed and put a cold object in her hand and told her to drink it. Oh no, it was his gross hangover drink. It tasted like moldy feet, but it worked like a charm every time. He used lots of greens, some minced garlic, orange juice and some other weird things, including an egg. She held her nose and gulped it down. When it was all gone, she started coughing and almost lost everything she just drank. Luke rubbed her back, telling her it would kick in soon and she would feel much better.

"In the meantime, let me get you out of those clothes," Luke said.

"Oh, I'm fine babe; come here and I'll give you a hand job," Molly said, while feeling around for her favorite dick in the world.

Luke kissed her hand and said, "Later, right now I'm getting you out of those clothes."

Molly looked down at herself and gasped. God, she was an embarrassment. How Luke could still look at her with loving eyes was beyond her. She wanted to break up with herself she was so embarrassing.

Her shirt and bra were nowhere to be found and her mini skirt was up around her breasts, barely covering her nipples. She was wearing underwear, thankfully, but there was something sticky in her hair.

"Luke, did you ejaculate in my hair last night?"

Luke shook his head in amusement and said, "No, that would most likely be some of the 'drink' you tried to make for yourself last night. I found mayonnaise, apple cider vinegar, peanut butter and a Laffy Taffy wrapper on the counter and the gross mixture in the blender this morning."

"Oh fuck, that sounds disgusting. I hope I didn't drink any of it."

"I think you did because you seem to have formed a pinky-brown crust on your upper lip. Care to explain what you were trying to make?"

Disgusted, Molly said, "And you want to marry me why?"

Luke grabbed her arm and started rubbing it. "Because there's never a dull moment with you. Come on, I'll take another shower if you're involved. We need to get you looking and feeling human again, because seeing you in that mini skirt barely covering your tits has got me all hot and bothered."

Molly playfully pushed Luke and grimaced in pain. "There's something wrong with you, Luke."

He shrugged, pulled her mini skirt down, exposing her breasts, and ripped her underwear off. He just stared at her naked body for a minute and then scooped her up to carry her to the shower. He whispered in her ear, "Even when you have a hangover and have puke drink crusted on your upper lip, you are still by far the sexiest thing I've ever laid eyes on."

Molly whispered back. "Scoring big points, big boy…you've graduated yourself from a hand job to full-on pussy action. I'll bend over in the shower, and you can have your way with me. If you're lucky, I'll even grant you tit access."

Jane

Jane just got out of the shower. She had to rinse off the oils the masseuse used on her body. That was one of the best massages she'd ever had. She felt brand new and not like she went out drinking the night before and passed out on her phone while her boyfriend was trying to figure out if something happened between her and her friend.

God, Brady must be a saint for not getting jealous and throwing her coffee table through the wall. That was what George would have done, or something to that extent. He wasn't really macho, so maybe he would have pulled his pen out of his pocket protector and flicked it at the wall instead.

As Jane dried off, her doorbell rang. She wrapped the towel around her and looked through the peephole. There was a man holding a box wrapped in a ribbon; Brady's doing most likely. She took the box, thanked the man, and shouted with glee as she flung herself on her bed to open the box like a teenager. She ripped open the ribbon, pulled the top off and found a little note.

Jane,
I saw this and thought of how damn sexy you would look in it. Please consider wearing it for our date tonight.
Brady
P.S. There is lingerie at the bottom that I EXPECT you to wear.

Jane blushed. What did he purchase for her? She ripped the tissue paper to the side and gasped. He bought her the new Valentino deep teal V-neck dress. It was gorgeous! Of course she was going to wear it. Was he crazy? She pulled the dress out and held it up to her. Oh, it was perfect. It was going to be a tight dress, but she never minded showing off her curves and it was just long enough that she was not going to look like a hooch.

She looked in the box to find the lingerie he picked out for her and laughed. She pulled out the skimpiest thong she had ever laid her hands on; how they even got lace on it was beyond her, and there was a matching black lace bra to go with it. The bra was a push up bra with barely any nipple coverage; she hoped everything got covered up. She was going to wear them, no matter how uncomfortable they might be, because Brady picked them out and she wanted to fulfill his every fantasy.

She couldn't wait for their date tonight. Not only was she going to be with Brady physically for the first time, he was taking her out, and after three days of him being out of town, she really needed some Brady time. They talked on the phone every night, which kept her sane, but she could really use some physical action and she planned on getting as much as possible tonight.

CHAPTER FIFTEEN

Brady

Brady pulled into Jane's apartment complex. She really lived in a nice area, but he thought, how nice would it be if she lived with him? Wait, what? Live with him? Where did that thought come from? They hadn't even had sex yet and he was already picking out wallpaper for the both of them? Slow down, buddy, one step at a time.

The thing was, he thought he could really spend his life with Jane. She made him laugh again, and she didn't treat him like some rich baseball player. She saw his soul and appreciated who he was as a person, not what he did or how big his bank account was. Yes, he did lavish her with gifts, but he wanted to. It was the people who expected material possessions from him who he didn't like buying things for. She didn't expect expensive items, romantic getaways or pricy dinners from him. She just wanted him for who he was.

He walked to her apartment and heard something rustling around in the bushes next to the door, which nearly sent him falling down the stairs. God, he was skittish tonight, must have been Mr. Mendez's cat. That thing was always prowling the apartment complex, pissing on everything in sight. Brady gathered himself and knocked on Jane's door. When she opened the door, Brady was taken aback by Jane. She instantly took his breath away.

She was wearing the dress he picked out for her, and she looked more beautiful than he ever expected. The dress was cut just low enough in the neckline where he got a great view of the amazing rack she had, and the dress was just short enough where he got a great look at her slim tan legs. She wore black glittered high heels and her cute little toes that peeked out were painted the same color as the dress. She had a radiant smile plastered across her beautiful face and her hair begged for his fingers to run through it. Yup, he was a goner. She had him wrapped around her little finger.

She pulled him inside, grabbing the lapels of his jacket and pulled him down toward her. Her lips encased his and he lost all thought. When she finally pulled away, his eyes slowly opened. He most likely looked like some lovesick puppy, but he didn't care. She was amazing.

"Jesus, you look gorgeous," Brady said in a raspy voice.

"You look pretty good yourself, handsome," Jane smiled.

He was wearing black pants and a white button-up with the collar open a little at the top and a black suit jacket. Nothing too fancy and nothing compared to her.

"Do you like the dress?" Brady asked, while spinning Jane around. She had so much grace it was incredible. Her hair floated and bobbed in curls while her eyes glistened with lust.

"I love the dress, thank you so much. You seriously didn't have to buy it for me. I feel bad I have nothing for you."

"You don't need to give me anything but yourself." Brady rubbed his thumb pad against her jaw and tilted her head up for another kiss. He couldn't get enough of this woman. "Did you like the lingerie?" Brady murmured in between kisses.

Jane squeezed her body closer to him so she leaned right against his crotch and whispered. "I loved it. I was planning on going commando until you sent these over to me. I must say, my tits look spectacular and my ass is looking damn fine in the thong you picked out as well. I hope you're ready for it?"

Brady cleared his throat and nodded. He couldn't seem to get any clear thoughts in his head. He took her hand and helped her lock up her apartment. While she locked her door, he ran his hands up and down her body and kissed the back of her neck. Then there was a flash of light. Startled, they both looked at each other in confusion.

"What was that?" asked Jane.

"I don't know; that was weird." Brady didn't like the feeling he was getting. "Let's get going, we have places to be."

They walked out of the apartment complex just as a man jumped out of the bushes and started taking pictures of them and asking questions about who Jane was and where Laney was at the moment. Brady's blood instantly boiled. He made Jane duck as he put his hand up.

Do not punch this guy's lights out, just get to the car, he thought. Brady opened the door for her, swearing under his breath. This was exactly not what he needed or wanted. He wanted to give Jane a romantic, calm night; the last thing he needed was the paparazzi following them around. Brady climbed in his car and slammed his hands on the steering wheel. Jane jumped out of her seat.

He leaned over and looked at Jane. She looked terrified. He grabbed her hand and said, "I'm sorry babe, I didn't mean to scare you. I'm just frustrated right now. I had such a great night planned for us, but anywhere we go, this ass fuck is going to follow us and document our every move."

Jane rubbed her thumb against his hand. She looked at him with loving eyes and said, "Brady, you don't have to impress me anymore. I don't mind skipping the plans you had for us; I just want to be with you. Is there somewhere else we can go where we can be alone?"

Brady smiled at Jane, yes there was. He put the car in drive and took off, leaving the dickhead in the dust.

Jane

Jane was feeling more relaxed once the tension in Brady's jaw loosened up. She could understand how he felt. She couldn't imagine being in the public eye, being scrutinized for every move he made and every person he dated.

All of a sudden, a horrible thought went through her mind. Was he so mad because he got caught taking out a girl like her? Was he embarrassed because she wasn't the celebrity type he was used to dating? She couldn't help herself, she had to ask because she needed to clear her head of those thoughts.

Jane cleared her throat. "Brady, umm...did you not want to proceed with your plans because the paparazzi spotted you and you were embarrassed of me?"

Brady nearly crashed the car. He pulled off on the side of the highway and whipped his whole body around so fast she thought he looked like some action hero in a movie.

"You're kidding me, right? You're not serious with that question."

Jane looked down at her lap and replied, "I don't know. You seemed to be in an awful hurry to shield me away from the camera and then you cancelled everything. I guess I'm just a little self-conscious. You are this amazingly gorgeous, famous man, and I'm just an event planner who happened to get lucky."

She could feel Brady's eyes burning a hole through her, but she couldn't look at him. She was ashamed for asking the question, but couldn't help herself. She couldn't be with someone who was embarrassed of her.

Brady took her head in his hands and looked her directly in the eyes. "Jane, I'm by no means even close to being embarrassed of you. I'll show you off to everyone I know if you want, but I'm nervous all the guys would be drooling all over you. I was trying to protect you. You shouldn't have to deal with stupid editors making up stories just to sell some shitty magazine. You are beautiful inside and out, and I love the fact that you're making a name for yourself. You're so strong-willed. I just don't want our dating each other to screw up any hard work you've put into your business, so I was trying to protect you. Do you understand me?"

Jane nodded her head. She turned toward him and looked into the green valleys that were his eyes. They were full of concern for her well-being. She felt stupid for asking that question, but she was glad she knew the answer. She kissed Brady gently on the lips. She thanked him and entwined her hand with his. She believed him; she just had to make sure he wasn't ashamed of her. He'd made it very well known that he was attracted to her, but there was always that little voice in the back of her head that made her think, because she wasn't in the limelight like he was, she wasn't good enough. She stashed away those thoughts as they rolled up to what looked like a miniature mansion.

"Where are we?" Jane asked.

Brady turned to her and smiled. "My house."

"House?" Jane said, breathless. "Oh my God, it's amazing. I could never imagine living in a place like this."

Jane briefly thought she saw Brady cringe, but he continued to smile and park the car. He opened her door for her and led her inside.

The foyer was grand. It had a huge wrap-around staircase

and a beautiful crystal chandelier hanging in the center. It was very sleek and stylish. He didn't have much color, though, nor decorations. It was very plain, very much a bachelor pad. Brady set his keys on a side table and led her to the backyard. There were candles floating in his massive pool and flowers everywhere. Off to the side, there was a table set for two, and what seemed like food under metal containers. Light intimate music was playing through outdoor speakers. She turned to Brady and he grinned like a fool.

Jane playfully nudged him and said, "You planned on taking me here all along, didn't you?"

Brady nodded. "Yes, I did. I wanted you all to myself. I really was pissed about the photographer though; that was not in the plan. I could have taken you to a million different places, but what I really wanted was to be intimate with you in our own setting."

"It's perfect, Brady, beyond perfect."

"Shall we?" Brady waved his hand toward the table. She nodded.

The table had the most gorgeous linens she had ever seen in deep purple hues. There were flowers in all jewel-toned colors spread throughout the pool area and draped over the table. If she didn't know any better, she would have guessed Brady hired someone to decorate, but knowing him, he did everything himself.

He pulled her seat out for her and lifted the metal container off her dish. She laughed out loud. Sitting on her plate was fried chicken, mashed potatoes, and corn bread.

"Nothing like a good southern meal to set the mood," Brady said.

Jane took her napkin, tied it around her neck and said, "Agreed!"

She dug in, but she didn't eat too much. She knew what the plan was for tonight, and she didn't want to feel all gross and bloated from the fried chicken. She loved fried chicken, but she needed to be at her sexiest.

Brady put a stop to her thought process when he asked her, "What are you thinking about over there, sweet thing?"

"Oh dessert, of course," Jane said winking.

"How do you know there's going to be dessert?"

"Oh, there's dessert and I'm looking right at it." She licked her lips, boy she couldn't wait for dessert. Brady looked so good tonight. The glow of the candles beamed off his bare chest that seductively poked through his white button up shirt. He'd left a couple buttons undone, nearly making her pass out. He had the best looking chest she'd ever seen on a man, and she couldn't wait to run her hands all over it tonight.

Brady gave her a very sexy grin that would turn her legs into jelly if she was standing. "All in good time, sweet thing. Now tell me, water or land?"

He was cute. He wanted to get to know her better. She was a little frustrated, because she wanted to move along with the night. She was really looking forward to showing off the scandalous items Brady bought her.

She sighed, taking her napkin that was wrapped around her neck and placing it on the table. Fine, she would play his games, but she didn't know how long she could last. Jane replied, "Water, I grew up on the Chattahoochee."

"Sweet or Green tea?"

"Sweet, of course"

"Country or Rock?"

"Hmm…all of the above."

"Star Wars or Star Trek?"

"Wars, give me a break. Do I look like I carry around a pocket protector?"

Brady chuckled. "There definitely is no room in that dress for one. Lacrosse or baseball?"

"That's a dumb question. Lacrosse, of course, all the pansy athletes flock to baseball," Jane teased.

Brady got out of his chair and lifted Jane to her feet. He ran his hands up her arms, sending a chill through her body. He wrapped his arms around her waist and slowly started dancing with her. "Is that so? So, are you calling me a pansy?"

"I don't know," Jane said, playing with the buttons on his shirt. "I haven't seen a lot of manly action from you."

"What qualifies as manly action?"

"Oh, you know, ripping trees out of the ground, grunting occasionally, eating a whole pizza in one swallow…fucking your girlfriend."

Brady gulped and asked, "Top or bottom?"

Jane thought for a second, the sexual tension between them was incredible. She replied, "Whatever makes you come faster." Oh yes, she was definitely feisty tonight, delivering that kind of answer. Molly would have been extremely proud.

"Ah, a girl after my own heart," Brady replied. "If you could choose three words that you could only speak for the rest of your life, knowing you have sign language to communicate, what would be your three words?"

Jane pondered that question for a couple of minutes. She looked into his satiny green eyes that were full of pure male rawness. He was going to have his way with her tonight, and she couldn't wait. She knew he would be amazing in bed just from the way he gently touched her. His hands were like magic, hitting every erogenous zone she had. He knew how to please a woman.

She grabbed his shirt and pulled him down so her lips were barely caressing his and said, "My three words would be: Fuck, Me, Now."

Brady

Brady didn't need much more of an invitation than that. He crushed his mouth down onto Jane's and drove his tongue into the depths of her mouth. She replied with her own scorching tongue. God, she tasted and smelled so good.

He moved his hands up her back and into her hair…one of his most favorite things about her. He could get lost in her hair for hours. It was thick and smelled like coconut on a tropical island in the Caribbean. She started to unbutton his shirt, and he stopped her.

"Let's take this to the bedroom, shall we?" Brady said.

Jane giggled a little and replied, "What a cheese-dick line, but I'll take it."

She intertwined her fingers with his as he led her up to his bedroom. He had candles set up in there as well. He really wanted the atmosphere to be romantic and memorable. He'd put his satin sheets on his bed earlier. They always seemed to heighten the mood. He went to the store right after he left Jane's in the morning and stocked up on every type of condom he thought she might like. He wanted to make sure he had plenty of protection, so they could ride each other all night. Jane caught her breath when they walked in the bedroom.

"Brady, it's so dreamy in here." Jane pulled him close and

ran her hands up his arms, grabbed the edges of his suit jacket and took it off. She grabbed him and motioned for him to get on the bed. Brady sat on the edge with his legs hanging off. Jane put her hands on his chest, kissed his lips lightly, and moved her hands slowly down to his waist.

Whoa, buddy, take it easy, don't get too excited too fast. Jane kneeled on the floor and hovered right over his erection. She eased her hands down his thighs all the way down to his feet and started taking off his shoes and socks. Thank God because he hated fucking with socks on; he felt like an idiot, because remembering to take them off in the heat of the moment was always so difficult.

Jane moved her way back up Brady's body and started unbuttoning his shirt. With each pop of a button, she lingered her hand on his bare chest. Just having her barely touch him was such a huge turn on. Shit, he was not going to last long at all. She unbuttoned his entire shirt and slowly slid it off him and began to kiss his chest very softly. Shots of pleasure rolled through his body. She flicked his nipple with her tongue, and he let out a low grumble from his mouth. Fuck, she was such a vixen.

She worked her head all the way down to his belly button, sticking her tongue in it and then gently placed a kiss there. If she got any lower, he was going to explode. She unbuckled his belt and whipped it off. He noticed there was one thing wrong with this picture.

"Hey, I can't be the only one getting undressed here," Brady announced.

"All in good time, handsome; be patient," Jane replied.

Brady growled. He wanted it to be slow too, but he lost more room in his pants each minute. She unbuttoned his pants and tore them off. There he was in all his glory, wearing only his Calvin Klein boxer briefs with a massive hard on. Jane purred in approval, turned around and sat on his lap. She leaned her head back on his shoulder and asked if he could unzip her dress.

Hell YEAH!

He grabbed the zipper to her dress and very slowly tore it down, revealing the lacy bra he got her and getting a sneak peak of the brilliantly miniscule thong he found.

She stepped away from him, still with her back toward him, wearing her sexy glitter heels. She slipped the dress off both of her shoulders and let it fall to the ground. Brady's eyes widened. The thong he picked out left nothing to the imagination. Her ass was a perfect little bubble of erotic flesh. He wanted to reach out and bite into it.

He leaned back on his elbows and marveled at the woman he was so lucky to have. Then he nearly came on command when she bent over right in front of him and slowly worked her way back up. Her hair flung back on her shoulders and she turned around to face him. She grinned because she knew exactly what she did to him.

He looked her up and down and couldn't take it any longer.

"Baby, if you don't get over here fast enough, I'm going to combust. I'm throbbing so hard for you right now."

Jane sashayed over to him and sat on his lap. She curled her legs around his waist and gave a little wiggle. Oh, he was not playing this game anymore. He picked her up and threw her on her back. He was instantly stretched over her.

Jane purred. "Mmm, Brady, I love a man who takes charge."

"And I love a good striptease, especially performed by you, but I don't think I can take much more."

Jane rolled him over and pinned him to the bed. "But I wasn't done."

She pouted while she pulled one of her bra straps off her shoulder, letting the weight of her breast take control. She let the other one fall as well, then dipped down and did a wave like motion across his bare chest leading her up to his lips. She lightly nibbled at his bottom lip, and then raised herself and started rocking her pelvis back and forth on his arousal. She grabbed Brady's hand and slowly lowered it into the front of her thong. His hand touched her very wet and very bare pussy.

She threw her head back and said, "Brady, feel how wet you make me."

Brady nearly came right then and there. She felt beyond amazing in his hand. And, holy crap, was she wet. Brady didn't think he'd ever been more turned on in his life, and they were only in the beginning of their first sexual experience together.

Jane

Jane was about to have an orgasm from just sitting there. His heated length was pounding on her door, begging to enter her warm center. She unclasped her bra and let it completely fall off. The look of pure sex in Brady's eyes turned her on even more. She throbbed so hard; she needed him in her, and she needed him now.

She moaned, "Brady, please, take me now; I need you inside me."

Brady twisted her to the bottom and ripped the thong right off of her. He started to kiss her all over her body. His hands came up to her breasts and he started kneading them with his expert hands. He sucked them into his mouth one at a time, lavishing her nipples until they felt raw. She felt his erection glide with his movements, and she desperately wanted him inside her, so she spread her legs for him. Brady groaned and slipped a hand down to her clit. He massaged her wet center, gently flicked her clit, and then drove his fingers inside of her. Jane's body started to take over as waves of pleasure were encompassing her whole frame. The first wave of pleasure shot through her and made her entire mind go black.

She moaned, "Oh fuck, Brady, yes!" She laid there, stunned by the amount of pleasure rushing through her body, when she noticed Brady was taking his briefs off. She caught her breath in her throat. She had waited for this moment for a very long time. She couldn't help herself; straining her voice she said, "Brady, please, I need you inside me; take me, please."

"I'm going to, baby, let me grab a condom first."

"No need," she said, exasperated. "I'm on the pill, and I haven't had sex in years. I trust you."

Brady let out a little moan and gently spread her legs wider. "Please tell me if I hurt you." She felt the tip of his penis tease the outside of her center. She thrust her hips at him and he laughed. Slowly, he entered her moist sex. Jane instantly felt the girth that was Brady Matthews. Oh crap, could she do this? Oh, it felt so good.

"Fuck, baby, you are so tight. Are you okay?"

"I'm going to shove you in there if you don't do it yourself soon, please, Brady," she begged.

He laughed and entered her more, inch by inch. He kissed her and played with her nipples to help her relax until he was fully inserted.

They both breathed heavily. He placed his arms on each side of her head and they just stared at each other, feeling their inner most parts connect. His dick was enormous; it stretched her out a little past her comfort zone, but the pain was nothing compared to the pleasure that was rippling through her.

Brady stared into her eyes and asked, "How did I get so lucky?"

Jane replied, "I was just thinking the same thing, handsome."

He lowered his lips onto hers and had his way with her mouth as he slowly rocked in and out of her. There was no urgency in his kissing, he took his time and explored every last inch of her mouth. She wrapped her legs around his hips, so he could take her even deeper. She started to go numb, and blackness started to creep in. Brady thrust into her again, and she lost all control. She screamed at the top of her lungs as she felt Brady shoot his cream into her center and a moan escaped from the back of his throat. Two more quick thrusts and they were both shuddering together from the aftershocks of ecstasy.

Brady collapsed on her, but lifted his head so he was staring into her eyes. His hand stroked the top of her forehead and he said, "Jane, I think I'm falling for you."

Jane was shocked that he would make such a confession. Was it too soon to say things like that? Did she feel the same way about him? Never in her life had she ever experienced the passion and pleasure she just experienced with Brady. It wasn't just sex; it was a deeper connection they shared. A warm feeling spread throughout her body. Was that a post-sex feeling, or was she falling for Brady too? She'd never had this feeling after sex, so she chose the latter.

"I think I'm falling for you too, Brady."

Brady leaned down, kissed her on the forehead, rolled off her and pulled her close.
He breathed out. "Jane, that was amazing. I don't think I've ever felt like this before."

"I don't think I have either; it makes me nervous."

Brady propped himself up on one elbow and looked down at her with concern. "Why are you nervous?"

"I've never felt this strongly about anyone before and never this fast. It just seems too good to be true. You are too good to be true," she said, while she stroked his hair, circling his ear.

"I feel the same way, sweet thing. It's a little scary knowing you have strong feelings for someone and you don't know what the future might bring, but we just need to take this one step at a time, right?"

Jane sighed and cuddled closer to Brady. "Yes, baby steps. Although I do believe we took a huge step a couple of minutes ago." Jane brushed her hand against Brady's penis, and he jerked. "And I mean HUGE."

Chuckling, Brady said, "So I can guess you've grown fond of my manhood."

"You could say that. All I know is, I think I may have found my new best friend," Jane said, smiling and lightly stroking him.

Brady rolled on top of Jane and took her breath away when he plunged into her once again without any notice and, to her surprise, she was already wet with need for him. She laid her head back and let Brady roam his magic hands all over her body and plunge her into oblivion.

CHAPTER SIXTEEN

Michael

Michael stared at the ceiling while he lay in his bed once again. It was the last night before he had to take off for spring training. He was leaving Sunday afternoon. He wanted to get there a little ahead of time to get himself situated properly, since it was a new team. He wondered what Jane and Brady were doing right now. Most likely they were fucking the night away and falling in love. Damn, why couldn't that be him? Not just with Jane, but with any girl.

His wife, Kelly, was definitely cheating on him and he wasn't quite sure who with. He knew it was a football player on the Falcons, because she had suddenly taken up quite an interest in the team. She never cared about sports, let alone a specific team. He needed to find out for sure if she was cheating on him, because he was not going to deal with her shit if she was. He deserved better; he deserved someone like Jane, sweet, kind and sexy-as-hell Jane.

Once he got settled into his place down in Florida, he was going to hire a private detective. He needed to get to the bottom of his situation because, if she was cheating on him, he would divorce her sorry ass and use the evidence in court so she didn't get one penny of his money. He should ask Jane's friend Albert if he knew any good detectives; he had a lot of connections and could probably suggest someone who would be really discreet. He didn't need his name plastered all over the tabloids as the centerfielder who couldn't keep his woman happy. Fuck, what a mess.

Molly

Molly woke up to the sun shining on her face. She loved sleeping naked. Not only did she feel incredibly sexy sleeping naked next to the hottest man in the world, but the sheets rubbing against her skin turned her on tremendously. She rolled over to grab ahold of her man and rolled into a bunch of pillows.

What the hell? Where was Luke? She stretched out of bed and strolled to the bathroom to relieve herself. On the mirror, Luke had left her a note.

Good Morning Beautiful,
It took all my energy to get out of bed this morning; you looked incredible laying there completely naked. I did sneak a little grab of your tit before I left. You moaned and I almost drove into you. What a way to wake up. I went to the store to get some donuts and coffee for my sex kitten. Be back soon. I love you.
Molly's Man

Donuts, she could use a donut right now. She sure burned enough calories last night to earn one. She heard the door open and close. She strolled out to the living room, still completely nude. Luke turned around, saw her, and dropped his bags.

"Babe, that is so not fair to do to a man." Luke grabbed her and scooped her into his arms. He nuzzled his head in her breasts.

Molly laughed and pushed Luke's head away. "Are you fucking motor boating me right now?

Luke lifted his head and faked a shocked look. "Who me? Of course not, I'm just trying to get myself some milk for my coffee." He captured one of her nipples in his mouth and started sucking.

Giggling, Molly pushed his head away. "Man, I must have milked you dry last night."

"I thought I was the one who milked you dry," Molly teased. "By the way, did you have Mexican for lunch yesterday? I swear your cum was spicy in my mouth."

Luke threw her on the couch and laughed. "What is wrong with you, girl?" Luke ran his hands up her stomach, capturing her breasts in his hands. She let out a little moan as he began to rub her nipples in between his fingers. He suddenly stopped his movements and she grunted in protest.

"Oh shit, I almost forgot; you distracted me with your naughty ways. Look at what I found at the store."

Luke pulled a magazine out of his shopping bag and tossed it to Molly. She looked down at it and gasped in horror. There was a giant picture on the front of the magazine of Jane and Brady with the headline reading, "Brady's New Bimbo."

Holy shit! She opened the magazine and read the little blurb that went with the three pictures of Brady looking so mad he might spit fire and Jane scared as hell and trying to hide her face. The caption read:

Brady Matthews caught in the act of a possible new booty call? Looks like he's straying away from the blonde beauties and going for a new brunette bimbo. Only time will tell when Brady goes back to his typical blondes.

"Holy Crap! Why the hell did you buy this? You just supported this piece of shit magazine."

Luke threw his hands up in a defensive position. "Sorry, I didn't think you would have believed me if I didn't bring it back."

"You're right about that one. Please tell me it was the only one," Molly said with a pleading look. Luke didn't respond. "Luke," Molly carried his name out "Please tell me this was the only magazine with pictures of Jane in it."

Luke shook his head. "No, this one looked like the least offensive. Are you going to call Jane?"

"Well, fuck, like I even have a choice. Damn it, this totally ruined my morning. I was hoping to get some action from your tongue and maybe eat a donut off your dick." Molly huffed into the bedroom to go grab her phone.

Brady

Brady woke up to the most amazing feeling in his arms, Jane. It was like she was made specifically for him. She fit perfectly in his arms. He pulled her closer as she started to stir. Her perfectly blue eyes opened and stared straight into his soul; a gorgeous little smile formed on her face.

"Good morning, gorgeous. How did you sleep?"

"Well, what sleep I got was perfect. You have quite the

stamina, Mr. Matthews."

God, she was sexy, he couldn't get enough of her. He could see a future with this woman. She was driven, sexy, intelligent, sweet and caring, and everything he would look for in a wife. Whoa, wife? Where did that come from? God, do not say that out loud. That would scare her away for sure, he thought. All of a sudden, something was stirring his balls. He looked down and saw Jane grinning like a fool, that little vixen.

She ripped the covers down, exposing both their bodies to the morning air. Her nipples went instantly hard and his dick bobbed upward. Jane slid on top of his body and started shimmying her way down.

"What do you plan on doing down there pip-squeak?"

"I'm always thirsty in the morning, mind if I take a sip?" Brady could only muster a husky grunt of approval.

Jane slid all the way down his body and planted her head right at his throbbing arousal. She spread his legs so she had easier access. She lightly started to caress his balls and placed the other hand on the base of his cock.

Fuck, she barely touched him and he was ready to come. She lowered her head, pressed her tongue to the tip of his velvet erection and started doing slow circular motions around the tip. Brady had to concentrate not to thrust his dick down her throat. She closed in around his cock, moving in and out, slowly pulling up and down with her hand and caressing his balls at the same time. There were too many sensations to even think about. His whole body started to tingle and his limbs went numb. His dick was throbbing faster than his heart. He was about to explode.

Brady caught his breath and squeezed out, "Baby I'm going to come, you might want to move your mouth."

She smiled with his dick in her mouth, licked the pulsing vein running the length of his shaft, then closed in on it with her mouth again and gave it one last suck and jerk with her hand. He was a goner. He felt like a douche bag, since he blew his load in her mouth, but she didn't move, and there was nothing he could do about it. She excused herself and went to the bathroom. He felt like a teenager; he would go in there, but he couldn't move…she made him immobile.

Brady threw his arm over his head in embarrassment. "Jane, I'm sorry. That was such a douche bag thing to do."

Jane straddled him, how did that happen? She came out of nowhere. She ran her hands up to his chest. "Whatever for, handsome?"

"For blowing in your mouth, it's disrespectful."

"Oh really? Well, I didn't mind." She licked the corner of his mouth and whispered, "I like the way you taste."

Brady shook his head in astonishment. "You are one of a kind, Jane Bradley, but no more of that, you hear me?"

"Fine, no more blow jobs."

Brady was just about to shout in protest when Jane's phone started ringing. She ignored it and let it go to voicemail. Her stomach rumbled, begging for some food.

Brady laughed, "You hungry, pip-squeak?"

"Starving, you know how to give a girl a good workout, and I barely ate any dinner last night because I didn't want to be bloated during our extracurricular workouts."

Jane's phone rang again. "Ugh, who is trying to interrupt this perfect moment?" She looked at her phone. "It's Molly, do you mind?"

"Of course not. I don't think I have any authority over you after what just you did to me a couple of minutes ago."

Jane answered the phone and talked to Molly, while still straddling Brady. He reached up and started playing with her breasts, turning her nipples into tight little nubs. He threw her on the bed and she giggled as he kissed her neck up and down, then all of a sudden she went completely stiff. He lifted his head to look at her and her eyes were empty, her face completely white. She looked like she just saw a ghost.

Jane

Jane froze; Molly must be joking. This was a joke, right? Her whole body went numb. She could not believe what Molly just told her. If she was telling the truth, this could ruin Jane. She didn't want any bad press to focus on her, especially since she'd worked so hard to get her business where it was today. Maybe the media attention she got would not affect her business. Maybe it would just affect her personal life, like that was any better.

Molly spoke up on the phone. "Jane, are you there? I'm so sorry, honey, please say something. It's not that bad...I'm sure it will blow over. Do not let this ruin anything between you and Brady, you hear me? You are stronger than that. Jane, please say something."

"I've got to go, Molly, thanks." Jane threw her phone against the pillow and buried her face into Brady's chest, crying like an idiot.

"Hey, look at me, what's going on?" he asked, concern lacing his voice.

Jane got up and separated herself from the man who was partially responsible for plastering her face all over the gossip magazines. She rummaged through Brady's drawers, found a pair of mesh shorts and a Braves shirt, grabbed his keys and went straight to his car. She didn't care if she drove his BMW like a lunatic. She needed to get to the store as soon as possible.

She drove to the local supermarket, raced inside and gasped in horror as she went up to the checkout line to see all the pictures of her face on display. She grimaced as she looked through all of the magazines with her face plastered on them. The headlines were horrid and read; "Brady Goes Brunette?" "Baseball Brady Batting Around" and "Brunette Booty Call." She grabbed one of each and went through the self-checkout line. To hell if she would be checked out by some employee only to be mocked and ridiculed.

Jane sat in Brady's car for a while, reading all the articles, taking in all the nasty comparisons between her and Laney. One magazine actually had two pictures side by side, one of her and one of Laney. Just the sight of the pictures of the two of them made Jane feel disgusted in herself for thinking she could ever be with Brady. She was nothing compared to Laney, and the magazines made that quite clear. Brady was slumming it when it came to dating Jane.

Jane tossed the magazines to the side and looked at her phone. She noticed 12 missed calls, all from Brady. Crap. She drove toward his house and kept thinking about all the horrible headlines and comments written about her. When she pulled into Brady's driveway, she saw him run out to greet her. He flung the car door open and pulled her out.

"Don't ever fucking do that again. You scared the shit out of me," Brady said, shaking her by the shoulders. "What's going on, Jane? Tell me right now."

Jane didn't have to say anything, she just grabbed the magazines, threw them on the hood of
Brady's BMW, and walked into the house. She heard Brady swear under his breath and come after her. Before she reached the door he spun her around. "Where do you think you're going?"

"I'm going inside, heaven forbid I should be outside and not get my picture taken." She yanked her arm out of his grasp, went inside, ran to his bedroom, flopped on his bed, buried her face in his pillows, and cried.

Brady sat next to her gently and pulled her into his warm embrace. He smoothed her hair down while whispering calming words into the side of her head. They sat there for a long time, just holding each other. Jane didn't know if she could handle the spotlight that came along with Brady. He brought her back from the dead, made her remember how to laugh, have fun, and enjoy the feel of a man, but could she deal with the publicity that came along with him?

She knew the magazines were pure gossip, just trying to sell some rubbish, but at some point, she even believed what the magazines wrote. Who's to say they won't make something up and people will believe the rumors written about her?

She pulled away from Brady's chest. "Brady, I'm sorry. I just don't know if I can handle this kind of attention like you can. I should probably go." Jane got up from Brady's lap and started gathering her things.

Brady

Brady sat there in shock. Was she serious right now? She was just going to throw away everything they had because of some fucking magazines? Anger started boiling in his blood as he stood up and stomped over toward Jane. He took the objects in her hands and threw them on the ground.

He ran his hand through his hair and shouted, "Are you fucking kidding me right now, Jane?" She started crying again. Ignoring the sadness in her bright blue eyes, he continued. "You're just going to take the easy way out and walk out like nothing happened between us? Like you could give two shits about me?"

"You know that's not how I feel about you, Brady."

"Please enlighten me, Jane. How do you feel about me?

Because, frankly, I'm a little confused. You're willing to throw away everything we have because of some stupid gossip magazines? Damn it, Jane, you're breaking my heart here. In case you haven't noticed, I'm falling in love with you."

Fuck, fuck, fuck. Why did he say that? Instantly regretting his words, he turned around and walked out of the bedroom and into the master bathroom.

"Don't forget your thong that's hanging off the lamp when you walk out." And with that, he slammed the bathroom door and turned on the shower.

Jane

Jane fell to the ground, feeling completely helpless, as she bawled her eyes out. Brady just said he was falling in love with her and she felt the same exact way. Brady was everything she had ever dreamed of; he was perfect for her. She needed to get over herself and deal with her problems head on, instead of running away from them. If she wanted to date Brady, which she did, she would have to grow tougher skin. She peeled her body off the ground, stripped down to nothing and walked into the bathroom to join Brady in the shower.

Brady stood under the showerhead, leaning his head against the wall, looking completely defeated. She walked into the oversized shower, wrapped her arms around his waist, and rested her head on his back.

He stiffened at first, then slowly melted into her embrace. He turned in her arms to face her; not saying a word, he grabbed the shampoo and started to wash her hair for her. She rinsed it out and tried to do the same for Brady, but she was too short; she couldn't even reach the top of his head. She stepped back and rested against the shower wall, shaking her head.

"Brady, I'm sorry. I don't know why you put up with me. Please don't feel like you need to do me any favors and stick around because you feel sorry for me. I have too much baggage. But if you're willing to deal with all my bullshit, I would like to work together to get through the tough times."

Brady wrapped Jane in his arms as he caressed her hair. "Pip-squeak, what am I going to do with you? You drive me crazy. One minute I want to shake sense into you and the next minute I want to kiss you senseless. I know this is new for you, but we have to work together. You just have to remember, we know what is going on between us and that is all that matters. People can have their opinions, but all that matters is what is actually happening between us. You can't just keep running off; it breaks a piece of my heart every time you do."

Jane felt awful; she was still learning how to deal with her emotions and Brady was incredible for being so patient with her. She saw the hurt in Brady's eyes when she came back from the store and then announced how she wasn't sure she could handle being with him. She never wanted to cause him that kind of pain again.

Jane nodded in understanding. "Thank you, Brady, for putting up with me. I really do want to see where this goes, where the future takes us."

Brady answered simply, "Me too, babe, me too."

Brady

Brady was grateful they were able to put the morning behind them and enjoy the rest of the day together, lounging in his pool naked, making love on the kitchen counter while making lunch, and talking about their childhoods while lying in bed. It was perfect up until now. He'd been dreading this moment. He had to get to the airport to catch his flight to Orlando.

He pulled up to Jane's apartment to drop her off and walked her to her door. Thankfully, no paparazzi lurked in the bushes or around any corners, which was surprising given the amount of publicity they stirred up this morning. She let them in the apartment, set her stuff down, and leaned against the wall.

"This isn't fair. Why couldn't we have met a little earlier?" Jane asked.

"I've been thinking the same thing, pip-squeak. I wish I had some more time to make this relationship a little stronger. I'm nervous you're going to get scared and run away from me."

Jane took Brady's hands in hers and kissed them gently. "We talked about this earlier. I promise you, if I start to get scared, I'll call you and talk to you about it instead of running away. I want this to work between us."

Brady believed her, but he still felt uncomfortable leaving

her so early. He was just going to have to have faith. He was excited to get started with the season; he was starting to get a little restless. He just wished he could take Jane with him.

Wouldn't that be perfect? Baseball during the day then coming home to Jane at night; he would be in heaven. He would ask her to go with him if she wasn't working so hard at making her business a success. He knew she needed to make her company work. It was a big part of who she was now, and she needed to prove to herself that she could make it on her own.

"So, you are going to come visit me, right? I have some plane tickets with your name written all over them."

Jane ran her hands up his chest, kissed him gently on his mouth and whispered, "You can bet your ass I'll be there. I expect there to be some more lingerie waiting for me."

Lingerie? Hell yeah!

"So you like my taste in underwear then?"

"Well, you are a bit of a slut when it comes to thongs, but your choice of bras shows off your classy side. I thought you were a tit man until I saw what kind of underwear you chose for me. You're an ass man through and through."

"You got that right, pip-squeak, and you have the most perfect ass I've ever seen."

Brady reached down and gave her butt a good squeeze. Jane turned around so he faced her back, dropped her phone on the ground, bent down to pick it up, and as she proceeded back up she rubbed her butt on Brady's crotch all the way up.

Jesus, great, he now had to go to the airport with a hard on.

"Thanks, babe, can't wait to walk through airport security with this hard on, having to explain to them that, in fact, it is my penis and not a gun."

Jane laughed and pulled him closer. He caught her mouth with his and devoured her whole. God, he was going to miss the taste of her. She felt so good in his arms. She filled a massive void that was missing from his life, and he didn't want to let go yet. He planned on spending some fantastic weekends with her, though. All he had to do was get through the week, which was hopefully going to be easy, since he would be busy training.

He slid his hands up and cupped her face. He had to just go for it, what did he have to lose? He had never felt like this about a woman before. She made him happy every second they were together and, even when they were apart, he was happy because he knew she was waiting for him. He wanted to tell her how he felt and he couldn't hold it back anymore.

"Jane, these past couple of weeks have been such a roller coaster, but one that I've enjoyed tremendously. I just wanted to tell you before I leave for training…I uh, just wanted to say, shit what I am trying to say here is…fuck, I love you Jane."

Brady held his breath and watched Jane's eyes roam, looking deeply into his soul, possibly for sincerity. Her eyes started to fill with water while she gave him the biggest, sexiest grin he had ever seen. She threw her arms around his neck and leaped up so her legs were wrapped around his waist. She planted a huge kiss on his lips and leaned her forehead against his.

"I love you too, Brady."

He sighed with relief. She loved him. She actually told him she loved him. She was his woman and no one else's. He knew it hadn't been long at all, and some people might call them crazy, but he knew his life had changed the minute he saw Jane in Deuces wearing that red dress. From that moment, he knew he was in trouble and he needed to convince the girl in the lace dress that they were meant to be together. He couldn't believe he did it. She loved him. He wanted to click his heels together in joy.

He felt confident taking off to Florida. They'd confessed their love for each other. They still had a lot to accomplish in building their relationship, but they had a solid foundation now. Things were going to be just fine. He knew it.

CHAPTER SEVENTEEN

Molly

Molly had a meeting with Jane to go over wedding details. Jane moped around most of the week, now that Brady was gone. Jane told Molly that she hadn't heard from him very much because he'd been busy with the start of spring training, getting settled in, and talking to the press about the upcoming season. Molly felt for Jane, because she knew exactly how it felt to have the man you love gone for periods at a time. Luke was gone for a week for training, once again, but a week was nothing compared to months or even a year. So a week was doable.

She began to feel really excited about their wedding. Luke said he would love to get married on the beach in Savannah…that was Molly's number one choice too, but she thought she would ask Luke what he preferred. It was his wedding too, even though his attitude was whatever made his Molly happy. He was such a doll.

Molly had a present to give to Jane. When Molly was shopping the other day in the mall for some new lingerie, she saw something in the store window Jane just had to have, and Molly couldn't wait to give it to her.

When she arrived at Jane's office, she was pleasantly surprised to see Albert there too.

"Hey there, bitches. God I've missed you both." She planted huge kisses on both of their cheeks.

Albert wore some ridiculous gold leather jacket with tassel fringe. Molly wanted to know where the hell he even got clothes like that.

"Albert, are you here to go over wedding details with us?"

"I actually came by to make our friend Jane here eat something. She hasn't been eating properly because she misses that hunk of a first baseman. I threatened her that I would tell him she hasn't been eating if she didn't eat the hot dog I shoved in her face."

"I have been eating, Albert, but thank you for your concern," Jane interrupted. "Why don't you stay and help us plan a wedding."

"I would love to. I have nothing else planned for today."

"Great!" Molly cheered. Before we get started, I have a little something for our Janey bear." Molly handed the present over to Jane and waited in anticipation as she opened it.

Brady

Brady sat in the ice bath cooling off from his morning conditioning. He had to work himself hard this year. He had expectations to live up to from the media, fans, and his teammates. He was sexually frustrated, since he hadn't seen Jane in a little while. It hadn't been that long, but it was like giving a child a little taste of candy and then not letting them have any more. He needed more of Jane; it wasn't fair to have had a little taste of her and then be ripped away.

Marc came in and fist bumped Brady as he walked by to grab ice from the ice machine. Brady and Marc had been friends for a while. Brady would say Marc was probably his best friend on the team, along with Michael now. He trusted Marc and could tell Marc anything because Brady knew it would not get spread to anyone else.

Marc was twisting off a bag of ice when he asked, "How's the little lady back home?"

"She's great. I never thought I would get back into a serious relationship again, but I can't help myself; she's amazing."

"When are you going to have her visit?"

Brady slumped in the ice water. "I don't know. Either I'm too busy with pre-season or she has an event. I won't see her for a while. It's killing me. I didn't get enough of her before I had to take off, and now I'm about ready to fuck a bagel I'm so horny."

Marc Laughed. "I'll make sure to keep my breakfast far

away from you. But, you see, that's where you screwed up, man. You should have stayed single through pre-season and landed some chicks down here in Florida."

Brady shook his head. "You know that's not how I work anymore. I worked really hard to get myself out of that kind of spotlight, and it's still following me around. I don't need that reputation when I'm 60 and being inducted into the Baseball Hall of Fame."

Marc punched Brady in the shoulder. "Oh, you think awfully highly of your capabilities, don't you?"

"Hey, I'm just telling the truth, and you won't be next to me at that podium until you get that swing of yours under control," Brady smirked. He knew Marc had one of the best swings on the team.

"Oh, fuck off. All you do is stand on a padded white object in the ground while everyone else does the work shuttling balls over to you. Now if you were actually good at baseball, you would have been a catcher...that's where all the talent lies."

"Yeah and bad knees. Good luck fucking when you're 45 and crippled," Brady joked.

Marc chuckled. "That's why you don't see me tied down now, just getting all I can get now."

"And why am I the one the tabloids are after?" Brady asked.

Marc tapped him on the cheek and said, "It's those boyish good looks you have. Your gene pool fucked you over. You're too damn good looking to not draw attention."

Brady just shook his head. Marc pulled a seat next to Brady's ice bath and dunked his legs in so the water was just past his knees, while he put the bag of ice on his shoulder. Brady felt bad for Marc. He was getting older and more beat up each season. He was still one hell of a catcher, but he could tell Marc's catching days would be coming to an end in the next couple of years. Brady was just about to comment on Marc's age when his phone beeped.

Laney: I thought about you all last night, big boy. I miss your dick. I'll be near your training field later today if you want to go out to dinner and then eat me for dessert.

Brady groaned and slammed his phone shut. What the

fuck? He told Laney to stop texting him and to leave him alone. He got another text message.

Laney: You can't tell me that little brunette is keeping you satisfied. There's barely anything on her. What you need is a real woman with curves and the ability to make you scream. Don't deny that is me. I'll let you do anything you want, just like we used to.

"Hey, is Jane sending you dirty texts?" Marc asked, interrupting Brady's thoughts of anger.

Brady was so mad he didn't even know what to do. "No, fucking Laney keeps texting me. She apparently has had a revelation and thinks that we belong together. She won't leave me the hell alone. This is the last thing I need."

"Oh God, not her again. She is such a whore bag. It's unbelievable the rest of the nation doesn't realize it. Have you told Jane?"

"Fuck no! Are you crazy? She wouldn't handle it very well. You should have seen Jane's reaction when the magazines compared her to Laney; it was not good. I want to tell her, but she's already so sensitive and, with me not being there, I don't know what she'd do."

Marc thought for a second before he replied to Brady. "Dude, I really think you should tell her. With your luck, something will go down and Jane will find out about Laney texting you and then you'll be in more trouble than telling her now. At least if you tell her now, you're being honest. I'm sure honesty is a big thing with her, given her previous relationship."

Brady knew Marc was right. He needed to tell Jane. He just hoped she didn't distance herself from him.

Jane

Molly didn't have to get her anything, but she was not one to turn down a present.

Jane screeched and pulled out a T-shirt jersey with Brady's last name on the back, as well as his number, seventeen, of course.

"Oh, Molly, this made my day, thank you!"

"You're welcome, pretty girl. I saw it and knew you just had to have it. Even though almost every woman in Atlanta owns the same one, since you're dating the hunk of the Braves yours actually counts. You're the one that holds his heart."

"Thank you, you have to take a picture of me in it so I can send it to Brady."

Jane changed into the shirt that was extremely small, but she knew Molly got it small for a reason; she wanted to show off her curves. Fine by Jane, all the other girls could eat their hearts out.

She looked in the mirror in the bathroom and was startled when she saw how big her boobs looked in the shirt, good Lord it was a tight shirt. She should cut a slit down the front and turn it into a sexy shirt to wear for Brady at night. No, she would just wear it to the games.

She posed for the picture so her back was toward the camera, but turned her head over her shoulder and gave the camera a kissing face. Albert and Molly laughed, took the picture and handed back her phone. She sent Brady a message.

Jane: Look at what Molly got me today. I think I can pull it off. What do you think?

Jane hugged Molly for her present then got down to business. Luke and Molly planned on having their wedding on the beach in Savannah and renting a house for the reception. They didn't want anything big at all, just a small celebration with their closest family and friends. Jane's phone beeped back. She didn't want to be rude, so she distracted Molly with some books so she could respond to Brady.

"Molly, here's a book of floral arrangements, look through it and mark anything that you like."

Molly was too smart for her. "More like, Molly distract yourself so I can text my hunk of a boyfriend back," Molly said in a mocking tone.

Jane stuck her tongue out while tapping her phone to read her text.

Brady: You more than pull that off, pip-squeak. You look fucking hot with my name on your back.

Jane's toes curled. Ugh, she hated how much of a lovesick

teenager she looked like right now, but she couldn't help herself. She tried to play it cool in front of her friends, but they saw right through her. There was no use trying to hide her excitement.

Jane: Thanks, it's my new favorite shirt. I miss you terribly.

Brady: I know, I miss you too. I wish I could see you this weekend.

Jane: Me too. When are you going to start getting days off?

Jane hadn't seen Brady in a while and she was getting antsy. When Brady first told Jane about spring training, she didn't think they were going to be apart this much. Either he didn't have the time to see her or she had an event on the weekend. They talked every day, but it was nothing compared to the real thing. Jane received a message back from Brady.

Brady: Soon, I hope. Our manager is riding us hard this year. I'm so sore I can barely move.

Jane: My poor baby, I wish I was there to massage you all over.

Brady: You and me both, babe.

Jane started thinking about her and Brady together in his giant whirlpool tub with only bubbles covering them. She would massage every inch of his body, running her hands up and down his muscular thighs all the way up to his very impressive arousal. She nearly jumped out of her seat when Molly interrupted her daydream.

"Uh, earth to Jane."

Jane startled at Molly's voice. She felt herself begin to flush from the naughty thoughts she was having. Jane was being rude to Molly and Albert, but she couldn't help it; she missed Brady.

"Sorry Molly. I don't know how you do it…handle being away from Luke for so long. It's been a week and I can barely function without thinking about Brady."

"After a while, it gets easier, but I know how you feel. You're fresh off the love boat and all you want to do is be naked with each other, screwing your lives away. I still feel like that whenever I see Luke and when we're together, we make the most of it. We try not to pick stupid fights and just work on enjoying each other's company."

"Well, I have a lot to learn from you, because if I ever have a relationship that is half as good as yours and Luke's, I'll be a happy lady."

"Oh my God, I'm going to puke all over my new white leather loafers," Albert chimed in. "Blah, blah, blah, who cares about love? Let's talk about what I'll be wearing to the wedding."

The girls laughed. Molly asked Albert to perform their wedding ceremony. He was ordained on the internet a couple of years back so he could marry his gay friends, but he never knew he was going to be so popular. Word spread and he was now a hot commodity in the reverend business.

It surprised Jane that he performed ceremonies and was involved in weddings because, ever since his partner and love of his life, Ricky, passed away, he'd pretty much shut off all feelings in the love department. Albert never talked about Ricky much; it worried Jane. She was afraid Albert bottled up all his emotions and something would happen one day. Molly and Jane tried having an "intervention" with him one day because they were concerned. He lost a lot of weight and dropped off the face of the earth when Ricky passed. Jane needed to remember to take Albert out for lunch one day soon and see how he was doing.

"Don't give me your crap about love," said Molly. "I see you with boys all the time in the bars, making out and passing around phone numbers."

"Molly, you should know better than anyone else, that's all for show. A girl has to keep up her reputation in these parts," Albert replied shyly.

Jane really felt for him, here she and Molly were flaunting their relationships in front of him and he, most likely, was still hurting inside.

Jane gently asked, "Alby, are you doing alright? I know things might be hard for you now that Luke is home and I'm in a new relationship…"

Albert cut her off, waving his hand at her, picked up some magazines and said, "Oh, I'm fine. Stop worrying about me. I'm just an old used up queen; you are the girls we need to focus on. Now, what the hell am I going to be wearing?"

Molly exchanged glances with Jane and Jane just shrugged to indicate they should continue with the planning. Jane grabbed some dress books she snagged from a couple of local bridal shops. She tossed them over to Molly and Albert and asked "Are you thinking dress or pant suit Alby?"

He looked over at Molly, they smiled at each other and both said dress at the same time. Jane laughed, dress it was then, time to go shopping!

"If that's the case, let's head over to Dolly's Dresses. I know they just love you there, Alby."

Dolly's Dresses was a dress shop specializing in drag. It was one of their favorite places to go because Albert always insisted on giving them a fashion show, and they never found more flamboyant clothes then they did at Dolly's.

Albert was what they called a "bear" in the gay community. He was a bigger set guy with no fear of showing his chest hair, but he loved to dress up and bring out his inner queen. He was the most fabulous hairy man in a dress you would ever lay your eyes on.

The girls took off to go look at some dresses for Albert. They arrived at the store and were instantly greeted by the saleswoman, who handed them some champagne in rainbow-tinted flutes. If you wanted some good gossip, Dolly's was the place to go. The salesladies knew everything before the media did. The owner had "connections" in every major city that was swarmed by celebrities, another reason why Jane loved going there.

When you walked into Dolly's, you were instantly smacked in the face with glitter, tulle and sequins. The guts of the building were supposed to mimic the streets of Paris, clean lines, wrought iron and facades in every corner. The walls were white because Dolly said the real art was the dresses and, boy, was she right.

The dresses were fit for the taste of ice skaters, RuPaul, and drag queens in general. Jane looked over at Albert as he twirled around, holding up an extremely short tutu with a full zebra print leotard encrusted in sequins. Jane cringed a little; she loved it when Albert dressed up, but she needed to pull back on the reins a little for Molly's wedding.

"Isn't this just divine, ladies? Oh, I think I'm in love," Albert said, as he twirled.

Molly pointed at Albert while saying to Jane, "This coming

from the guy who just shit on love half an hour ago."

Jane laughed and told Albert to try to look for something a little more wedding-y and less the gay version of Black Swan. While Molly and Albert continued to look around, Jane leaned on the counter with her champagne and talked to Dolly.

"So, Dolly, tell me what's been happening lately, any good gossip?"

"Sweetie, you know there always is. I see you made the headlines with that Brady boy. Oooeee is he a fine piece of man meat."

Jane blushed. "Yeah, we are seeing each other; it's been great."

Molly yelled from across the shop, "Don't let her fool you, Dolly. They're fucking up a storm every chance they get."

Jane turned white. "Molly! Jesus, do you need to shout that?"

Dolly patted her on the hand and laughed. "Girl, if I were you, I'd be shouting that across the roof tops. Good for you, but I hope there is nothing too serious between you two, because haven't you heard?"

Jane looked confused. What hadn't she heard? Was Dolly about to tell her that Brady was gay? She was standing in a drag queen's dream, and if anyone knew information on what celebrities were in the closet, it would be Dolly. Jane was going to set her straight if she tried to tell her Brady was gay. She knew for a fact that was not true; she had proof on many different occasions.

Jane asked quizzically, "Haven't I heard what?"

Dolly leaned over the counter and brought her voice to about a whisper. "That Laney girl saw the picture of the two of you together in one of those magazines and was not very happy. She told my friend and confidant, who is her hairdresser, that she was going to get Brady back. She said letting him go was one of the biggest mistakes of her life."

Jane sagged in defeat. "Laney? As in Laney Johnson, Brady's ex-girlfriend? Beautiful blonde movie star?"

Dolly nodded, patted Jane's hand and started to walk away to open a dressing room for Albert, who had a handful of clothes and said, "I'm sorry honey, but as everyone knows, whatever Laney wants, Laney gets."

With that, Jane sank into a deep purple, velvet chair. Was

Dolly right? Was Laney going to try to win Brady back? Would he take her back? She didn't see why not; that woman was a life-sized Barbie doll. Who wouldn't want her back? She probably did things for Brady Jane could never live up to.

No! She wouldn't do this. Brady told her he loved her, that he was falling for her, Jane Bradley. She had his heart, not Laney Johnson. She had to give Brady the benefit of the doubt and trust that he was serious about her and no one else. But Laney could most likely be very persuasive if she wanted to be. Jane had seen the *Maxim* that Laney graced the cover of; she even drooled herself from the cleavage Laney sported. Hands down, there was no denying that Laney was more beautiful than Jane, but maybe Jane beat Laney in personality? She laughed at herself, okay.

Jane excused herself to go outside for a moment. Albert told her to hurry up because he was ready to blow her bra off with his catwalk. Jane pulled her phone out and dialed Brady's number. Brady always told her to call him when she felt insecure or sad. She waited in anticipation as his phone rang. Damn, it went to voicemail. She left him a message.

"Hey, handsome, it's Jane. I, uh just wanted to call you, um, because I heard something and I don't know…it's stupid, crap…sorry, forget I called, erase this message. Say hi to Michael for me. Bye."

Ugh, she just sounded like an idiot. Good job Jane, after he heard that riveting message he would for sure be more inclined to date Laney. Laney probably left messages in a Marilyn Monroe type voice.

She probably would have said in a sultry voice, "Hey Brady (rolling her "r") it's me, I was just calling you to tell you how sexy you are and that I am naked in bed thinking about you caressing my body. Call me later." Then she would have giggled and hung up.

Jane felt like she could puke. She needed to get a grip with her life. This was so not healthy.

CHAPTER EIGHTEEN

Brady

Brady finally got out of the video room and rubbed his head, hoping it would help clear the fog that eclipsed his brain from being in there too long. He hated looking over scouting videos of pitchers he'd face in the upcoming season. He knew they were helpful and when the time came that he had to go up against them he would be ready, but it was still hard to pay attention to them for hours.

Earlier, when Jane texted him the picture of her in his T-shirt jersey, he thought about telling her about Laney contacting him, but decided to do it in a conversation on the phone instead. That was not a text kind of message to relay. He wanted to make sure he heard her voice when he told her, so he could tell if she was upset or not.

He stopped by his locker to grab his belongings. He checked his phone and had one voicemail. Shit, Jane called hours ago; he hoped it wasn't important. He listened to her voicemail.

"Hey, handsome, it's Jane. I, uh just wanted to call you, um because I heard something and I don't know…it's stupid, crap…sorry, forget I called, erase this message. Say hi to Michael for me. Bye."

Brady stared at his phone and thought that was one weird message. Jane seemed rattled by something. What was she doing today? He was pretty sure she was hanging out with Molly and Albert, so why did she seem rattled? Brady had to go back to the training room, so instead of calling Jane, he sent her a text message.

Brady: Hey, baby, I got your message, are you okay?

Jane: Yeah, sorry about that. Just forget it.

Brady: Okay…how was your day?

Jane: Fine.

Yes, something was definitely going on that she wasn't telling him. She was being very short and vague with him; he could tell she was pulling away from him and he needed to call her out on it. He needed to know what had happened while he was looking at scouting videos. He hated not knowing when something bothered her, especially when he wasn't there to console her.

Brady: Jane I know something is wrong. Please don't pull away from me.

Jane: I'm sorry Brady, you're right. There is something that is bothering me. I was at Dolly's today and she told me some unpleasant news.

Brady: Dolly's?

Jane: You know, the drag queen shop. Albert needed a dress for Molly and Luke's wedding.

Brady chuckled to himself. Oh, of course Albert needed a dress for Luke and Molly's wedding. He wished he could have been a fly on the wall while they shopped. He would have loved to see the obnoxious clothing deemed worthy by Albert to put on. The guy had quite the ostentatious style and, if he was in a drag queen's paradise, Brady could only imagine what Albert would pick out. He focused back on Jane and what was bothering her.

Brady: What did Dolly tell you?

Jane: She said her friend, who is Laney's hairdresser, said that Laney was bragging to everyone about how she's going to win you back and letting you go was one huge mistake.

Crap! Brady ground his teeth together and made a low growl in the back of his throat. That was the last thing he wanted to hear. Laney did not stop until she got what she wanted and, most likely, Jane had thought about that.

And what did Laney mean "letting" him go? Was she deranged? She cheated on him. She was the one who fucked up. She probably saw the pictures of Jane and was jealous that Jane was getting publicity instead of Laney.

Laney also liked the challenge of trying to get what she didn't have. She wasn't saying those things because she actually cared about Brady or loved him. No, she was saying those things so she could get some free publicity. God, he hated her. Brady sent a message back to Jane and hoped she believed him.

Brady: You have nothing to worry about, sweet thing. You know you are the one who owns my heart.

Jane: You promise?

Brady: Yes, are you kidding me? I couldn't even focus on the scouting videos today because I kept thinking about your sweet smile, sky-blue eyes, and bodacious body.

Jane: Ha, bodacious body. That's a throwback word.

Brady: You liked it. Damn, I need a Jane fix soon or I might explode.

Jane: I know what you mean. Do you know when you'll have some time off soon?

Brady couldn't imagine being without Jane for months on end. He was barely making it now and it had only been a little over a week. He would have a weekend off soon and he knew exactly what he was going to do with it. He wanted to spend time with Jane, but he also wanted to get to know her friends better, as well and prove to them that he was the perfect fit for her. He should talk to Michael and plan something where he surprised Jane...Molly could help as well. Brady sent a message back to Jane to throw her off...yes, he loved surprises.

Brady: Probably not for a while, sorry baby.

Jane: Ugh, I thought you said you were going to at least get one day off a week.

Brady: So did I. We're just so busy, I got to go. I'll talk to you later.

Brady couldn't be texting Jane right now when he needed to make plans for a surprise this weekend. He hoped if he saw her this weekend, it would help her forget the rumors about Laney. He decided not to tell Jane about Laney right away; the timing wasn't right, especially after she heard about Laney from Dolly. If he told her Laney had been texting him...that would really send her flying off the edge. No, he would wait a little bit and let this new information blow over first.

Now he needed to make plans to surprise her. First things first, he needed to talk to Michael and get in touch with Molly.

Jane

Jane started to get quite busy with work and decided that it was time to hire an assistant for additional support. It would a big moment for her. She had worked incredibly hard to get to the point where she needed to hire additional staff. Granted, it was just one person, but it was still a huge stepping stone for her business.

It felt like yesterday that she had found the empty office space in the popular neighborhood of Decatur. It was the perfect little space for her. Her office was small with exposed beams that gave off a rustic feeling. She'd separated the office into two spaces; the main entrance where she did consultations and the back where she kept her personal desk and office equipment. Jane would set up a small desk in the front for the newcomer, so they could greet clients and take care of any incoming traffic and phone calls.

She had a couple of interviews today and hoped to hire someone to start next week. She knew it was a pretty tall order, but she had an event coming up that she could not do by herself, unless she had the ability to split herself in two and be in two different places at the same time. She didn't get the memo on how to accomplish such a feat, so she decided it was time to hire someone else.

She had a lot of inquiries and resume submissions, which

surprised her, given the fact that she was such a small business. She was nervous because she had never conducted an interview before, and she wanted to come off as a strong and confident businesswoman. She hadn't talked to Brady much in the last day or so; he had been really busy with spring training. She sent him a quick message.

Jane: Hey, handsome, hope you have a good day. I have my interviews today. Wish me luck.

When Jane looked through all the resumes that were submitted for the position, there was one that pulled her attention the most. A girl named Patty O'Neil, great Irish name, seemed like the best candidate. She had experience in catering and had been part of a wait staff. She also majored in event planning and interned with a small event planning company in New York. In her cover letter, she said she wanted to relocate down to Atlanta. Jane was interested to find out the reason for the switch. New York and Georgia were pretty different. Maybe she had a husband or boyfriend that relocated. Jane's thoughts were interrupted by a text message. It was Brady.

Brady: Hey, sweet thing, good luck today. I'm proud of you.

Jane's heart melted as she sighed.

She interviewed two candidates and they were both very nice and accomplished, but she didn't feel a connection with either of them. One of the candidates, Martha, had the most irritating nose twitch and sniff. Every time she did it, Jane cringed. There was no way in hell she would be able to deal with such an irritating habit on an everyday basis. The other candidate, Juan, was a gay man to the fullest. He was very entertaining, too entertaining actually. She was afraid that he would be so busy cracking jokes and being the center of attention that he would distract attention from an event or forget that he was actually there to work. Her next interview was with Patty. She hoped this was the one.

Patty's interview was at 1:00 pm and it was 1:10 pm. Patty was late. Well, there went the idea of thinking Patty was going to be a good hire. You can't be late to an interview and expect to get the job. Jane was annoyed and started to pack up her things when a person came bursting through her door. Startled, Jane looked up and saw a girl with strawberry blonde hair and fair skin who looked like a younger version of Amy Adams. Her hair was a windblown mess and her clothes were completely disheveled. She wore high heels and one of them had a broken heel, so when she walked, she had what looked like one serious limp. What the hell had happened to this girl?

She brushed her hair to the side with her hand and held out the other for a handshake.

"Hi, I'm Patty O'Neil. I'm extremely sorry that I'm late. My car broke down five streets down and I sprinted all the way here. It seems like I need to work out a little more, since I'm ten minutes late."

Jane couldn't help but smile at the girl. She looked like one serious train wreck, but Jane was intrigued. The girl ran from five streets over in heels and a pencil skirt. She was determined…Jane would give her that. Jane offered her a seat and grabbed some water for the heavily breathing girl.

"Well, I'm glad you didn't hurt yourself running over here. Usually, I don't deal with people who are late, but I'm interested to hear more about you after seeing your determination just to make the interview. Tell me what brings you to Atlanta?"

Jane saw a dark cloud pass over Patty's eyes. Jane wondered if her move to Atlanta was a sensitive subject for the girl. Patty took a second to gather herself and answered the question.

"I needed a fresh start and my best friend, April, lives in the area. I thought it would be a good move for me."

Jane was interested, there was definitely some history there. She wasn't going to push her for the details right away, but if she did hire her, she would get to the bottom of that conversation.

Jane asked, "How do you like it in Atlanta so far?"

Patty perked up a bit. "Oh, I like it much better than New York. The weather is amazing and the people are so much friendlier. The area is great too, so much to do."

Jane asked her some more questions about her history. She found out she actually played basketball for Marist College, where she attended school. She was a point guard, since she was the shortest on the team and the best ball handler. Jane liked that she was on a team because it showed Patty could handle responsibility and could be a leader if Jane needed her to be. Her wait staff and catering experience was a plus and her internship gave her great experience working in all different types of event atmospheres. They got a little off-track when they started comparing chicken salad sandwiches and egg salad sandwiches, but Jane didn't mind. It was great to actually feel a connection with someone.

Patty seemed extremely determined to make it on her own and reminded Jane of herself. She admired that about Patty. Jane knew how hard it was to make a name for yourself and, if she'd had any help, it might have been a little less stressful on her. She decided that Patty was in the same boat she was a couple years back, but Jane wanted to offer this girl the help Jane wished she'd had.

"You're willing to work weekends, right?" Jane knew it was stupid question because, if you're into event planning, you could bet two tits and a ball sac that you would work weekends.

Patty replied, "Of course, I expect to work weekends and I'm very flexible. I have nothing holding me down right now."

Jane was curious. "No husband, children or boyfriends in the mix?"

"Nope, completely single and so not ready to mingle. My friend April likes to take me out to meet guys, but I'm just not ready yet. I got mixed up in a very abusive relationship and I'm not ready to take on more than I can handle. Right now, I'm focused on nothing but myself and my career."

Very interesting. Yes, Jane wanted to help Patty. Jane offered her the job on the spot, which made Patty jump up and hug her. Jane couldn't help but laugh and hug her back. They talked about her pay scale, said their goodbyes, and Jane sent Patty on her way. Jane was excited to have Patty working with her. They both had the same mindset and they were both very much determined. Jane thought, with both of their strengths, they had the possibility to really take JB Events to the next level.

Jane was so excited and there was only one person she truly wanted to share it with. She called Brady. She hadn't talked to him on the phone in a while. They mostly communicated through text messages because he was so busy or too tired. It started to worry her. Was he already bored with her? Brady's phone went to voicemail. Jane groaned out loud and waited for the beep.

"Hey Brady, it's me. Just calling you to let you know I hired someone. Her name is Patty O'Neil and I think she is going to be great for my business. She looks like Amy Adams, so you better not drool all over her when you meet her. Um, kind of sad you didn't answer your phone. I miss your voice and I miss you. I guess I'll talk to you later. I love you, handsome. Bye"

Brady

Brady's heart pained when he listened to Jane's voicemail. It killed him not to talk to her, but he really wanted to throw her off. If he talked to her on the phone, he knew he would spoil the surprise.

He was so happy for her that she hired someone and had the opportunity to be able to take her business to the next level. She did everything on her own and used the resources she had to prevail. She was one hell of a businesswoman.

Brady had to get packed. His plane was going to leave in a couple of hours and he was still sweaty from practice and had nothing packed. If he had it his way, he would pack nothing because he would have preferred to be naked with Jane the entire time he was there, but he knew that was not an option. He had a plan and the plan required clothing. He sent Jane a quick message.

Brady: Got your message baby, so happy for you. Sorry, I can't talk right now. Going into a meeting, don't know how long I will be. Love you.

Brady hated misleading Jane, but it was all for a good reason. If anything went seriously wrong, he knew Molly would have his back and rein in any negative thoughts Jane might have about their relationship. He could just see her start to freak out because they hadn't talked on the phone in a while. Little did she know, she would talk to him in person in just a short time

CHAPTER NINETEEN

Molly

"He's cheating on me, I know he is. Molly, what am I supposed to do?"

Molly listened to her friend freak out while flailing her arms about and pacing, practically naked, in her room. Boy, was she going to regret what she was saying right now. Brady called Molly a couple of days ago saying he wanted to surprise Jane, but he needed her help. Molly came up with a great plan to throw Jane off by limiting the amount of calls Brady made to Jane. She suggested that she convince Jane to go out to Deuces, since that was where they first met and he would be in the VIP area waiting for her with all their friends. She knew Jane would freak out, but little did Molly know her friend would drive her up a wall with the constant questions about her and Brady's relationship. She wanted to wring Jane's neck.

Brady backed off a little with Jane because he was awful at keeping secrets and said he was so excited he might let something slip. So, he kept their conversations to simple text messages and quick calls at night, if any. Because of that, Jane had the impression that he was either no longer interested or was cheating on her. Granted, that was how George wound up cheating on her, so she understood Jane's conclusions, but she wanted to flick her friend in the head and shout *he fucking loves you, moron!*

"He is not cheating on you, Jane, now get dressed. Albert is waiting on us and Luke is meeting us there. I don't want to be late.

Jane groaned. "I don't even know why I agreed to going out with you tonight. I'm so not in the mood. I just want to sit on my couch, listen to 'Chicken Soup for the Soul' on tape and drown myself in pudding."

"Jane, that is so pathetic I can't even take listening to it. You're not 80 years old with a crusty vagina; now get dressed. I'm sick of staring at your underwear choice, even though I appreciate the red. It's hot."

"Thanks, it was a present from Brady. He loves picking out my undergarments. What should I wear?"

"Wear that sexy red dress, the same one you wore when you met Brady. It will match your bra and thong perfectly. Although I have been examining that strip of fabric covering your lady cactus and I don't even know if that falls under the classification of underwear. Seriously, you've become quite the slut and I'm loving it!"

Jane laughed, grabbed her dress and went in the bathroom. Brady asked Molly to make sure she wore that dress. He told her how he so wished he could re-enact that night because it got ruined by George. Jane was going to lose her mind when she saw Brady. Molly couldn't wait to see her friend's reaction. Jane stepped out of the bathroom looking sizzling.

"Damn, chica! I might get a little frisky with you tonight."

"It would be the most action I've had in weeks. Let's go before I change my mind."

Brady

Brady waited in the back of the VIP room Albert had set up for the night. He decided that he was going to come up from behind and surprise Jane, instead of waiting for her out in the open. It was going to be hard to not run up to her right when he saw her, but it was worth the surprise. He received a text message from Molly saying they were five minutes away. Brady had brought Michael, Marc, and Austin, the rookie, back home with him. They waited in the back with Brady as well.

Brady felt like puking and taking a leak at the same time. God, what was he so nervous about? It wasn't like she would slap him in the face when she saw him. She would be excited, right?

Brady saw Molly walk in and then he spotted Jane. Damn.

She looked dick-throbbing good. She was, by far, the most attractive lady in the joint, and she had on the dress she wore when they first met. It hugged her curves perfectly and gave her the most amazing cleavage he had ever seen. All he wanted at that moment was to bury his head in her chest. She had done some kind of twisty concoction with her hair and stuck a red flower in the back. Yeah, he would be ripping that out later and watching her hair fall over her shoulders.

Molly and Jane went straight for the bar and grabbed drinks. He watched every guy turn his gaze at Jane as she sashayed her way through the bar. It took all his energy not to go up to each and every one of the creeps and yank their heads off.

Albert called the girls over once they'd received their drinks and sat them down at his table with Jane's back toward Brady. Perfect. Brady let them get their pleasantries over with and start a conversation before he came out from hiding, so that Jane was distracted and didn't notice him approaching.

He couldn't wait any longer. Molly lit up when Brady approached Jane, which made him nervous; he needed Molly to stay calm and not give him away. He placed his mouth right next to Jane's ear and whispered, "Fuck, Chuck or Marry; Brad Pitt, George Clooney and Matt Damon?"

Jane

Jane felt someone creep up behind her as she talked to her friends and just hoped the creep was not going to linger around for too long. If he did, she knew Albert would take care of him. Then she heard Brady's voice and her heart fluttered, she screamed and turned around.

There he was, grinning like a fool at her, along with Michael and two of his other teammates. He flew out here to surprise her? Oh my God, and she had just bitched about him earlier, accused him of cheating on her. She was an idiot. She had never been so excited in her life. She missed Brady so much and just seeing him in person eased all the tension out of her body.

God, he looked good. He wore some nicely fitted darker jeans and a button-up shirt untucked with the sleeves rolled up. Mmm, she just wanted to rip his clothes off right there.

She jumped up, flung herself around him and wrapped her

arms around his neck and her legs around his waist. She felt her dress slide up to just under her ass, but she didn't care if she was showing her vagina at that point, her Brady was home. She captured his mouth with hers and kissed him senseless. She let out a slight moan in her mouth when his tongue slid against hers and played with her lips.

Molly shouted, "I'm going to start charging people to come in here to catch the soft porn act we have going on right here if you two don't stop. I'm getting all hot and bothered just looking at you."

Jane laughed and let herself down, resting one hand on Brady's chest while the other wrapped around his waist. She playful swatted him and said, "I'm mad at you."

Brady looked at her with shock and replied, "What? Why? I fly out here to be with you and you're mad at me? What am I missing here?"

Jane laughed and said, "Because I'm assuming you've been here for a while and we could have at least fucked twice by now."

Molly shouted, "That's my girl, a round of shots on me!" Luke grabbed her from behind and made her sit on his lap.

Everyone gathered around the table as Brady made introductions. Jane was in heaven; she was in Brady's arms with her friends at her side. Brady announced, "Who's ready to get wasted?"

Everyone cheered and the shots started rolling in. Jane looked over at Molly, who smiled at her. Molly gave Jane a little wink. Molly clearly had something to do with Brady's surprise; jeeze, Jane thought they told each other everything. Although, she was glad Molly kept this a secret because it was one of the best surprises she had ever received.

Jane leaned back on Brady and he whispered in her ear. "You never answered my question, pip-squeak."

"Brad Pitt, George Clooney and Matt Damon? Are we talking Ocean's Eleven here?" Brady nodded his head. "Well then, fuck Brad Pitt, marry Matt Damon and chuck George Clooney."

Brady shook his head. "Wrong answer. You should have said none of the above. I have you and that's all that matters."

Jane rolled her eyes. "Wow, I didn't know you were going to turn into a woman and make cheese dick comments like that when you went off to spring training."

Brady laughed, squeezed her and turned her toward him.

He stared into her eyes and all she saw was pure love coming from him. He loved her and it was the greatest feeling. This man would do anything for her, and she had never felt luckier than at this moment right now.

He interrupted her thoughts when he said, "God, I've missed you." He tucked away a stray strand of hair behind her ear and lingered his fingers on her jaw. He was just about to kiss her again when a shoe hit Brady in the shoulder, Albert's shoe to be exact.

"You can pork later. Come on, we have some drinking to do," Albert said.

Jane was irritated; now that Brady was here, she just wanted to go back home, but all their friends came out tonight for them. The least she could do was hang out with them for a while and toss back a couple of drinks.

Brady tossed Albert's shoe back to him and said, "Alright, the name of the game is Did You Just Queef?" Everybody stared at him like he had three dicks dangling off his head. He chuckled and said, "From the blank faces you're giving me, I'm going to assume you've never played. This is how it works: it's a game of questions. You basically go around asking each other questions one at a time, but they have to have some kind of sexual connotation to them, and it has to be quick. You get two seconds to ask another question, if you don't ask a question to someone in the allotted time, then you must drink."

Brady ordered a bottle of Jack Daniels and a shot glass. "The person who asks the questions and stumps a person gets to come up with a rule for the group. Everyone must follow this rule. No matter what, if you don't, you must drink. Any questions?"

Luke asked, "When asking questions, do we have to go in order around our circle here?"

"No, no order at all. It's all in the element of surprise and then when someone starts getting drunk, it's fun to focus your attention on them and make them drink even more. Since I introduced the game, I'm going to start off with one rule; you must say the person's name before you ask the question, that way we can avoid confusion. Is everyone ready?"

They all nodded their heads. Jane was excited. Her clever boyfriend was teaching them a drinking game. Oh boy, she needed to pull herself together. She was fawning all over him for coming up with a damn drinking game. Yup, she was a goner. Brady started.

"Alright, Luke how big is your dick?"

"Jane, is my dick bigger than Brady's?"

"Molly, remember when you showed me a picture of Luke's dick?"

Molly gasped then said, "Brady, did you know Jane described your dick to me in detail?" Jane could have stretched across the table and flicked her friend in the forehead. How embarrassing!

Brady laughed, "Jane, do you have an infatuation with my dick?" Jane diverted the attention away from herself.

"Albert, do you even have a dick?"

Albert was caught off-guard from the repartee and didn't know how to answer. Jane replied, "I take that as a no." Everyone laughed and Brady handed the first shot to Albert.

"Oh, sweet banana hammocks, that was gross." Albert shuddered from the taste. "And for the record, I do have a dick and I will bet one ball sac and two tits that my dick is the biggest one at this table."

Jane chuckled, "I know it, sister. So I get to make a rule, right?" Brady nodded. "Hmm, if you choose to laugh, you must snort like a pig instead."

Molly cursed, "Fuck me, I'll be oinking all night like a damn porker."

Albert got to start the next round, since he messed up. "Michael, do you have a man-gina?" Michael looked a little caught off-guard, but recovered quickly.

"Austin, have you ever tried blowing yourself?"

"Brady, are Jane's tits really as big as you say?"

Jane swatted Brady, he oinked. Men! "Jane, are you upset I described your tits?"

"Michael, remember when you had man boobs when you were young?" Everyone oinked and Michael playfully scowled.

"Brady, how many women have you fucked?" Hmm, Jane thought about that one, how many women had Brady actually had sex with? Jane only had three ever in her life. Brady's had to be higher, but she was too afraid to find out, so she put that thought on the back burner.

"Luke, have you ever titty fucked Molly?"

Luke shook his head, filled the shot glass with the powerful alcohol and took a shot. He then announced, "I'm only taking this shot because I want the record to be known. Yes, I have titty fucked Molly and, yes, she got off on it."

Everyone laugh-oinked. "I'm not ashamed to admit it. When you have a torpedo like his bobbing toward your face, it's hard not to come on his command."

Jane muttered under her breath. Brady chimed in, "Alright, I get to make the next rule, no pointing."

The game started up again. It was hard for Jane not to point at someone who laughed instead of oinked, so she had to take some shots since she broke the pointing rule. Molly almost fell on the ground from laughing too much. Three more rules were installed in the game where you had to suck your beer bottle like it was dick after you asked a question, if someone yelled "yeast infection" everyone had to grab their crotch (thank you, Molly) and the thumb master. Brady, of course, came up with that rule so whenever he put his thumb on the table everyone else had to place their thumb on the table, leaving the last person to notice the grand prize of taking a shot. Rule penalties started to stack up and everyone got drunker and drunker.

Michael leaned his head against his chair; he got screwed over by the thumb master. Austin and Marc rocked back and forth, unable to steady themselves. Albert wore his shoes on his hands. Luke and Molly made out like crazy in between questions and rule penalties. Brady was the only somewhat normal one and Jane found herself giving Brady a lap dance by slowly moving her ass in circular motions on his lap. She knew she was doing a good job, because he was very hard underneath her.

"Alright, one more round and then I'm taking this vixen home. She has me harder than a rock right now."

Everyone oinked together. Brady made one last rule; you have to end every sentence with the word izzle. Brady began.

"Molly, do you wax your ass-izzle?"

"Yeast infection-izzle," shouted Molly. Everyone grabbed their crotch. By then, Marc was just holding his crotch because he kept getting caught off-guard.

Molly continued, "Marc, would you give your coach a blow job–izzle?"

"Albert, would you ever touch a pussy-izzle?"

"Jane, did you just queef-izzle?"

Molly laughed, Jane pointed, Marc held his thumb on the table which left Michael to be the last one to pick up on it, and Albert never sucked his beer bottle after he asked a question, Austin pointed at Albert because he didn't suck his bottle, Molly shouted yeast infection, Luke pointed at Molly and said, "You didn't say yeast infection-izzle izzle," Jane pointed, Luke laughed at Jane for pointing which led Marc to point at Luke for not oinking, leading Albert to shout yeast infection-izzle, Marc forgot to grab his crotch, Michael rolled on the floor oinking when Brady put his thumb on the table, which left Michael unable to see the thumb once again which caused Jane to oink laugh, Marc pointed again and Molly just sat on Luke's lap as she oink laughed and sucked her beer bottle.

Brady

Brady called the game off because they looked like a bunch of idiots and were starting to attract some major attention. Everyone rolled in their chairs as they laughed. Now was the perfect time to snag Jane away and head back to her place. He whispered in her ear, "Do you want to go back to your place?"

Jane straddled him and said, "No, I want to dance. We never got to finish our dance last time we were here."

Jane was completely drunk, but he thought he might as well dance some of the booze out of her, so she didn't pass out on him when they got home. He had lots of plans for them when they got home.

Brady led her out to the dance floor with her hands entwined in his. Brady was such a lucky man, all the guys stared at her and he knew they wished they were in his place. Jane pulled him close, one of his legs in between hers as she pressed her center against his. Brady instantly thought how he wasn't sure he could last that long out on the dance floor. It had been a couple of weeks since he'd been with Jane, and he was very excited as he anticipated what would come of them when they finally got some privacy.

Jane wrapped her arms around his neck and swayed to the booming beat. Brady didn't really have to do anything but move back and forth, Jane did all the work and made them look good. She slid one of her hands up his shirt and started playing with his waistline. He bent down so his lips were touching her ear.

"Babe, I would suggest you remove your hands from my pants, or I might want to bang you right here on the dance floor." Jane gave him a devilish grin and slid her hand down his pants, briefly touching the head of this throbbing manhood.

Brady jerked away, looking at his teasing girlfriend. "You're in so much trouble when we get home, you hear me? You are getting a spanking."

Jane put her finger in her mouth and faked a sad look. "Oh, have I been naughty?"

Brady was just about to pick Jane up and haul her outside when he was practically tackled from behind. He went flying across the dance floor and ran into the bar chairs. What the hell? He turned around, ready to punch the crap out of whoever just slammed into him when he saw Luke grinning like the Grinch at him. Then, Luke grabbed him and tried to waltz around the club with him.

Oh Jesus, Brady needed to call him a cab. He looked over where Molly was rolling on the couch in the VIP area as she laughed hysterically, her skirt lifted so everyone got a good shot of her choice of pink underwear for the night.

Brady danced Luke over to Molly and said, "Dude, you might want to get that soon-to-be-wife of yours home. She's showing everyone her who-ha."

Luke immediately grabbed Molly and put her over his shoulders. "Come on Britney Spears, I don't want any other peep shows coming from you tonight unless I'm the one fucking your peep."

Molly laughed and blew kisses with both hands rapidly to everyone. As Luke carried her past Brady, Brady thanked her for her help. He could not have pulled this night off without her.

Brady really enjoyed Jane's crowd. They were his kind of people and didn't treat him any differently because he was in the public eye. He really felt like he was part of the gang. He had his baseball crowd, which was nice...he got along with all the guys and had friends on different teams, but it was nice for him to step out of that world and have a little bit of normalcy as well.

Jane was the best thing that had happened to him in quite some time. He was extremely lucky to be able to play his favorite sport for a living, but sometimes he got so consumed by it. It was nice for him to take a step back and enjoy normal life…not in the spotlight. Jane grounded him and gave him that sense of security he'd been looking for.

He could see himself marrying her one day and having kids. He knew she would be the best mom and, by far, the hottest MILF in Atlanta. Now, if only he could get Jane in the same frame of mind as he was. He could tell that she was still a little apprehensive to take steps forward in their relationship, thank you George, but she had become much better and really had given her whole heart to him. He just needed to help her stop second-guessing everything in their relationship.

Brady had Marc and Austin take Michael back home. Poor guy, he'd been having such a hard time and tonight must have been a nice release for him, but now Michael had to go back home and face, what did he call her? Ah yes, Hot-lanta's hooker.

Brady leaned over to Jane, wrapped his arms around her from behind and leaned down into her ear. "You ready, sweet thing? I want you so bad."
She turned around, pressing her body against his and lowered her hand to his crotch. She gave it a little squeeze. He took that as a yes and bolted out the door with the love of his life.

CHAPTER TWENTY

Jane

Jane woke up the next morning when her phone beeped in her ear. She opened her phone and saw a message from Albert.

Albert: Oooo darling, I almost got a hard on looking at the pictures of you and Brady from last night. They're all over the Internet.

Jane groaned in annoyance. She didn't even remember seeing anyone taking pictures. She needed to talk to Deuces and see if they had a policy of letting paparazzi into the bar. Although, nowadays, everyone had a camera on their phone...nobody was safe with modern technology. Brady was still sleeping, so she snuck out of bed and pulled out her laptop.

She went to a well-known celebrity gossip blog and saw what Albert was talking about. God, she did look hot. Jane was not a self-absorbed girl and didn't by any means think she was sexy, but by golly did she look good last night. She looked amazing with Brady. She stared at the pictures and realized, not only was she staring at Brady and herself, but she saw two people completely head over heels in love with each other. She swore it could have been Luke and Molly in the pictures.

Was she really at that point in her life where she'd found the perfect person for her? Every time she thought of Brady, her heart skipped a beat and she couldn't stop smiling. She was so in love with him; he was perfect for her. He took care of her, supported her, loved her and treated her like she was the only woman he would ever have eyes for.

She felt Brady walk up from behind her and she cringed.

"Fuck, who took those pictures?" Brady huffed angrily.

"I don't know and I don't care." Jane turned around and wrapped her arms around Brady's bare chest. "What I see in those pictures, Brady, are two people who are in love with each other. That's all I care about. People can say what they want to say, but the pictures speak for themselves. Whoever took that picture captured a moment in our lives, a moment that I will never forget. Last night was remarkable, Brady, and I am so amazingly in love with you."

Jane felt Brady melt into her. He leaned down and kissed her on the head. "I'm so in love with you too, pip-squeak."

Jane playfully swatted him, grabbed his hand and pulled him into the bathroom. She lifted her T-shirt over her head, exposing everything she had to offer and turned the shower on. Brady raised an eyebrow at her when she got closer to him and pulled his boxer briefs down. She watched as his already-hard penis sprung from his shorts and bobbed upward. Jane tried to have self-control, but she lost it very quickly.

Brady

Brady instantly got excited when Jane took her shirt off. How could he not with a body that perfect? He could never get tired of staring at her. They walked into the shower together and he watched as water slowly started to drip down Jane's body as she reveled in the spray. She threw her head back with her eyes closed and let the water stream down her body. Brady licked his lips and gulped, that was enough of that.

He grabbed Jane and pulled her closer. "I've dreamed of taking showers with you and, so far, it's better than anything I could have imagined."

"You must not have high expectations," she replied.

"Oh, I had high expectations, but you exceed them by far. Now, do I get to lather you up in all your crevices?"

Jane purred, "I expect you to."

Brady tilted Jane's chin up so he had better access to her lips and slowly started to nibble at her mouth, working his way down her neck across her collar bones and back up again. Jane made a faint moaning sound and started to run her hands up through his hair and down his back; she gripped on a little tighter than usual, but he liked the way her fingers dug into him. His erection pressed hard against her core, telling her he was turned on immensely.

Jane threw her head back and Brady took that opportunity to close in on her delicious breasts. He captured one in his mouth and sucked every last inch of it until her nipple was raw and vulnerable. He did the same thing to the other, while Jane moaned some more.

"Oh, Brady, oh I need you inside me. Please feel how wet I am for you."

Brady spread her legs with his and lowered his hand to her warm wetness. He could tell it was wet, not just from the shower, so he started to stroke her in short motions that made her catch her breath. He took two fingers and worked his way into her hole and dove in, reaching for her g-spot. He knew he got it when she clenched around his fingers and threw her head back groaning. Brady started to slightly scoop inside her and used his thumb to stroke her clit at the same time.

Jane quickly abandoned everything to Brady. She screamed his name out, moaning yes at the same time. Brady couldn't believe he'd made her come so fast and so hard. He pleased his woman and that meant more to him than anything. She flung herself against him, wallowing in the aftershocks of her orgasm. He just held her while she breathed heavily.

Jane looked at him, her eyes were big, bright and full of mischief. She grabbed his dick with her hand.

"Mmm, still hard, just the way I like it." She took him by surprise when she pressed him up against the wall of the shower, hopped up on him, wrapped her legs around his waist and pressed her hot center down on his hard shaft.

Brady couldn't help himself, he moaned and thrust up into her.

"Fuck, baby, why are you so tight? It makes me not able to last as long as I want to."

Jane laughed and said, "Well, if your dick wasn't so huge, maybe it wouldn't be a problem, but I'm going to come again any minute now, so I'm right there with you."

And she was. After a couple more thrusts into her, they

shook together as their joined orgasms took over their bodies and propelled them somewhere else. Brady had to set Jane down, because his whole body went numb with pleasure and he couldn't hold her up any longer. They leaned into each other and stood under the water until they were ready to float back down from their cloud of ecstasy.

Michael

Michael found himself lying on his couch, fully clothed, shoes still on. God, his teammates were jerks; they couldn't even take his shoes off? Lord knows his wife wouldn't be home to take care of him.

He strolled into the kitchen and grabbed a PowerAde to re-hydrate. He didn't need to wreck his body so he was trash on Monday when he got back to spring training. His manager would not be happy. He went upstairs to take a shower. When he entered his room, he noticed a huge line-backer was in his bed with his wife Kelly, who was bouncing up and down on top of him. Michael hated that he thought Kelly looked hot at that moment. Her fake boobs were bouncing up and down, her flat stomach was more amazing than ever and her hair floated on her shoulders. Fuck.

They both turned and looked at him in surprise. Michael pulled out his phone and took a picture.

Shocked, Kelly grabbed the sheets and pulled them over herself and screamed, "What the fuck do you think you're doing, you sick bastard?"

"Just sending proof over to my lawyer that you are, in fact, cheating on me and don't bother covering your body up. I'm your husband, remember? I've seen everything you have to offer and paid for that massive rack of yours."

Kelly scrambled to her feet while the linebacker awkwardly got out of bed. He grabbed his clothes, got dressed, and started to walk down the stairs.

Kelly yelled to him, "Call me, Dayshon."

God, she had no class at all. Did she not even care about Michael one bit? What kind of evil bitch yells out to her boyfriend to call her with her husband standing right in front of her?

Kelly punched Michael in the arm and said, "What the fuck are you doing here? Shouldn't you be at your stupid training playing with your balls?"

"Very clever, Kelly, good to see you too. Glad to see you're making friends."

"Dayshon is not my friend. We're in love and we're going to run away together. What do you have to say about that?"

Michael pondered that for a second. Kelly and Dayshon? Well, good luck Dayshon! The poor man had no clue what he was now wrapped up into. When Michael first met Kelly in New York, she was incredibly sweet, shy, and supportive of his sport. They formed a foundation together to help kids who were diagnosed with Leukemia, visited hospitals, and were known as the power couple. The cameras started to flash at them, and that was when she started to get her hair and nails done more often. A little something new to wear on occasion turned into full-on shopping sprees every week. She drew away from Michael, physically and emotionally. All she wanted was camera attention.

Never in his wildest dreams did he think Kelly would develop an obsession with becoming famous. She craved the camera and attention any chance she could get it. She even wanted to start singing, but Michael made sure to put the kibosh on that; she couldn't carry a tune and he didn't need her to embarrass him anymore than she already had.

When he was traded to Atlanta, he thought maybe they could have a fresh start. He thought he might just have a chance to save their marriage. People would ask him where she was and he'd just say that she was upset, she missed her family, or she was at a book club meeting. He lied to everyone because he was so ashamed he couldn't make his marriage work. He felt like less of a man because of it.

He turned to Kelly and said, "I want you out of this house by the time I come back from spring training. You can count on hearing from my lawyers. We are over. You are a dirty, self-absorbed, tramp and I don't need you in my life."

Kelly started to punch him and screamed how he was a bastard and had ruined her life and she regretted the day she ever said yes to marrying him. Those were cheap shots to a man's ego. He tried to not let her words affect him, but deep down inside, he knew he'd failed as a man. He wasn't good enough for Kelly; he'd tried and he failed. Good thing he never tried to really pursue Jane, because he would have failed her as well, and he didn't know if he could stand to fail Jane.

Molly

Molly stretched her arms above her head and let out a little yelp. Luke pounced on her and started to tickle her all over. Molly thrashed around, trying to get him off, but he wouldn't let up. Finally, she grabbed his naked cock that bobbed on her stomach, which backed him off real fast. He instantly went hard.

"Whoa, cowboy, don't get any ideas. I don't think I can handle another pounding from you right away. That last one was a doozy. Where did you even learn how to twist me like that? I felt like a human pretzel with all my sensitive spots exposed."

Luke had her tied up last night with her butt hanging out in the open and breasts on display. She had never felt more vulnerable in her life, but she was extremely trusting when it came to Luke. He would never hurt her, but he did deliver her multiple orgasms more intense than she had experienced in a while. She needed a bit of a break from his body to regain her strength.

"I've never heard you scream like that, babe. I was nervous I was hurting you at one point," Luke said.

Molly stroked his cock lightly and said, "You would never hurt me. It was just so intense." Molly continued to stroke Luke slowly and watched how his arousal got harder and harder with each movement. She loved it when a simple touch could turn him on; he was so responsive to her and it made her feel like a million bucks.

She needed to talk to him about the wedding plans and what she and Jane had developed. Molly didn't like to talk about it that much, with anyone really. She felt stupid that she wouldn't have anyone on her side to support her. Her parents were gone and she was an only child. She never really got to meet any aunts or uncles and, clearly, her grandparents had passed a while ago. She was practically an orphan, which embarrassed her.

She felt Luke jerk his hips up and she noticed there were some juices glistening from the head of Luke's arousal. His eyes were closed and he was breathing heavily. She continued to run her hand up and down the veiny part of his length, she reveled in the soft velvet of his penis. Luke occasionally thrust at her hand, and Molly just giggled at his absentminded response. She was torturing him, she knew it and he knew it, and they both enjoyed the sensation.

Luke started to groan in the back of his throat. Molly knew that as Luke's I'm-going-to-come-any-second-sound, so she stopped stroking.

"Uhhhhh, fuck Molly!" Luke groaned in a husky voice.

Molly giggled and blew a little on his bobbing arousal, which caused him to jerk up. He scooped her under him, ready to press his length in her center and said, "We can do this one of two ways, I can plow into you, leaving you raw, or you can take that sweet little hand of yours and finish what you started."

Molly knew she should talk to Luke right now about the wedding, but hell, she wasn't going to turn down a good distraction to get out of an awkward conversation that she wanted to avoid having. She smiled and spread her legs for Luke. His head slouched down and he laughed.

"You are incredible, you know that?"

"I know, now show me how incredible you are, big boy!"

After Luke finished off and, once again, delivered another orgasm to Molly, she checked her phone. She'd received a text message in the midst of pleasing her man. It was from Jane.

Jane: I don't know about you, but I fucked myself up an appetite. Meet us at Massimo's at 1?"

Luke laid on the bed with his hands crossed behind his head, naked as hell, as she reveled in his ability to have such a healthy libido. Molly turned to him and said, "Lunch with the Matthews at one?"

Luke laughed, "They're not married yet, Jesus. Don't let Jane hear you say that; she would freak the fuck out."

"I don't know," replied Molly. "Jane is really beyond smitten with Brady. I truly think she would consider marrying him."

Luke shrugged and got up to go to the bathroom. "I'm up for some Greek if you are babe, plus I enjoy Brady's company. I could see a bro-mance forming in our near future."

Molly rolled her eyes and sent Jane a message back.

Molly: You're on, girl. P.S. Luke just said he could see having a bro-mance with Brady. I almost puked.

Jane: Haha, OMG Brady was saying how much he liked Luke earlier. Maybe we should step aside for them.

Molly: No, they need us because they wouldn't know how to live without tits.

Jane: Brady surely wouldn't. He thinks mine are like magical orbs that appear on my chest.

Molly: Well, I've seen them and I can honestly say he is one lucky man. I'd be touching them all the time if you were my girlfriend.

Jane: You do touch them you hoe-bag, every chance you get.

Molly: I'm jealous, so what? I have to live through you and your ample cleavage.

Jane: I'll make sure to wear something low cut to lunch then.

Brady

Brady waited in Jane's living room sweating bullets. He'd made a key for his house to give to Jane. He wanted to be with her as much as possible and wanted Jane to feel at home in his place. In the near future, he wanted Jane to live with him, but he knew he needed to take baby steps. He didn't plan on receiving Jane's key in exchange for his. He just wanted her to have his so she could freely go over to his house as much as she wanted.

Jane walked into the room looking fantastic. She wore little denim shorts, a yellow T-shirt that showed off her amazing breasts, and her hair was up out of her face. He preferred when her hair was down so he could run his fingers through it, but she looked gorgeous with her hair up as well. He pulled her down on his lap and circled her waist with his arms.

"Hey, beautiful, when are you going to stop taking my breath away?"

Jane's eyes turned wide with shock and then transferred into lust. "You are one sweet man, Brady Matthews. Are you ready to go?" She tried to pull him up, but he didn't let up on his hold around her. "What's going on? Is everything okay?" she asked in a worried tone.

"Everything is perfect, baby." She relaxed a little. "I just want to give you something."

Brady pulled out the spare key to his house, placed it in the palm of Jane's hand and closed her fingers around it. Jane looked at him in surprise and her eyes started to glisten. Was she going to cry? That was a good thing, right?

Brady cleared his throat and said, "Listen, don't feel pressured or anything, I just wanted to give you the spare key to my house. I want you to come and go as you please; the more you're there, the better. I want my home to feel like your home."

Jane stared at the key and then back at him. She didn't say anything, oh shit. Big mistake buddy. How could he take this back without making it incredibly awkward between them? He started to say something when she placed her finger on his lips.

"I can't believe you're giving me your key," she said. "I don't know what to say."

Brady stiffened. "Is that a good thing or a bad thing?" Brady realized he was holding his breath.

"Oh, Brady." She grasped his head between her hands. "It's the most amazing thing ever."

Brady let his breath out in relief.

"Jesus, I thought you were upset," Brady said, relieved.

"Why in the world would I be upset? You opened your home to me. I don't know what to say. I love you so much, thank you."

Brady's heart melted into a pool on the floor. Hell yeah! He was one step closer to his ultimate goal: to make a life with Jane. She kissed him until he couldn't breathe anymore. He was about to move his hands up her shirt when she stopped him and shook her finger at him.

"We have lunch plans. I promise to give you full access when we get back."

Brady groaned, "Uh, why are we going out in public again? I thought we were just going to stay in bed together the whole time I was here."

"We have to eat, silly…and hey, you get to see your new boyfriend, Luke."

"Well in that case…" Brady jumped up and nearly

knocked Jane into the wall. "Let's get going, I don't want to be late for our date." Jane laughed at him. If only he could bottle up that sound and save it forever, he would. He was so in love it hurt, damn. It sure did creep up on him, but he wouldn't change it for anything in the world.

Molly

Molly and Luke arrived before Jane and Brady. How wonderful was this? Her best friend had an amazing man, she was about to marry the love of her life, and things were going great. She just wished she could get over the empty feeling of not having any family. Weddings should be fun, but the closer it got, the worse she felt about it.

Jane and Albert planned her bachelorette party to be in a couple of weeks, and then the wedding would be here before she knew it. Luke had to go off to training in North Carolina, but he would make it home in time for the wedding.

She didn't want Luke to be gone the last few weeks leading up to their wedding. She already felt vulnerable with no family; Luke was all she had, she needed him to be there and help her. Although, he couldn't help her unless he actually knew what was bothering her.

Jane and Brady strolled up to the table where Molly and Luke were sitting; Jane radiated love and Brady's chest could not get any bigger with pride. It was funny to see the two of them so much in love; it poured out of them.

Luke stood up and gave Brady a hug, they embraced for a second and Luke leaned in and said, "You can lead one hell of a waltz, my man."

Brady laughed and patted him on the back. "I know how to two-step my way around a dance floor. How are you guys faring this afternoon? I know this little pip-squeak I have with me had a serious headache this morning."

Molly scoffed, "Oh, that's because she's a pussy. We veterans don't get headaches."

Luke laughed and replied, "I beg to differ. I clearly remember a couple of weeks ago finding you on the kitchen floor with only your mini skirt covering your nipples from exposure."

Molly swatted him. "Whatever, you still got fucked that

morning."

Molly looked over at Jane and noticed that she couldn't stop smiling. Either she got some real good action before they came over, or something was going on. Would they be engaged? No, it was way too early for that. Jane was not emotionally ready for that kind of commitment. Funny, Jane wasn't emotionally ready, but she would have all the support she would need from a family. Molly was way more than emotionally ready than Jane, but had no family at all to support her. Why did it matter to her so much?

It must be all those romance novels she'd read and romantic comedies she'd watched that instilled in her mind that she needed her mom at her side while she picked a dress and her dad holding her arm as he walked her down the aisle. She would have neither.

Molly shook the thoughts out of her head and turned her attention to her friend. "What's with the smiles over there Jane?"

Jane held Brady's hand and looked over at him. Oh my God, they were engaged. She couldn't believe it.

"Brady gave me a key to his house today."

Oh. A key, well Molly jumped the gun on the old engagement thought. Note to Molly, do not tell Jane what she thought she was going to say. Molly didn't need to make things more difficult for Brady.

She put her congratulations face on. "That's great you guys. I'm so happy for you. Does that mean you're going to move in?"

Jane's face went a little white...oh shit, wrong question.

Brady chimed in. "Jane knows I would love for her to move in, but we're taking baby steps, so she can come over whenever she wants. If she wants to move in after a while, Lord knows I'll be the first one packing her boxes, but we're taking it one step at a time."

Molly watched Jane as Brady explained the new development in their relationship. Jane instantly melted and became warm again. Brady was so great for her. He knew her problems, worked with her, and was patient.

"Well, that is great, man," Luke said. "Congratulations. How much longer will you be at spring training?"

"We have three and a half more weeks left, then we start

our season at home against the Mets. We'll have pre-season games during the next three weeks, so there'll be more traveling. It'll be a little difficult for Jane and me, but then we'll get back into a regular schedule."

"That's great, so do you think you're going to make it to the wedding?" Molly asked.

"I plan on it. That is, if Jane will take me as her date," Brady said jokingly.

Molly watched Jane pretend to consider someone else. "I don't know Brady. I think I really had a connection with Austin the other night."

"Don't even think about it, pip-squeak, you're all mine."

They ordered their food and talked about the wedding, why Albert wore his shoes on his hands last night, and the upcoming bachelorette party while they ate lunch. Molly was having such a good time...she loved these people. Even though they weren't blood related, they were connected through their souls and that might just have to be good enough for her.

Jane

They were all about to get up from the seats they had outside of the restaurant when Jane backed her chair into someone. She turned around and, to her surprise, ran into Patty. Patty was with an incredibly gorgeous strawberry-blonde with blue eyes. She was definitely taller than Jane and had a fantastic muscular body. She must work out every day for hours to have a body like that. Jane apologized for hitting Patty with her chair.

"That's okay, I guess I should watch where I'm going," Patty replied. She pointed to her friend and said, "This is April; she's the friend I was telling you about." Jane shook hands with her and made introductions all the way around. Jane watched Brady closely when he shook hands with the girls. He showed no sexual interest in them whatsoever, which made Jane feel incredibly good about herself. Brady truly only had eyes for her.

Patty commented, "Gee, Jane, I didn't know you were dating the Braves' starting first baseman. That's a little intimidating. So, that means you know all the players, even Marc Sullivan?"

Jane laughed and replied, "Well, to me, Brady is just some hunk of meat that I'm currently stuck with. I don't know all the players, but I have met some, including Marc." Brady playfully gave her a little pinch. "And, speak of the devil," Jane said, pointing behind them.

What were the odds that Jane would not only run into her new co-worker, but her co-worker would express interest in a baseball player she knew, who just showed up at the same restaurant? Jane couldn't help but get excited about a possible love connection.

Brady gave a handshake to Austin and Marc. "What are you guys doing here?"

Marc looked at the girls, he lingered a little longer on Patty and said, "Uh, we heard they have great food here and thought we'd give it a try."

Jane noticed how Marc looked at Patty. Jane introduced everyone once again and couldn't help but smile. Marc was a very good looking guy and fun. She would maybe talk to Brady and see what Marc's status was. Maybe she could get Marc to ask out Patty. Whoa, Patty expressed she was not interested in having a relationship. Now that Jane was in love, she apparently wanted everyone she knew to be in love as well.

Patty did say she didn't want a relationship, but the way she turned bright red when she shook Marc's hand and continued to stare at him, gave Jane the impression that her new co-worker not only wanted to be in a relationship, but she had eyes for Marc Sullivan. She couldn't blame Patty…the Braves had some amazingly gorgeous men on their team.

They all parted ways and Jane made sure to wish the boys good luck with spring training and told Patty she would see her on Monday. She watched Patty walk away and glance back at Marc. Poor girl, Jane knew exactly how Patty felt.

CHAPTER TWENTY ONE

Jane

Jane and Brady spent the rest of their hours together in bed, where they held each other, pleased each other, and even ate off each other. Jane had never felt so good in her entire life. Even when she was with George, he never truly made her feel as feminine as Brady did. Brady treated her with respect and showered love on her whenever she was near him.

She was upset that he had to leave, but after this visit they just had, she had never felt more confident in her life about a relationship. Brady made it quite clear that she was his and he wasn't interested in anyone else. In the back of her mind, she always wondered if Laney Johnson would ever take action to win Brady back, but she knew it wouldn't work. Brady would never give Laney the time of day...right?

Brady put his head on her stomach and looked up at her. "What are you thinking about, sweet thing? I lost you a little."

"Oh, I was just thinking about how this has been the best day and a half of my life."

"Mine too, baby. I hate that I have to leave so soon, but time is going to fly by, right?"

Jane thought about all the things that she had to accomplish in the next week. She had an event next weekend that she had to put on for a major pharmaceutical company in the area and then, of course, she was in crunch-time with Molly's wedding and her bachelorette party. Time really would fly by.

"It will fly by." Jane stroked Brady's hair. "When do you

have to go?"

Brady sighed, sat up and pulled her close. "My flight leaves around eight. I wish I could stay longer, but I'm pushing it as it is."

"I understand. So, now that I have a key, does that mean I can go in your house, paint the walls pink, and put fake flowers everywhere?"

Brady laughed and then got extremely serious. His eyes burned into hers and she shivered in place. "Babe, you can do whatever you want to my house. I'm serious. I want you to be comfortable and I want you to think of it as yours as well."

Jane was taken aback. She was only kidding. She didn't expect Brady to say she could actually make herself at home. She knew he gave her a key, but just so she could come over whenever, not to set up and play house. Was he serious? He really wanted her to come into his house and decorate?

"Brady, you're not serious. You don't want me going into your house and messing up your vibe."

Brady grabbed her hands and rubbed the tops of them with the pads of his thumbs. "Jane, I'm dead serious. I want you to do whatever you want to the house so you feel at home. Right now, the house is just a house; it's not a home. You will make it a home. You know I want you to move in with me, but I'm giving you your space. When you're ready, you can start making it a home for us."

Jane's breath caught in the back of her throat. Were they moving too fast? He didn't say she had to move in right away; they could take their time and slowly move her in. Although, there was a little voice in the back of her head that was screaming yes, yes, yes! A little part of her, the not overly cautious and conservative part of Jane wanted to move in with him so badly, but the old, hurt Jane was extremely cautious.

She simply replied, "We'll just see what happens. Can you hold me for now, until you have to leave?"

"Of course, sweet thing; come here."

Brady grabbed Jane and pulled her close to him. She laid her head on his shoulder and wrapped her arms around his bare waist. They were skin on skin, but nothing erotic passed through her mind. She just wanted human contact, Brady's love.

Molly

Molly was dreading today. Luke was leaving for training to Lord knows where. They were scheduled to go to North Carolina first and then to some non-disclosed location. She assumed it was in a jungle area because he'd packed his woodland camouflage. Luke seemed more anxious than usual, especially since he was just going on a training session. He acted like it was an actual mission. She wondered if it was an actual mission, and he didn't want to tell her because he didn't want to make her nervous. Missions were more unpredictable and it could be possible that he would miss the wedding.

If Luke missed the wedding, it wouldn't be that big of a deal. The wedding was a small one, so it wouldn't be a big hassle to move it to another day. Maybe they should just move it to another day anyway. She thought the more she put it off, the more she wouldn't have to worry about not having any family there.

Molly gained some courage and asked Luke, "Do you just want to move the wedding so you have plenty of time to get back and you don't have to rush?"

Luke stopped in his tracks and whipped his body around. "Are you serious right now?" Molly just nodded her head. "Jesus, Molly, are you having second thoughts about us?"

Molly saw every ounce of Luke's love for her fall flat to the ground, and he went completely pale. She grabbed him by the arms and shook her head.

"No, not at all. God, I love you and want to be your wife more than anything. It's just…" Here goes nothing. Luke tilted her chin up so she looked him in the eyes. "I love you, Luke, and I want to be married to you, but this whole wedding thing has just made me realize that I'm all alone; I have no family. I'm an orphan. When a girl gets married, it's supposed to be this glorious celebration with her family, and she's supposed to pick a dress out with her mom and be told how beautiful she is by her dad right before she walks down the aisle. I won't have that."

Luke wrapped his arms around her and rested his chin on her head. If Molly could stay in the little cocoon Luke formed around her, she would be happy for the rest of her life. When she was wrapped in his arms, she didn't have to worry about anything.

"Oh, baby, I didn't even think about how you would feel

about not having your family here to celebrate with you. I'm so sorry, but you know, a wedding isn't only about celebrating with family, but it is also about starting a new life with your soul mate. You know you have family, not by blood, but by heart. Jane, Albert, and even Michael and Brady are your family. Most importantly, I'm your family and that's all that matters. Instead of focusing on your family not being there, focus on starting a new life with me."

Molly knew Luke was right. She had family all around her, but just a different kind of family. They loved her, supported her, and would be by her side on the most important day of her life. Molly just nodded her head against Luke's chest.

"Believe me, I can't wait to start a new life with you, buy a house, and start making some really cute babies. Those are my top priorities right after we say our I do's. What do you say babe? Are you in? Will I forever be Molly's man?"

Molly's man. She couldn't think of anyone else who could fill that position. Of course he would be Molly's man, he always had been and always would be. Luke was right. She just needed to think of their wedding as the start of a new chapter in their life together. When she thought about it that way, she couldn't wait...she wanted to get married right away.

"Yes, Luke. No one else will ever come close to filling that role. Three weeks and we'll be married. I can't wait. Now, enough with all this talking, it seems to me like you're taking off and that calls for a goodbye blow job."

Luke instantly dropped his pants and told her, "I'm ready, woman, when you are."

Molly threw her head back and laughed. Yes, this would be a very interesting new chapter in her life, but it would be the best thing that ever happened to her.

Brady

Brady got back to his apartment in Florida and was hit in the face with an empty and lonely apartment. No big blue eyes to stare at him, no crystal clear smile that said 'I love you' or warm embrace to help him relax. Damn, he had it bad. He tried to text Michael to see how he was doing, but Michael never sent him anything back, which was weird. Last time he saw Michael was at

Deuces as he rolled on the ground laugh-oinking. Austin and Marc said they got him home alright. They just dropped him off on his couch and assumed his wife would take care of him.

That made Brady nervous. Brady knew Michael was struggling with his marriage and was having a difficult time; he only hoped that Michael would open up to him about it. He hoped Michael had made it back to Florida for practice. After practice, he was going to take Michael out, provided he was here. It seemed like Michael needed to get some things off his chest.

At Deuces, Brady noticed that Michael was quieter than usual and he drank a lot more than everyone else. He wondered if Michael still had feelings for Jane. He hoped not because what was going on between Brady and Jane wouldn't be messed with. Brady knew he'd found the woman he was supposed to spend the rest of his life with, and nothing could mess that up.

Brady's phone beeped on his way out of the apartment and he looked down at his phone. It was a message from Jane.

Jane: Hey, handsome, just thinking of you. Hope you made it back alright. Thank you so much for one of the best weekends ever.

Brady's whole body went warm. Yeah, nothing would break them up. Hopefully, while he was gone, she'd go over to his house and start to make herself comfortable there. He really wanted her to start to move her things in there, but he knew that might be moving a little fast for Jane. When he got back to Atlanta, he would go buy some of her favorite products, a tooth brush and maybe some spare clothes for her, so she didn't always have to have an overnight bag. He sent Jane a message back.

Brady: Hey, sweet thing, I had the most amazing time. I miss you. I'm headed to practice now. I'm hoping to catch Michael after and grab a bite to eat.

Jane: That should be nice. He's been weird lately. I hope everything is okay.

Brady: I noticed the same thing. That's why I wanted to take him out.

Jane: You're a good guy, Brady Matthews.

Brady: I try to be. I'll call you later tonight. I love you.

Jane: I love you, handsome.

Brady headed to his car to drive to the ball park and had just placed his phone in his pocket when it beeped again. He got in his car and cranked up the air conditioning. It was surprisingly very warm in Florida for the time of the year. He pulled his phone back out of his pocket and hoped Jane had sent him a picture of her or maybe a naughty text. When he saw a strange number again, he swore under his breath.

Brady boy, you have not gotten back to me. I'm going to find out where you are and just jump your bones myself. Come on, baby, I know you want me.

Brady was about to throw his phone when he received one last text message. Fuck! It was a picture of Laney, completely naked, holding a bat as it rested on her shoulder. He instantly deleted the message.

He was shaken from the erotic picture that popped up on his phone, not because Laney was a hideous looking person, but because if Jane ever knew Laney sent that picture to him, he could possibly lose her forever. He needed to remind himself to block that number.

Holy hell, if Jane knew about that picture, he would be in a lot of trouble, then that reminded him…He never told Jane about the texts from Laney. Crap. They had such a good time he didn't want to ruin it with a conversation about his deranged ex-girlfriend. He needed to remember to tell her when he got back from training. He decided he wanted to tell her in person, so she didn't flee on him.

Jane

Jane went to work that morning feeling refreshed. She was so happy she got to see Brady, even if it was just for a little bit. She had a hard time saying goodbye to him when he left; she even cried like an idiot, which she knew tore Brady apart from the inside out. He told her he would call her every night, and they even planned to Skype. Something she had never done before. She didn't know how she felt about seeing him and not being able to touch him all over; if she wasn't careful, she might start humping the screen of her computer.

Jane told Patty to come in a little later than normal so she could get ready for her. Jane set up a desk at the front for her, equipped it with all the necessary supplies and a brand new laptop as well as some fresh flowers. It was always nice to have fresh flowers around; it always put Jane in a good mood. Jane's phone beeped. It was a text from Brady. Her heart flip-flopped. When would that stop?

Brady: Baby, you were right! Marc just asked me about Patty. He asked if she was available. What should I say?

Jackpot! Jane knew it. Marc was looking Patty up and down the whole time they were talking outside of Massimo's. He should have been a little more discreet, but knowing him, he wanted Patty to know about his interest. She sent Brady a message back.

Jane: I know she isn't attached to anyone, but I don't know if she wants a relationship. She said she just wanted to focus on her career.

Brady: Sounds to me like you hired a miniature Jane.

Jane knew she hired Patty because they had similar values. It was going to be easier to work together, knowing they thought the same way about things.

Jane: Yeah, and look at what happened to me. I'm caught up with the likes of you!

Brady: Just admit it, pip-squeak, I'm the best thing that has ever happened to you.

Jane knew Brady was joking around with her, but when she sat back and thought about it, Brady really was the best thing that ever happened to her. He made her feel loved and needed again. He truly brought her back to life. Jane replied.

Jane: You are the best thing to ever happen to me, handsome, and I mean it.

Now I have to go. Have a good practice. I love you.

Brady: Good luck with Patty's first day. I love you too and P.S. you are by far the greatest thing in my life past, present and future.

Jane got choked up when she read Brady's text message. Where the hell did he come up with one-liners like that? Did he have a book of them or something? There was no way a man was that romantic.

Jane was just checking her eyeliner in the mirror for any smudges when Patty walked in. She looked fantastic, wearing a nice pair of black dress pants and a cranberry colored blouse; it really brought out the red highlights in her hair.

Jane greeted Patty and showed her around the office. She showed her the ins and the outs of the business, as well as described her expectations and Patty's different responsibilities. They went over the pharmaceutical event they had this weekend. Patty jumped right in and tossed some ideas around with Jane. To Jane's surprise, they were all great ideas and would help make the event run smoother.

They broke for lunch and Jane ordered salads from the place around the corner. They delivered, which was perfect because Jane wanted to talk to Patty for a little and get to know her better. Maybe even question her about her interest in Marc.

Jane paid for the food when it arrived and asked Patty, "So, why is a pretty thing like you deciding to be single?"

Jane saw Patty sigh. "Well, since we'll be spending a lot of time together, I might as well tell you." Jane was intrigued. Patty continued, "Back in New York, I dated a guy named Gino. He was ruggedly handsome, Italian, very loud and very proud of his job. He was into selling bonds and whatnot. I didn't really know all the details, all I knew was that he made a lot of money. We started dating in high school, made it through college together, and then into the real world. He was always very opinionated with me and made sure I always took his opinion because 'he was always right.' It didn't faze me at the time because we had so much fun together it didn't matter."

Patty took a sip of her water and continued. "It wasn't until he started making more money that he started to get verbally abusive toward me. He would call me stupid, useless, pathetic, and a worthless excuse for a woman, and I just took it all in. By then, I didn't know any differently. I had been with him since high school. It seemed normal to me."

Jane knew exactly how Patty felt, trapped in a man's wrath. She went through the same thing with George, and it could be incredibly hard to remove yourself from the situation when you'd been living in it for so long. Jane grabbed Patty's hand and urged her to continue.

"When I got home one day from my internship, Gino was furious. He'd had a bad day at work and lost a bunch of money. He took his anger out on me, physically. He beat me pretty good that night. I was so shocked, I didn't know what to do. I've always been a strong woman, thanks to basketball, but Gino took over that girl and made her weak and feeble. It wasn't until the fifth time he beat me and he cracked one of my ribs by kicking me continuously until I couldn't breathe, that I realized I needed to get out of there. I called my friend April and removed myself from the situation and haven't looked back since."

Jane teared up. She couldn't imagine what it was like to be beat by the person who was supposed to love her. Patty was even stronger than Jane could ever be. Jane gave Patty a huge hug and thanked her for sharing her story.

To lighten the mood, Jane said, "Well, you're doing great now. You can go brag to Gino and tell him you have a major league baseball player interested in you."

Patty's face went bright red and she asked, shocked, "Who?"

Jane couldn't help but laugh. "Marc Sullivan, girl. Are you blind? He couldn't take his eyes off you the other day, and he even asked Brady about you."

Patty's mouth hung open. "Marc Sullivan, catcher for the Atlanta Braves, asked about me? You're kidding, right?"

Jane shook her head and said, "Nope, he asked if you were seeing anybody. I told Brady you weren't. I hope that was okay?" Patty was silent for a second. She played with her leftover salad and looked up at Jane. Her face was stiff and not as welcoming as before. "Well, that's fine that you told him that, but I don't plan on getting involved with anyone. I'm done with men."

CHAPTER TWENTY TWO

Brady

Michael was, thankfully, at practice, but he was very quiet and kind of out of it. His swing was off, which was uncommon for him. It was like someone sucked all the energy out of him, leaving only a corpse of a body walking around. After practice, Brady pulled Michael to the side in the training room while they iced off their abused muscles.

"Michael, hey, do you want to go get a bite to eat after this?"

Michael looked a little annoyed at Brady. What was that about?

"Uh, I don't know Brady. I'm really not in the mood for company," Michael replied. Brady just watched him as he iced off his shoulder. Michael wouldn't look him in the eye.

Brady grabbed Michael's shoulder and made Michael turn toward him. Michael shoved Brady away from him and pushed Brady into the ice machine.

"What the fuck, dude?" Brady yelled.

Michael looked like he was about to rip someone's head off. Marc and Austin appeared, as if out of nowhere, and made sure no one would get hurt or into any trouble. The organization didn't like players getting in fights with each other.

"Just back the fuck off, Brady. I don't need your charity."

Charity? Why would Brady treat Michael like he was charity? Brady thought they were friends. What the hell? Something must be really bothering Michael. Brady decided to push Michael a little further to see if Michael would open up more. Michael wouldn't get over whatever was bothering him until he got it all out in the open.

"I thought we were friends, Michael. Are you being a complete dick right now because you're still in love with Jane?"

Next thing Brady knew, he was on the ground; Michael was on top of him with his arm cocked back, fist clenched, ready to punch Brady in the face. Austin and Marc grabbed Michael instantly and pulled him off of Brady. Brady was pissed.

"Don't stop him," Brady said to Austin and Marc as he got up. "Let him punch me, let me be his punching bag for whatever the fuck is bothering him. God forbid he should actually talk to us about it."

Austin and Marc let Michael go. Michael just stood there as he breathed heavily; rage burned in his eyes. He stood up straight in front of Brady, inches from his face. Brady just whispered, "Do it, you know you want to."

Michael

Michael couldn't help himself. He punched Brady square in the jaw. His hand stung like hell, but for a moment, it felt so right. For just that moment, all his problems faded into black and there was instant gratification from the punch he threw at Brady. But it was just temporary.

Shit, he needed some more ice. Brady took the punch like a man and then asked for more. What was his problem? Why did Brady want to fuel his fire? Michael went to go punch him again and Brady grabbed his hand, twisted his arm and turned him around so his back was against Brady's chest.

Brady wrapped his arms around him and whispered in his ear, "Go ahead, try again."

Michael lost all control. His mind went black. He could kill Brady right now he was so mad. Why did Brady get Jane and he got stuck with Kelly, who turned out to be a giant hooker? Brady didn't deserve Jane. He was just a good looking guy who swept her off her feet. Michael was the one who had an emotional connection with Jane; he was the one who deserved to be with her.

Michael elbowed Brady in the chest, Brady buckled over and Michael was about to punch Brady in the head when two sets of strong arms came around him and pinned him to the wall.

Austin and Marc.

Fuck. He started to flail his arms around and kick whatever was in his range, but no matter how hard he tried, he couldn't connect with anything to relieve the pain that was flowing through his chest. Austin and Marc pinned him to the ground and told him to calm down.

Michael shouted, "Don't tell me to fucking calm down. Let go of me. You're not the ones with a wife who is cheating on you with some guy named Dayshon. You don't even deserve her Brady. You're just some pretty boy who always gets what you want. You don't have a connection with her like I do and you never will. If it weren't for me, you never would have had a chance at being with Jane. You're just some lucky fuck who landed a girl that's too good for you."

Brady

Brady stood next to the ice machine, hunched over and gasping for air. Michael definitely knocked the wind out of him with the quick jab to his stomach. Fuck him.

Brady listened as Michael spilled his guts. His wife was cheating on him? That explained Michael's piss poor attitude, sulking, and inability to have the bat make contact with the ball during practice. Brady actually felt bad for Michael, until he said Jane was too good for Brady and that he didn't deserve her. That crossed a line.

Even though Brady didn't want to talk to Michael at the moment, Brady did need to set him straight.

"Michael, I'm sorry about your wife, but you have no right to talk about my relationship with Jane like that. I know you're hurting, but that doesn't give you the fucking right to make me feel like I'm not good enough for Jane. Both you and I know that I have done nothing but help Jane get through the problems she accumulated while dating that jackass George. Now, if you want to actually talk about what's going on in your life and stop blaming me for your problems, I'm ready to listen. Until then, you can fuck off."

With that, Brady grabbed an ice pack and left the training room. Michael seriously could fuck off. Yes, Brady was lucky that

Jane gave him the time of day, but it wasn't like he came in and swept her off her feet. No, he worked his ass off trying to prove to her he was a good guy and helped her realize that she was amazing and deserved to be treated the way he treated her. It hadn't been easy. George really screwed her up, but Brady worked hard to eliminate all the damage George created.

Brady was beyond pissed and his jaw became really tight from clenching his teeth so hard. He grabbed his phone and typed in Jane's number.

"Hey, handsome," Jane's excited voice rang through Brady's ears and instantly calmed him. Her voice was so sweet. He wished she was with him so he could hold onto her and be wrapped in her tender embrace.

"Hey, baby, God I miss you." Brady tried to sound normal, but he came off as weak and needy.

"Brady, are you okay? You sound upset."

She knew him too well. "Michael and I got in a fight. I let him punch me so he could let some anger…"

Jane interrupted him. "You what?! Where did he punch you? Are you okay? Oh my God, I'm going to kill him."

Brady couldn't help but chuckle. Jane was five foot nothing and Michael was all muscle and towered over her. She didn't stand much of a chance.

"I'm fine, babe. He got me on the jaw…"

"Oh my God! He punched your face? Don't worry, I'll catch the next flight out there."

Brady laughed out loud this time, then was interrupted by Jane. "I don't find this very funny, Brady Matthews. So I don't understand why you are laughing when I'm over here about to either cry or have a panic attack."

Great, now Brady felt like a giant ass. He didn't want to worry Jane, he just needed to hear her voice. He wasn't feeling too hot, and he just needed some reassurance about their relationship. Although, it was nice to hear that she would jump onto the next flight just because he got punched in the jaw.

"Aw, baby, I'm sorry. I didn't mean to upset you. Michael just said some things that made me feel a little off and I needed to hear your voice."

"What did Michael say to you and don't tell me not to worry about it. I want to hear exactly what happened, Brady. I don't like that my boyfriend is fighting with one of my best friends."

Brady exhaled. He should have known Jane was going to want to know everything. He didn't want to tell her what Michael said, but Lord knows she'd find out at some point. Brady took the next couple of minutes to relay everything that happened, why he pushed Michael into getting physical and why he let Michael punch him.

He could tell Jane wasn't happy, because she was dead silent on the phone when he finished.

"Babe, please say something."

Jane

If Brady was in her view right now, she would punch him right in the gut, then kiss him all over. Why would he provoke Michael to punch him? She never would understand why guys had to be all macho with each other. They might as well have pulled their pants down and compared the size of their wieners.

"Brady, I appreciate you trying to help Michael out, but I wish you had gone about it differently. I don't like that you're willing to get punched in the face. I plan on looking at that mug of yours for the rest of my life and I don't want it all battered and bruised."

Did Jane just say the rest of her life? Did she mean that? She must have if it just flew out of her mouth. Most likely Brady was going to pick up on that comment.

"The rest of your life?" Brady replied.

Damn, could he have paid attention to anything else she said? No, he had to pick up on the one little sentence she wished he didn't. Did she want to spend the rest of her life with Brady? One thing she knew for sure at that moment was that she couldn't imagine life without him.

Jane threw in the towel and said, "Yes, Brady, I have plans for us too. I know I'm taking it slow, but all I know right now is, I have to be with you and I can't imagine you not being in my life. I'm committed to you."

Brady was silent for a second and then she heard him exhale. "Jane, you don't even know how great that makes me feel."

"Can you just do me one favor?" Jane asked.

"Anything, sweet thing, name it."

"Please make things alright with Michael. He's one of my best friends, and I can't imagine having to get in between the two of you."

"You got it, babe. I'll stop by his place tonight and fix things."

Jane felt relieved. Brady would make everything okay. She just hoped Michael would talk to Brady. Michael could be stubborn sometimes. Normally, Jane would talk to Michael and find out what was going on because he would tell her everything, but she sensed that might not be the best idea. It seemed like Michael thought Jane belonged to him. She wanted to keep this fight between the boys and maybe Brady could start to help Michael out, instead of Michael always relying on Jane to help him.

"Thank you, handsome. Hey, by the way, I've been doing some thinking."

"Good thinking or bad thinking?" Brady asked hesitantly.

"Good thinking. When you get back to Atlanta, I think I want to maybe go pick out a new comforter for your bedroom, you know, since I'll be spending the night there more often."

"What, you don't like my comforter?" Brady asked, chuckling.

"It's not my favorite. You would think someone with as much money as you and the potential to bring girls home would have a really nice down comforter, but no. You have one that looks like it's from the 90s with geometric shapes and Aztec patterns."

Brady laughed. "Hey, I never said I was good at decorating. Maybe when I get back, we can do a little shopping and you can help me pick some things out, things that will make the house more ours rather than mine."

"I would like that a lot."

Jane got excited. Yes, she could see herself moving in with Brady sometime in the near future. She would give it a month. She wanted to move in now, but she didn't want to seem too desperate. One thing she realized being away from him while he was at spring training was the time they had together was precious and they should not spend it apart in separate places. Brady wanted to open his house to her and she should take advantage of it, so she could be closer to him whatever chance she got. Maybe she should move some things in there before Brady got back to surprise him.

Michael

Michael lounged on his couch, sipping a beer and eating pizza when someone knocked on his door. Irritated, he got up to answer it. He didn't want any company, and he by no means wanted to talk to anyone after what happened earlier in the training room. He opened the door and deflated. What was Brady doing at his apartment? Didn't he get enough earlier in the training room?

"What the hell do you want?" Michael asked.

Brady looked sincere when he said, "Listen, Michael, I just wanted to come over and make peace with you. I don't like fighting with my teammates, and I'm truly concerned about you."

Damn, Brady was an annoyingly good guy. Michael got pretty heated in the training room and let his emotions get the best of him. He thought he would be happy to get away from Kelly and her open for business pussy, but he still couldn't help but feel like he failed.

He was so mad about Kelly that he took his anger out on Brady. Michael was jealous that Brady was with Jane. Michael wasn't sure if he was jealous because Brady took Jane away or if he was jealous that Brady was in such a great relationship; maybe a combination of both. That didn't mean he had to be a dick to Brady, though. Brady had been nothing but nice and accepting toward him ever since Michael was traded to the Braves. Brady took him in and made him feel welcome.

Michael shook his head in embarrassment and let Brady in. "I'm sorry, man," Michael said, while he rubbed his jaw. "I said some things that I shouldn't have and took my problems out on you."

"It's alright, bud. Now tell me what's going on."

Michael was shocked that Brady accepted his apology just like that, as if nothing had happened between them. Brady was a much bigger man than he was. Michael would have at least put up a little bit of a stink. Damn, he felt like a total idiot.

Michael tossed Brady a beer and offered him a piece of pizza. Brady grabbed a slice and sat on the couch. Michael started from the beginning, how Kelly used to be this amazing girl and then the spotlight changed her completely. He told him about the move and how he noticed she started to distance herself and the lies about where she was during the days and even the nights. He told Brady how he walked in on Dayshon and Kelly fucking in his bed and how he asked Kelly to be out of the house by the time he got back from spring training.

Brady sat on the couch and listened intently until Michael was done. God, he felt a little better. It was nice to get all his pent-up anger off his chest. Damn, he hated to admit it but to share his feelings with someone other than Jane wasn't bad. It felt good to talk to Brady, because he was able to understand where he was coming from about failing at being a man and a husband.

Brady chimed in, "Bud, you didn't fail. I want you to know that. Kelly was the one who failed you. You did everything you could to make things better between you two, and that was all you could do. She was the one who failed you, broke her vows, and disappointed you. It hurts, I know. I've been there, but what you need to take away from this is that you tried your hardest, and sometimes you can do everything in your power to make things right, but if the other person isn't in it, the relationship is going to fail. It takes two to make things work."

Michael thought about that for a second. Brady was right. Michael did everything he could to try to make Kelly happy, but it was never good enough. How could he ever live up to her standards when she set him out to fail no matter what? Maybe the only thing Michael failed at was his judgment of character.

"Thanks, man, you're right. Once she got a taste for the spotlight, there was no way I was going to be able to salvage what we had."

Brady took a swig of his beer. "It happens to the best of us sometimes. Some people aren't strong enough to survive the pressures of being a celebrity. It takes over their bodies. The same thing happened to Laney Johnson, the girl I was dating. She became a media whore."

Michael knew about Laney Johnson; she would do anything for a little bit of publicity. He wasn't quite sure how a nice guy like Brady got wrapped up with the likes of her, but that was a story for a different day.

"You know, Brady, you're a pretty good guy. I'm sincerely glad Jane is with you. If she couldn't be with me, I guess you'll do," Michael said jokingly.

Brady gave him a playful shove. "I appreciate you bowing

out for me."

They both laughed and spent the rest of the night joking around, drinking beers, and watching *Sports Center*. Michael was glad Brady came over; he sent a text message to Jane.

Michael: Hey, Janey bear, thanks for encouraging Brady to come over tonight. I know you had a part in that.

Brady looked over his shoulder and asked, "Are you trying to steal my girl away again?"

Michael laughed. "It wouldn't be very hard," he said jokingly.

Brady playfully punched his arm. "Ha, you wish!"

Michael thought, he did wish, but if he couldn't have her, Brady was a perfect replacement. He got a message back from Jane.

Jane: You know I like to keep the peace. I hope everything worked out.

Michael: Yeah, Brady helped me deal with some demons I've been facing. He's a good guy.

Jane: I seem to think so as well. Tell him I love him for me.

Gross, Michael wasn't going to say that. Brady seemed to notice Michael's face and asked, "What did she say?"

Michael joked, "Oh that she wishes she could jump my bones right now, but wanted to make sure I didn't tell you."

"In your dreams, buster. She prefers white chocolate."

Michael laughed, that she did.

CHAPTER TWENTY THREE

Jane

Jane put together some items to take over to Brady's house. He would be home tomorrow and she wanted to surprise him with some fresh flowers throughout his house, some pictures of them together and some new edible lotions she found at a specialty shop.

The last couple of weeks had been hard, but Brady and Jane talked every night, they even tried phone sex once. Jane couldn't help but giggle, and she could tell Brady got a little irritated on the phone from her lack of maturity. She couldn't help herself, though. She felt awkward describing the way she would pleasure herself to him. He said that they would practice when they got home, because he didn't know if he could survive on the road without it. He was just a horn dog and needed to learn to control his urges.

Things with Michael and Brady were going great. Brady said they were getting along and had really grown close. Brady helped Michael through his divorce emotionally and, in return, Michael supplied the beer. Men!

Patty was the best thing that had happened to Jane's business in a while. She was a very take-charge kind of girl. She didn't act like the boss, by any means, but she got things done before Jane could even ask. If Patty didn't slow down, she'd have to give the girl a raise.

Patty worked on a new website for JB Events and helped with marketing the business. Marc continued to show his interest in

Patty. He sent her e-mails and tried calling the office a couple of times. Patty was polite and talked to him, but never really showed him any interest in return. She stood strong with her no men policy. Poor Marc.

Luke left for his training; Molly thought he actually went on a mission, but just told her it was training because he didn't want to worry her. Jane was worried for Molly no matter what, even if it was just training. The government didn't really care what went on in their operators' personal lives and Jane had a bad feeling that Luke would miss the wedding. The thing that really frustrated Jane was that she didn't know how Molly could do it. The poor girl didn't get any correspondence from Luke at all, so they would have to approach her wedding week having no clue if the groom would be able to attend.

Molly's bachelorette party was tomorrow night, and Jane was excited about it. Albert reserved their usual room at Deuces, but decorated it with dick paraphernalia. Jane knew it was tacky and cliché, but nothing would be better suited for Molly. She worshipped the male genitalia. Albert also booked a male stripper, which made Jane cringe. Was she the only girl who didn't want to have a random man's dick flapping in her face? Maybe she would have to help replenish food when the guy showed up. What did Albert say he was? A policeman or a fireman? They really wanted Mr. Ex-rated commando, but apparently he was all booked up.

It was going to be a good night. Jane couldn't wait, and after the penis festivities were over, she hoped to join Brady at his house for some much-needed cuddle time. He wanted her to come over for sure, but she said that she would most likely stay with Molly, so she had someone to watch over the drunken mess she was going to be, but there was a slight possibility she might be able to go to him. Albert stepped in and said he would take puke duty because he knew how, in his words "horny" Jane was. She didn't care. She was so excited to see Brady.

Jane gathered her items and went over to Brady's house to set them up. She couldn't wait. She only wished she could be there to see his reaction. She kind of wanted to move everything in and she knew Brady would be the first one to help her, but she wanted to make sure she felt comfortable at his place first before she did anything too permanent.

Tomorrow night would be great. She was going to

celebrate with her friends, and then she was going to go get her some Brady Matthews.

Molly

Molly still hadn't heard from Luke, but that wasn't a surprise; she very rarely did when he was training. She was lucky if he sent her a quick note. She wasn't going to worry about Luke tonight, though, because it was her bachelorette party. She was so excited, even though she felt bad that Luke didn't really get a bachelor party. She promised him a fantastic striptease when he got back.

Molly put on the skimpy hot pink number she got on clearance from Macy's. It was short, tight and completely inappropriate, but so perfect for the bride to be. She put on her yellow high heels and was on her way.

She wondered what the place was going to look like. She didn't want the party anywhere other than Deuces, that was her go-to bar, and she wouldn't dream of going anywhere else. If Albert had anything to do with the planning, there would be dicks everywhere and definitely a stripper. She got giddy just thinking about all the dicks that would be flying about tonight.

Molly got to Deuces and Jane greeted her outside.

"Hey gorgeous, look at you…you are one big slut bag tonight!" Jane said.

Molly laughed, "Did you expect any less from me? I'm so fucking pumped for tonight I can't wait to get liquored up. Hey, have you seen Brady yet? Didn't he get back today?"

Jane sighed, "Yes, he did. I haven't seen him yet because I've been doing things for you, silly. I'll see him later tonight when I'm all loose from the booze. Albert said he'll be going home with you tonight. He enjoys watching you make a fool out of yourself when you're wasted."

"Oh great, I should expect to see pictures of my drunk ass online tomorrow then. He is notorious for getting the ugliest shot of you and then posting it for the world to see," Molly said.

"Yeah, but don't worry. We'll get that little queen back one day."

They walked inside and Molly was fantastically surprised when she walked into their room. Not only was there a dick on every corner of the wall, but all the food was dick-shaped as well. Oh, how she loved her friends.

"This is perfect! I've never seen so many dicks in my life; I'm in heaven."

Jane handed her a drink and said, "You are one strange girl."

Jane

Jane felt pretty good by now, they had played pin the dick on "Luke," match that dick (which was basically matching a dick to its corresponding ball sac) and they had suck-the-dick contests. That was what really sent Jane over the threshold from tipsy to drunk. She didn't know she had it in her to suck so hard. The harder you sucked, the faster you drank, the faster you drank the more the other team had to drink afterwards. It basically was a game designed to make everyone drunk off their asses.

The stripper came, and that was Jane's cue to go see how Brady was doing. She stepped outside to give him a quick call. The phone rang twice and went to his voicemail…that was weird. She left him a message.

She was about to walk back inside when someone tapped her on the shoulder; she turned around and came face to face with George. Shit!

"Well, well, well, if it isn't Miss Popular. How's your baseball player boyfriend?"

George slurred his words and wasn't able to keep himself standing still, although she wasn't faring so well in that department either. He'd let his hair grow out, so it curled behind his ears and his beard was two days past a shave. His clothes were disheveled and he reeked of alcohol.

"What do you want, George?"

He pinned her against the wall and whispered with his scotch-soaked breath, "You." He started to slide his hands up her arms and she screamed. He clamped his hand over her mouth.

"Don't you fucking dare scream right now. I have about 100 pounds on you, and I'll take you down so fast. I just want to see what the big deal is. I was going to marry you and don't remember you being so special that a famous baseball player would want anything to do with you."

George slid his hand across her breasts. She tried to kick him, but he pinned her legs down with his and then she gasped from his erection pressing against her center. No. This could not be happening right now. The only thing she could think to do was press dial on her phone again, maybe Brady would pick up and hear them.

"You've lost weight; you're all skin and bones. No one likes to fuck a skeleton. Does your boyfriend get his jollies from fucking a pile of bones? There must be something completely wrong with him."

Jane shook her head and freed her mouth. "George, get the fuck off of me; please don't do this."

"What do you think I'm going to do? Rape you? Get real. I'd rather go fuck a rusted old tin can right now. You're trash, always have been and always will be. You really think I was going to marry you? I just proposed to you to get a promotion, but then you fucked that up by walking in on me and Rebecca. God, does she have delicious tits," George said as he reflected. "You think you're all special because your business is still afloat? Well, reality check you dumb bitch…you are going to fail. You'll never be anything more than a sorry excuse for a woman. Do that baseball player a favor and go jump off a cliff."

Jane couldn't help herself; she began to cry like an idiot. George knew how to press all the right buttons. He knew exactly how to hurt her, and he was doing a pretty good job of it at the moment. Jane just wanted to go see Brady. George was wrong. Brady loved her and saw her for who she was. He didn't think she was trash or worthless.

Jane tried to push George away, but instead, he stopped her from moving and slapped her right across her face. The entire right side of her face lit up in flames. Holy crap that stung. She thought her eye swelled shut right away, but it was just hard to move it.

George slammed her to the ground, which made her wince in pain, and he said, "Good luck with lover boy. News is, his girlfriend Laney is in town. Now that is a woman Brady belongs with, not some white trash nobody like you."

With those parting words, George left her on the ground in the alleyway of the bar. She stayed there for a while and cried her eyes out. Was George right? Did Brady really deserve someone else? Was she not good enough for him? She was just about to get up when she heard a scream and then all of a sudden, soft hands touched her side.

"Oh my God, Jane, are you okay? What happened?"

Albert was at her side, caressing her back, and pulling her into his arms. She broke down again in tears. Albert rocked her back and forth and whispered in her ear that it would be okay. He asked again, "What happened, sweetie?"

Jane, in between sobs said, "George...found...me."

Albert swore under his breath and pulled her in tighter. "What did he say to you?"

Jane could barely get any words out, she was so upset. She just shook her head. She didn't want to talk about it. All she wanted was Brady and his loving arms.

Albert must have sensed that she didn't want to talk about what happened, because he said, "Listen, girl, you go to Brady's and have him take care of you, alright? Give him a call on the way over."

"I can't leave Molly; it's her bachelorette party."

"Sweetie, she's talking to her shoes right now, because she thinks they're her friends. I highly doubt she will even know you left."

Jane nodded and started to get up, Albert helped her. He walked her to her car. George had slapped the sober back into her and she was ready and alert to drive. Albert gave her a kiss on the cheek and told her to take care of herself. She pulled out her cell phone and tried to call Brady again; his phone went to voicemail once more. What was he doing that was so important he couldn't answer her phone calls?

CHAPTER TWENTY FOUR

Brady

Brady was in his pool swimming around. He didn't even bother to put his trunks on. When he got home, he just stripped down to his briefs and jumped in. He noticed all the little touches Jane made to his house when he was gone at spring training. His heart melted when he saw she'd put pictures of them around the house...and fresh flowers. Even though he wasn't a flower kind of person, they still made the house homier and more like Jane.

He loved to take a late-night dip in the Atlanta heat. Plus, he hoped Jane would be done with her maid of honor duties soon and take part in a little late night skinny dipping with him. God, he couldn't wait to see her. He unlocked the door for her so she could just pop in.

As he floated on his back, he heard the sliding glass door pop open. He lifted his head and started to swim to the side to go greet Jane when he stopped in his tracks.

"Hey, hot stuff, spring training has served you well."

Laney Johnson.

"What the fuck are you doing here?" Brady asked, as steam blew out of his ears.

"Well, I was expecting a different greeting, but I'll give you that one. I heard you were back in town and wanted to see if you wanted to take me for a go around the bases? I've been practicing third base and I'm ready to make you squirm. I've missed you."

Brady got out of the pool and grabbed his towel to wrap it around his waist. God, just the sound of her voice made him cringe. No way in hell did he want those plastic lips of hers anywhere near his dick.

"Have you completely lost your mind? Get the fuck out of here! I want nothing to do with you, Laney. Don't you remember you cheated on me? Why the hell would I take you back?"

Laney got closer and rested her hand on his chest, Brady tore away. "Oh, come on, Brady, you never used to shy away from my touch before. You know you want me. I know how hard your dick would get when I would strip for you or suck your dick till you had nothing left inside you."

Brady needed to get her out of here. He would admit it…she did turn him on when they were dating, but now he had no feelings for her at all. Whenever he saw her, all he could think of was how ashamed he was that he ever dated and fell for such a cheating fame-whore. He didn't need Laney, he had Jane who was sweet and sultry with no yearning to be in the spotlight whatsoever. He was in love with Jane and nothing would change that.

Brady grabbed her by the arm and escorted her toward the door. Laney pulled away and wrapped her arms around his waist.

"Seriously, Laney, get off of me. I'm with someone else. Someone who I love more than anything; I plan on marrying her, and there's nothing you can do to stop us."

Laney slid her arms up Brady's chest and wrapped her arms around his neck, "You want to bet?"

Right when Brady was about to push her aside, Jane walked through Brady's front door. His breathing completely stopped at the sight of her. Her makeup was smeared from crying and she had what looked like the start of a very serious black eye. What the hell happened to her? Did she try to call him? Fuck, his phone was inside when he was in the pool.

The look on her face made his heart shatter into a million pieces. It was like someone reached through her mouth down her throat and ripped her heart out. Brady threw Laney to the side and told her to get out.

Laney smiled, blew him a kiss goodbye and said, "You know how to get ahold of me." As she walked past Jane, Laney added, "I hope you know, I've been texting your boyfriend for a while now and even sent him a naked picture of myself, but I'm sure he told you all about that." And with that, she walked out of the house.

FUCK! This did not look good at all. Not only was Laney implying that something happened between them, but he was also wearing a towel around his waist and was bare-chested while she had her arms wrapped around him. Brady went to go grab Jane and tell her it wasn't what she thought, but she stormed off to her car.

He chased after her and put his hand on her door before she could open it fully. He grabbed her by the arms and turned her toward him. "Jane, please listen to me."

She pushed his arms away and screamed, "Don't you fucking touch me! Don't you dare come near me, Brady Matthews. You are a liar and a cheat, and you disgust me." She tried to open her door again.

"Jane, please listen; it's not what you think at all."

"Isn't that what they all say? It's not what you think, baby, I swear," Jane said in a mocking voice. "Do NOT come near me; I'm not kidding Brady. I want nothing to do with you. You are a fucking liar. You swore you would never cheat on me. You told me how you would never cheat because you got your heart broken the same way. I'm so stupid for listening, because here you are in some passionate embrace with your ex. Well, congratulations asshole, you broke my heart. I hate you! We are through. Don't even try calling me."

And with that, she got in her car and drove off. Brady stood in his driveway, completely stunned. His whole life was over in a matter of minutes. Everything he worked so hard for was just washed away. Jane was gone and wanted nothing to do with him. He could barely breathe, his heart was hurting so badly. What could he do, and how the hell could he explain what happened?

He saw flashes of light from the bushes in the distance. Fucking fantastic. The paparazzi must have documented the entire encounter, most likely thanks to Laney and her loud mouth.

He went inside to put some clothes on, so he could run over to Jane's place. He wasn't going to let her continue to think he'd cheated on her with Laney. There was no way he'd let Jane end things with him over something that never happened between him and Laney. He got inside his house and saw his phone on the counter in the kitchen. He looked at it, three new voicemails.

Fuck.

First voicemail...

"Hey, handsome, it's me. I just wanted to call you and tell

you I can't wait to see you later. Molly is completely wasted right now. She was going around the whole room at one point grabbing everyone's crotch. I should be leaving in an hour or so; I can't imagine Molly lasting any longer than that. I love you so much. Bye."

He hoped to God that wasn't the last time he would hear her say those three perfect words to him.

Second voicemail sounded like there were two people scuffling around. Then he heard a man's voice. Who the hell was that? There was no way she would cheat on him. Brady listened harder and noticed the guy was being a real dick to Jane and said some awful things, things he could never imagine saying to a woman, even Laney. Then he heard Jane say George's name. Brady's body went completely numb with anger. Son of a bitch. He heard a loud slap as the phone sounded like it tumbled to the ground. All Brady wanted to do was reach through the phone and kill George. That mother fucker slapped her across her face. Brady's blood boiled. He wanted to nail that bastard. He didn't even want to hear the third one, but he listened to it anyway.

"Hey Brady, (sniffling) I'm coming over now. George attacked me in the alley and said some really awful things. I really need you right now. I know we haven't seen each other in a while, but I just need you to hold me and tell me how much you love me. I'm not doing so well right now. See you soon."

Fuck, fuck, fuck.

Jane

Jane's heart pounded so fast she thought she might have a heart attack. She drove like maniac and didn't even know where she was headed. She sure as hell wasn't going home, because that was where she assumed Brady would go. Molly's place wasn't an option, because Jane couldn't deal with Molly's drunk ass right now and Albert would be taking care of Molly; therefore, he wouldn't be home. Maybe she could go to Michael's house?

Her phone rang, and she looked down at the caller ID; Brady was calling her. There was no way she was going to talk to him, so she ignored his phone call.

She could barely see through her tears. The road was completely blurry, thanks to her tears and bruised eye. She needed to try to focus on the road. The last thing she needed was to get in a car accident. She wanted to call Michael, just to make sure he was home and not in any kind of argument with his wife. That would be awkward to walk in on.

Jane pulled her phone out and started to dial Michael's number when she looked up real quick to make sure she was still on the road, and that was when her heart sank. A little black and white dog ran out in the middle of the road, causing Jane to swerve so she would miss him. She slammed on her brakes to slow down her out-of-control car, but was too late because she ran straight into a telephone pole.

Her air bag exploded in her face as her head flew forward. Her leg instantly started to shoot pain all the way through her body. She couldn't move it, because it felt like her car formed a vise grip all the way around it. She blacked out from the immense pain she felt.

She didn't know how long she was out, but when she woke, she woke to sirens and flashing lights surrounding her car. A man in a uniform tried to open her door, but had no luck. He asked if she was alright through the car window. She gave him the thumbs up and nodded her head, then regretted the movement instantly. Her head and neck were throbbing with pain and she could no longer feel her leg.

The paramedics had to use the Jaws of Life to get the door off her car and get her out of the smashed-up interior. When she was in the ambulance hooked up to a bunch of different machines, they asked if they could call anyone for her. She thought about it for a second. Well, she wasn't going to call Brady…that was for damn sure. So she told them to call Michael Banks, whose number was in her phone.

Michael

Michael's phone rang and startled him from his sleep. What time was it? He looked at the clock on his nightstand, noticing the late hour. When he reached for his phone and saw it was Jane, his heart sank. He answered frantically.

"Hey, is everything okay?" He was confused. Wasn't she with Brady?

"Is this Michael Banks?" said a strange man. Michael's

heart sank even further than he thought possible. Who the hell was he talking to?

"Yes, this is. Is everything okay? Where's Jane?"

"Jane is on her way to the hospital. She got in an accident and asked us to call you. The ambulance is taking her to St. Joseph's hospital."

"Shit, is she okay?"

"She'll be okay, sir. When you get to the front desk, just ask what room she's in."

"Thank you."

Michael ended the call on his phone and raced around his room trying to find clothes to put on. Holy crap his heart was pounding fast; he thought he might have an anxiety attack. Why did she call him and not Brady? Something must have happened between the two of them for her to call Michael instead. Did Brady even know that Jane got in a car accident? He should know, even if he did something to piss her off. He deserved to know. Michael called Brady.

Brady answered the phone, "Is Jane with you?" He sounded panicked. "I'm at her apartment, and she's not here. I'm starting to freak out, man."

So, something did happen. Man, if Jane got in a car accident because of Brady, he would want to kill himself.

"She's not with me right now." Michael heard Brady swear. "But, before you hang up," Michael added quickly, "I got a call from the paramedics who had Jane's phone. She got in a car accident and is on her way to the hospital."

"What?" Brady shouted in Michael's ear; he had to pull the phone away for a second, so he didn't lose his hearing from Brady's yelling. Brady continued. "Is she okay? Why didn't she call me? Holy shit, I think I'm going to have a heart attack."

"Brady, calm down; she's alright. I don't know why she called me. Did you guys get in a fight tonight?"

Brady swore some more. "You could say that. Shit, Michael, my life is falling apart at the seams. The one thing that is supposed to be constant in my life is in some hospital right now." Michael could hear Brady's voice starting to break. He felt bad for him. Whatever happened tonight must have been some serious miscommunication.

"Hey, listen, meet me at the hospital; you can wait in the

waiting room with me and you can tell me what happened. Listen, though, I'm not going to let you see her until she wants to see you, and I'll make sure the nursing staff knows that. If she's mad at you right now, we don't need her any more upset than she is, understood?"

"I understand, thank you. Where are they taking her?"

"St. Joseph's, meet you there."

Michael hung up the phone. This was not what he expected to do tonight, but his friends needed him. His friends, who had been helping him deal with his own problems. It was his turn to return the favor.

Brady

Brady never drove so fast in his life. He didn't give a flying fuck if he got pulled over. God damn it…he caused Jane to get in an accident. He would never forgive himself for this. He loved her so much. He couldn't believe this had happened. He should have fought harder instead of letting her take off in her car while crying hysterically. He should have held her to the ground and explained everything to her. No, instead he let her take off when she was crying her eyes out to the point where she got in a fucking car accident. Brady slammed his hand on the steering wheel.

Please, God, don't let her be hurt that badly, Brady silently prayed. Brady wouldn't know what to do with himself if she refused to talk to him when he got to the hospital. Brady's throat started to get really tight as he held back tears. He couldn't even imagine what she must be feeling. He couldn't imagine what she thought when she saw Laney in his house holding him around his neck while he only wore a towel. She didn't know he had his boxer briefs on underneath, let alone that he'd been swimming in the pool beforehand while he waited for her to get naked with him and take a dip. Damn it!

He pulled into the parking lot of the hospital, tore himself out of his car, and raced for the entrance, where he ran directly into Michael. He looked just as worried as Brady. Michael clasped Brady's shoulder as they walked through the front doors together and asked the front desk receptionist where they could find Jane Bradley. The receptionist was taken aback a little by the sight of them. She probably didn't expect to see two starting Atlanta Braves players standing in front of her. She sent them in the correct direction.

When they got to the elevator, Michael turned toward Brady asking, "How're you doing man?"

Brady ran his hand through his hair and shook his head. "I feel like I'm going to puke any second now."

"Hang in there, buddy, I'm sure she's going to be okay."

They got to the desk where they'd been directed, and they were told she was in surgery. The attending nurse was nice enough to tell them that she'd crushed her foot in the car accident and had to have some pins put in to stabilize her leg. She also had some cuts that had to be stitched up. Other than that, she was going to be very sore, but alright.

Brady felt a slight bit of relief wash over his body, but he still would be on edge until he could hold her, stroke her hair and tell her how sorry he was and how much he loved her. Until then, he wouldn't feel right. Brady could tell Michael felt awkward.

"Thanks, man, for calling me. I know you didn't have to. I really appreciate it."

"I thought you deserved to know. So, what happened?"

Brady let out a long breath and told Michael everything that happened a little bit ago, but what seemed like hours ago. Reliving the events was torture. All he could picture in his mind was Jane's face of total destruction. He put his head down and massaged his forehead. Michael didn't talk for a little after Brady finished explaining.

"If only I had my phone with me when I was in the pool…"

"Brady, you can't start with the 'what if's.' It's a huge misunderstanding and I'll back you up on that. I know how much you love Jane and that you would never ever get back with Laney. Not after the conversations we've had about our exes."

"Thanks, Michael, you're a good friend. She probably had the worst night of her life because of me and Captain Skinny Dick, George. The things he said to her touched every one of her sensitive spots. She was already so vulnerable and upset when she was driving to my place, then she saw me with Laney and all of her insecurities probably came flooding back to her."

A man in green scrubs came up to Michael and Brady and interrupted them. "Mr. Banks?" Michael and Brady stood up.

"Yes?" Michael answered.

"Miss Bradley is doing just fine. We had to put some pins in her foot and ankle; it was smashed by the engine in the accident. She suffered a concussion, as well as some pretty nasty scrapes from glass on her arm and leg. We stitched her up pretty well, though, so we don't think there will be much scarring. She was pretty lucky. If she swerved any further, she would have flown over the guard rail and rolled down the hill. She owes her life to that telephone pole. She should be ready to take visitors in a little bit."

They both said thank you, and Brady collapsed in his chair. She could have died tonight? He could have lost Jane forever tonight. He was completely at a loss for words. He was so grateful she was going to be okay, but he still couldn't stop thinking about what he could have done differently. What if he told Jane about the texts from Laney prior to the whore showing up at his house unexpectedly? What if he didn't unlock his door and just let Jane use her key? What if he'd brought his phone out to the pool with him?

Michael patted his leg and said, "It's going to be okay, man. Try to relax."

Yeah, that was the last thing he planned on doing right now. He needed to see her. He needed to hold her. "When can we go see her? I can't take this waiting. I need to see for myself that she is okay."

"I'll go in and check on her. Remember what I said; you're not seeing her until she's ready. She doesn't need to be stressed out right now."

All Brady could do was nod his head. He didn't know how he'd react if she didn't want to see him. Didn't serious events like this in a person's life bring them together? Maybe she would want to see him after all. Please, God, let her want to see him, he thought. He felt like his gut was turning itself inside out. He excused himself to the bathroom and throw up in one of the stalls.

Jane

Jane knew she was in the hospital from all the beeping sounds that were rolling through her brain, but why couldn't she see anything or remember anything? Was she sleeping? Was she in a coma? She felt strong hands touch her arm. Her throat was really dry, but she squeaked out a measly, "Brady?"

"No, Janey bear, it's Michael."

Michael, why was he here? Where was Brady? Wait, she told the fireman to call Michael. That's right, Brady didn't give two shits about her; all he wanted and cared about was Laney Johnson. That stupid bitch.

Why couldn't Jane open her eyes? The one side of her face burned badly. Why was it only one side? Her eye felt swollen...oh wait, George. She was attacked in an alley by her ex-fiancé, then she caught her new boyfriend cheating on her with his ex, and then she got in a car accident. Fucking fantastic. But Michael was there; at least he cared about her.

"Brady is here, do you want me to go get him?"

Jane went rigid. Brady was here? Why the hell was he here? She didn't want to see him. She barely opened her eyes. Her one eye wouldn't open at all. She saw Michael's brilliant smile and gave him what she thought was a little smile back.

"No, I don't want to see him." She got choked up. "I hate him so much, Michael." She let out a sob. "I hate him so, so much, but damn me for loving him even more."

Michael grabbed her hand and squeezed it. "Janey, he's hurting out there. He told me what happened, and you have to listen to him."

"I don't want to hear his excuses. I was beaten up by George and he wasn't there for me. Why didn't he answer his phone? Why wasn't he there? Why didn't he tell me about all the texts that bitch sent him?" Jane couldn't stop crying. "Instead, he was with that slut, practically naked in his house."

Michael sighed next to her. "Let's not talk about that right now. You just were in a very bad accident, and we don't need you getting worked up. Are you feeling okay?"

Jane tried to push Brady out of her mind, but that was pretty much impossible. She wanted him to be by her side, to hold her, to tell her how much she meant to him, but that was not going to happen because, right now, she couldn't even stand the sight of him. When she saw Laney hanging all over him, her heart broke in half. She would rather have George beat her and rape her than see Brady with Laney.

Jane realized she hadn't answered Michael's question. "I'm feeling the best I can feel after a car accident. Thank you for coming, Michael. I really appreciate it, but I kind of want to be alone, plus don't you have your season opener tomorrow?"

"Yeah, but that's okay. You're important to me. I want to be here for you."

"Thank you, but you can go home; it's late and I'm tired. Tell Brady to go home too. I don't want to see him, ever."

"Okay, Janey, but please consider letting him see you at some point. I seriously have never seen him like this. He can barely function right now. He loves you so much. You should really listen to him."

"Thank you, Michael, but I don't want to hear his excuses. Good luck tomorrow."

Michael shrugged and gave her a kiss on the cheek. "I'll visit tomorrow, sleep tight."

Jane watched Michael walk out the door, leaving her alone. Once he left, she broke down and cried. This was, by far, the worst day of her life. She had hit rock bottom. She couldn't even talk to Molly or Albert, because they were wasted from Molly's bachelorette party, and the one person she needed the most was the one person who'd betrayed her and broken her heart. Brady was her soul mate, the one person who brought her back from the dead, and he was the one person who broke her heart when she needed him the most. She was so stupid for thinking that she could have someone like Brady. George was right; she was trash and would always be trash.

CHAPTER TWENTY FIVE

Molly

Molly woke up to a beeping in her head. Oh fuck, she was in bad shape. She felt big hairy arms wrapped around her waist. Oh Jesus, she felt around and realized she was in bed with Albert; he was always a spooner. She nudged him to get off her. He released her, stretched his body to the length of the bed and said, "Jesus, Mary, and Boy George am I in pain. Girl, you sure know how to party and grab a crotch."

Molly laughed, "Yeah and you're a little too frisky. I think you held onto my tit all night. If you didn't like the cock so much, you could count on Luke beating you up for your groping hands."

"And I would have loved every moment of it."

Molly slapped his shoulder playfully and called him a pervert. Her phone beeped again. Ugh, who was texting her this early in the morning? She looked at her phone and noticed it was a message from Brady. Molly opened her phone and nearly threw up from the text message she read.

Brady: Jane got in an accident last night and is at St. Joseph's hospital.

She bolted out of bed like a crazed lunatic, threw clothes on her body and tossed her hair up as fast as she could. Albert looked at her with a perplexed facial expression.

"What's going on?"

"Jane got in a car accident last night and is at St. Joseph's."

That got Albert out of bed in seconds. He started to grab

clothes too. He borrowed a sweatshirt from Luke and they jumped in Molly's car and took off toward the hospital.

The whole car ride to the hospital was dead silent. Molly prayed to herself that everything was going to be alright. Jane was her best friend, and she couldn't afford to lose Jane after she had lost so many other important people in her life. When they got to the hospital, they saw Brady in the waiting room. Molly ran up to him.

"How's she doing?"

Brady looked like shit. He definitely did not sleep at all. His eyes looked like he had aged twenty years, and his face was pale white.

"I wouldn't know; she won't see me." He sat down and rubbed his eyes. Had he been crying?

"Brady, what's going on?"

Brady proceeded to tell her that Jane went outside to call him last night during the bachelorette party and, when she was outside, she ran into George. She heard Albert swear under his breath. Come to find out, George had beat up Jane and left her in the alleyway.

"Damn, I can't believe I didn't remember about Jane and George last night. I was so busy taking care of your drunken ass," Albert said to Molly.

Brady glared at Albert, "You knew about George?"

Nervous from Brady's tone, Albert said calmly, "I came out looking for Jane, because she was gone for a while…that's when I found her in the alley…lying on the ground crying. I rushed over to her quickly and took care of her the best that I could. She said she just wanted to be with you, Brady. So I helped her into her car. Is that when she got into a car accident?"

Brady shook his head and continued his story. Apparently, he was swimming when Laney let herself in his house and tried to get Brady into bed with her. Brady wanted nothing to do with it and tried to push her out the door when Jane walked in. Brady became really quiet as his voice faded in and out from holding back tears. Molly could tell he was in an extreme amount of pain. He tried to stop Jane, but she drove off.

Brady ended his story and looked like he would lose his cookies. Molly sat next to him and held his hand.

"I believe you, Brady. I know you'd never do anything to

hurt Jane. You love her so much."

Brady choked on his words. "I do…I don't know what I would have done if I lost her. I can barely function right now, and I have a game tonight. I don't think I'm going to play. I wouldn't be any good for the team right now."

Molly squeezed his hand and said, "Let me see what I can do. Come on, Albert."

They left Brady slouched over in his chair. Her heart was broken for him. She couldn't imagine being in his place. The love of his life was in the hospital, and she refused to see him. Molly wondered how Jane was doing. Was she just refusing to see him because she was so hurt or because she was being stubborn?

Molly and Albert walked into her room. Jane was watching some TV when they saw her. She looked over and her eyes welled up with tears instantly. She looked terrible. Molly tried to put on a brave face for her friend, but her lip started to quiver. Jane's eye was almost swollen shut and she had little cuts everywhere. There were some bandages in places, and her foot was all wrapped up.

Molly flung herself at her friend and began to cry; she couldn't help it.

"Oh, Jane, I'm so sorry this happened to you and I wasn't there. I feel so terrible." Jane squeezed her arms around her and Albert joined in on the group hug.

"I'm so glad you guys are here. I get to go home today, and I was hoping you guys would take me."

"Of course. We'll do whatever you need," Molly said. "I just can't believe this happened. We talked to Brady outside, and he told us everything."

Jane went stiff, "Brady is still here?"

Molly stroked her friend's hair. "Yes, Janey. He's been here all night; he looks like pure shit and is as pale as a ghost. He has a game tonight, and I think he's calling his manager to tell him he can't start tonight. I don't really know how that works. You need to talk to him, Janey."

Albert chimed in, "Yes, you do. Did you listen to him at all?"

"No, and I don't need to; I know what I saw. He broke my heart right in front of me when I needed him most. I can never forgive him for that. I don't want to talk about this. Will you please send him away and take me home. I need to get out of this bed."

Molly nodded and told Albert to watch over Jane while she talked to the nurse to find out any specifics of taking care of Jane. When she left the room, she saw Brady stand up and look at her with hope. God, she needed to help him somehow.

She walked over to him and said, "She still wants nothing to do with you. I'm sorry, Brady. She won't even talk about it."

Brady looked defeated. He sank back in his chair and put his head between his hands. "Molly, I don't know what to do. I'm losing myself here. If I don't see her soon, I might go crazy. I have to see her. I have to hold her and make sure everything is alright. Please help me."

Molly looked at Brady as her heart dropped for the poor guy. She believed him and knew he deserved to see her; he did nothing wrong and deserved a chance to explain himself. She pulled him to his feet and told him to come with her. They talked to the attending nurse together and found out the specifics of Jane's care and what prescriptions needed to be filled.

Molly turned to Brady and told him she had a plan. "I want you to be able to talk to Jane, so we're going to make sure that happens. Albert and I are going to take her home. I want you to fill her prescriptions while we take her back to her place and get her settled in. When you get the prescriptions and come back to her apartment, Albert and I will act like we're going to go fill the prescriptions, and we will let you in her apartment. That will give you a chance to talk to her, and no one will be around to interrupt you two."

Brady wrapped his arms around Molly and spun her around. "Thank you so much, Molly. You don't know how much that means to me."

"Hey, I know you would do the same for me. You two deserve each other. You just need a little help from the outside."

Brady squeezed her hand and took off to go to the pharmacy. Molly went to go grab Jane and fill Albert in on the switch-a-roo.

Brady

Brady grabbed Jane's medication, some flowers, her favorite chocolates, drinks, and magazines he thought she might like. He was nervous as hell, but no matter what, he wouldn't leave her side…no matter what she said. He talked to his manager and he wasn't happy at all, but knew Brady would be useless tonight anyway, so his manager made up some story about Brady having a tight hamstring. Brady didn't give a damn what his manager said, as long as he got a chance to win Jane back.

He sent Molly a text saying he was outside the door and ready to come in. A couple of minutes later, she popped out of Jane's apartment, gave him a hug and whispered good luck. Brady walked into Jane's apartment and almost broke down. Just the smell of her apartment made his knees weak. He missed her so much, he could barely stand. He placed the bags of pharmacy items he got on her counter and quietly walked to Jane's bedroom. He poked his head in and saw her sleeping on her bed.

The instant he saw her, he rushed to her bedside and started to cry. He didn't care if she saw him cry…he was full of a mixture of emotions, happy to see her, angry about the abuse from George, and incredibly heartbroken to see the love of his life in her bed completely helpless. He gently grabbed her hand, laid his head next to her, and cried.

Jane stirred next to him. "Brady?" She jerked her hand away. "What are you doing here?"

Jane

Jane was shocked to see Brady at her bedside, and even more shocked to see his bloodshot eyes as he cried. She was torn in two; she loved him, but was so heartbroken she could barely look at him.

"Jane, please, I beg you, please let me talk to you."

"Brady, I don't want to see you; I thought I made that clear earlier. Don't you have a game to go to?"

"I called my manager and told him I couldn't play tonight; I need to be with you."

Brady wouldn't miss his game because of her? Lord, if the fans knew he missed the season opener because of her, she'd be tarred and feathered by everyone in Atlanta. He was, by far, one of the favorites on the team, and he was idolized in Atlanta.

"Well, go call him back, because you're not staying here. Go home, Brady. I have nothing to say to you."

Brady looked so pathetic she had to turn away. If she

looked at him any longer, she was going to give in and hold him. She couldn't though; he was with Laney.

"Jane, you need to listen to me, please." He cried some more, his voice was tight and full of sorrow. She couldn't even listen to him…it made her heart hurt so badly. She couldn't say anything, because her throat was tight as well. He continued.

"I will never forgive myself for what happened to you. I've been beating myself up about it."

Jane let out a little sob. "Oh, so you do actually care about me; I thought you just liked to go around breaking my heart."

Brady cringed at her nasty tone. "Baby, I care about you more than anything; you have to know that."

"Do NOT call me baby. I'm not your baby; we're done here Brady. You know how I feel about cheaters. If you don't get out of here in the next five minutes, I'm going to call the cops."

"Jane, don't do this to us; please, let's just have a conversation about this."

Jane flashed a death look at Brady and gritted her teeth, "There is no more us, Brady. The sooner you recognize that, the better."

Jane lifted herself out of her bed, grabbed her crutches, and headed toward the kitchen. She noticed a bunch of bags on the counter from the pharmacy. She swore Molly's name and cursed her out for putting Jane in this position with Brady. She opened her front door in the most awkward way possible, thanks to her crutches, grabbed the bags of "sorry items" Brady had gotten her, and threw them in the hallway.

She turned to Brady, pointed one crutch out the door, and said, "Get the fuck out of here and stay the fuck out of my life."

Brady bowed his head in disappointment and walked out. She slammed the door shut and then she fell to the ground and sobbed. She just kicked the man she loved out of her life. She hated that she still loved him. Why did she still have to love him? It wasn't fair to still have feelings, strong feelings, for someone who ripped your heart out. She wished she could just turn her feelings toward Brady off; life would be much simpler then.

CHAPTER TWENTY SIX

Brady

Brady played in his opening game and the opening series. He was present and in the lineup, but his head was nowhere close to being in the game. Jane hadn't answered any of his phone calls, text messages, or e-mails, and she didn't open her door when he came by her apartment. He tried talking to Molly and Albert, but they said they needed to respect Jane's wishes, even though they believed him. Michael was the same way. Brady felt lost, alone, and didn't know what to do.

He had the worst start to his season he'd ever had. He hadn't hit one ball and had committed a handful of errors that normally he never would have made. He was starting to get booed at the stadium and lose all credibility. They had to head out to play the Phillies, and Brady didn't know how he would be able to manage, especially since he would be so far away from Jane.

Life turned into a robotic routine for him. He woke up, worked out, and headed to the stadium. He avoided all press because, thanks to Laney, his face was plastered on all the gossip magazines, as well as Laney's, along with Jane's beat up face when she stood in Brady's driveway. He couldn't get the images out of his head, and the media didn't help.

The sports channels started to nail him in the highlights for letting his personal life affect him, which was true, but in every report, they never failed to show a picture of Jane in the corner of the screen. He could give two shits about the press ragging on him about his game, but why plaster Jane's face everywhere? That was most likely another reason why Jane wouldn't talk to him.

Michael was a decent guy and kept Brady updated on Jane's recovery. It physically made him ill that he was not there, holding her, taking care of her, and making sure she was okay. He had to rely on everyone else to make sure she received the best care she could get. Michael said she hadn't started back at work yet, but Patty held down the fort like a pro and put out all fires that might have started while Jane was away.

The team was supposed to leave tonight to go to Philadelphia. Brady had to pack, but couldn't muster the energy. His phone started to ring and his heart dropped; he prayed Jane might be calling him. Fat chance. It was his manager, Deek Jones.

"Hey, Deek," Brady answered.

"Matthews, I need you in my office in an hour."

"Is everything okay?" Brady started to get nervous. He knew his contract protected him from being traded, so that wasn't a concern he needed to worry about, but he still felt nervous whenever his manger called him into his office.

"Just get here in an hour." Then Deek hung the phone up.

Crap! That wasn't good. Most likely, Deek's phone call was about Brady's performance. He was so not in the mood to be yelled at by his manager. Deek Jones could be one terrifying guy if he wanted to be. Deek had a bit of a pot belly and one serious mustache. He played many years ago and was decent as a ball player, but was, by far, a better manager. He was well-respected and everyone listened to the man and didn't question his actions.

Brady groaned, got up, and started to pack for Philly. He might as well pack now, because he most likely wouldn't have a chance to get back to his house before the team left.

Michael

Michael walked up the steps to Jane's apartment. He had flowers with him and chocolate, per her request. Jane was not faring well. Physically, she was improving every day, but emotionally she was a wreck. She was still madly in love with Brady, no matter how much she denied it; she wasn't fooling anyone.

Michael let himself in with the key she gave him a couple of days ago. It was easier for him to have a key than for her to have to get up and crutch her way to the door to let him in.

He walked into her apartment, enjoying the smell of Jane. Helping her out these last couple of days had really brought up some old feelings he harbored for her, but he had to make sure to keep them under control. He knew his feelings couldn't turn into anything between them; he had no chance with Jane. He'd closed that chapter of his life a couple of weeks ago when Brady helped him through the complications of his marriage.

Michael walked over to Jane, gave her a kiss on the cheek, and delivered her chocolates. He loved the way she ate them. She poked every single one and, depending on what came out, she made her decision if it was worthy enough for her delicious lips. Okay, enough Michael. Feelings about Jane are in the past.

Jane moaned as she put a chocolate in her mouth and Michael nearly keeled over. He searched Jane's kitchen for a vase to put the flowers in, while she destroyed the box of chocolates he brought her.

"These are hitting the spot, thank you Michael," Jane said, with a mouth full of chocolate. "Although, I should probably not be eating these, since I have no way to work them off. I'm going to become a big old fatso, thanks to this bum leg of mine."

Michael placed the flowers in a vase and disagreed with her. "Jane you've had the same rocking body since I met you in college. Believe me, and don't forget I watched you go through your ice cream sandwich for dinner every night phase, I'm pretty sure you're going to be okay with a couple of chocolates."

Jane laughed and patted the seat next to her for Michael to sit down. He sat down and tried to keep his distance. He still didn't trust himself completely, even though he knew he'd tried to shut that part of his brain off.

"When do you leave for Philly?" Jane asked, putting another chocolate in her mouth. It looked like an orange cream filled one, one of his favorites.

"In a couple of hours. I wanted to stop by your place and make sure you were all set for the night. Molly is coming over later, right?"

"Yeah, she has Jane duty later. I feel like such an idiot being waited on. I really can get around on my own, you know."

Michael knew, and he also knew how stubborn Jane was. She would break her other leg just to prove she could do things by herself, but Michael and Molly both agreed that they and Albert would take shifts in watching Jane, because they were nervous about her break-up with Brady. She cried straight through the day the first couple of days, but today, she'd actually started to look human again.

Michael knew Brady felt the same way as Jane, if not worse. Michael wished Jane would just let Brady speak to her. He knew Brady had played terribly because he was completely at loss when it came to love, and Brady couldn't function since he'd hurt Jane so badly.

Jane interrupted his thoughts when she placed her hand on his thigh and her head on his shoulder. "Thank you so much for being there for me, Michael. You've always been there for me, no matter what…even when I was a complete bitch during my George years."

"Well, you do still owe me from dealing with your alter ego," Michael joked, as he tried to get the thoughts out of his head regarding Jane's touch that radiated heat through his body.

She started to rub his leg up and down and sighed. "What am I going to do, Michael?"

Michael didn't know how to answer her question, so he just let it hang in the air. Her touch was starting to affect him a little, so before he embarrassed himself, he got up and asked if she wanted anything to drink.

"You don't have to get me anything, but since you're up, I will take a ginger ale if there are any left. Albert was sucking them down the other night with gin mixed in. Apparently, me crying hysterically was too much for him to handle."

Michael laughed, "Well, you have been a handful lately, but we're here because we love you."

"You mean that, you love me?"

Michael shut the refrigerator door, placed the drinks on the counter, and leaned over the bar as he looked Jane in the eyes. "Jane, I have always loved you, you know that. I have loved you as a friend and I have loved you as more. I always have and always will."

What was he doing? He should just shut up. What happened to closing that chapter of his life? He brought the drinks back to the couch and handed Jane hers. She set it on the table without taking a sip and turned toward him.

She stroked his jaw lightly with her delicate hand and said, "Oh, Michael, I'm so sorry I put you through such hell."

Michael couldn't help but get lost in Jane's eyes. They were full of sorrow and sadness. He knew the sadness was not for him, though; it was for the loss of Brady in her life, but he couldn't help but imagine what it would be like to have the love of Jane that he always wanted. Jane pulled Michael in for a hug. Her breasts pressed against his chest, and he started to get hard. He needed to pull himself away from this situation before he let his feelings take over his actions.

"Jane, don't think twice about it; that's what friends are for."

Michael was about to get up when Jane grabbed his face with both her hands, her face mere inches from his. "Have you ever wondered what it would be like to be more than just friends?"

Michael's heart stopped beating and his breathing was non-existent. Was she for real right now?

"I think about it every day, Janey Bear." Michael was honest with her. He knew he could never have Jane's heart like Brady did, but he knew that if he never said anything, he would regret it.

"Jane, you are the most amazing woman I have ever met and I know I will never meet anyone who comes close to you, but if being your friend is what gets me close to you, then I will forever be your friend and nothing more."

Jane's eyes were watery, and then she did something he never thought she would do. She put one hand on his chest and the other behind his head and pulled herself on his lap. She slowly lowered her hand on his chest as she stroked his muscles up and down.

Michael didn't dare breathe; any slight movement might scare her away. She began to cry, which Michael thought was strange, but she'd been crying a lot recently. She lowered her mouth toward his, and he licked his lips right before her plump lips met his. She slowly kissed him on his mouth, nothing intrusive, just sweet kisses. There was no passion behind them; just the touch of human on human, like their relationship had always been.

Michael couldn't help but think that the passion she had for him would never be at the same level as the passion he had for her. He separated himself from her, and set her on her side of the couch. Breathing heavily, Michael ran his hand over his face.

"What's wrong, Michael? Did you not enjoy that?"

"Jesus, of course I did. I'm so hard for you right now, it's ridiculous." Michael watched Jane blush. "But, the fact is, Jane, you were not enjoying it. I know what it feels like to be kissed by someone who is madly attracted to you and someone who is kissing you out of pity. I'm not mad at you, but you were not kissing me with passion. I don't need your pity, Jane. I've always been fine with being friends with you. I don't want to be your toy to play with to get back at Brady. I don't deserve to be treated like that."

Michael knew he was being harsh, but he needed to be honest. His heart was not hers to play around with. Maybe Brady's, but not his. Jane looked furious; she didn't move for a second and then, out of nowhere, her hand slapped the side of his face. What the hell!

"How dare you accuse me of using you?"

Michael was astonished at first, but once he got his wits about him, he realized what was happening. Jane wanted to turn this around on him. Oh no, he was the one being fucked around with. He shot off the couch and paced the living room.

Finally, he shouted, "If you're not using me, then what the hell are you doing, Jane? You can't sit there and tell me you're not in love with Brady still. I know you are. It is all over your face. What I don't get is why you won't see him and end everyone's misery."

Jane grabbed her crutches and started to get up. "Well, I apologize for making your lives so miserable. I didn't ask for you guys to babysit me twenty-four-fucking-seven. I can do things on my own, so you can take the pity party you've been throwing me and take it somewhere else."

Michael was furious with her. She was being so ungrateful. She started to the door to let him out, but he stopped her in the hallway.

"Really, Jane? Playing the woe is me card a little early, aren't you?"

"Fuck you, Michael! Get the hell out of here."

Michael didn't move a muscle; he wouldn't leave her like this no matter how mad he was. He turned, grabbed her, knocked her crutches down and threw her over his shoulder. He carried her to her bedroom, while she kicked and screamed the whole time, then he threw her on her bed and went back to the kitchen to grab her some food and the ginger ale she never touched. He came back and she was curled up on the bed crying. Michael sighed and sat on the bed next to her. He touched her shoulder and she pulled away.

"Jane, listen I'm sorry I accused you of using me…"

Jane interrupted Michael, "Michael, stop. You were right. I was using you, and that was so beyond fucked-up of me. I'm so sorry."

Jane cried in her hands as she rocked back and forth. Shit, he was right. She was using him. He couldn't help but be furious. He tried to calm himself before he spoke because he didn't want to say anything he would regret later.

"Jane, I'm going to leave; I don't want to deal with this right now. I'm done being in the middle of your relationship with Brady. If you're still in love with Brady, then grow up and deal with your problems. If you don't want anything to do with him, then put the guy out of his misery and tell him. Either way, stop being a child and face your problems head on. It's about time you stop hiding behind everything and using excuses for your problems. I'll let Molly know I left early from your apartment. I'll talk to you later."

Michael grabbed his keys and left Jane to think about what he said. He decided to just drive to the stadium and, hopefully, Brady would be there, because it was about time Michael paid him a little visit.

Jane

Jane just laid there on her bed for a while and thought about how her life had gone from perfectly in love to crying in her bed with a broken leg and her friend yelling at her. She knew she was wrong in using Michael. She felt like a complete shit because she kissed him and, when she kissed him, she knew she felt nothing, nothing at all.

Jane thought about what Michael said. She was not entirely sure what she wanted in her life. She knew her career was right where she wanted it. Her love life, on the other hand, was a pile of trash. She still hurt from seeing Brady with Laney and hearing about how she had been contacting him for a while. Why didn't he tell her? Duh, Jane, because he didn't want her to know he was cheating on her. She felt so much worse than when she found George humping Rebecca's brains out.

She actually trusted Brady and believed him when he told her he would never hurt her. He told her he wanted to be with her forever and make her his wife. Was he fucking Laney when he was telling her that? Or was that just a recent development? Either way, she couldn't seem to stop loving him. She wanted to so badly, but it wasn't like a switch she could just turn on and off.

She realized she had to go to the bathroom, but her crutches were all the way in the hallway near the front door. Annoyed, she crawled off the bed and headed for the bathroom. She was too tired to make it to the bathroom, so instead, she just laid down on the floor for a while and cried as she felt the coldness of the tiles touch her face. Man, she'd hit rock bottom if her bathroom floor was the one soothing thing in her life.

Brady

Brady got to the stadium and went directly to the clubhouse. He dreaded this meeting with his manager, but he had to just get it over with. He knocked on his manager's door, and Deek answered in a gruff voice to come in. Brady entered the office and was instantly smacked in the face with the musky cologne of Deek Jones. He wore a brand that all the guys in the clubhouse called Deek's stink. They were not sure where the man got it, but it must have been fifty years old and out of production. The guys were almost positive that when the company that made the cologne shut down, Deek bought out all of their remaining inventory.

Brady tried to ignore the stench filling his nose and sat down. Deek stood up and paced behind his desk; he looked extremely irritated. He rummaged under some papers on his desk and threw a magazine in Brady's direction. It had Brady and Jane's faces plastered all over the front with the title, "Naked Dispute: Brady's Brunette Exchanged for Blonde Bombshell." Fuck!

"Please tell me this is not the fucking reason you have not had one hit in the last three games and the piss poor excuse for your fielding skills," Deek yelled.

Double Fuck. Anyone who knew what Brady was going

through right now, knew that the reason his performance on the field was so terrible was because of the situation with Jane. Brady could barely function in everyday life, let alone on a field with thousands of people watching him. Brady didn't know how to answer the question. All he could focus on was the picture of Jane on the magazine cover with the look of horror and heartbreak on her face. Brady just lowered his face and shook his head.

"Jesus Christ, Matthews. Are you shitting me? You're seriously letting a girl affect your performance? You're supposed to be a leader on this team, and there you are pussy footing around because your heart is broken. Well, get used to it; it happens to all of us. It's the people who separate their personal lives from the ball field who are the greats. Are you going to be someone who's taken down by their personal life?"

Brady was so furious by now, he was about to lose it. He wanted to reach across his manager's desk and punch him several times in the face. Deek had no clue about the hell Brady had been through in the past couple of days. Brady just shook his head in agreement and didn't look at the bastard.

Deek continued, "Seriously, Matthews, no hits and five errors in three games is beyond pathetic. When did you become such a damn softy? Do I need to coddle you and rock you back and forth, stroking your forehead, while telling you everything is going to be okay? Do you need me to warm you some milk and put your fluffy slippers on your feet and talk about your feelings? Shall I call your mummy and tell her that her little Brady boy needs his mummy? Should I tell the cameras to not focus on you in the dugout so you can suck your thumb in between innings like an infant? I should bench your ass for such poor performance, if it wasn't for your…"

Brady couldn't take it any longer; he jumped out of his chair and threw it across the room.

"Then fucking bench me! I don't give a shit if you don't like the way I've been performing. You have no clue what I've been through in the past couple of days. My girlfriend, who I thought was going to be my wife one day, got beaten up by her ex, she found Laney trying to take me to bed when I wanted nothing to do with her, then Jane wound up getting in a serious car accident, and all I want to do is make sure she's okay, but oh no, she won't fucking see me because she thinks I cheated on her with that bitch, Laney, who set me up and had paparazzi standing outside my house ready to capture the whole disgusting encounter that is now so eloquently displayed on your fucking desk. So, if you want to bench me, please do so. If you want to trade me, please, by all means, go right on ahead. If you want to end my career, please put me out of my misery, because it couldn't be any worse than what I'm going through right now."

Brady turned to leave Deek's office when Deek shouted to him to pick up the chair he threw and sit down. Brady was about to ignore Deek, but something in his head told him to listen. He grabbed the chair and sat down, as he stared the man in the eye.

"Are you done with your temper tantrum?"

Brady just gritted his teeth; the man was one hell of a manager, but had zero compassion. Brady just nodded, not wanting to be sucked into another screaming match with the man.

"Good, I know you've been through a lot. I talked to Marc yesterday after the game, and he told me everything. I'm sorry to hear about Jane."

Holy shit, was that compassion from Deek? The stone-faced shit head? Brady almost passed out in surprise.

"I'm not married, and I never gave my love life a chance. I was too busy focusing on my career; I regret it now. I don't want to see the same thing happen to you. I'm putting you on the temporary disabled list. You have fifteen days to figure your life out."

Brady couldn't believe what he was hearing. Was his manager actually giving him time to fix his life? Was that something that could actually happen?

Deek continued, "I expect you, in this time off, to fix your life and to continue to train. If things don't work out the way you want them, I don't want it showing in your performance. Do you hear me? I need you this season, so that's why I'm giving you this time off. Get your shit together, Matthews."

Brady was shocked. "Thank you, sir, are you sure this is okay? What's the media going to say?"

Deek waved his hand in the air, "Don't worry about those blood suckers. I have a conference with them later, and I'm simply going to say you have been nursing a sore hamstring and, instead of pushing it, we're letting you strengthen it before we get too far into the season. You have fifteen days. Fix things, Matthews!"

"Yes, sir, thank you." Brady shook Deek's hand and left his office.

He couldn't believe his manager just gave him fifteen days off to try to get Jane back. How was he going to do that? She wouldn't even let him in her apartment. Brady went to his locker to grab his bag he was going to take to Philly and ran into Michael. He looked terrible.

"Hey, Michael, how's Jane?"

Michael scowled at him. What had happened? "Oh, just fine, just using me as a toy in her plans to get back at you."

Get back at Brady? What did she do? Brady's blood started to boil; Michael better not have touched her. He just about ran to Michael's locker and asked him in a stern tone, "What did you do to her?"

Michael pushed Brady away from him and said, "Fuck you, man. I did nothing to her but care for her and take care of her while you were sucking it up on the ball field."

"You piece of shit! You know I'd give anything to be with her, but she won't even let me near her. You think this has been easy on me?"

Michael interrupted him. "Easy on you? What about me? I'm her second choice, always have been. I get to sit there and take care of her, but never get the love I give her in return. How do you think that makes me feel? I'll never be good enough for her, but I'm good enough for her to kiss when she wants to get back at you."

Brady's vision went red. He kissed Jane?

Michael added, "What, you want to punch me now that you know she kissed me? Well, guess what, dickhead? I stopped her. I knew what was happening wasn't right because she had no passion behind those gorgeous lips of hers. So, you win; she wants nothing to do with me. I always knew it, but it felt great to have it confirmed mere hours ago."

Brady watched Michael dig into his pocket and pull out a key. He flung it at Brady and said, "Here it is, a key to her apartment. Why don't you go patch things up because, Lord knows, all of us are sick and tired of dealing with your little melodrama." Michael gathered his stuff and left.

Brady had so many different feelings flowing through his body right now. Jane kissed Michael? Why would she do that? He

245

could go find out. He finally had access to Jane; there was nothing standing in his way. He had to go see her and get his woman back. He sent Molly a quick text to say he would take care of Jane and to not worry about her shift. No matter what Jane did, he wouldn't leave her sight. He had fifteen days to make things better, and he only planned on using a couple of hours to fix things, and the rest of the days to make up for lost time. First, he would stop by the store and get some items for Jane he knew she'd enjoy.

CHAPTER TWENTY SEVEN

Jane

Jane was still lying on her bathroom floor when she heard someone come in the front door. That was weird. She didn't expect Molly for a while. Did Michael lock up before he left? She heard heavy footsteps, and she rapidly started to panic. She curled in the corner of the bathroom between the toilet and the shower. She pulled her hairbrush off the counter and positioned it in front of her as a weapon. The footsteps grew louder and traveled into her bedroom. Jane wanted to scream, but decided to stay quiet. Hopefully, the intruder wouldn't look into the bathroom.

"Jane?"

Who was that? Was that Brady? Jane couldn't do anything but cry...

Brady

Brady heard crying in the bathroom and ran in that direction. When he walked in her apartment and saw her crutches sprawled out in the hallway, his heart dropped. He didn't even have to use the key Michael threw at him because the door was already unlocked. Brady's heart panicked, and that's when he started to run around the apartment looking for Jane. When he didn't see her in her bed, he almost threw up because his mind went straight to thinking some crazed fan found out where she lived and abducted her.

It wasn't until he heard someone crying in the bathroom that he realized he hadn't checked there yet. He threw the door open and saw Jane curled in a tiny ball holding a hairbrush out as if she was going to defend herself with the hair-filled bristles. Her eyes were bright red from what looked like crying, and her bad foot was not in the most comfortable looking position. Even though she was a complete mess, he had never seen anything more beautiful.

He walked toward her and started to bend down to pick her up when she waved her hairbrush in front of his face and said "Don't come near me. What are you doing here? Leave, I don't want you here."

Brady refused to play games this time. He grabbed the brush from Jane, put it in the sink, and picked her up. She started to kick and fling her arms about, saying something about how, just because she was small, didn't mean she could be manhandled. He brought her over to her bed and grabbed some pillows to place under her bad foot to give it elevation. He was pretty sure the position she had it in on the bathroom floor wasn't the best angle for her foot.

Jane dropped her head and shook it in despair. "Brady, please just leave."

"I'm not going anywhere; you're just going to have to deal with me being here and, if you feel like talking about what happened between us...that would be preferable."

Jane

Jane did not want Brady in her apartment. She was too weak. The minute she heard his voice, she lost what control she had left in her body. She just wanted to curl into his strong, comforting arms. She was about to when images of Brady and Laney together, holding each other, flashed through her head.

She got furious and shouted, "You want to talk, Brady? Alright, let's talk about how you cheated on me. How you shattered my heart to pieces and left me alone on a night that I was beaten by my ex-boyfriend. Let's talk about that."

Jane saw fury pass through Brady's eyes. She didn't think she'd ever seen him so mad before.

Jane was nearly blown over by Brady's anger. "God damn it, Jane, I did not fucking cheat on you! You really think, after being cheated on myself, I would go and do it to you, especially after I knew your relationship background? Do you honestly think that poorly of me?"

Jane didn't know what to say. He was so angry with her. Why was he the angry one? She was the one who was hurt, not him. She fought back.

"Then, why don't you enlighten me. Tell me why the night I was abused by my ex, I found my boyfriend, the man that I love, wet, in a towel with his Hollywood ex wrapped around his neck."

Brady lowered his head and shook it. "I don't know why I'm even here. You're never going to believe me. You've already made up your mind. You don't even want to listen to me. When did I lose that trust, Jane?"

"You lost that trust when I walked in on you and Laney holding each other intimately," she retorted.

"You walked in on nothing!" Brady yelled, as he threw his arms in the air. He got up and started to pace the room. "When I got home, I noticed all the things you did to my house and couldn't wait for you to come over later. I decided to go for a swim and I unlocked the door…"

Jane interrupted him. "I don't want to hear it, Brady. Just leave. I've heard all the excuses in the book."

Brady sat on her bed and grabbed her by the shoulders. "I'm not giving you excuses. You are going to sit here and listen to what I fucking have to say, damn it. I'm not leaving here until you hear what I have to say…then you can kick me out."

He continued, "I unlocked the door so you could just pop in and join me in the pool. I left my phone in the kitchen, which come to find out, would end up being one of the biggest mistakes of my life. When I was swimming, I heard the sliding glass door open. I thought it was you and beamed in excitement. When I turned to look, it was Laney. I instantly got out of the pool, wrapped the towel around my waist and told her to get the fuck out. She kept throwing herself at me, but I kept pushing her away. I was just leading her out the door when she tried one last time to hold on to me, that's when you walked in. I know it looked bad and the look on your face is forever ingrained in my brain. I should never have let you drive away. I'm the reason you're like this right now, and I will never let myself live it down."

Brady became very quiet and stroked her arm. "I'm so sorry Jane, I'm so fucking sorry. Please believe me."

Jane looked away; she started to cry like an idiot. She

wanted to believe him; she wanted to so badly. Both Molly and Michael said she needed to listen to him. Did they believe him? They must have, or else they never would have let him speak to her. So, if her friends could believe him, why was she having such a hard time doing the same thing? Oh, that's right, because he hadn't even told her about the text messages he'd been receiving from Laney for Lord knew how long.

"What about the text messages and naked picture, Brady? How come that was such a big secret? I thought we were open and honest with each other."

Brady ran his hand over his face. "I was planning to tell you…"

Jane interjected, "Oh, how convenient."

"For fuck's sake, Jane, just listen, please!"

Jane just waved her hand in front of him, indicating for him to continue.

"Jesus, I was going to tell you, but our relationship was already on rocky ground when Laney first texted me, and I didn't want you running on me, so I decided to tell you when our relationship was a little more stable. I was going to tell you the day you went to Dolly's, but then you freaked out about the gossip you heard about Laney and, clearly, that wasn't a good time. You can ask Marc; I wanted to tell you. I hated keeping it from you. It ate away at me. I just couldn't find a good enough time to tell you, and then everything fell apart so fast. I haven't been able to function."

Jane just sat there. Why did she believe him? Probably because he was so sincere when he told her how everything went down. His eyes were crystal clear when he looked at her and, when he told her, he looked directly into her eyes and spoke to her soul. She knew he was telling the truth.

"Please speak to me, Jane. Please say something."

Jane turned her head and tears filled her eyes. Brady wiped her face with his thumb pads. His touch was so warm, so familiar, everything she craved. All she could say was, "I hate you so much, Brady." She watched Brady drop his head to the side of the bed, as if he symbolically surrendered.

Brady

She hated him; Brady lost all hope. His heart fell to the

ground and he couldn't even move. There was no hope; he had to learn to live without Jane. He didn't think that was possible. The last couple of days were horrific. He couldn't imagine life getting any easier without her, not after he experienced a small glimpse of what life would have been like with her. Then, Jane spoke again.

"I hate you, Brady, but I still love you so much it hurts."

Brady thought he had a minor heart attack. Did she just say she loved him? Did he actually still have a chance? He put his head on her stomach and cried. He didn't care that he was crying...by now, he had lost all shreds of his dignity. Then, the most amazing thing happened...Jane gingerly put her hands on his head and ran her fingers through his hair.

It was the smallest of gestures, but her touch was all he needed. He just needed a little bit of hope from her to believe that everything would be okay between them and that was what she gave him: hope. He looked up and saw that she was crying as well. Brady reached up and grabbed her head carefully.

"I can't tell you how sorry I am about what happened to you." Jane just shook her head. "Do you believe me, Jane? Do you believe that nothing happened and that there is no one else on this earth for me besides you?"

Jane didn't answer. She just laid there and cried. Brady got up went around to the other side of the bed and climbed in. He took a big risk by climbing into bed with her. If she refused him, he might die inside, but he needed to do this...he needed to see if she would let him closer to her. He laid right next to her and put his arm over her shoulder, pulling her in close to him so she could rest her head on his shoulder. She didn't pull away, one small victory.

Instead of pulling away, she nestled her head into his shoulder and cried some more. They stayed just like that for a while. It started to get dark and, at one point, he noticed Jane had fallen asleep...fine by him. As long as she didn't kick him out of the bed, he would hold her all night long. He wanted to hold her all night long.

Brady drifted off for a little bit, but was disrupted when Jane pulled away. No, please don't pull away. Please, God, don't let her pull away, he repeated in his head.

"I don't know if I can do this, Brady. I'm so hurt and so scared. I cannot get the image of you and Laney out of my head. "

He tried to pull her close again, but she wouldn't budge.

So, instead, he tried to talk to her. "I know, Jane. You don't even know how much I wish this would all go away. I have never felt so low in my entire life. I wouldn't even care if I never played ball again, as long as I knew I had you in my arms for the rest of my life."

"Don't say things like that, Brady."

"It's true. I wouldn't just say stuff to blow steam up your ass, Jane. I truly mean it." Brady hoped she believed him. He waited a while for her response.

"Why didn't you answer your phone, that night? I needed you Brady. You were the one person I needed the most, and you weren't there. I hate you for that," Jane said, as she punched him and cried. Brady grabbed her arms to pull her in close. She struggled for a second, but then relaxed and rested her head on his chest as she cried some more. Brady tried to soothe her. He couldn't imagine how she felt that night. If he was in her shoes, he would have tried to distance himself just like she had.

"Shhh…I'm sorry. God, I'm sorry. My phone was in the kitchen when I was swimming. I wish I could take that day back…I wish I had my phone by me, I wish I was never in the pool, and I wish Laney and George got what was coming to them for fucking with people's lives. They deserve to be taught a lesson."

Jane held onto the collar of his shirt and nestled her head into the crook of his neck. Brady pulled her closer and made sure not to let up his grip. He had her in his arms and could feel how close he was to winning her over again. He wouldn't let up now.

Jane

Jane believed him…she did. Molly had told her Brady would never cheat on her and so did Michael. They both said what Brady said. He was cheated on and knew how it felt, why would he ever do that to the person he was in love with and wanted to spend his life with? She also believed him about the text messages. She did remember the moments he pointed out and they would not have been the most opportune moments to break the news that, in fact, his ex was trying to win him back and texting him. She understood his reasoning; she still wished he had told her, though.

She was so sick of fighting. She just wanted to find out, once and for all, if Brady really was in this for the long run or not.

"How much do you love me, Brady?" Jane asked in between sniffs.

Brady pulled her away to look deeply into her eyes. His eyes were sad and tired, but there was a hint of hope in them. "I love you more than anything, baby, more than baseball, more than life itself. I would do anything for you, and I promise to do anything for you for as long as you will let me. As evidenced in the last couple of days, I cannot live without you. You are my life, Jane, and you are the only thing I need to make me happy.

She couldn't help herself…she grabbed his face and lowered his mouth to hers. She paused right before their lips touched and swiped a tear from his cheek.

She whispered, "I believe you, Brady." Then his mouth closed in on hers. He kissed her ever so gently, barely caressing her lips with his. They pressed their foreheads together and just enjoyed the touch of their skin, as well as the moment of reconnecting with each other.

"Baby, I'm so sorry. God, are you okay?" He started to feel and examine her body as if he was checking for any extra wounds. "When Michael called me and told me you were in an accident, my entire world flipped upside down. I saw my future being washed away right in front of me."

Jane didn't know what to say; she was so happy that he told the truth, but she still had some sour feelings. Those would pass in time, she thought. She decided to just focus on the present and future.

"I'm doing okay. I wish I had some more pain meds. The way I was sitting in the bathroom was kind of a funky position. I think I really tweaked my leg."

Brady swore and leapt out of bed. He returned with a couple of bags from the local pharmacy. "I got your meds. I'm such an idiot. I sent Molly a text earlier telling her I was going to take care of you tonight. She was a little hesitant at first, but then caved in and told me to pick up your pain meds on my way to your place. I should have brought you your medicine earlier. Great nurse, aren't I?"

"Nurse? You mean you're staying? Molly isn't coming over tonight? She released her Jane babysitting shift to you?"

Brady got her prescribed amount of pills out of the bottle and opened a ginger ale for her. "Nope, you're all mine. I was never leaving…even if you kicked me with your peg leg. All Jane babysitting duties have been released to me. You are under my responsibility now for the next fifteen days."

Jane chuckled a little. "Baby…that's the best noise I've heard in a while. Your laugh makes my heart float," Brady said lovingly.

Jane smiled at him and then asked, "Fifteen days? What about your games?"

"Coach put me on the temporary disabled list and told me to pull my shit together. Apparently, I'm not a very good baseball player when the love of my life is not talking to me and all battered and bruised. He's telling the press I have a tight hamstring or something. All I know is that I have fifteen days of you all to myself, and I plan on taking advantage of it."

Jane grabbed Brady's cheek with the palm of her hand and pulled him close. She kissed him on the lips and whispered, "I love you, Brady."

Those were the most glorious words he had heard in quite some time.

Brady eyes watered again. "You know the first message you left me on the worst night of our lives? At the end, you said you loved me so much. I was afraid that was the last time I would hear those words come out of your mouth. I'm so glad I was wrong. I love you so much, sweet thing."

Jane smiled at him, gave him another kiss, and then asked, "Now, what's in those bags? Is that a Snicker's Peanut Butter in there?"

Brady laughed, "Can't fool you. Yes, I got you some chocolate bars, drinks, pain pills, and magazines I thought you might want to look at."

Jane couldn't help but beam with love as she looked through the magazines he chose for her. "You're adorable. You even got *Martha Stewart Weddings*."

"Of course, that bitch knows what she's talking about."

Jane patted the bed on the other side of her, Brady flung himself over and pulled her close. She opened the magazine and said, "Maybe we can look through this together and make some plans for the future." Brady's eyes almost popped out of his head.

"Are you saying you want to get married?" Brady said with his chest puffed out and hope shooting out of his pores.

"I'm saying it's in our future. Let's try moving in together first. I'm afraid I've become attached to your house. So, if you'll have me, I would like to live with you."

Brady smiled brightly. "Are you fucking kidding me? Of course I'll have you." He got up and started pulling things out of her closet.

"What are you doing?" Jane asked, confused.

"I'm starting to pack you up. What do you think I'm doing? You're moving in with me ASAP. I'll call the movers and get them over here. You can guarantee this is your last night in this apartment; you're stuck with me now, babe."

Jane chuckled and said, "Get over here, you big oaf." He went to her side and she grabbed his face. "I love you, Brady Matthews, my handsome, handsome man."

CHAPTER TWENTY EIGHT

Molly

Molly started to pack for their honeymoon. Her and Luke's wedding was in a couple of days and then they would fly to the Caribbean, basically to have sex on the beach all day. Luke joked about not getting sand in his crack, but she thought it would be well worth it. She still hadn't heard anything from Luke, but that was the norm. It wasn't very likely that she would hear from him until the last minute. She could just picture walking down the aisle as Luke parachuted in from the sky. He would cut it that close.

Molly talked to Jane earlier this morning on the phone. She and Brady were doing fantastic. Jane was all moved in and head over heels in love with Brady. Brady was taking care of her and being such a great nurse for Jane. Jane told her how Brady's nurse uniform was a Speedo, but not to tell anyone else because he didn't want to ruin his tough man persona. Molly scoffed at that, because it wasn't that long ago that she saw Brady Matthews cry in the hospital. He was just a big teddy bear. Molly thought about how Luke would never wear a Speedo; he always said he would rather wear nothing at all. Her kind of man.

Albert helped Jane bedazzle her cast for the wedding, and Brady bought her some designer crutches. Who knew they made fashionable hobbling sticks? Molly was ready to bust out the duct tape and make the crappy grey ones the hospital gave her a little bit more wedding appropriate. Molly joked about getting the new leopard print duct tape just to see the cringe on Jane's face. Jane would have to hobble down the aisle on the beach, but Jane said she didn't care. She wouldn't miss Molly and Luke's wedding for anything.

She was so lucky she had such a great friend, and even luckier that nothing serious or life-threatening had happened to Jane. Jane was the closest thing she had to a sister and couldn't have imagined how she would handle losing such a big part of her life. Molly would have lost her mind. She couldn't lose any more important people in her life.

Molly's phone beeped; she got a message from Jane.

Jane: Hey, girl, three more days and you are going to be married!!!

Oh, Jane, she was such a romantic. She had been texting Molly a countdown ever since the one week mark until the wedding hit. Molly thought it was silly, but secretly she got excited. It was only a couple more days until she got to see Luke and be married to the love of her life.

Molly: I know. I can't wait. More than anything, I can't wait for Luke to come home.

Jane: Have you heard from him?

Molly: No, but I didn't expect to. You know how he likes to surprise me.

Jane: Oh, I love his surprises. Do you have any plans for today?

Molly was about to text Jane back when there was a knock on her door. Molly's heart fluttered. It had to be Luke; it was just like him to wait until the last minute and surprise her. She could envision him standing at the door, holding a bouquet of flowers and a bag of condoms. She ran to the door quickly, unlocked it, and flung it open.

The smile that was plastered on her face quickly melted off. Her whole world went completely black as she fell to the floor. She was completely motionless and time seemed to stand still. In front of her were two soldiers holding a letter with sympathetic looks on their faces.

No, this couldn't be happening; this was not happening to her. Where was the rewind button? Please, God, don't let this be true. The taller of the two soldiers interrupted the darkness that was creeping over Molly. He cleared his throat and said, "Miss Myers? Ma'am, we are so sorry we have to tell you…"

Molly screamed and cried hysterically. She didn't even let the man finish his sentence. She could not hear the words that would rip her life apart. The soldiers bent down to the floor and pulled her to the couch. With one soldier gently stroking her shoulder, they embraced her the best they could. Molly started to shout whatever came to her mind.

"No, no, no. This is not real. Please tell me this is not real. Where is Luke? Please tell me he's coming home." She clung to the soldiers' shirts.

The taller soldier fumbled with his hat and said, "I'm so sorry, ma'am. Luke was on his way home from a location we cannot share with you when an enemy shot at his plane. No one survived the flight." He reached in his pocket and handed Molly Luke's dog tags. "This is all we could find left of him, ma'am. We're so sorry."

Molly grasped the dog tags in her hands and put her head on her lap. Luke was dead, her Luke. The man she was supposed to spend the rest of her life with and marry in three days; the man who was her one and only reason for believing in having a family, dead. She cried until she thought she had no more tears left.

"Please tell me he's coming back; we're supposed to get married in three days. He's coming back, right?" Molly knew she sounded desperate, but she was by no means ready to accept this news. Was this a sick joke someone was playing on her?

The tall soldier looked at the other one and shook his head in sorrow. "We're sorry. He was marked as dead, ma'am. There were no bodies found, just body parts. I apologize for being so graphic with you."

Molly threw her head back and wailed. She kept screaming no and shaking her head. This was not happening. Luke had to be alive. She could not survive without him. He was the love of her life. They were supposed to get married and go on a honeymoon and have sex until they couldn't have any more. They were supposed to grow old together, have children. They wanted to buy a house. Molly's life washed away, just like that. She didn't want to live. She needed Luke. Luke was her family. The one solid thing in her life taken away. Why did God take him away from her?

Was she supposed to be alone for the rest of her life? No, Luke was still alive. He wouldn't leave her behind like this. He only had a couple more years left in the army. He wouldn't leave her like this, by herself. He knew she didn't have any family and that he was it. He would never do this to her.

Molly thrust her head up; she knew she wasn't pleasant to look at, but she didn't care. Her eyes were burning, and her head was pounding like her brain was trying to break through her skull.

"You guys didn't look hard enough. Take me there. I'll look for him," Molly yelled.

The taller soldier patted her arm. "Ma'am, I know this is hard for you, but the government has an account set up for you that Luke left in your name."

"You think I give a fuck about money right now? You fucking bastards!" Molly said, while she punched them in their chests. "I can give two shits about money. I want Luke back. I want my life back. I want my family back!"

The soldiers just looked at each other, perplexed. "Ma'am, we understand how you feel. We've lost our friends, too. It doesn't go away...the pain you're feeling; you just learn to live with it." She cried into the soldier's shoulder as he handed her a letter. "Luke wrote a letter to you, just in case something like this happened. We were instructed to give it to you."

Molly looked down at the envelope in her hand and started to cry even more when she saw Luke's handwriting.

Molly looked at the soldiers and said, "Thank you, please leave...I would like to be alone." She could not have these men in her house anymore. They were too big, and the house seemed like it was closing in on her. She needed them out of her house, now.

The soldiers got up and, before they walked out the door, they asked if they could call any family for her...all she said in return was, "I don't have any."

Molly slammed the door, threw her back against it and slid down so she sat on the cold tile in the entry way. She had never felt so much pain before, not even when her parents died. It was like her heart stopped working, and her body functioned purely out of spite. Did she want to read this letter? It was the last connection she had to Luke...the last time she would ever hear from him. She wasn't ready to say goodbye, but she needed his comfort. She wished he was here. Why did he leave her? She opened the letter and started to read through her sobs.

Dear Molly,

When I saw you for the first time in Deuces, I knew you were going to be a hellion, but I was going to make you my hellion. You were the hottest girl in the bar, by far, and I was honored that you chose to dance with me that night. When I held you in my arms, I knew I was holding my wife. I just had to convince you of it.

You were a hard one to wrangle in, but I knew I had you after the first time we made love. The look on your face that night was incredible, it was something I will never forget. You gave me love I never thought I could have, and I will die a happy man knowing that.

I am so sorry I let you down and have left you alone. Please do not shut people out. I know I am your family and have left you, but don't forget you have so many other people who love you. So many people who will take care of you and make sure you get through this. I don't want you to shut down your life and lose your spirit that lights up a room when you walk in.

You are strong, baby, you can get through this. I want you to live your life and move on. You have a long life ahead of you. You are going to make another man the happiest man on earth and you are going to make a beautiful mom one day. Live life to its fullest and never forget me, but don't live for me. Live for yourself, baby.

You are the most beautiful woman I ever set my eyes on, and I am so grateful you chose me to spend part of your life with. Thank you for your love, your kindness, your body, and for being my heart, soul and pillar. I will love you forever, baby.
-Molly's Man

Jane

Jane was supposed to meet Molly at the florist for some final touch-ups for the wedding, but Molly missed the appointment. That was never like Molly. Jane was a little confused.

Jane and Brady decided to meet for lunch at Massimo's. Brady had the afternoon off and wanted to celebrate a big client Jane just booked. Jane waited outside of the restaurant when Brady grabbed her by the waist turned her around and kissed her senseless. She loved this man so much.

"Hey, handsome, that was quite a display of affection."

Brady grinned down at her. "I'm in love and everyone

needs to know about it."

Jane swatted his arm. "You're so corny; you know that, right?"

Brady just shrugged his shoulders as they went to go sit down at their table. Brady pulled her chair out for her, grabbed her crutches and laid them on the ground next to their table, out of the way so no one tripped on them.

"How was your workout this morning? That hamstring starting to feel better?" Jane joked.

Brady gave Jane a smirk and said, "Oh yeah, the hamstring is feeling much better. It really has loosened up these past few days."

Jane knew exactly why it loosened up. Brady hadn't left her side and had not let her leave bed. All the muscles in his tensed-up hamstring were relaxed pretty quickly the first couple of hours they were together again. Jane blushed just from the thought of the things they'd done in bed since they got back together. Brady interrupted her daydream.

"What are we having today, gorgeous?"

"I'm not sure. I do have a craving for you, though," Jane said, as she wagged her eyebrows.

Brady chuckled, "And you think I'm the corny one? How was your meeting with Molly and the florist? Did you tie up all the loose ends and make the perfect arrangements?"

Jane quirked an eyebrow at him and joked, "Have you been hanging out with Albert a little too much?" Brady laughed. "Actually, Molly didn't show up. I'm a little worried, she never just doesn't show up. Most likely, she lost track of time…either packing or shopping for the upcoming honeymoon. I'm going to send her a text to make sure she's okay."

Jane pulled her phone out and sent Molly a text message.

Jane: Hey, is everything okay? We missed you at the florist.

Brady just sat in his chair and grinned at Jane. Jane shook her head in embarrassment. "Are you just going to sit there and stare at me all through lunch?"

"I might, do you have a problem with that?"

"I might, you know there are other things you can look at that might be of more interest."

"Are you crazy? No, you are by far the most interesting thing here," Brady said, kissing Jane's hand. "Hey, did you talk to Michael? I talked to him the other day and he still sounded a little bitter about everything. I don't know if he will ever get over you."

Jane felt awful. She knew what happened between her and Michael not only hurt their relationship, but it also hurt Brady and Michael's relationship. She called Michael a couple of days ago, but he didn't answer the phone. She left him a message and a couple of text messages. It wasn't until the team returned back home and she went to his house and knocked on the door until he answered that she finally spoke to him.

"Yes, I went to his house and we talked...well, if that's what you want to call it. It was extremely awkward and uncomfortable, but I apologized for everything. I'm not sure he really accepted my apology, even though he said it was okay."

"It's going to take some time for him to get over everything, babe. You're going to have to be patient and persistent. Just continue to make sure he knows you still want to be friends."

"I will. I'm just not sure we'll ever be friends like we used to be. I'm sorry your friendship got messed up over this as well."

"Don't sweat it, babe. Guys get over things fast when it comes to their friendships. We aren't like girls...holding grudges against each other," Brady said with a smirk.

Jane playfully swatted his hand. "Not all girls are conniving bitches, just blonde busty ones that try to go after people's boyfriends."

"Aw, touché!"

They had just put their order in when Jane's phone beeped back. She opened it and her heart instantly dropped to the floor, and she felt like she was about to lose all the contents that were in her stomach. Brady noticed Jane's sudden change in appearance and grabbed her hand.

"What's wrong, sweet thing? Is everything okay?"

Jane couldn't even talk. She just shook her head and cried. What was she supposed to do? She turned her phone around so Brady could read what Molly sent her.

Molly: Luke is dead.

EPILOGUE

Molly

Molly got home from Luke's memorial and sat on the toilet while she held the bag she got from the store. She had thrown up every morning for the past week, but she thought it was because she was so upset about Luke. It wasn't until she realized she missed her period that she considered the fact that she might be pregnant with her dead fiancé's child. She opened the box that held the home pregnancy tests and peed on a stick.

Jane, Albert, Brady, and Michael had been more than supportive ever since they found out the news, and Luke's parents told her to visit whenever she could, but Molly couldn't face them; she barely knew them. They were Luke's parents; they were not her family.

She was able to shake Jane and Albert off of her for the afternoon, but she knew they would come back later tonight. They had been up her ass ever since they found out about Luke. She appreciated their support, but she just wanted to be left alone. She didn't want to talk to anyone, see anyone, or think of anyone.

Molly crawled into Luke's army shirt, the one she had worn ever since the worst day of her life and she laid on her empty bed with the test on the night stand. What would she do if she was pregnant? How could she raise a baby without Luke? Luke was the one who really wanted kids. He would have loved this child so much. He would have been an amazing dad. Damn it. She couldn't be pregnant. She could barely live and take care of herself, let alone take care of another human being…a baby no less.

Every couple of minutes, Molly's phone would go off…someone else just making sure she was okay. She wanted to scream into her phone saying, no she was not fucking okay. She just needed to be left alone; she wanted to be with Luke, and there was only one way to do so. If she ended her life, she would no longer have any more pain, she would be with her parents and Luke and she wouldn't have to worry about the loss of any more loved ones.

Molly stared at the picture of Luke she kept on her nightstand. It was his army-issued photograph. He looked so handsome in his dress blues. He was supposed to wear them on their wedding day, but instead of their wedding, she had a memorial service for him, her dead fiancé. She couldn't even bury him, because they had no body. She had no real grave to visit and no way of reconnecting with the person who made her feel whole again, who made her feel loved and cared for. Now she felt alone, and she slowly slipped into a dark abyss.

It had been a couple of minutes; the test results should be ready by now. She had a very large bottle of pills next to her, along with water, ready to be taken after she saw the results. She thought about ending her life and not even finding out if she was pregnant or not, but she thought she owed it to Luke to let him know when she united with him once again. It was the moment of truth. She looked over at the test and saw the results.

BOOK TWO (PLAYING THE FIELD) AVAILABLE NOW

BOOK THREE (WARNING TRACK) AVAILABLE NOW

Thank you for reading Caught Looking! I hope you enjoyed it. If you did, please help other readers find this book:

1. This book is lendable, so send it to a friend who you think might like it so she can discover me, too.
2. Help other people find this book by writing a review.
3. Come like my Facebook page: Author Meghan Quinn
https://www.facebook.com/meghanquinnauthor?ref_type=book

<u>mark</u>

4. Find me on Goodreads:

<u>https://www.goodreads.com/author/show/7360513.Meghan_Qui</u>
<u>nn</u>

5. Don't forget to visit my website: <u>www.authormeghanquinn.com</u>

ABOUT THE AUTHOR

I grew up in Southern California where I was involved in sports my whole life. I was lucky to go to college in New York where I met the love of my life and got married. We currently have five, four-legged children and live in beautiful Colorado Springs, CO.

You can either find my head buried in my Kindle, listening to inspiring heart ripping music or typing away on the computer twisting and turning the lives of my characters while driving my readers crazy with anticipation.

Made in United States
Troutdale, OR
11/28/2024

25365196R00149